WHAT DOESN'T KILL YOU

ALSO BY ED JAMES

WHAT DOESN'T KILL YOU

ED JAMES

 THOMAS & MERCER

Published by Thomas & Mercer, Seattle

www.apub.com

Amazon, the Amazon logo, and Thomas & Mercer are trademarks of Amazon.com, Inc., or its affiliates.

ISBN-13: 9781503942325
ISBN-10: 1503942325

Cover design by @blacksheep-uk.com

Printed in the United States of America

For Jon

Day 1
Night Shift
Thursday, 9th June 2016

Chapter One

DI Simon Fenchurch stepped out of his Mondeo onto the pavement, stretching out with one of those yawns that threatened to never end. Bishopsgate milled around him. Some suits carried giant coffees back to their City trader desks like ants returning to the colony, fuel for a busy Thursday evening. The yawn decided it'd had enough and Fenchurch nudged his car door shut with a thunk. 'I need my bed. These night shifts are killing me.'

'You're not the only one.' DS Kay Reed joined him outside the Bishopsgate Institute's front door, her own yawn twisting her cheeks. She covered her mouth and swept back her new haircut, a bob she couldn't yank into a ponytail. The deep red was bleeding white at the roots, not that Fenchurch could talk. She let her jacket hang loose. 'Wish I was in the garden on a night like this, guv.'

'Tell me about it.' Fenchurch hauled open the scarred oak door and entered the cool building, silent as an old cathedral. 'Much better in here.' Another set of doors led into the auditorium, while a corridor meandered off to the side street. No sign of—

'Evening.' DI Steve Clarke was just round the kink in the hallway. He raised his watch, chunky and with enough gold to refinance the RBS office across the road. His spray tan had shifted to a real one, no doubt picked up in Cannes or Nice, maybe even on someone's yacht off Monaco. His tailored suit was film-star tight, not the sort you'd want when chasing an idiot down a train line.

Bloody City cops . . .

Clarke did up the top button of his jacket. 'There's a green room upstairs but it's a somewhat unsecure location, so we're through in the café.' He thumbed behind him and set off. 'Thanks for lending a hand, by the way.'

Not that we had a choice . . .

Fenchurch followed him, giving Reed a flash of the eyebrows.

Halfway down the corridor, a hatchet-faced woman in uniform stormed towards them, flanked by two similarly armoured beefcakes. 'DI Clarke, it's a complete disaster outside.' She gave Fenchurch a frown and Reed a friendly smile.

Michelle Grove, something like that. DS in CO11, Public Order Operational Command. Riot Squad. She waved her arms wide. 'You've got two hundred angry cabbies spoiling for a fight out there.'

Clarke stepped to the side and grabbed her bulky forearm, puffing out his cheeks. 'You're here under my remit, okay? I don't care that you're Met and this is City ground, you're doing what I tell you.'

Grove clicked her fingers and waved her two officers off. 'The last time they did something like this, they got inside City Hall. We're heavily understaffed.'

'Well, your job is to make sure they don't get in here.' Clarke adjusted his cufflinks, big gold pound-signs shining in the spotlights. 'Now, Sergeant, I suggest you get out there and sort it out.'

Grove shot him a full-on police-officer glare, then smiled at Reed. 'Kay, good luck dealing with this.' She strode off down the corridor.

Clarke let out a breath, his tan whitening a couple of shades. 'If people just did their jobs . . .' He plastered a smile on his face and set off again.

Fenchurch followed the coffee smell like a thread through a labyrinth. He held the café door for Reed, yawning into his free hand.

Clarke stood just inside the almost empty café, his uniformed colleagues acting more like they were policing a World Cup final than an amiable panel discussion. Riot gear, sharp movements, helmets drawn, clutching shields and sticks.

Reed nodded at them. 'You really should go on the firearms training course, guv.'

'Me with a gun? Stroll on . . .' Fenchurch let her go first. Baking hot in here . . . Pockets of sweat formed on his shirt.

Should've been full of post-work diners, but it was empty, just a small squad of armed cops sipping at espressos, their Heckler & Koch carbines hanging from their padded shoulders. Bitter coffee smells lingered in the air, softened by the fruity tang of cakes heating in a fake Victorian oven set into the far wall. Shards of light blazed in through the floor-to-ceiling windows, flickering as suits of both genders passed. Behind the throng, a scrum of protestors propped themselves against the full row of Boris bikes, the red hire bicycles glowing in the evening sunshine. Should really be called Khan cycles now.

Most of the protestors were fatherly cabbies — red faces, white hair, faded denim jeans, a rainbow of polo shirts. Over by the RBS office, some old-school skinheads, English Defence League types by the look of things, were eyeing up the next-door *Pizza Express*'s windows, their hands hidden from sight. A wave cut into the protestors from the Bishopsgate end, the jeering muted by the glass.

'Here we go.' Clarke charged forward, gesturing with his fingers at an armed cop guarding the side entrance.

A dark-grey Bentley pulled up by the kerb, Batmobile-like, drawing the crowd towards it as much as the paint job sucked in the sunlight. Four officers surrounded the vehicle, pushing back the howling protestors.

Fenchurch waved a hand at the scene. 'And to think he's on their side . . .'

'Nobody's on anybody's side these days.' Clarke opened the door and let his officers part the angry sea. Two armed cops hurried in a group of men as the Bentley crawled off.

Clarke locked the door and left the officers guarding it. 'DI Fenchurch, DS Reed, I'd like you to meet Lord Gilbert Ingham.' He patted one of the men on the back.

Ingham's port-coloured cheeks were cut with red Stilton veins. His tweeds were more suited for a countryside shooting weekend than an in-depth discussion of the technological disruption of the taxi business. He was smiling at them, the sort of shit-eating grin that screamed, 'Don't you know who I am?' He gave Clarke a dark look. 'And these are?'

'Colleagues from the Met, sir.' Clarke beamed at Fenchurch and Reed like they were his kids at sports day. 'They're here in an advisory capacity as they have more experience with public security. I'm sure you'll have experienced that during your time in office?'

Ingham flashed another of those grins, cheeky and knowing. 'Well, Margaret caused a bit of a stir back in the day.'

'I imagine she did.' Clarke barked out a laugh, then led them back through the café, his officers' guns pointing at the floor as they walked. 'They're just about ready for us through here, sir.'

———

Fenchurch rested against the auditorium's cold side wall. The room lights were low, making their job that bit more difficult. Can't see a thing in there.

On the stage, the three figures were cast in a white-hot glow.

Yvette Farley, the *London Post*'s Managing Editor, sat in the middle, wearing a sort of pink trouser suit a flamingo would be proud of. 'Joining me this evening are two figures who should need no introduction, but I shall give one anyway.' She waved a hand at Ingham. 'Our first guest served in successive Conservative cabinets, first under Baroness Thatcher as Under Secretary of State for Social Security in 1989, then as Secretary of State for Trade and Industry under John Major until 1997. Lord Gilbert Ingham of Poundbury.'

Applause cannoned round the room.

Ingham sat on the left of the stage, looking like he'd escaped from Toad Hall, his frog tongue slurping all over his lips as he waited for the clapping to die down. 'I was a mere slip of a lad under Margaret.' He held up a hand. 'And we don't like to talk about 1997.' His laugh failed to set off any more echoes round the room.

'Quite.' Yvette smiled, more than a hint of politeness in it. 'And we're also joined by Mr John Q. Gomez, the CEO of Travis Cars, Inc.' She beamed at Gomez like she wanted to take him home with her. 'Our audience are probably more familiar with your competitors, so do you wish to give them an overview of your company?'

'Sure.' Gomez got up from his seat and paced around the deep stage, his black jeans and crisp white shirt barely moving. He stopped in front of Yvette, obscuring Fenchurch's view of Ingham. 'Gimme a show of hands. Who here's heard of Travis?'

Most of the audience raised their arms.

Fenchurch scanned through, still couldn't find anything like a threat. The worst of them would be outside, leaving the talk to City fund managers and the like.

Gomez raised his own hand. 'Okay, so some of you know all about us.' He grinned to himself, then steepled his fingers, creasing his forehead. 'We started Travis in San Diego just two years ago. Feels a lot longer, I can assure you.'

Laughter rippled through the crowd, though it didn't quite reach Ingham's lips.

'Our competitors do things their way.' Gomez chopped his left hand at an imaginary sparring partner. 'They disrupt.' Another chop. 'We set up our business to work *with* drivers.' He pulled his hands in from out wide to form a tight ball in front of his chest. 'Our mission statement is to *enable* established and *trusted* taxi companies to harness new technology. We're creating a platform so you guys can do your jobs. We want to support existing infrastructure and make it better.

Stronger. More integrated with modern life. With apps. Mapping and GPS. Real-time traffic.'

A loud cheer flooded the dark auditorium.

'I see we've got some fans here.' Gomez sucked in the applause as he paced over to the side of the stage, like a rock star letting the band play the opening bars to his biggest hit. 'The reason we're here in old London town is to enable you guys.' He waved theatrically at Ingham, who looked like he was already asleep, and grinned, his perfect teeth twinkling. 'Some people have vested interests, though, and don't want us to help the little guys.'

Yvette waited for the blast of applause to die down before motioning for Gomez to sit. 'Lord Ingham, that seems to be aimed at you. Do you have a response?'

Ingham wiped a tweed-clad arm across his forehead. 'It's an interesting position, that's for sure.' He ran his frog-like tongue around his lips. 'And I'm sure my lawyers would be interested in Mr Gomez's allegations regarding vested interests.' He sat forward and clasped his hands together, rocking slightly. 'But listen, Travis is dangerous.'

A jeer shot out of the audience. 'You're lying!'

'I assure you I'm not. Travis let any Tom, Dick or Harry drive your mother to the shops, or your daughter home from a nightclub.' Ingham waved a shaking hand around the auditorium. 'Mr Gomez says he's working with taxi drivers. *Some* firms can access their platform, providing they pay a healthy stipend, but they are in direct competition with his employees, who don't have to cover that monthly overhead, who get assistance purchasing state-of-the-art vehicles.' He shook his head as he spoke, his jowls wobbling. 'And these drivers don't go through "The Knowledge" to *understand* London.' He paused to nibble at his bottom lip. 'Customers get into a cab on the basis of a shiny app. But, instead of getting a licensed driver with a wife and children, they are merely rolling dice. Roll a six, you might get a normal cabbie. Roll a one, however, and . . .' He licked his lips again, slowly. 'Well, as you all know, women have been raped and killed by Travis drivers.'

Fenchurch whispered to Reed, 'Now I see why we're here. Ingham's turning this lot into a lynch mob.'

Gomez shifted in his seat and brushed some lint from his shoulder. 'Now *those* are some serious allegations.'

'They're facts, Mr Gomez.' Ingham loosely aimed a finger across Yvette at the CEO. 'And aside from the safety concerns, Travis are taking away jobs from Londoners and placing them in the hands of *immigrants*. You don't *care* what happens to taxi drivers or their families. Travis don't pay tax in this country. It's the worst sort of neoliberal, disruptive technological upstart.'

'That's rich.' Gomez smirked at Yvette, giving her a raised eyebrow. 'You were a journalist at the *London Post* in the eighties, correct?'

Yvette's cheeks flushed crimson. 'I was very young, I can assure you.'

'But you remember Lord Ingham here being in Baroness Thatcher's cabinet?' Gomez winked at her as he draped his left leg over his right. 'Along with the Reagan administration in my country, that government implemented the neoliberal policies.'

'Listen, sir.' Ingham spoke with his eyes clamped shut. 'I am, and always have been, a one-nation Conservative. Things must remain as they should be. Taxis should be driven by honest men, not by Johnny Foreign—'

'So you weren't on board with Mrs Thatcher's policies?'

'My memoirs are clear on the matter.' Ingham snorted, blasting a wave of noise through his microphone. 'It was a marriage of convenience to further the party's agenda at a time of dire straits for this country.'

'But you were involved?' Gomez waited for a response but didn't get one. The audience rippled with chat. 'And correct me if I'm wrong, but didn't you also oversee the demolition of the—'

'Right, that's the limit!' Ingham shot to his feet and tore at his microphone. He tossed it to the floor, a huge thud popping the speakers, and stormed off, heading straight for Fenchurch.

'We're on.' Fenchurch pushed away from the wall and tried to clear a path between Ingham and the audience. 'Sir, if you'll just—'

'Absolute disgrace.' Ingham barged past him and rattled the door. 'Don't they see what I'm trying to do for them?'

Clarke stayed with the squad of armed officers in the auditorium, guarding the exit. 'Go with him.'

Fenchurch followed Reed out into the cool corridor. 'Where is he?'

Reed waved over at the far wall.

Ingham was pacing around, barking into a Nokia museum piece a street drug dealer wouldn't hold on to for longer than a week. 'Giles, bring the Bentley round *now*.' He killed the call and pocketed the phone, yellowy eyes on Fenchurch. 'Inspector, I shouldn't have to put up with that sort of thing from an *American*!'

'I can only thank you for leaving in an orderly fashion, sir.' Fenchurch had to lock his neck muscles to stop shaking his head. 'Shit . . .'

A middle-aged man swaggered down the corridor towards them, like he was at a Stone Roses gig in the late eighties: draped in a St George's flag, honking on a plastic vuvuzela that must've seen service at the South African World Cup, silver hair in a quasi-mullet, grey shirt open to his gold chain. 'Got a bone to pick with you, sunshine.'

Ingham pushed himself back against the wall, eyes almost popping out on stalks.

Fenchurch stabbed at his Airwave, his other hand reaching for his baton. 'Urgent assistance needed at the side—'

'You Tory prick!' The protestor lurched forward, a flash of steel catching in the light.

Fenchurch lashed out with his baton and cracked it off the cabbie's hand, sending the knife flying across the marble floor. He raised it high, ready to slash down again. 'Stop!'

'What did you do that for?' The protestor stared after his fallen weapon. 'That prick killed this country!' He shot off, his Adidas Sambas squeaking against the floor.

'Oh, bollocks.' Fenchurch pointed at Reed. 'Kay, get Ingham out of here!'

Reed put her Airwave to her lips. 'All units, we need to get Lord Ingham out of Exit B. Delivery vehicle to Exit B!'

Four of the riot squad surrounded Ingham, each one grabbing an arm and lifting him clean off the floor.

Fenchurch jogged off, waving at Clarke as he burst through the side door. 'He's getting away!'

The protestor dropped his shoulder like an old-time winger and swung round a kink in the hallway, disappearing out of sight.

Fenchurch raced after him, his old man's knees grinding with each step. He screeched to a stop in the empty foyer.

The front door burst open and two armed officers stormed in from Bishopsgate.

Fenchurch paced over to them. 'Have you seen a man in a grey shirt?'

'Nobody's come out here, sir.'

'Shit.' The auditorium entrance was blocked off, but there was another door just past it. 'Oh, bollocks.' Fenchurch raced down the hallway and yanked the door open. A marble stairwell, footsteps ricocheting down from above. 'Follow me!' He clambered up, taking the stairs two at a time. Round the corner, then up again, panting hard. Another door at the top. He opened it slowly, sucking in traffic fumes. The building's roof, a wide, flat expanse, like an American prairie. Some big sheds lay at the far side like they were about to topple over.

Fenchurch raised his baton and stepped out, evening light bouncing off the nearby skyscrapers.

Where had the stupid bastard gone? Not like he had a chopper on the roof . . .

Something hit Fenchurch's shoulders from behind and he stumbled forward, sliding in the loose gravel. A dead weight crushed his knees against the concrete, the stones digging into his cheeks.

Bastard!

The protestor rolled off and got to his feet. He stabbed a finger at Fenchurch. 'You've no idea what he's done to people!'

Fenchurch stuck out a leg and tried to lever himself up. 'Try me.'

'No chance.' The protestor spun round and ran away again. DI Clarke burst out of the door, making their target veer away.

Fenchurch got up and sprinted towards the protestor, his limp easing off after a few strides. The protestor's eyes were on Clarke as he sped up, his shoes slapping off the concrete. He caught sight of Fenchurch and skidded as he tried to turn. Pebbles bounced across the roof. He rolled forward, tumbling towards the sheds. He thumped into one, crunching through the wooden slats.

A whine came from the shed, like a million tiny klaxons going off at the same time. High-pitched vuvuzelas. Small dots formed around the protestor, darting through the air at him.

'Ah! Ah!' He tucked himself into a ball. 'Get them off me! Ah!'

Fenchurch stepped forward, squinting.

A bloody beehive.

Chapter Two

Fenchurch clutched his paper cup, his other hand resting on the warm metal barrier. He basked in a little sliver of sun, Bishopsgate now mostly in the shadow of the towers. He took a scalding sip of tea. Not exactly the best drink for the weather. 'Reckon they're ready for us yet?'

Reed caught a coffee dribble on her chin. 'Probably.'

'Shame to leave this.' Fenchurch's personal mobile rang. He checked the display and answered the call, facing away from Reed. 'Liam.'

'Evening.' Liam Sharpe's voice sounded a flat cap and whippet more northern on the phone. 'Just a quick one to say I've just spoken with Yvette Farley.'

The Bishopsgate Institute was just round the bend. She was probably still in there, schmoozing Gomez into an interview. Or bed.

'What's this about, Liam?'

'She's running the story.'

Fenchurch's shoulders slackened off a notch.

'You've bagged the front page, mate.' Liam laughed down the line. 'Saving that Tory gimp helped.'

Fenchurch locked eyes with Reed and looked away. 'It wasn't a rally, Liam.'

'Well, whatever, you're a hero in her eyes. The magazine is all about Chloe.'

Fenchurch's stomach lurched. Over the road, a tall man marched past, bulging out of his navy suit, a black suitcase trundling behind him. Fenchurch cleared his throat with a thick cough. 'I take it my father's happy.'

'Over the moon. Just hope it helps.'

'Look, I've got to go.'

'Can we meet for breakfast tomorrow?'

'Text me where you want to meet.' Fenchurch switched his phone off.

'Liam Sharpe?' Reed took another sip of coffee. 'You're playing with fire, guv.'

'It's Dad that's doing it.' Fenchurch covered over a yawn and finished his tea, dumping the carton in the recycling point next to them. 'The boss is fine with it.'

'Is your wife?'

Fenchurch let the air seep out through his nostrils. 'Abi's not speaking to him.'

The station's front door opened and Clarke stepped out. 'The duty doc's just finished with him. Other than a few bee stings, he's ready for us.'

Fenchurch cracked his knuckles. 'We really need to get off, Steve.'

'Not my call, Simon.' Clarke led them back inside. He opened the door and let Reed go up first. 'We've assisted you lot a few times over the last six months or so. This is a bit of the old *quid pro quo*.'

'And we've returned the favour.' Reed stomped up the stairs, her flat shoes thwapping off the steps. 'Just don't get why you need us babysitting you on your own patch.'

'Charming as ever, Kay.' Clarke followed her up, the dirty sod staring at her arse. 'Did you enjoy the show?'

Reed spun round at the top, frowning. 'What, Ingham throwing his toys out of the pram?'

'Yeah. What do you make of him?'

Fenchurch shrugged. 'I wouldn't vote for him.'

'We're keeping an eye on this Travis lot. New kid on the block and all that.' Clarke stopped at the start of the short corridor. 'Anyway, like I said, the good news is our friend doesn't have an allergy to honeybees.'

Fenchurch pointed at the ceiling. 'Was that some sort of environmental thing on the roof?'

'Nothing to do with me. I just police the City.' Clarke raised up his hands, his palms almost white for once. Definitely a natural tan, then. 'Anyway, DS Reed, can you take Lord Ingham's statement?' He waited for the most grudging of nods, then grinned at Fenchurch. 'Now, let's you and me get in with Mr Nutwell.'

'Nutter?'

'Wayne Nut*well*.' Clarke rolled his eyes. 'I'll get things started.' He entered the interview room.

Reed crumpled her cup into a ball and chucked it in a bin. 'This is going beyond the scope of our job, isn't it?'

'Just a bit.' Fenchurch's turn to roll his eyes. 'Hurry up Ingham's statement, yeah?'

'Guv.'

'Cheers, Kay.' Fenchurch pushed into the interview room.

Inside, Clarke was resting on the table, blocking Fenchurch's view of the protestor. The digital recorder was already flashing away and the room smelled as if someone had blasted it with cheap deodorant, like some kid covering his dope smoke. 'DI Fenchurch has entered the room.' He stood and got out of the way.

Nutwell's left eyebrow was covered by a huge swelling, like the worst attack of acne ever. The skin was redder than his sunburn. He prodded it, then winced. 'This is *agony*.'

'The duty doctor has cleared you for interview, sir.' Fenchurch plonked himself down, like they were just chatting over coffee. 'We'd like to go over the events of this evening, if that's all right. Do you want a lawyer?'

'I don't believe in them.' Nutwell snarled at him. 'Like vampires, they just suck money instead of blood. They're scum, the lot of them.'

Fenchurch closed his eyes. We've got a live one here. 'Are you a taxi driver, sir?'

'What?' Nutwell pulled a face, patting at his welt. 'Just because I drive a cab doesn't mean I'm a mug. No. I'm an intellectual. I read a lot. Political science, economics. None of that neoliberal shit, either.'

Bet you don't . . .

Fenchurch got out his Airwave Pronto and stabbed the stylus on the screen to wake the device. 'Take us through what happened at the Bishopsgate Institute this evening.'

Nutwell leaned across the table and kept his voice low. 'You know who that scumbag is?'

Fenchurch smiled at him. 'Why don't you tell us?'

'Lord Ingham. Tory bastard, lining his own pockets.' Nutwell rubbed at his eyebrow, like he was squeezing the sting. 'Old money, but he's owned by the banks. Where there's money, there's corruption.' He sniffed. 'His sort have ruined this country. *Ruined* it. People like him want to tear us from the EU just to line their own pockets and rip up the human rights legislation. It's not perfect, but it's fixable. Meanwhile, they're spreading all these lies about immigration. What'll they replace the EU with? Do they even have a plan?'

Heard it all before so many times. Another idiot with a mouth but no idea how to fix anything.

Fenchurch tapped some notes into the Pronto, letting Nutwell's words echo round the room. 'Why were you at the talk this evening?'

'I'm actually a big believer in this Travis company.' Nutwell ran a hand across his chin. 'They're doing things the right way, you know? I get a few fares from them. Very nice earner.' He sniffed again. 'Lord Ingham's sort, they're stopping people taking control of their own destiny. He'd rather this city had automatic cars, I bet. So the taxi firms don't have to pay drivers. That's coming, by the way. You mark my words, all the cars on the road will be driverless by 2025.' His eyes narrowed, the left one disappearing behind the sting. 'That's what the Jews want.'

Oh, shit.

Fenchurch glanced at Clarke, his wince reflected.

'You listening to me?' Nutwell's gaze shot between the pair of them. 'Ingham's in their pockets. The Jews are in charge of all this. They did 9/11, you know? They want to steal our money and instigate the New World Order, just you watch.'

Fenchurch glanced at Clarke and clocked his eye roll. Here we bloody go . . .

———

'Well done for keeping a straight face, Inspector.' Fenchurch blew air up his face as he leaned back against the door. 'So he is a nutter, after all.'

'He had me going for a bit.' Clarke smoothed down a cactus of hair sticking up. 'Then, *boom*, it's all this anti-Semitic shit.'

'We get more than our fair share of conspiracy freaks on my patch. I'll send up some tinfoil hats, if you want?'

Clarke stopped fiddling with his hair, his hand floating in the air. 'Why would you wear a tinfoil hat?'

'Tinfoil's the only way to block the CIA's mind-control rays.'

———

Fenchurch trundled the Mondeo along the road, keeping pace with Ingham's dark-grey Bentley. The long street had a gentle curve, so you never saw the horizon, just the tall walls lining both sides, shrouded with taller trees.

The Bentley stopped outside an entrance bookended by oaks, their leaves dappling the sunlight. The gates slid open automatically and the car crawled through the gap in the brick, parking next to a sunbathing Range Rover on a paved drive bigger than most streets. A grey house loomed behind, offering size more than class or beauty.

Fenchurch pulled his car forward and blocked the entrance.

Reed slumped back in the passenger seat and folded her arms. 'It doesn't look like much, does it, guv?'

'Bet there's a swimming pool and cinema in there.' Fenchurch switched off the engine. 'Paid fifty million for it, according to Clarke.'

Another look from Reed. 'Shut up.'

'I'm serious. Must be worth double that now.'

Reed's expression darkened further. She jolted forward and wound down her window. 'Here we go.'

The house's front door flew open and two hulking giants in black suits emerged, eyes darting around. Ingham got out of the back of the Bentley, his toad face bunched up tight. 'You have my permission to leave!' He gave a flourishing wave in Fenchurch's general direction and marched off into the house.

'What a charming wanker.' Reed let her window grind up as she yawned. 'Didn't even bother to thank us.'

'Him noticing us ants is enough thanks, Kay. We should be grateful.' Fenchurch caught her yawn as he stuck the car in gear and twisted the key in the ignition. 'I suppose we'd better head back to the station.'

'If you insist, guv.'

Fenchurch pulled off. His phone started flashing. Docherty. 'What does he want?' He parked a few metres down the road and put the car in neutral. 'Evening, boss.'

'There you are.' Docherty's Scottish accent sounded like it could stab you over the phone. 'Been trying to call you all night.'

'Sorry. Phone's been off. Kay and I were doing that favour for DI Clarke.'

'That all done, aye?'

'For now.'

'Right, well, I've got no time for a handover tonight. I'm heading home, but a case has just spilled all over my lap.'

Fenchurch tightened his grip on the wheel. 'And you want us on it.'

'Aye. Body at a building site out at Bromley-by-Bow. Have fun.'

Chapter Three

'And I've got stacks of novels still to read. I'll fill my suitcase with paperbacks.' Fenchurch got out of the car into the balmy night, the air feeling heavy as a suit of armour. 'But it's the heat I can't stand.'

'Abi loves it.' Reed led down the pavement. 'Just another sacrifice you'll have to make, guv.'

'Tell me about it.'

The A10 rumbled behind them, three lanes of night-time traffic heading to the Blackwall Tunnel and south London. The developers had been working the other side of the road for years, turning the industrial land all the way to the City into new vacant towers. Now it was this side's turn.

A narrow row of boards advertised the 'BbB', like that meant anything to anyone. Artists' impressions rested under a dusting of harmless graffiti, glass-and-chrome penthouses overlooking the Thames. Just a splodge of waste ground between Bow School's Waterside Theatre and an older site, stuck next to the motorway but miles from the on-ramp. The nearest tube or DLR must be a mile or so. The next-door plot was a twenty-or-so-storey building, paired with a block half its height, both draped in scaffolding and not far off completion.

Fenchurch started down the thin pavement. 'Fished here with my old man.' He waved behind the building. 'Bow Creek and the Lea River join up here. Perfect spot for catching an old football boot or a used condom.'

A uniformed officer guarded a tall metal gate, wide open. She held a clipboard in front of her like it was the Ark of the Covenant. 'Sir.' She handed it to Fenchurch.

Fenchurch waved his warrant card and signed the form for both of them. He led Reed through the heavy-duty gates.

Rows and rows of bricks and blocks covered the rough ground. Further over, the earthworks dug deep, the dark-grey concrete foundations like dinosaur fossils. A streamer of police tape flapped in the gentle breeze that was sucking all heat down to the Thames.

A silhouetted figure eased himself out of a SOCO suit by tearing it into strips. His full beard flopped down over his dickie bow. Dr William Pratt.

Fenchurch sped up and stopped at the perimeter. 'What's up, William?'

'Simon . . .' Pratt waved a hand over at a huddle of Scenes of Crime Officers. 'Got ourselves a female victim. IC1. Twenties.'

Fenchurch stepped to the side to get a decent view through the huddle.

A young woman lay on the dry earth, the embodiment of IC1's cold classification of white northern European. Her raven hair spilled all over the sandy mud. Her blouse was blood red, the same colour as the cuts on her cheeks. Her knee-length skirt was pulled up, her sheer stockings torn down to her knees. Her suit jacket was half on, the other side draped on a bag of cement.

Every case felt worse than the last one. A descent into the pits of hell.

Fenchurch huffed out a breath. 'What do we know?'

'Nothing much at this juncture.' Pratt switched his pointing to one of the SOCOs. 'I've asked some of your chaps to find an ID. She had nothing on her.' He stepped his left toe on the right side of his leggings, mud caking the bottoms and his blue shoe covers, and kicked them off. 'I have inspected the body and I'm pretty sure the cause of death is manual strangulation.'

Fenchurch shifted round until the victim's dead eyes pierced his skull, nibbling at his soul. He flashed a smile at Pratt. 'Just pretty sure?'

'Usual drill, Simon. I shall confirm it during the post-mortem.' Pratt dropped the ex-suit into a pile and rested a stone on top. 'I'd say she was murdered elsewhere and dumped here, given the early signs of livor mortis on the girl's side.' He waved at the body. 'And she's lying on her back there.'

Dumped like a bag of rubbish. Fenchurch looked at the girl again. Those cuts . . . Must've been done at knifepoint. Meaning only one thing . . . 'Any signs of sexual assault?'

'The way her clothes are arranged would indicate that.' Pratt swallowed hard, not looking back at the body. 'There are marks around her wrists and knees, too.'

'Before or after death?'

'I'm afraid I don't know yet.'

'Done *in situ*?'

Pratt looked down at his beige medical bag. No idea what was so fascinating about it. He huffed out and finally shut the bloody thing, the clasps clicking. 'I don't think so. There's nowhere near enough mud on her for a start.'

A fresh battalion of white-suited SOCOs emerged from the road. 'Have you any idea who called it in?'

Pratt waved over at a pair of Portakabins stacked on top of each other. 'The project manager.'

The office stank of caked-on mud and instant coffee. Maybe the whiff of Cup-a-Soup and rotting oranges, too.

Arthur Hillier blinked hard as he supped from a 'World's Best Project Manager' mug, like he was just that one cup away from absolute focus. Checked shirtsleeves rolled up, wiry hair almost covering his Apple Watch like a forest surrounding a stone monument. Red tie undone and hanging loose. Grey hair, with a pen stuck behind his ear. 'I need to get my guys working first thing.'

'That's not going to happen, sir.' Fenchurch was standing by the open window overlooking the site from the second storey. Felt like the safest place in the rickety structure. At least he could jump out, if need be. 'My Scene of Crime team will be here tomorrow as well.'

Hillier raised his fist, like he was going to slam it on the desk. 'That's unaccept—'

'You might be in luck, Mr Hillier.'

'What? How can you—'

'It's likely that poor girl's just been dumped here.' A flash from a SOCO's camera bounced off the victim's body. Fenchurch waited for Hillier to take another slug of coffee. 'If that's the case, we won't have to raise up your foundations.'

Hillier sprayed coffee across the desk, coating both project and building plans. 'Tell me you're joking!'

'I can't promise anything.' Fenchurch tapped the window, pointing at the adjacent site. 'If that's your lot working next door, your boys might find gainful employment there.'

'Listen to me.' Hillier fished out the pen from behind his ear and tossed it on the desk. 'Do you understand the amount of pressure I'm under here?'

Fenchurch let a smile creep over his face. 'Try me.'

'I've been in here till midnight all week.' Hillier unrolled blue tissue and dabbed at his paperwork. 'We're owned by a hedge fund, and they just love their data and they *love* changing their reporting basis every single month.' He wiped the building plan clean and dumped the tissue in an overflowing bin. 'First time I've worked for one. Never again, I swear.'

Fenchurch gave him a sympathetic smile, letting him feel the shared pain across two industries. 'You got any CCTV here? Never had any scaffolding poles going walkabout of an evening?'

'Of course.' Hillier balled up some more tissue and chucked it in the bin. 'Hadn't turned it on yet.'

And none of that sounds at all fishy . . .

Down at the site, Reed was briefing a squad of uniforms and a few plainclothes. The SOCOs were erecting a tent near the victim, ready to drape over her and protect the scene from the elements.

Fenchurch folded his arms and fixed a glare on Hillier. 'Sir, a young girl's turned up dead on your building site. I need to ask if you have anything to do with it?'

'Excuse me?' Hillier dumped his tissue roll on the desk and walked up to Fenchurch. 'Listen, *mate*. The first time I saw . . . her was when I went outside for a cigarette. Okay?'

Fenchurch stepped forward, clacking the toes of his shoes against Hillier's. 'Persuade me.'

'I'd been in here all night, hammering away at spreadsheets and PowerPoints, gasping for a smoke, promising I'd treat myself when I finished.' Hillier stepped back and took a Zippo out of his pocket, then started playing with the lighter, flicking the lid back and forth. 'I was just sparking up when I saw a car shooting off.'

'You *saw* it?' Fenchurch tilted his head to the side. 'You hadn't heard it?'

'It must've been one of those electric thingies.'

Across the building site, the gate was hidden by a row of JCBs.

'So you just missed seeing this girl's killer?'

'I'm telling you I saw a car. If it was her killer, then . . .' Hillier shrugged and held up his cigarettes. 'Do you mind if I . . . ?'

'I do, as it happens. Wait until we're done.'

Hillier tossed the pack onto the desk. They skittered to the floor. 'Right.'

'Did you see the car's plate?'

Hillier bent down to pick up his cigarettes. 'It was all a blur, sorry.'

'A blur? It can't have been travelling very fast.'

Hillier dug his knuckles into his eye sockets. 'My eyes aren't very useful after twelve hours' straight laptop work.'

'What time was this?'

'Just before eight.'

Fenchurch went over to the door. You can see the site entrance from here. 'So you were here?'

Hillier joined him outside, putting a cigarette between his lips. 'This exact spot.' He pointed with his right hand, wrapped around his lighter. 'It shot off.'

'And what, merged with the traffic heading south?'

Hillier waved past the JCBs and the gate. 'Gillender Street's one-way. Then it joins the A12 at the roundabout.' He sparked the lighter and lit the cigarette. 'From there, you're either going into the tunnel or . . . Could've gone anywhere from there, really.'

Fenchurch gave him a long, hard look. 'When did you see the body?'

'Right after.' Hillier took a deep suck on his cigarette, careful to exhale away from Fenchurch. 'I saw her down there.' His shaking hand pointed down to the crime scene. 'Just lying there. I ran down and saw she was dead.' Another long drag. 'I mean, I checked for a pulse to confirm. Then I called it in.'

Was he telling the truth? Hard to figure it out. Makes sense, but don't they all?

'I'm going to need a full statement from you, sir.' Fenchurch beckoned to the nearest DC, some new start pissing about with his phone whose name he couldn't remember. 'And anything that can back up your movements over the last few hours.'

'I've been here all that time.'

'And I need you to prove it to me.'

Hillier stamped over to his desk and picked up a black laptop, half a dozen cables hanging out of the back. 'I can show you my save log into Dropbox.'

'How does that prove anything?'

'I'm an obsessive saver. I hit CTRL-S every two seconds. I've lost a shitload of documents over the years.'

Fenchurch tramped away from the Portakabin, careful to avoid the puddles.

Reed was speaking to a SOCO, not far from the body but just outside the inner locus. She broke off and marched over, arms folded tight. 'You get anything, guv?'

'Square root, Kay.' The tower of Portakabins was draped in the shadow of the nearby buildings. Hillier stood at the door, sucking on a cigarette as he talked to the DC. 'Don't trust him, but there's nothing concrete so far. Can you dig into the statement?'

'Guv.'

Fenchurch tried to spot anything close to evidence or a lead. 'We getting anywhere? Found a handbag? Phone? Work pass?'

'Nothing yet, Si.' The SOCO unzipped his suit and pulled it down. Mick Clooney, the lead. The front of his white T-shirt was filled with the old Adidas logo, three stripes slicing through three rugby balls. Footballers' tattoos butched up his skinny arms, a mishmash of women and Celtic knots and . . . stuff. 'No dice just yet.'

'So we've got a dead body and no ID?'

Reed placed her hand on his arm, gripping tight. 'I've got people going through the MisPers from the last day or two. She might be in there.'

'And she might not.' Worry gnawed away at Fenchurch's oesophagus, the acid reflux bubbling up. 'Shit, this can't be another—'

'Whoa, calm down.' Clooney arched an eyebrow. 'Jumping to conclusions much?'

'Paid to do it, George.'

'Yeah, and annoy me with that nickname.' Clooney held up an evidence bag and let it hang in the breeze. 'I did find this.' The sort of Samsung you'd see political fixers using on TV shows these days. He ran his finger across the fractured screen, covered in a spiderweb of cracks. 'That's not just a drop. I'd say a hammer did that.' He flipped it over to show the open back panel. 'The SIM's gone, too.'

'So we're bollocksed?'

'Might not even be hers.' Clooney popped it back into the evidence bag. 'Either way, we might be able to get something off this.'

Fenchurch wrapped his fingers together and held them in front of Clooney's face. 'Then I'll get the whole team to cross their fingers and toes.'

'You do that.'

Another SOCO sprinted over towards them, muffled speech coming through their mask.

Clooney waved a circle around his mouth. 'Mandy, I can't hear you.'

Mandy tore at her mask. 'We found a handbag over by the bricks.' She held up a large evidence container, a leather bag inside. 'Gucci, by the look of things.'

Clooney gave it a once-over before handing it to Fenchurch. 'Put your gloves on when you rifle through it.'

Fenchurch reached into his jacket pocket for his nitrile gloves, Viagra blue. He pulled the ziplock apart. The handbag was full of crap. Painkillers, tampons, mints, a black brolly. A lint-covered iPod Nano with a cracked screen. 'No purse, no work ID. Nothing.'

'Give it here.' Reed snatched it off him and stared inside. 'Honestly . . .'

The girl's body was now exposed, the area surrounding her clear of SOCOs. Someone had dumped her here like an old telly. Smashed her phone. Taken any identification and tossed her bag.

The main road droned behind the boards, just the tops of buses and lorries hurtling past.

Assuming her killer had raped her, he'd take her someplace quiet. So he knew this place'd be empty. Close enough to the trunk road to act as a dumping ground with a quick getaway. Probably saw the gate open as Hillier worked at his spreadsheets, itching for a fag. The project manager was still puffing on the Portakabin's steps, the DC still writing away.

Assuming it wasn't him. Assuming he was telling the truth.

The electric car, though. The lack of an engine would keep it quiet.

Feels like a hell of a lot of premeditation . . .

And it'd be the longest day in, what, two weeks? Less? Dumping her at that time, not even dark. Not even dark now. Pushing the assumption nobody'd be at the site right up to danger levels. Add arrogance to premeditation.

'Got something, guv.' Reed held up the handbag, a business card sucking up to the ziplock. Dirty white text on bright blue. 'Victoria Brocklehurst. Works for some firm called Ogden & Makepeace.'

The victim's pale, dead skin was exposed to the evening air.

'Think that's her?'

'I assume she's either our vic or she's had some contact with her.' Reed stabbed a number into her phone.

'What are you doing?'

'What do you think?' Reed held her phone to her ear.

A mobile ringtone blasted out, over by the Portakabins.

Nah nah nah, nah nah na-nah nah.

Fenchurch raced over, listening hard for the direction. That Kylie Minogue song. What was it called? 'Can't Get You Out of My Head'?

Nah nah nah, nah nah na-nah nah.

Where the—?

There. A faint glow beneath the steps leading up to Hillier's office.

Fenchurch crouched down and reached forward with his still-gloved hand. The light died, the sound still echoing around. He spun round to Reed. 'Call it again!'

She hit a couple of buttons and the music blared out again, louder. *Nah nah nah, nah nah na-nah nah.*

Fenchurch grabbed the glowing phone. A BlackBerry, the screen fractured but otherwise still intact. 'Bloody thing's locked.'

Clooney held out an evidence bag. 'Thought we had her mobile? The Samsung?'

'That's probably her personal one.' Fenchurch grumbled to his feet and dropped it into Clooney's bag.

Reed grabbed the bag from Clooney. 'So it looks like our victim could be Victoria Brocklehurst?'

'Could be.' Fenchurch's gut churned. 'Want to call that company?'

Chapter Four

Fenchurch drove down the tight streets of the ancient City, the grand Georgian buildings screaming out, 'Money!' The road was a Y shape, splitting at a modern block with the thousandth Pret A Manger in the square mile. Roadworks hissed behind them, blocking off the street. He could almost taste the deep tang of the bitumen. He parked on the double yellows and stuffed his **ON POLICE BUSINESS** sign onto the dashboard. 'Still ringing out?'

'Afraid so, guv.' Reed put her Airwave away. 'Still nothing from Clarke?'

Fenchurch checked his own handset. 'Shit.' Two missed calls from him. He hit dial and waited. 'Steve, sorry. We were driving.'

'I know.'

Something clapped on Fenchurch's window. Clarke was waving in, his tan darkened by the street lighting. 'You two coming out to play?'

'Only if we use my ball.' Fenchurch ended the call and got out to stretch. Another yawn. 'So where is it?'

Clarke nodded behind Fenchurch. 'Diagon Alley is just through there.'

'Austin Friars' was etched into the stone of an arch over an innocent-looking lane. It curved almost immediately, as if to hide the top law firms' billions from prying eyes. Two artificial torches lit up tall box plants outside the only building. Could be a gentleman's club.

Fenchurch flashed him a grin. 'So where do I go for my broomstick and my owl?'

'Follow me, Master Potter.' Clarke put his hands in his pockets and led them onwards. 'Forgot to say, we tore up that Nutwell geezer's flat and found a load of nasty shit there. Anti-Zionist books. Nine-eleven truther stuff.'

'There's still a lot of stupid people out there.' Fenchurch followed him down the tunnel. Really did feel like they were entering a magical world. The lane only revealed another block before it kinked to the right again. Across the way, a statue of a monk holding a Bible was inset into the wall. Not the darkest magic around these parts.

'Here we go.' Clarke stood by a door just beyond the statue, an innocuous-looking oak entrance to an ornate Victorian building. 'Ogden & Makepeace. Leave your cauldron at the door.'

Fenchurch winced, something stabbing at his gut. 'Aren't those the ambulance-chasers who are always in *Private Eye*? Super-injunctions and all that shit?'

'Slowdown & Makecash, I think they call them. One of their sins, yeah. Only a small part of what they do, mind.' Clarke rapped on the door and stood back, fidgeting with his jacket buttons.

The door shuddered open with a groan and a man blinked out into the summer night, blond hair framing his Anglo-Saxon face, almost a perfect rectangle. His face was lined with anger as well as laughter. Shifty little eyes and a long, bulbous nose. His thin lips slid into a grin as the door opened wide. 'Steve.' He clapped Clarke on the shoulder. 'Good to see you, my man.' His accent sounded like it cost a small fortune in school fees.

'Gerald.' Clarke coughed. 'Sorry, Mr Ogden.'

Ogden beamed, a frown glancing onto his forehead. 'What's the matter?'

Clarke waved at Fenchurch and Reed. 'I've got some Met officers who want a word with you, if that's okay?'

31

Ogden tilted his head up to inspect him. He stepped back inside the building. 'Very well.'

——— ———

'In here.' Gerald Ogden led them through a door heavy enough to guard against an army of orcs. Inside, the office was like an Oxford college's dining hall, all ancient flagstones and dark-oak panelling. He sat down behind a marble desk and folded up some paperwork, setting it off to the side. 'Please, have a seat.'

Fenchurch let Reed sit first, then took the chair on the left. As expensive as it was uncomfortable, no doubt.

Ogden shrugged off his suit jacket, a navy affair with a thick yellow chalk-stripe and crimson lining. His giant iMac was the only allusion to the modern world, though he'd stopped short of writing with a quill on parchment, his black fountain pen resting on a silver stand.

Clarke stood next to a heavy bookcase, the sort that wanted to hold hunting trophies but had to settle for a few hundred law books instead. 'You alone, Gerald?'

'You know I'm married to the business. I'll be here for another few hours.' Ogden glanced at the grandfather clock in his office as it chimed ten. 'Be lucky to get away at midnight.' Another look at the clock. His impatience was growing. Clearly a man not used to listening to shaggy-dog stories. 'Now, what's this all about?'

'DS Reed and I work for the Met's Major Investigation Team, sir. Our remit is east London.' Fenchurch stabbed the stylus on his Pronto's screen, waking it up. 'Earlier this evening, we were alerted to a body at a building site, not far from the Olympic Park.' He dragged up a few crime-scene photos onto the machine, careful to conceal them from Ogden. 'While we've not formally identified the body yet, the victim was carrying a business card for one Victoria

Brocklehurst. When we called the number, a BlackBerry rang at the crime scene.'

'Good heavens.' Ogden crunched back on his office chair, the mechanism giving an odd squeak. 'Is it her?'

'What was Ms Brocklehurst wearing today, sir?'

Ogden switched his gaze to his desk, like that stored the memory of his employees' attire. 'A grey suit, I think. Pin-stripe. Skirt, of course. Always a skirt with Victoria. Stockings, regardless of how hot it was. And a red blouse.' He looked up and his shoulders slumped. 'It's her, isn't it?' He wheeled over to the far side of his desk and rummaged around in the drawer, pulling out a photo frame. 'Here you go.'

Fenchurch took it and examined it closely. Gilt-edged, weighed more than it looked. Pretty much definitely the girl from the building site, though, give or take a few slashes and a strangled neck. And a whole lot of life. He handed it to Reed, trying to keep his expression Switzerland-neutral.

Ogden reached over and seized the photograph back from Reed. 'Is it her?'

Fenchurch settled back in the chair. Still uncomfortable. 'My initial assessment is the photo could match the victim's body. We'll need her next of kin to give a formal identification.'

'Sweet Lord.' Ogden pinched his nose and shut his eyes. 'That'll be me. I'm Victoria's godfather. The only family she's got left. She was an only child and her parents sadly passed away last year.' He stared deep into the photo and caressed the glass with a wavering finger, his head shaking in absolute denial. 'What happened?'

'I'm sure you can appreciate it's early days with this case.' Fenchurch tapped out a few words on the Pronto. 'When was the last time you saw her?'

'This evening.' Ogden set the picture down and cleared his throat. Sounded like he had a ton of tar down there. 'She left about seven, maybe ten past?' He walked over to the window looking onto a narrow passageway lined with stone buildings probably built by the Romans. 'We're up against it with a client. Victoria and I stayed late to complete the filing for first thing tomorrow. I'm still here putting the final touches to the document.'

Fenchurch stabbed the details into a timeline. 'So the last time you saw her was in this office?'

'Not quite.' Ogden walked back to his desk and picked up his cigarette case, running his finger along the lip. James Bond would be proud of it. 'Victoria had summoned a Travis car.'

Fenchurch looked up from the Pronto. 'Did you say Travis?'

'Indeed.' Ogden dropped the case onto the table. 'Our corporate policy is to avoid black cabs. Travis are cheaper and the app keeps everything neat and tidy, gives a nice little audit trail.' He raised a finger. 'But we don't get access to the data until three days later.'

Fenchurch typed in a reminder. 'Did you see her get into the cab?'

Ogden gave a tight military nod. 'I needed a cigarette, so I joined her on Throgmorton Street. It was one of those . . . electric cars. Barely made a sound.'

Drums thundered in Fenchurch's ears as he stabbed it into the Pronto, underlining *electric*. 'And she definitely got in?'

'Saw it with my own eyes. Some Japanese thing.'

'You didn't get a model?'

'I'm afraid not.' Ogden reached into his drawer again and produced a small card. 'If there's anything I can do to help, please don't hesitate to call. Day or night.'

'I appreciate it, sir.' Dark-grey card, very thick. Even higher quality than Victoria Brocklehurst's. Must've cost a pretty penny. 'I'll need—'

His Airwave chimed out — Pratt.

'Sorry, sir, I need to take this.' Fenchurch left the office and headed back into the corridor. A man in a suit lugging a briefcase smiled at Fenchurch as he passed. 'William, I think we've got an ID.'

'Well, that's a relief.' Pratt's sigh echoed his words, like a whole load of tension poured out. 'I was calling to let you know that the body is on its way out to Lewisham as we speak.'

'I'll send the next of kin.' Fenchurch beckoned Clarke over and nodded into the office, where Ogden was staring at the photo again. 'Any chance you can give Lord Malfoy here a lift out to Lewisham?'

Clarke rolled his eyes. 'Can't you?'

'I've got a crime scene to manage.'

'Been a long day . . .' Clarke scratched his chin, thin dots of stubble breaking the surface of the tan. 'I *was* going to head home . . .'

'I think you still owe me for this evening, Steve.'

———⌣———

Fenchurch zapped his Mondeo and got in, stretching out in his seat, as Reed wandered around in a circle on a phone call. Clarke's BMW pootled down the street, the red lights ghosting in the mist.

What next? Head to Lewisham and cramp Pratt's style? Head back to the station and set up the Incident Room? Visit Victoria Brocklehurst's flat?

The passenger door opened and Reed got in, stuffing her Airwave in her suit jacket. 'Want the good news or the bad?'

'Is the good anything to do with connecting her Travis cab to the electric car?'

'Sort of. I've just been on with that new Roads and Transport Policing Command. CO five million or something.' Reed tucked her hair behind her ears, still not quite used to the new cut. 'Thought I heard someone say they've got a line into the taxi companies. Turns out they do.'

'Including Travis?'

'Part of the deal to let them operate in London, apparently.'
Reed pocketed her Airwave. 'Gives us full access to their database,
full co-operation from their management. Everything.'

Fenchurch waited for the other shoe to drop. 'And the bad?'

The New Scotland Yard sign spun around as ever, sitting in front of the
bright-blue security entrance, waiting to move to the new HQ.

Fenchurch rolled past and parked on the single yellow between yet
another Eat and The Feathers pub, pretty much the only decent one
round there. 'You still won't tell me who it is?'

Reed just drew a zip across her mouth and tossed the key.

'Bloody hell.' Fenchurch slammed the door as he got out, then
stomped past the TSB branch. *Haven't even locked the car.* He zapped it
once Reed was out, then entered the Yard's corner entrance. 'Oh, shit . . .'

DI Jason Bell stood beside the security guard, chatting away like
they were old mates. He'd put on even more weight, just a space princess
on a chain short of being Jabba the Hutt. His tiny little peanut head
scanned around the room, the strip lighting bouncing off his glasses,
those stupid darkening lenses kicking in at this hour. He waddled away
from the guard and thrust out his hand. 'Simon!'

Fenchurch shook it and recoiled. *Sweaty as hell.* 'String.'

Bell wagged a finger in the air. 'You can't call me that any more.'

Who does he think he is?

Fenchurch glowered at him. 'Course I can.'

'It's insubordination, Inspector.' Bell flashed his warrant card. 'I'm
Detective *Chief* Inspector now.'

Fenchurch followed Bell and Reed along the corridor, his ears burning white hot.

How the hell had that useless prick got a promotion? They should be kicking him off the force, not rewarding his . . . ways. Cut him out like a worm from an apple. Turn all that blubber into soap.

Fenchurch stood outside the meeting room, fists clenched, eyes drilling into Bell at the head of the table. Henry VIII without the wives.

'You not sitting down, Simon?'

'I'm fine standing.' Fenchurch closed the door behind him and leaned back against it, folding his arms across his chest. 'You're obviously dying to tell us about the promotion.'

'I've got a much wider remit.' Bell's native Brummie accent receded with each rank. 'My old team are still targeting mobile-phone theft, but Tom's given me the technology side of unlicensed-taxi crime.'

Whoever Tom was.

'That doesn't make any sense to me.'

'They're related, Simon.' Bell stretched out in his seat, his shirt stretching the buttons almost to popping. 'It's all gang activity.' He flashed a smile at Reed, like that would sweep her off her feet. 'We're prosecuting a large gang of mobile-phone thieves.'

'What?' Fenchurch couldn't move back any further without passing through the door. 'That was my case! You lot sat around, twiddling your thumbs, while we caught a murderer and took down a gang.'

'Simon, the actions my team took would've secured the conviction had he not . . . you know, been killed in prison.' Bell was talking with his eyes shut, the lids flickering like the strip lights. 'Look, I've cut thefts across London.' He ran a hand along his shoulder, as if there were a Chief Inspector's epaulets there. 'The senior officers gave me the promotion, *Inspector.*'

Fenchurch sat down at the opposite end of the long table and opened his jacket.

Reed was halfway between them, her face pinched tight. 'I gather you know why we're here, sir?'

'Travis, right?' Bell got out a notebook and flicked through the pages. 'They're the bane of my bloody life just now. Yesterday morning, I had to brief Sadiq on them.'

Don't rise to it.

Don't rise to it.

'Sadiq Khan?'

'Yes, Simon, the new mayor of London. Charming fella, as it happens.' Bell smirked at himself. 'Anyway, I was telling him how the digital economy affords as many opportunities to criminals as it does to the man on the street. They find new ways to exploit people, which is why they need officers like Jason Bell leading things.'

'Listen, I don't need your mayoral campaign for 2020, Stri—' Fenchurch snorted. 'We just want to confirm whether a potential murder victim caught a cab, okay?'

'I've met Sadiq three times since he took office. Got another session tomorrow, which is why I'm here so late.' Bell splayed his hands on the table, palms up. 'He's taking this whole business very seriously.'

Big wow.

'From what I hear, Sadiq was at your little incident this evening.' Bell gurned a toothy smile. 'You saved someone's life, didn't you? Very well done, Simon.' He gave a round of applause.

Fenchurch let the drums cannon around. Give the scrote his time in the sun. 'Jason, we just need to speak to this Travis lot. We've got a victim out east, last seen getting into one of their cabs.'

'Shit on it.' Bell scribbled something down in his notebook. 'I'll get back to you in the next couple of days, then.'

'This is a murder, Stri—' Fenchurch broke off. Close to running over and booting the git in the head. 'Jason, I need to speak to them tonight. The driver is our main suspect. I shouldn't have to tell you about the first twenty-four hours, should I?'

'I hear you, Simon. And I'll get back to you.' Bell snapped his notebook shut. 'Okay?'

Chapter Five

A stream of red lights lay ahead of them, cars idling in the night air as drills rattled the ground beneath them. Tower Hill was further up, just behind the gardens and a queue of traffic. Punters flooded out of the All Bar One on the left: chucking-out time.

Fenchurch snapped two pills out of their blister pack and swallowed them down with some stale water from a bottle he'd slung in the door pocket. That'll fix those drums for a bit.

Just one bloody car made it through the change of roadworks lights.

He punched the steering wheel hard enough that it unlocked and wobbled about. 'Shit.' He clipped it back in, not quite at the right height. Then he tried again. Still not right. 'Should've gone south of the river, Kay.'

Reed looked up from her Airwave, smirking at him. 'You going to shift forward?'

A car-length gap had opened up in the traffic. He slid in to fill it. 'Who needs this Cycle Superhighway anyway?'

'Boris Johnson did. Could've built it when he was still in office, I suppose.' Reed winked at him. 'Want me to get DCI Bell to have a word with *Sadiq*?'

Fenchurch tried the steering wheel again. That'll do. 'We did all that work. Did that fat bastard get covered in soot? Did he almost get electrocuted? Did he have an officer lose—?'

'He played by the rules, guv.'

'Kay, I caught them. I solved that case. That little weasel doesn't deserve to be a Sergeant, let alone a bloody DCI.' Fenchurch hit the horn a couple of times. 'Should've gone up by the Barbican.'

'Are you angry because the victim reminds you of Chloe?'

'No.' Fenchurch kicked into gear and trundled up another car length. Two cars managed to not arse up driving through some lights for once. Not long now . . . 'It's got nothing to do with that, okay? I'm over it. It's done. We're moving on with our lives, Kay.'

'Right, guv.'

Fenchurch's personal mobile blared out Led Zeppelin's 'Kashmir', the tinny speakers not quite giving it the menace it deserved. Unknown caller. What the hell? He answered it. 'Hello?'

'Simon!'

Fenchurch mouthed 'Bell' at Reed and pulled the phone away from his ear, the thudding building up. 'How can I be of assistance, *sir?*'

'Less of the lip, Simon. You should be thanking me.' Bell left a pause. 'I've managed to get some time for you with Travis.'

'Already?'

'If you don't want it . . .'

'No, that's good. Thanks.'

Bell cackled down the line. 'Well, where are you, then?'

'Been stuck in traffic for the last half an hour.'

'At this time?'

'It's a flash mob working on the cycle path.' Fenchurch grinned at Reed. 'Should get your mate Sadiq to cancel it.'

'You overestimate my importance, Si.'

Don't I just.

'Simon, I'm at Leman Street. I'll see you when you get here.'

Fenchurch scowled. 'How the hell have you got there so quickly?'

'I went up by the Barbican. Much quicker.'

Fenchurch pulled into East Tenter Street, the grey bulk of Leman Street station looming over them, the rear entrance lit up like a motorway services as an Armed Response Unit mobilised. He killed the engine. No sign of Bell.

'Miracle him still being in at this time, guv.' Reed stifled a yawn. 'All that important PowerPoint shit he's doing for *Sadiq* . . .'

Up ahead, a brand-new Lexus flashed its headlights, the sort of bling they flog between football matches on Sky, soundtracked by some grime music. It drove up to them, stopping window-to-window. Bell sat behind the wheel like he thought he was a player. The window wound down almost in time with Fenchurch's. 'So you've finally got here.'

'Where we headed?'

Bell pointed upwards. 'Up there.'

Fenchurch craned his neck to see where Bell was aiming his stumpy finger. The Aldgate Tower climbed above them, glowing in the night sky. Still new enough that less than half of it was occupied. 'They're next door?'

Bell burst out laughing. 'Don't even need a Travis to get there.'

Wanker.

London's night flickered in the pitch darkness through the floor-to-ceiling windows, Tower Bridge lit up, the London Eye twinkling behind it in the distance. The City's new skyline was over to the right, the orange sky silhouetting the Gherkin, the Cheesegrater, the Walkie-Talkie and the surrounding towers, as yet unnamed. The outline of Canary Wharf flashed in the darkness to the left.

The floor was packed, even at one in the morning. The pine air freshener squished out of the ceiling every minute, drowning out the bitter coffee smell. Might be the busiest time for a cab company — drunks calling in or drivers stuck halfway to Amersham, only to find the dual carriageway is shut.

Pavel Udzinski wore mirror shades at night, two small copies of Fenchurch and Reed in his lenses. His dark hair was swept back like a Mafioso, a vague goatee covering his chin but venturing no further up his face. Tiny traces of Polish amid his barrow-boy London accent. 'Jason, does your existing warrant really cover *this*?'

'Of course it does.' Bell was sitting behind Udzinski, his gut hanging over his trousers. 'Give us the information and we'll be on our merry way.'

Fenchurch smiled at Udzinski. Weird as hell seeing your fake grin reflected like that. 'We just need some help verifying a trip made from the City this evening by one of your customers.' He let the smile slip. 'Her name is Victoria Brocklehurst.'

'Very well.' Udzinski hammered a few keys and shifted his glasses to focus on his monitor. 'I've got someone by that name. Tell me where she lives.'

Fenchurch checked his Pronto. 'Bermondsey.'

'I have someone by that name in Shad Thames.'

'That's just next to Bermondsey.' Fenchurch glanced at Reed, his frown mirrored on her forehead and in Udzinski's shades. 'That'll probably be her.'

'"Probably" isn't good enough.'

Fenchurch glared through the glasses. 'She was picked up near Austin Friars in the City at about seven o'clock this evening.'

'Let me see.' Udzinski drew his finger down the screen. 'That's correct.' He scraped his fingernail across the monitor's surface. 'Okay, the co-sign is Steven Robert Shelvey.'

Fenchurch jabbed the name into his Pronto. '"Co-sign"?'

'Our direct drivers, as opposed to those who are employed by a third party, such as a taxi company.'

'What can you tell us about him?'

43

'Hm.' Udzinski swivelled round to look at Bell. 'This feels like a non-standard case, Jason.'

'This is a standard, Pavel. Standard.'

'But he is only with us for a few months.' Udzinski's accent slipped. 'That is non-standard.'

Fenchurch got between them, blocking Bell out of the view. 'Mr Udzinski, we found that passenger's body at a building site a couple of miles down the road. She'd been strangled. Possibly raped.'

Udzinski's gaze was unwavering. He swallowed. 'By my co-sign?'

'I don't know if your *driver* did it or not. Yet. But we need to speak to him.'

'Travis Car Inc. can't accept any responsibility for the actions of our co-signs.'

The Police National Computer check came back empty. Fenchurch dumped his Pronto onto the desk. 'What's his address?'

'All I'm at liberty to divulge is that the individual had recently passed the same enhanced criminal-record checks that all private-hire and taxi drivers in London go through as part of Transport for London's licensing process.' Fenchurch couldn't see the script Udzinski was reading from. Udzinski lifted up his shades and rubbed his eyes. 'In addition to these checks, we apply our own rigorous search of numerous databases to identify convictions, such as CCJs and sex offences.'

Fenchurch tapped his foot. 'I just need Mr Shelvey's address.'

'And I told you that Travis Car Inc. can't accept any responsibility for the actions of our co-signs.' Udzinski stopped typing. 'Our CEO is in the country. I can set up some time with him to progress this matter tomorrow.'

'Son, I need you to listen to me.' Fenchurch wheeled his chair closer and peered at him. 'The only option I'll have to track down Mr Shelvey will be through a public request for information via the news media. It'll be very difficult to keep his employer's name out of the story.'

'Fine.' Udzinski battered the mouse. The printer next to him whirred into life.

Fenchurch took the page from him. 'Is he still working?'

Udzinski hit the keyboard again and clicked the mouse button with enough force to snap it in half. 'He clocked off at eleven.'

'—and you're sure? Okay.' Reed put her Airwave away and let her seat belt rise up. 'Control haven't got this Shelvey guy on record, guv. So what's the plan?'

'Usual approach, Kay.'

Burford Street was a long row of two-up two-downs near where West Ham became East Ham. Some roughcast, others painted, but mostly just bare brick. A few even had those over-sized Polish satellite dishes.

Shelvey's address was a double-glazed house halfway down. Plain brown door, wheelie bins instead of a garden, a downstairs bay window the only embellishment. A Vauxhall Corsa was wedged between two work vans. Opposite, two motorbikes blocked in a Toyota Prius.

Fenchurch tapped the Prius's plate into the PNC search on his Pronto. Bingo. He held the device up and pointed across the street. 'That's his motor, anyway.'

Reed typed something onto her own Pronto. 'I'll get someone checking it against the CCTV from the streets near the building site.'

The victim was dumped at eight, killed before. If it was Shelvey, there was a good chance he'd taken a few more passengers since his motor had been at Bromley-by-Bow. Raping and killing someone, just dumping their body . . . Then going back to work. If it was him, he was an arrogant bastard.

Still a huge, huge if . . .

'The plan, guv?'

Fenchurch looked over at Reed. 'Let's wait for the cavalry to turn up, then grab him and have a little word with him down the station.'

'Right.' She tapped the window, pointing at the wing mirror. 'Here we go, guv.'

A panda car pulled up behind them and two uniforms got out, both of them snapping their batons out in time. Another car in front flashed the lights and the passenger got out.

'Come on then.' Fenchurch checked his baton was in place and joined them in the street. He gestured for two of them to stay and opened the gate with a screech that could wake a drunk desk sergeant. Then he walked to the door and hammered on it — rap rap, rap rap. 'It's the police! Open up!'

Curtains twitched in both neighbours' houses — the poor bastards' main bedrooms faced the street.

Footsteps rumbled down the stairs inside the house and the door opened a crack, a bleary eye peeking out, yellow and bloodshot. The door widened out. A woman in her mid-fifties, give or take. She gave Fenchurch the up and down. 'What?'

'Police, madam.' Fenchurch showed her his warrant card. 'We need to speak to a Steven Shelvey.'

'Why?'

Fenchurch stepped forward, trying to get a foot between the door and the outside. 'Is he in?'

The door pushed shut, bouncing off his toe.

Fenchurch beckoned the spare uniform over.

Inside the house, 'Steve!' boomed out.

More clumping on the stairs. 'What?'

'Police for you. What have you done now?'

Fenchurch waved off the uniform.

The door opened again, filled by a six-footer in a Union Jack T-shirt, his fingers twitching at his drainpipe jeans. Tattoos, skinhead, baby face. Sunburn lashed his face and arms. 'What?'

'Steven Shelvey?'

He gripped the door and sneered at Fenchurch. 'Ain't done nothing.'

'Well, we still need a word with you about a passenger you picked up earlier this evening.'

'I'm off duty. Come back in the morning.' Shelvey slammed the door.

Fenchurch's toe caught the weight of it. Stung like a bastard. Shelvey pushed it again and it shut.

'Good work, guv.' Reed put her hands on her hips and exhaled, shaking her head. 'What's the plan now?'

Fenchurch drilled his gaze into the door. 'We're speaking to him tonight.'

'Not without probable cause, we're not.'

A window clattered open above them. 'Oy! What's going on?' An old man loomed out, glowering at them.

'Police, sir.' Fenchurch waved his warrant card. 'Can you please go back to bed?'

'Not until you lot bloody shut up. I've got to get up at half five!'

'I can only apologise, sir.'

Reed's Airwave blasted out, the sound bouncing off the buildings. She answered it and paced back down the path. 'Lisa, you got anything?' Then squinted at the Prius. 'Yep, you're right. It's a P. No, papa. Okay, thanks.' She killed the call and put her Airwave away. 'That Prius matches the car on the CCTV. The one that project manager saw.'

Fenchurch hammered on the door again. 'Open up!'

The man at the window shouted down again. 'Give us a break.' He disappeared inside.

Fenchurch hit the door. 'Mr Shelvey, I need you to come out.'

'Piss off!' Shelvey must've been just behind the door, probably pushing back against it. 'I know my rights! You can't come in here without a warrant!'

'Sir, we need you to answer some questions regarding your movements this evening.' Fenchurch left a few moments' grace, the drums building up in his ears. 'I need you to come with me.'

'Piss off!'

Fenchurch looked round at Reed. 'Where's the nearest Enforcer? Leman Street?'

'Think Brick Lane have one.'

Fenchurch checked his watch. Half past one. No time. Then he thumped the door again. 'Sir, you need to come with us.'

'Piss off!'

'Kay, stay here.' Fenchurch stormed off down the path, then headed for the patrol car. He waited for the window to buzz down before leaning in. 'Can one of you two get—'

'Ow!' Reed toppled over by the front door, light blazing out of the house. Footsteps pounded across the street, away from the squad car.

Shelvey was making a run for it.

Bloody hell!

The lights on his Prius flashed. He tore at the driver's door and got in.

Fenchurch got there just in time to grab the door. Shelvey lay on his back, bracing his feet against the inside of the door and tugging at the handle for all he was worth. The door crept shut.

Uniformed hands grabbed the door and helped Fenchurch tear it open. Then Reed got in on the act, her lip split, a trail of blood dribbling down her chin. Fenchurch kicked out and cracked Shelvey's wrist. Shelvey let go of the door and tumbled backwards into the car.

Fenchurch reached inside and grabbed a fistful of Shelvey's T-shirt. 'I'm done asking nicely.' He yanked him and twisted Shelvey's arm round his back. Then started a pat-down with his left hand. Wallet, keys.

'You can't do this!'

About seven quid in coins.

'This is police brutality!'

No weapons.

Fenchurch flipped him round and pinned him against the car. 'Sir, I need you to answer a few questions about one of your passengers this evening.'

A glob of spit hit Fenchurch's chin.

'I need you to stop that, sir.'

'Make me.'

'Guv.' Reed got out of the passenger side. 'You want to see this.'

Shelvey's eyes bulged. 'See what?'

Fenchurch pushed him towards the uniform and joined her on the pavement.

Reed pointed into the car. Just above the glove box, a small compartment had popped open. 'He must've kicked it by accident.' She snapped on a glove and pulled out a white plastic tub. She tore off the lid and rattled it. Thing was filled almost to the brim with blue pills. 'Looks like Viagra.'

Shelvey was barely out of his teens. Can't be using it, can he?

'Think he's dealing them?'

'I've seen knock-offs before, guv.' Reed held a pill up to the streetlight. 'These are fakes.' She passed it to Fenchurch. 'See how they're stamped with Pfizer on the top and VGR100?'

'Pfizer's the manufacturer, right?'

Reed winked at him. 'You've never had to take one, guv?'

'Not for a while.' Fenchurch squinted at the tablet, the blue greyed by the street lighting. 'So how do you—?'

'See how the "f" tapers off? The fake pills can't get it right, something in the process or what they're laced with. Or they're just rat poison.'

'So they're fakes?'

Reed smirked. 'You want to try one? Won't work on me.'

Fenchurch laughed. 'Maybe later.' He stomped back to the other side of the car.

Shelvey snarled at some onlooking neighbours as he was cuffed from behind. 'What did you plant?'

Fenchurch passed him the knock-off Viagra. 'This yours?'

'You planted them, you fascist bastard!'

Fenchurch rolled his eyes, then nodded at the uniform. 'Get him to Leman Street as soon as, yeah?'

'I WANT A LAWYER!'

Chapter Six

Fenchurch pulled in on Leman Street outside The Oliver Conquest, the pub's recent hipster transformation still struggling to shrug off its cop clientele in favour of stray City boys and girls. 'You okay?'

'He just caught me on the ear, guv.' Reed rubbed at the side of her skull. 'Nothing I haven't had a hundred times or more.'

'Your lip's bleeding.'

'What?' She dabbed at it. 'Bloody hell.'

'Make sure you see the duty doc, right?' Fenchurch locked the car and followed Reed down the street, the night breeze cooling his neck. For once, the drums were quiet.

A couple in shorts and T-shirts walked hand in hand ahead of him, dawdling like only the young could. No mortgages, missing daughters or—

'Simon!' Paul Temple was standing on the steps, barely visible above the handrail. An old college mate of Reed and Fenchurch's wife, he looked a few years younger than either, his blond hair and designer suit giving him the sort of image a public prosecutor shouldn't have. Maybe that's why he was so good at his job. That, or his lack of height induced some weird psychosis in the judiciary. He trotted down the stairs and offered Fenchurch a fist bump. 'How's tricks, amigo?'

'Fine, actually.' Fenchurch bumped knuckles. 'What brings you here?'

'Given our recent fun and games, the Crown Prosecutor's asked me to get in on the ground level on this case.' Temple shot Reed a wink as he patted her lip. 'Simon taking his anger out on you?'

She dabbed at it again. 'All part of doing a real job rather than prancing about in court.'

Temple chuckled. 'Well, it's nice to see you smiling for once, Kayleigh.'

'It's Kay, Paul*ine*.'

Fenchurch frowned at Reed. 'What's going on?'

Temple grinned back at her. 'Do you think Kayleigh has—'

'—a resting bitch face?' Reed folded her arms, scowling. 'Well?'

Fenchurch shot his gaze between them. 'A resting what?'

'Resting bitch face.' Reed forced a wide smile onto her face, completely unlike her. 'Paul says I've got one.' Her face slackened, a scowl dancing across her features, then back to the fake grin. 'Well?'

Definitely.

Fenchurch raised his shoulders. 'Not that I've noticed.'

Reed prodded Temple in the chest. 'See?'

Temple's eyes twinkled in the sodium light. 'He just doesn't want you mashing his balls, Kayleigh.'

The squad car parked and the two uniforms hauled Shelvey out onto the street, the cabbie walking with the slumped-shouldered gait of the guilty. The *usually* guilty . . . 'I want a LAWYER!'

Reed grabbed his wrist and pulled him up the steps, the uniforms following. The four of them wobbled in the mirrored glass as the left-hand door opened. One final push from Reed and Shelvey was inside.

Temple hugged his briefcase like a small child. 'So how's this one seem?'

'Dodgy as hell.' Fenchurch rested against the handrail. Felt like it would give at any moment. 'We've got his motor leaving the crime scene. Not that it's indicative or anything, but we found a tub of fake Viagra in his cab.'

'Dealing?'

'Most likely.'

'Well, if you need a warrant . . .' Temple held up his briefcase. 'Any timeline on the prosecution yet?'

Fenchurch checked his watch. 'Another hour for his lawyer to turn up, then an hour taking an initial statement. Should be able to book him by three, with a good wind behind us.'

'No chance I'm getting any more sleep tonight, is there?'

'You get used to it.' Fenchurch frowned at him. The handrail groaned a bit. 'What are you doing here, Paul?'

'This is the CPS taking a different approach.' Temple scratched at a rash on his cheek. 'Given events at Christmas, and with our friend Kamal dying on remand . . .' He reached over and patted Fenchurch's shoulder. 'You believed him when he said he knew what happened to Chloe, didn't you?'

'I hoped he knew something, I guess.' A breeze blew through Fenchurch on its way down the long corridor of a street. 'One sharpened toothbrush was all it took to shut him up for good.'

'Frontier justice, amigo. Our job is to stop it happening.' Temple yawned and held out his fist for another bump. 'I'll see you inside, yeah?'

'Sure.' Fenchurch bumped knuckles again, sucking in the dark night air, and watched Temple bounce up the stairs.

Bloody CPS pissing all over our chips again. Like we need micromanaging.

Fenchurch's throat tightened up. Another death on a case. Another lead into what happened, gone. Just like that.

His Airwave blasted out, cutting through the street's silence. Lewisham Support Centre.

What the hell?

'Fenchurch.'

'Sir, it's Bill on the front desk at Lewisham. A Gerald Ogden is still sitting here. Not very happy.'

Dr Pratt tightened his red gingham bow tie, lost behind his thick beard, which exceeded the current hipster fashion by a good foot. Deep grooves dug into his eye sockets. His skeletal fingers played with the edge of the white sheet covering the slab and the rough contours of the body beneath.

Fenchurch gave Ogden a once-over. 'Are you ready, sir?'

Ogden stroked a finger down his long nose, his gaze scanning up and down the shape on the slab. He ran a hand through his blond locks, eyes closed. Then the smallest nod.

Fenchurch passed it on to Pratt.

'Very well.' The pathologist eased back the corner of the sheet, tucking it over Victoria Brocklehurst's chest to preserve what modesty she had left.

Patches of thick soil covered Victoria's dark hair, like she was still lying at the crime scene. The blood on her cheeks was dried, the gouges darkened in contrast with the pale skin around them. Her lips were blue where the lipstick was smudged aside. A burgundy ring surrounded her neck, choking her collapsed windpipe.

Ogden rested his hand on the slab and brushed his hair back again, leaving it splayed across his head, stuck there with sweat. He was panting, his teeth welded together. 'Vicky . . .'

Fenchurch snatched back eye contact. 'Is this is your goddaughter?'

Another tiny nod, eyes shut. 'It's Victoria.'

Fenchurch rested a hand on Ogden's shoulder. 'Can I get you a cup of tea, sir?'

'I don't need *tea.*' Nuclear fire burned in Ogden's eyes, locked onto Fenchurch. He stood up tall, pretty much the same height as Pratt. 'Some *animal* has butchered my Vicky, and you—' He broke off, fingers covering his eyes. 'Vicky . . .'

Fenchurch made eyes at Pratt to cover Victoria again, then led Ogden out of the room, the lawyer following like a small child, his head bowed. He sat him on a wide settee in the empty waiting area, dark and gloomy.

Three uniformed officers chatted by the door, bored but at least doing something other than watching DVDs through their night shift.

Fenchurch perched opposite, nudging a box of Kleenex across the table. 'Sir, these might help—'

Ogden glowered at Fenchurch. 'Tissues won't bring Victoria back.'

'Sir, I'm not—'

'You're not doing anything!' Ogden jabbed a finger at the door through to the mortuary. 'I was her only family and now I'm going to have to bury her, like I buried her parents. Do you have any idea what that's like?'

Fenchurch gritted his teeth and had to look away. 'I have some experience, sir.'

'What?' Ogden tore off a Kleenex and blew into it, honking like a tenor sax. 'Seeing this sort of thing a few times in the line of duty isn't the same as living through it.'

'I'm sorry, sir, but—'

'How can you *possibly* know what I'm going through, eh?' Ogden tossed the tissue onto the table, the paper skidding across and landing on the grey carpet tiles. 'I let her down and there's *nothing* I can do about it. How can you possibly know, eh?'

Fenchurch made eye contact again, his heart thundering, acid burning in his gut. 'My own daughter . . . She was kidnapped from outside my house.'

Ogden shut his eyes. 'Christ.' He reached for another tissue and dabbed at his cheeks, avoiding looking anywhere near Fenchurch. 'Forgive me, I—'

'It's fine, sir.' Fenchurch tried for a conciliatory smile. 'Now, I need to know that, beyond any doubt, the woman—'

'It's Victoria.' Ogden dropped the tissue onto the table, though this one stayed there. 'I wish it wasn't. And I wish me saying it's not her meant that she's still out there. But it's her. She's . . . She's dead.'

'Thank you, sir.'

'The stuff you were asking earlier.' Ogden tore off another tissue and honked into it. 'About Travis? Have you got anything from that?'

'We're still actively investigating Ms Brocklehurst's death, sir, and have a number of open avenues of inquiry.'

'Spare me.' Ogden huffed out a deep breath. 'So much of my time is spent working with abstract legalese. I like to deal in the concrete, Inspector. Please, do you have a suspect?'

'I can't comment on it just now.' Fenchurch slipped a business card out of his wallet and held it in his clammy palms. 'Is there anyone else we should be speaking to in relation to Ms Brocklehurst's death?'

'I'm afraid there's nobody I can think of.' Ogden tugged at his nose again, like one of those monkeys, and raised his shoulders and hands in defeat. 'Sorry.'

'There's nothing to be sorry for, sir.' Fenchurch beckoned the uniforms over. 'My colleagues here will take you home.'

'Okay.' Ogden flicked his tongue from side to side. 'Does it get easier?'

'Does what?'

'Dealing with her loss?'

The acid felt like it was going to jump up and attack Fenchurch's throat again. 'It gets easier when you let people help you.'

Chapter Seven

F enchurch stalked across the interview room to lean in front of Shelvey, getting right in his face. He just got a blast of garlic breath for his trouble. Drizzle of garlic oil on his pizza, most likely. He stood up tall and sucked in the silence of the room.

Shelvey sat back, facing away, and glanced at his lawyer.

Anna Xiang didn't look like any of her ancestors had even left London, let alone been from China. Mid-brown hair, mid-thirties, mid-everything. Her wedding and engagement rings glinted under the strip light. 'Inspector, I'm here on the understanding you have some evidence to present to my client supporting the allegations you've concocted.' Scratch that — the shrillest voice this side of a not very fondly remembered primary teacher. Like nails down a blackboard. 'I'd appreciate it if we could get started.'

Reed produced a sheet of paper and handed a copy over the table. 'Do you own a Toyota Prius, licence plate LK16 VKP?'

Shelvey sat there, mouth clamped shut. He picked it up and shrugged.

'For the record, the interviewee has just given a shrug.' Reed held her own page in front of her face. 'Mr Shelvey, you'll be glad to know we've done some digging into this vehicle. The Borehamwood DVLA Office registered it on the eighteenth of April this year in the name of one Steven Robert Shelvey. Now, is that you?'

Shelvey drew his mouth into a straight line. 'It's me.'

'Okay, so we're getting somewhere, then.' Reed opened an evidence box and produced the first bagged item: the tub of blue pills. 'You know what we found in your car?'

'Enlighten me.'

'Viagra.' Reed rattled the pills around. 'Fake ones at that.'

'Never seen that in my life.' Shelvey pointed at Fenchurch. 'You planted that in my car when you assaulted me.'

'Really?' Reed held the bag up to the light. 'We've got some prints off this and we'll be running them against yours. It's usually easier if you just admit they're yours, rather than waiting for our Crime Scene Investigators to waste hours analysing it.'

Nothing more, just a glare.

Reed squinted at the tub, her right eye shut. 'I hope for your sake that they're the real McCoy.' She pointed at a pill through the plastic. 'Something like seventy-seven per cent of the pills on the street are fake. They won't give you a strong hard-on. More likely to make it drop off.'

'They're mine.' Shelvey folded up his polo-shirt collar. 'And it's real stuff.'

'It's illegal to sell it without a prescription, you know?'

'They're for personal use.'

Reed flashed him a coquettish grin, coupled with a wink. 'Young fella like you shouldn't need any help getting it up.'

Shelvey just snorted, his sunburn spreading to his ears.

Reed put the pills down on the table. 'Bet you don't have a prescription for them, though, do you?'

Shelvey did a double-take at the door.

Clooney was standing there, hand poised to knock. 'Got a minute, Si?'

Fenchurch got to his feet and whispered to Reed, 'Keep him talking.'

She spoke into the microphone. 'DI Fenchurch has left the room.'

Fenchurch eased the door shut behind him. 'What's up, Mick?'

'Got something of interest.' Clooney rubbed at his ear, setting his earrings jangling. He yawned, his jaw shuddering. 'Christ, I hate it when you work nights. Always keep me out of my bed.' He blinked hard a few times, then stretched out his eyes with his fingers. 'Right. I got some fibres off the girl's backside and her tights. Done an initial test and, while this won't stand up in court yet, they match a Prius. A 2015 model, specifically.'

Fenchurch's gut lurched. Upwards, for once. Good news, no doubt about to be pulled from my paws. 'And that model would have '16 plates, yeah?'

'That's the badger.'

'Tell me there's evidence she was raped in that car.'

'It's on her bare buttocks, Si.' Clooney grimaced. 'Unless she was wiping her arse on the back seat, but I can't find any—'

'Yeah, yeah, yeah.' Never change, Mick.

'What about any signs of penetration?'

'Spoke to Pratt. He's got traces of spermicide in her vagina. Some pubic hairs that don't belong on her. Not that she had many.'

Fenchurch's turn to grimace. 'I need to know if that sex was consensual.'

'Think it's a safe bet it wasn't. I shall confirm at the post-mortem, though.'

'What about the knife?'

'Still not found it, Si. Could be anywhere. Mandy and Nina are checking the fibres in the motor as we speak. DS Nelson's there from your lot.'

'Good stuff.' Fenchurch opened the door and waited until Shelvey looked over, then clapped Clooney on the shoulder. 'I owe you a beer, Mick.'

'You *know* I don't drink.' Clooney slouched off down the corridor, shaking his head.

Just no pleasing some people.

Savour this moment. Don't let it disappear. That little trickle of happiness sliding down to your gut. The spring in your step. That's yours, sunshine, nobody else's.

Fenchurch made eye contact with Shelvey again, stopping him mid-sentence. Got you, you raping bastard. He opened the door and stood near the edge of the table.

'—pills, I bloody swear.' Shelvey was ignoring Fenchurch now. 'You're not listening to me, Sergeant. I need them to get an erection. I was in an accident when I was little.'

Reed spoke into the mic again. 'DI Fenchurch has re-entered the room.'

Sweat dripped from Shelvey's forehead. Guilty as that college rapist in America.

'Son, you've been lying your arse off to us.' Fenchurch sat opposite him and left a few seconds' gap, drowned out by the thunder of the drums in his ears. 'That girl was raped before she was killed. And we've found fibres on her body matching a Toyota Prius.'

Shelvey pleaded with his lawyer, eyes wide. 'This is bullshit! I didn't do anything to her!'

Fenchurch grabbed the pills and rattled them in his face. The garlic stench was even worse. 'Didn't pop one of these before you—'

'I didn't do nothing!'

'Let's go through this from nine o'clock yesterday evening again, shall we?' Fenchurch leaned over the table. 'You picked her up on Throgmorton Street, right?'

'That's the thing, right?' Shelvey sat forward, animated for the first time. His heavy eyebrows twitched. 'I was driving her home, yeah? Then she started having a go at me, said I should've gone over Tower Bridge.'

'Well, she was right.' Fenchurch cracked his knuckles. 'You went the wrong way, son. She lives in Bermondsey, not bloody Greenwich.'

'There was some incident on London Bridge, so I thought Tower'd be rammed.' Shelvey shifted his monster eyebrows into a frown. 'So I was heading for the Rotherhithe Tunnel instead.'

Fenchurch ran his tongue over his teeth, trying to suss out whether the kid was as stupid as he seemed. 'And what happened before you raped her?'

'I didn't rape nobody.' Shelvey waved his hands around. 'She was shouting at me, man. Telling me I was an idiot. Calling me a prick and everything.'

'Was that when you were raping her?'

'Ain't you listening to me?' Shelvey huffed again, half of his collar flopping down. 'I just let her out onto the street.'

'Where?'

'Shadwell?' Shelvey peered around the ceiling, like that's where Victoria Brocklehurst was. 'Not far from the DLR stop. Outside an all-night Paki's.'

Fenchurch flicked up his eyebrows. 'You dropped a lone woman in Shadwell just after nine o'clock?'

Shelvey burped, his face twisting up like he was disgusted with himself. 'I'm telling you, man, she could handle herself.'

Fenchurch let the slur hang. 'You're lying, son.'

Another burp, Shelvey blinking hard. 'I'm not, man. I let her . . . Let her out on the street.' Burp. 'I know you're talking out of your arse. I never raped anyone. That bitch . . .' Burp. 'That bitch was crazy, man. Crazy.'

'Evening, guv.' DS Jon Nelson was lurking by the Shelvey house, having a sly suck on his vape stick. He pocketed the e-cigarette. His purple shirt contrasted as ever with his beige suit and black skin. Didn't look anything like a cop, more like a management consultant. An overweight one who abused the weights at the gym. 'Did Temple come through?'

'Don't know how he does it, but he's always got a magistrate waiting by the phone.' Fenchurch unfolded the search warrant.

'You want me to lead in here, guv?'

'No, Jon, I'll take this.' Fenchurch knocked on the pale-brown front door. 'Mrs Shelvey, it's the police.'

She pulled the door open and stood there, hands on hips. Fully dressed now in tracksuit bottoms and a baggy T-shirt. A little Yorkie barked at her ankles. 'Have you let my son go?'

Fenchurch held out the search warrant. 'No, we've got a warrant to search these premises.'

'What for?'

'Drugs, weapons. Whatever your son's got—'

She prodded him in the sternum. 'What are you scumbags saying he's done?'

'Rape and murder.' Fenchurch let it sink in. 'Now, I need you to let me and my officers inside.'

'What the hell's going on here?' A lump of bone and anger lumbered through from the living room. Tight jeans strained to contain a pale-yellow work shirt hanging open, a silver St Christopher tangled up in white chest hair. 'You think you can come in here, do you?'

'It's not just think, sir.' Fenchurch stepped into the hall, his foot squelching on the carpet. Christ knows what that was. 'And you are?'

'Pete Morris. Barbara's brother.' He loomed tall, like a giant searching for a beanstalk. 'You saying my nephew's raped a girl?'

'I just need to get on with this, sir.' Fenchurch waved for Nelson to barge past and get up the stairs. A SOCO stood behind him, straining at his lead. 'On you go, Jon.'

'You need to give us space.' Morris tried to block Nelson, but Fenchurch got between them. 'Get back here, you bla—'

'No, you don't.' Fenchurch got in the guy's face, just a few inches too short. He had that uncle-y cigar smell you didn't get often these days. 'Keep out of our way.'

'I'll smash you into next week, you punk.'

'Try it.' Fenchurch reached round for his baton and detached it from his belt. 'I'm sure you'll get on well in Belmarsh.'

Morris stepped back and dusted himself off. 'You fascist bastards.'

Fenchurch pointed through to the living room. 'I need you to get in there and stay there. Okay?' He turned round and gestured for the squat uniformed officer to guard the door. He took a few seconds for the thunder in his ears to calm down.

That could so easily have turned nasty.

He bounced up the stairs, each step squeaking as he put his foot down. Three doors led off the landing. The bathroom door hung ajar. A second was shut. Nelson was standing next to the third one, waiting for the SOCO to nudge it open. The walls were covered in *Nuts* and *Zoo* posters, busty girls in the all-together on beaches and in hotel rooms. A Charlie the Seahorse poster, him smoking a joint, his eyes turning inside out. A few pictures of blokes in sharp suits — Charlie Sheen, Johnny Depp, Ray Winstone, Tom Hardy. Crystal Palace bedspread.

'See the bedding, guv? Geezer's maybe not so bad after all.' Nelson was over the other side of the double bed, careful not to sit on it. He rummaged around in the chest of drawers under the watchful eye of the SOCO. 'Oh, here we go . . . I've got something.' He held the drawer open for a photograph.

Fenchurch got a look. Some black fabric, frills around the edges. 'Is that . . . knickers?' His flashlight bounced off the material. 'Tell me these aren't Victoria Brocklehurst's.'

'Could be, guv. I'll get Clooney on it.' Nelson bagged them up, the camera pulsing light over every movement. 'Hang on, what's this?' He crouched down and lifted up the bed's valance. A small plastic ziplock bag lay there. Triangular wraps and some white powder in baggies. 'Bingo!'

'Now we're talking.' Fenchurch patted Nelson on the back. 'Good effort, Jon. What do you think, coke and speed?'

'Way more than enough to stretch beyond personal use, especially if you include the Viagra.'

Fenchurch peered over Nelson's shoulder into the drawer. Underneath an old mobile charger was a long strip of pale-blue fabric, UNICEF stencilled on it in white letters. He reached his gloved hand in and picked it up as the SOCO documented it. Plastic rattled as a work pass tumbled out. Something else clattered to the floor.

Dark hair shrouded her narrow eyes, a frosty smile on her lips.

VICTORIA BROCKLEHURST, OGDEN & MAKEPEACE.

Fenchurch swung it around to Nelson. 'What a stupid, stupid bastard.'

'This is gold dust, guv.' Nelson was crouching again. He pointed at a knife, the serrated edge lined with blood.

Fenchurch couldn't keep his eyes off it.

The SOCO logged it and photographed it. 'I'll get this to Mick Clooney, sir.'

Fenchurch's Airwave blasted out. Reed. 'Better take this.' He stabbed the button, but still couldn't take his eyes off the knife. 'Kay, what's up?'

'Couple of my guys have been looking into this Shelvey bloke.' Reed paused on the line, that infernal Rihanna tune playing in the background. 'Think we might have something. Shelvey worked for Flick Knife last year.'

Ice crept through Fenchurch's veins. 'Frank Blunden?'

'That's right. I'm round here just now, checking up. Blunden's here working, but . . .' Reed clicked her tongue a few times. 'As you'd expect, he'll only speak to you, guv.'

Chapter Eight

Fenchurch spotted Reed's car outside Frank's Cabs. Just an anonymous residential street in the better part of Mile End. 'Anywhere here.'

'Sir.' The uniform pulled in a few car lengths up and let Fenchurch out.

Reed got out of her Fiat and joined him. 'Morning, guv.' She ran a hand through her hair and let it fall into the new shape, then pursed her lips, a thick dark scab in the middle.

Fenchurch stopped dead. The DLR tracks sat silent above them, lit up on a Victorian railway bridge. 'You okay?'

'I'm not going in that office unless you order me to.' She tugged her hair tight round her ears. 'Said it has to be you, and you alone.'

Blunden.

'Didn't say why?'

'Just called me a bitch.'

'You shouldn't have to put up with that, Kay.' A shard of light crept out of the gap between the houses. 'Give me five minutes, okay?' Fenchurch set off, passing a pair of silver Škodas and a black cab on the street. He was tempted to key at least one of them. He marched beneath the arch and knocked on the door of Frank's Cabs.

It flew open and Frank Blunden peered out, almost as wide as he was tall. His snakeskin suit formed a chessboard pattern, twisted round by forty-five degrees, crinkling as his hands fell to his sides, flapping off his barrel body. 'Fenchurch . . . Nice to see you, me old mucker.'

Fenchurch ignored the counterfeit friendliness, instead pointing at the suit. 'Must've been a bloody big snake.'

'It's fake. Don't want any animal-rights tossers round here. Come on in.' Blunden ushered Fenchurch into his office through the darkened reception area, the white glow from a battered computer monitor the only light in the room. He rested against his desk, shunted round to the other window, facing out of the room instead of in. 'Have a seat.'

03:16 burned in large red digits on an old clock radio. 'You've long since burnt all the midnight oil, Frank.'

'I'm actually in early.' Blunden eased himself back onto the desk. 'I'm not sleeping so well these days.' He sneezed into his hand, then ran it down his trousers. 'Prostate cancer.'

Fenchurch's throat tightened up. 'You're serious?'

'Inoperable. Spread to my liver. Docs give me three months. We'll see how that goes. I'm not rotting away in some *hospice*.' He spat the word out like it could make the cancer worse. 'That's not for Frank Blunden.'

'Not sure working all night will give you any longer, though.'

'I've got a lot of thinking to do about what happens to this place after I've gone.' Blunden swept his hand round the grotty office like it was a country mansion with two sides of a family at loggerheads over the inheritance. 'They call it "advanced care planning", you know? How I'd like to die. Who inherits my empire.'

'Got anyone in mind?'

Blunden tapped his nose.

'Have to say, you don't seem too bad, Frank.'

'I'm one of the very lucky ones. I don't seem to be getting the biting pain a lot of my fellow sufferers get. It'll come, though.' Blunden picked up a newspaper and waved it in the air. 'Got a copy of the *Post* at the petrol station on my way in. Very interesting reading.'

Fenchurch's mouth dried up. He tried to swallow something down. Anything. 'What you talking about?'

'Front-page story, eh?' Blunden stabbed at the cover, his finger bouncing off it. 'Saving that old Tory bastard from what was coming to him. Can't stand him. Public-school pansy, arguing about stupid stuff like it matters to the man on the street.'

'Just doing my job, Frank.'

'Bet you were.' Blunden opened the paper fully and let the magazine section fall out. 'Oh, what have we got here?' He picked it up and winked at Fenchurch. 'Looks very much like an article about your daughter.'

Fenchurch shut his eyes, the thundering drums taking over. 'I'm not in the mood, Frank.'

'Really?' Blunden tossed the paper down on the desk. 'Makes the old heart bleed, doesn't it? Only bit of me that's not riddled with cancer, I tell you.' He sucked in breath and coughed it out. 'This why you're here?'

Fenchurch raised an eyebrow. 'That mean you know something about it?'

'Always quick with that, aren't you?' Blunden grinned, his tongue darting around the bottom of his nose. 'Like I keep telling you and that stupid bastard father of yours, I know nothing about what happened to your daughter.' He switched the smile to the sort of frown you'd give a small child. 'Terrible story, mind.' He sniffed as he rummaged around in his trousers. 'So why are you here?'

'Steven Shelvey.'

Blunden groaned like Millwall had conceded a last-minute own goal. 'What's he done now?'

'You know him, then?'

'Afraid I do.' Blunden did some more fiddling. 'Shelvey . . . Now he was a bit of a lad.'

'How'd you mean?'

'Got involved in those protests. You remember? All those cabbies crowding out town hall? He was eighteen but he was like a sixty-year-old shop steward, I tell you.' Blunden snarled. 'Unsightly business, mind. Just need to let that shit wash over, let things stabilise. This Travis lot, now that's stability. I love them, get a ton of work through them. Less hassle than answering the phones. Means I don't need a girl through the night. Plus, our rating's really high so we get even more business. Win bloody win.'

'Shelvey was doing a Travis run tonight. Wasn't for you?'

'I'd heard he'd gone direct with them.' Blunden glowered at the window. 'Now that is a scam. That lot loan these geezers fifteen grand or whatever to go buy themselves an electric car.' He chuckled hard, his squat torso rocking. 'An electric car, I ask you. Heard that ponce was driving around in a Prius like he's some Californian hippie.'

'He definitely doesn't work for you?'

'No, he bloody doesn't. I got shot of the punk last year.' Blunden's arms almost met in the middle of his huge chest. 'No, that prick tried it on with one too many girls in one of my cabs.'

Here we go.

Fenchurch grimaced. 'What do you mean by trying it on?'

'Oh, never anything too naughty. But, every few weeks, I'd get an angry husband, boyfriend or father showing up here asking me a few difficult questions.' Blunden picked up the paper and split out the sport section, covered in build-up for the Euros. 'Pestering these girls for dates, cheeky little grab of their thighs. Couldn't have that, now, could I? So I let him go.'

'You didn't come to us about any of it, I notice.'

'That's not the game I'm playing, Inspector.' Blunden held up the front page of the sport section, Wayne Rooney, Harry Kane and Jamie Vardy dressed in their official suits. 'I'm thinking we'll get knocked out in the second round. Probably to Portugal. You?'

'Don't follow international football.'

'Not a patriot?'

'Not a nationalist.' Fenchurch spotted a tatty St George's cross over by the door. 'I like my Hammers, that's about it.'

'Bunch of bloody thugs.'

'You're Millwall, aren't you?'

'For my sins.' Blunden folded the paper in half. 'I passed all that stuff about Shelvey on to some contacts in the local nick. Brick Lane. I don't know if they did anything with it.'

'Very public-spirited of you. Got their names?'

Blunden smirked at him. 'Smith and Jones, as it happens.'

'Very funny.'

'It's the truth, Inspector. Big lumps, the pair of 'em. Can see their skulls through their skinheads.'

'Sound like your sort of cops.'

'Oh, I couldn't bribe 'em if I wanted to. These boys are honest as the day is long.' Another smirk. 'Unlike you.'

'Inoperable?' Reed stopped outside Brick Lane station and killed the engine. 'Is that karma or something?'

'Of the instant variety.' Fenchurch undid the seat belt and tried to open the door. Her car was smaller than a hen cage. He got out and marched up to the door. Inside, the place was still packed with drunken fighters, even at this hour. He rested against the charred melamine counter and tapped the buzzer. Then gave Reed another glance. 'You get anywhere while I was with Blunden?'

Reed hovered behind him and grimaced. 'That reminds me . . .' She wandered off with her Airwave.

The side door opened and the Desk Sergeant hobbled over to sit on a stool, like he was running a Victorian factory. Huge whiskers veiled his eyes, darting around like he was fed up with modern life. Then they settled on Fenchurch and he groaned. 'Yes?'

Fenchurch flashed his warrant card. 'I need to speak to two of your officers.' He looked away. 'Smith and Jones.'

'Smith and Jones?' The Sergeant's eyes narrowed at Fenchurch. 'You having a laugh? We ain't got a Smith and bloody Jones here.'

Reed rested her hands on the counter and grinned at the Sergeant. 'Morning, Bunk.'

'Kay.' Bunk, if that was his first or last name, grimaced at the recognition. 'So you're here, are you? Finally got what's coming to you, then.'

Reed rubbed at her lip, then flashed him a grin. 'This is about a cab driver who killed a girl out by Bromley-by-Bow earlier on our shift.'

'You guys caught that one?' Bunk's eyes flicked between them. 'Heard it come through. Sounded nasty. That sort of case can take weeks to even get a suspect.'

'Well, we've got one in custody, we're just chasing up a lead.' Reed tilted her head, like she was trying to draw Bunk's eyes towards the computer. 'Problem is, our lead told us he'd reported some sexual assaults to these cops, who he called Smith and Jones.'

'Right, right.' Bunk hammered at the keyboard like it'd been sleeping with his wife for eighteen months. 'Smith and bloody Jones. You don't get any better, Kay, I swear.'

'This came from Frank Blunden.'

'Blunden? Cheeky bastard.' Bunk dug his fingers into his sideburns. 'Always a little nugget of truth in what he says, mind. Like a bit of sweetcorn in your morning dum—'

'You got anything yet, Bunk?'

'Yeah, here we go. You daft buggers.' Bunk rolled his eyes at Reed. 'It's not bloody Smith and Jones, it's Naismith and Johnson.'

Reed raised her eyebrows at Fenchurch, inches from pissing herself laughing. 'And have you got any idea where Naismith and Johnson are now?'

'Clive's upstairs.' Bunk buzzed the security door. 'Watching DVDs, if I know him.'

Reed winked at him. 'And which one's Clive?'

DC Clive Naismith sat in the station's tiny canteen, the room reeking of Indian food, like most of Brick Lane outside. Tall and heavy-set, his stubbly skinhead adding to the layer of psychotic he was born with. Sharp suit, though at least he'd covered it with a napkin. 'Don't mind me.' He hovered over a clear plastic tub, jabbing his fork in to skewer a gristly chunk of lamb floating in a beige sauce. 'Lovely grub.' The surrounding tables were filled with blue bags.

Reed couldn't take her eyes off the food. 'Take it you didn't pay for it?'

'Hardly.' Naismith finished chewing and swallowed it down. 'Fight in one of the curry houses up the street earlier on. Daft buggers let in a rugby team at one in the morning. Never learn, do they?' He tore off a strip of naan and dipped it into the sauce. 'Always letting in pissed-up drunks at all hours. Always a surprise when they chuck food and chairs at each other. Caught one lad pissing in the ladies' sink. Can you believe it?'

The coconut aroma was tying Fenchurch's stomach in knots. 'Don't quite understand how a DC gets involved in local policing matters, though.'

'Bit quiet on a Thursday night shift till the clubs start chucking people out.' Naismith took another slab of naan. 'Helping plod fills the time, you know? Only so many forms you can complete before you nod off, am I right?' He opened a tub filled with pakoras. 'Help yourselves.'

'You'll regret that.' Fenchurch took two of them, saliva almost dribbling onto his chin, and ate the first in one go. A lot hotter than he expected. Lovely. 'You ever speak to Flick Knife?'

'Frank Blunden?' Naismith stopped eating, his plastic fork hanging in the air waiting for Fenchurch's nod. 'I hear the poor guy's not so well these days. Cock cancer or something.' Another mouthful of curry, chewing the beige slush with his mouth open, his lips slapping together. 'We speak to him a fair amount, as it happens. Occasionally has some good gen on the street.' He held up his fork. 'He's not on our Covert Sources log, if that's what you're after.'

Fenchurch bit the second pakora in two and swallowed the first half down. 'What sort of things does he help you with?'

'All the horrible little crimes that aren't sexy enough for you rock stars.'

An answer for everything.

Fenchurch ate the other half. 'These are lovely.' He took another from the tub and scoffed it in one go. 'Does the name Steven Shelvey ring any bells?'

Naismith pushed the curry away, brushing his tongue between his teeth. 'What about him?'

'So you know him?'

'Quit it with the games, sir. What do you want to know about him?'

'Frank Blunden mentioned him.' Reed got out her notebook and opened it up. 'What do you know?'

'Main thing is when those cabbies swarmed City Hall. Few of them got in. Shelvey got arrested, from what I remember.' Naismith licked his fork clean, his serpentine tongue running down the tines to the point. 'Got a bit over-exuberant, started thinking he could take down the Met on his own. So we picked him up, stuck him inside.'

'Why's he not still inside?'

'No idea.' Naismith folded his naan bread over, still rubbing at his teeth. 'Thought he was a shagger, that's for sure.' He stared into his curry. 'Blunden fired the little scrotal sack when he went too far with this Indian girl. Way I hear it, he had the child locks on, got in the back of the cab and tried it on with her.' He stirred the sauce with the plastic fork, then dropped it in, almost up to the end of the handle. 'She scratched his cheek, he punched her.'

'Did he rape her?'

'No, he just left her at a building site and pissed off.'

Fenchurch leaned forward. 'A building site?'

'Yeah, down Woolwich way.'

Fenchurch stabbed it into his Pronto. 'And you didn't do him for this attempted rape?'

'Girl wouldn't testify.' Naismith shrugged, like he was saying, 'What can you do, eh?' 'See that a lot. These girls get frightened easy.' He snapped the plastic lid back on the curry. 'What's Shelvey done, anyway?'

'Looks like he's raped a girl, then murdered her.'

Naismith pinched his nose. 'Shit.'

'Anything you've got on Shelvey would be greatly appreciated . . .'

'Oh, I've got a bucketload . . .'

Chapter Nine

Leman Street's rear door buzzed. Fenchurch held it open and hauled it out of the way.

Naismith lugged the evidence folder under his left arm, the big bag of leftover curry in the other. 'You're going to clear this with my DI, right?'

Fenchurch fixed him a glare. 'In the morning.'

'Look, I've got import—'

'Constable, you're pissing about with curry houses, so don't give me the old "I've got a critical task on, sir". Okay?' Fenchurch folded his arms and gestured at the door. 'Now, get up the stairs and start organising what you've got on Shelvey. DS Nelson will be up shortly.'

'Sir.' Naismith trudged off, his shoulders low.

'You can leave that food.'

'Here, then.' Naismith held out a blue bag. 'I'll dump the rest in the canteen, okay?'

'Thanks.' Fenchurch watched him trudge off, then opened the bag. 'I'm starving. Kay?'

Reed tried peering inside. 'What have you got?'

Fenchurch fished out a box and tore off the lid. 'Mixed pakora, I think.' He ate one in a single bite. 'Mushroom.' Then he grimaced. 'Bloody hot, too.'

Reed frowned as she took one. 'Thought they were bhajis, guv.'

'They're the same thing. One's north India, the other's south. Can't remember which is which.'

'Right.' Reed blew out as she chewed. 'What do you think about this Naismith character, guv?'

The upstairs door clanked shut, rattling round the stairwell. 'I don't trust him.'

Reed rested against the wall, munching on another pakora. 'What's the—'

'Simon!' Clooney was jogging down the hallway, his trainers squeaking off the floor, earrings jangling. 'Where have you been?'

'Doing our job, Mick.' Fenchurch swallowed his pakora. 'What's up?'

Clooney sniffed the air, the spicy tang already replacing the corridor's usual bitter smell. 'Been out for a ruby?'

Reed hefted up the bag. 'There's more up in the canteen.'

'I could eat a horse.' Clooney picked out a pakora and bit into it, eyes closed. 'Heaven.' He ate the second half and cleared his throat. 'Anyway, Nina found some more knickers in a bag under the boy's bed.' He held up three small bags containing three pieces of fabric and lace.

'Jesus Christ.' Reed inspected them. 'Hiding stuff from his mum is different to hiding it from us.' She shifted the contents around. 'He could've raped a few women.'

'Let's be careful about assumptions.' Fenchurch handed the bag back, shaking his head at Clooney. 'Take it you've got the budget to test them?'

'Doing that when I get back.' Clooney grabbed another pakora. 'I'll run any DNA I find against any unsolved rapes, okay?'

'Right.' Fenchurch wiped grease off his lips, succeeding in covering his hands. 'You getting anywhere with the knife yet?'

'Mandy's running it now.' Clooney stuffed two pakoras in his mouth.

'I need to know ASAP, okay?' Fenchurch waved Clooney off and grabbed the evidence file. 'You think Shelvey knew Victoria?'

Reed's gaze trailed after Clooney. 'The alternative is she just got in the wrong cab at the wrong time. Don't know which is worse, guv.'

Fenchurch's mobile rang, the opening drone of 'Kashmir'. He checked the display — an unrecognised number, but not a hidden one. 'Better take this, Kay. Can you find Jon and get him to supervise Naismith?' He walked off and answered the call. 'Fenchurch.'

'Ah, Inspector.' A snuffle filled the line. 'I was wondering if there was any news?'

Fenchurch caught his reflection in the glass and let his forehead slacken. Made him look slightly less homicidal. Slightly. 'Sorry, who is this?'

'It's Gerald Ogden.'

'Right, right.' Fenchurch brushed his hair back, restoring the bed-head. 'Thanks for calling me, sir. I can't—'

'Have you caught whoever did this to my Victoria?'

We caught the scumbag who raped and killed your goddaughter, sir. And we've no idea how many others he's done . . . How can I push him back to tomorrow?

Fenchurch coughed, the pakora's fire loosening something. 'I'll need to ask you a few additional questions, sir. When would be convenient?'

'Well, I'm at home now and I can't seem to sleep.'

The lights on Vauxhall Bridge Road were still stuck at red. Up ahead, two new towers marked out the north shore of the Thames, square glass on the right, rounded concrete on the left. Alien towers setting up camp opposite MI6's headquarters. A mishmash of towers camped on the south bank in both directions, barely any blank lots remaining, certainly none without cranes marked by blinking lights. The Vauxhall Tower was outlined in blue like something from *Tron*, though the Eye of Sauron wasn't in flame tonight.

Fenchurch stuck the car in neutral. 'Hardly recognise this city any more.'

'Is that senility or something?' Reed's grin was lit up by her mobile in the pre-dawn darkness. 'Still think you should've taken the Lambeth Bridge, guv.'

'Not that shit again. After the cycle-lane roadworks, I'm not taking another chance.' Fenchurch put the car in gear and set off from the lights, powering over Vauxhall Bridge. He turned right after the station, then the next left, navigating the web of chicanes by the park. 'Quiet tonight.'

'It's half four in the morning, guv. The post-club cottagers will have gone home.'

'I'd pick you up on that if it wasn't true.' Fenchurch trundled round the bend in the dark street, the mix of grime and luxury you'd expect in Vauxhall, and came to a long row of terraced houses leading back to the main road.

'Think that's it there.' Reed waved at a gate stuck between two lead-roofed columns. Behind it, a sprawling old factory was floodlit from below. Beige brick with a giant clock tower, once there to keep the workers right, now just a rich man's folly.

Fenchurch pulled in, blocking the gates. He got out of the car and set off towards the building's entrance. The pattern of lights inside and the way the bricks had been cleaned made it look like it had been subdivided into flats, just not too many.

'Three mill a flat, I reckon.' Reed tapped at her phone as they walked over. 'Shitting hell. Last sale for the penthouse was eight point four five million.'

Fenchurch blew air up his face, shaking his head. 'If you had eight and a half million quid, why would you live in *Vauxhall*?'

'Your guess is as good as mine.' Reed stopped by a wide door and hit the buzzer.

The door ground open and Gerald Ogden blinked out into the morning light. His face was lined with anger, fire burning in his eyes, doused by the tears slicking his cheeks. He wore a smoking jacket over silk pyjamas, but his feet were bare, his left middle toe missing. 'Inspector.' A smile flickered across his lips as his eyes took in Reed. 'Well, come on in. Please.'

He led inside the house, straight into a colossal room that belonged in Buckingham Palace a hundred years ago. Double height and painted white, grand portraits hanging from the walls. A black wrought-iron staircase crossed the face of a giant brick chimney that dominated the room. He led them through a large dining area to three sofas arranged in a U-shape around a crackling fire. The air-conditioning unit hissed above it.

Ogden collapsed onto one near a small TV.

Reed sat opposite Ogden, while Fenchurch took the one facing the fire. A picture of a stag on a misty Scottish moor hung from another chimney. Place was full of the bloody things.

Ogden perched forward, tugging his gown tight. 'So you wanted to speak to me?'

Fenchurch gave Ogden a slow nod. 'We've identified the driver who collected Ms Brocklehurst from outside your office. There's some evidence pointing to him sexually assaulting her.'

'Good heavens.' Ogden shut his eyes and pushed the heels of his palms deep into his eye sockets. His breath came in short gasps. 'Did this animal murder her?'

'We're unsure yet.' Fenchurch waited for eye contact. 'Does the name Steven Shelvey mean anything?'

Ogden opened his eyes again and blinked hard. 'Is this the creature who raped and killed Victoria?'

'We're holding him in custody. Does the name mean anything?'

'Absolutely nothing.' Ogden got to his feet and paced around, fists clenched, fury burning his neck red. 'He's a rapist and murderer . . . And Travis just let these people drive their cabs?'

'I can't comment on—'

Ogden thumped the TV screen, Boris Johnson giving an opponent a withering look. 'They employ murderers?'

Fenchurch sat forward on the seat. 'Did Ms Brocklehurst ever mention him?'

'Never. And she would have. We were close, Inspector.' Ogden tightened his gown as he rested on the chair. 'Victoria had some dalliances, but never anything serious. And if some taxi driver was stalking her, she'd have come to me, after she'd reported it to the police. Victoria had her head screwed on very tight.'

'This could be a chance thing, Mr Ogden.' Reed's forehead creasing. 'It sounds like, tragically, Victoria just got in the wrong taxi.'

'Is that supposed to console me? Are you trying to provide *any* comfort?'

'Mr Ogden, I can only apologise.' Fenchurch shot Reed a shut-the-hell-up glare. 'How often did she get a cab?'

'Most nights. Like I told you earlier, Victoria was a hard worker and worked late.' Ogden drilled his focus into Reed. 'Do you think you'll be able to prosecute this Shelley character?'

'Shelvey.' Reed smiled at him. 'We'll certainly do our best, sir.'

⌣

The Leman Street canteen was otherwise empty, not even the early-shift uniforms burning toast or superheating porridge in the microwave. Place reeked of second-hand Indian food.

Reed put yet another box of pakora down on the table. 'Found this in the fridge, in case you're still hungry.'

'Ravenous.' Fenchurch mopped up the last of his curry with some third-hand naan bread. Just about edible. Could really have done with some bite, but the hot-sauce bottle in his desk was empty. And the old acid reflux was rearing its head.

'Guv.' Nelson plonked himself down between them. 'Want me to send Naismith home?'

'Fed up of him already?'

'A bit.' Nelson puffed on his vape stick. 'Spent more time on his phone than on those case files.'

'Texts or calls?'

'Texts, I think.'

'Send him home, but keep a close eye on him tomorrow, yeah? I'll clear it with Docherty.' Fenchurch spooned more curry from the tub onto his plate and tore off some more naan. 'Has he found anything yet?'

'Far too much, guv.' Nelson picked up the pakora box and fished out another mushroom one. 'Problem is, it's all unsubstantiated. About twelve rape cases stalled because the victims wouldn't come forward.'

Fenchurch dunked his naan into the curry. 'Any evidence Shelvey was intimidating them?'

'Maybe. Nothing we can use immediately . . .' Nelson patted the wad of paper files. 'Might be something in here. People who'll speak if they know he's going away.'

Fenchurch finished his second seconds. 'Sounds good.'

Reed reached over for another pakora. 'I'll get Lisa Bridge on it. She's still twiddling her thumbs.'

Fenchurch grabbed a pakora. 'Why?'

'Still a hold-up on the CCTV from the street by the crime scene, guv.' Reed picked at her teeth. 'Bell.'

'Bloody hell.' Fenchurch swallowed down the pakora. 'I'll have a word with Docherty in the morning.' That one packed some heat. 'He must have donkey pic—' He stopped himself. Then tapped the wad of paperwork on the table, just missing a splodge of curry sauce. 'Going back to this lot, anything?'

Nelson picked up a file and flicked through it. 'Naismith's got photos and case notes. Mostly background on Shelvey.'

'Why didn't any of this go to trial?'

'Like he said earlier, guv, the witnesses didn't want to commit to court.'

'So what's the plan? Get out there and change their minds?'

'Not a bad idea.'

'There's another option.' Fenchurch finished his curry and dumped the tub in the recycling. The lamb had stuck between pretty much all of his teeth. 'We could go in there, armed with that, and try and railroad him. Get a confession now.'

'Think that'll work?'

'Ninety per cent chance.' Fenchurch stood and stuffed the folder under his arm. 'Jon, can you get on to the CCTV?'

'Guv.'

'Thought I'd find you lot here.' Temple was standing over Fenchurch, though he was looking eye to eye. 'Nice feed?'

'Help yourself.' Fenchurch waved at the spread on the table. 'Pretty tasty, but not hot enough.'

'That means it'll be far too spicy for mere mortals like me.' Temple sat down and spooned out some curry onto a paper plate. He bit into some lamb and tossed his head from side to side as he chewed. 'Not bad.' He dolloped another mound. 'What did you make of that Ogden fella?'

'How did you know we were visiting him?'

'Kay told me.' Temple unbuttoned his suit jacket. Then he yawned. 'I know him of old.'

'Any juice on him?'

'Lawyers like him, the ones in this for the money, they're usually sociopaths.' Temple scooped some curry into his mouth. 'Very easy to confuse them with normal people, but deep down they just don't care.'

Fenchurch speared a chunk of lamb off Temple's plate. 'I thought that was all lawyers.'

'Very good.' Temple dipped a pakora into the sauce. 'I'm serious. Most City lawyers are sociopaths who don't care how the money's made.'

'Can't disagree with that.'

Temple stretched out, a yawn still grabbing hold of him. 'Don't know how you lot can work all night.'

'You get used to it.'

'I'll take your word for it.' Temple eyed the pakora box again. 'Been meaning to say . . . This Shelvey guy's lawyer has been speaking to me. Anna something or other?'

'Xiang.'

'Right. She's saying she's going to fight tooth and nail over the incident at his house.'

Fenchurch scowled at him. 'What incident?'

'You knocking his door down, chasing him along the street and twocking him in his car.'

'Jesus H. Christ.' Fenchurch stuffed his hands into his pockets, getting grease all over the fabric. 'First things first, that little shit gobbed all over me. It was like Rudi Völler and Frank Rijkaard at Italia '90.'

Temple reached out for another pakora. 'Is that your colourful way of saying you spat back?'

'No.' Fenchurch scratched at the stubble on his chin. 'I mean, Shelvey was like both of them. Gobbed twice on me. Maybe three times.'

'I'll add that to the charge sheet, but get whoever was with you to straighten up their notebooks, okay?' Temple tapped Fenchurch on the shoulder. 'Good news about the knife, though.'

Fenchurch dropped his pakora. 'What?'

'Positive against the girl's blood type.' Temple snatched up a couple more pakoras. 'See you later.' He wandered through the canteen and stopped by the door.

Fenchurch got out his personal mobile. Three missed calls from Clooney. 'Bugger.' He showed his phone to Nelson. 'Jon, can you chase this up? Get a print and we'll meet you at the interview room.'

'Guv.' Nelson grabbed the half-full pakora box off him and fished out his mobile, stabbing at the screen, then putting it to his ear. 'Mick, got a sec?' He nodded his head and gave the thumbs-up.

———

Reed entered the Custody Suite and looked around. 'His lawyer was still lurking around when I last looked in, banging on about his human rights.'

'Right.' Fenchurch followed her in.

'*Nnnngahh.*' The Sergeant lay back in his chair, his mouth hanging open, honking out a snore. '*Nnnngahh.*'

Reed prodded him in the chest. 'Come on, Martin. Wakey-wakey.'

Martin blinked hard, slowly, yawning like a stag the morning after the first of three nights in Magaluf. 'What's up?'

'Need to take Shelvey up to interview.'

'He's in six.' Martin got up and grabbed his keys.

'Cheers.' Fenchurch had caught Martin's yawn, another of the never-ending ones. Reed joined in.

Martin unlocked the door to room six, then thumped it with his palm. 'Out you come, Mr Shel— Shit!'

Shelvey was convulsing on the cell floor in a pool of blood, moaning, eyes flickering.

Chapter Ten

S tanding back was the only option.

Fenchurch got out of the cell and let the duty doctor do his magic. Didn't look good — Shelvey was still shaking, his torso twisting in ways it just shouldn't. Smelled like the guy had shat himself.

'Out of the way!' A Northern Irish accent foghorned from behind, accompanied by the rattle of a gurney. 'Coming through!'

Fenchurch skipped to the side and hugged the cold wall, letting them get access to the room. The paramedic, what was his name? Not Pratt, but similar. Platt, that was it. Cream flashes on his NHS glasses, hair slicked back to cover his creeping baldness.

The doctor got to his feet, jacket sleeves rolled up to the elbows, the grey suit covered in fluff like he'd cleaned it in a washing machine. He grimaced. 'We're losing him.'

Platt took one look at Shelvey. 'What do you think it is?'

'Could be anything. A fit, though it's not an epileptic seizure with all that blood.' The doctor stroked his chin, like there was any time for that now. 'I'm thinking poisoning.'

Fenchurch's spine tingled, shredding the nerves up his back. His stomach acid boiled like a cauldron. 'Poisoning?'

'I've never seen it before, but you read the textbooks and—'

'Okay, okay. Let's get him to the hospital.' Platt lowered the gurney, the mechanism squealing as he pumped it. 'I'll mobilise a specialist while we're en route. Okay?'

'That's . . . That's fine with me.' The duty doctor had all but given up. Standing inside the room was the only action he could take, aside from rolling his sleeves back down. 'Where are you taking him?'

'University College.'

A figure slouched against the wall in the Custody Suite. Martin, the bloody inept Desk Sergeant who let someone get poisoned while he slept off six pints. He kept trying to peer inside the door. 'What's going on?'

'That's a potential crime scene and you need to keep clear.' Fenchurch snorted as he tugged at Martin's arm and pulled him through to the Custody Suite, passing some rubbernecking prisoners pressed up to the open hatches. 'You're neck-deep in the shit. You'd better get someone to lock that cell down and start going through the CCTV in there to find out who's done this.'

Martin got behind his desk and tapped at his computer. His breathing was short and fast, his eyes bulging like he might have a heart attack any minute. He slammed the mouse on the wood. 'Shit, shit, shit.'

'What's happened?'

'The sodding CCTV's been wiped.' Martin pointed at the monitor. The time at the bottom was correct but the screen was black. 'Well, it's not been deleted. The cable's come out. It's just been recording—'

'Was it you?'

'Hardly.' Fire burnt Martin's neck and ears. 'As you know, I was asleep.'

'So someone's got in here, frigged the security system and killed him?'

Martin pinched at the skin on his throat. 'Has he been killed?'

'Someone's tried.' Fenchurch pulled his shirt away from his back, now a wall of sweat. 'You need to find out who's been in there, and fast.'

'Right.' Martin rubbed a hand down his face, pulling his eyelids down. Then he shook himself and clicked wildly with the mouse. 'Okay, here's the visitor log.' His fingers ran down the screen, his face glowing white in the reflection. 'There's nothing obvious. Two of my lads fed him at two . . . His lawyer's seen him.'

Fenchurch joined him on the other side of the desk. 'Anna Xiang?'

'That's the bird's name, yeah.' Martin scratched at his chin. 'Just wanted to see him, kept banging on about his human rights.'

'She didn't give him anything?'

'What, like a poisoned apple?'

'I'm being serious here, Martin. Did she give him anything?'

'I was with her the whole time. Didn't even get in the room, didn't even open the door. Just wanted to see he was being treated right.'

Fenchurch held his gaze, trying to tease out any crumbs of truth in there. 'And was he?'

'Are you saying I've got something to do with this?'

The cold wall leeched through Fenchurch's damp shirt. 'What was he fed?'

'A sandwich. Tuna, I think. Came from the canteen.' Martin burped into his fist. Mostly. 'I had half of it. Wish I'd waited for that ruby—'

'For once, I'm thankful for your gluttony.' Fenchurch tried to structure his thoughts into something coherent, fighting the tiredness like it was a rising tide.

A cabbie probably rapes and most likely kills a lawyer. Looks guilty as sin. Catch him without much effort, find drugs and the murder weapon.

Then this happens.

Who did it? How did they get in there? Did it happen before the arrest? Or after?

He glared at Martin. 'This the first time you've lost a murder suspect?'

'You what?'

'You heard me.' Fenchurch leaned in close, almost tasting his sweat. 'Has this sort of thing happened on your watch before?'

'Look, Inspector, that boy's still alive. Nobody's lost anything.'

'I saw you sleeping.' Fenchurch grabbed hold of his shirt. 'It's your bloody job to spot if there was something wrong with him. It shouldn't be up to me.'

Martin seemed to shrink away, his shoulders hunching and his chin digging into his chest. 'I can only apologise . . .'

'I'll tell that to the boy's mother, shall I? Big Martin sends his apologies.' Fenchurch hauled him to his feet. 'Is this the first time?'

'Whatever's happened here, it ain't my doing.'

The door juddered open and Nelson stormed in, his face twisted into a dark scowl, Naismith following.

'Jon.' Fenchurch stood up straight and puffed out his shirt. 'Constable, I need to know your movements over the last few hours.'

Nelson folded his arms across his chest. 'Except for when we were having a catch-up, guv, he's been with me all the time.'

'And while you were doing that, I had a chat with that SOCO geezer.' Naismith shrugged his shoulders. 'The one with the piercings. Clooney or something?'

Fenchurch curled his lip at Naismith, flashing teeth. 'Constable, I want you to fill out a statement detailing your movements, okay?' He nodded at Nelson. 'Jon, same with you, and I need it all confirmed.'

'Guv.' Nelson led Naismith away from the Custody Suite.

Fenchurch watched them leave, shaking his head. He got out his phone and dialled DCI Alan Docherty.

Took a few rings before it was answered with a groan. 'Si, do you know what time it is?'

'Got some bad news, boss.'

Through the window, London was a sea of light. The last night bus blurred along Euston Road, the top deck half full, trailed by taxis, like a presidential motorcade of drunks.

'You can talk to me, Simon.' Temple sipped from his machine tea. 'You do know that, right?'

Fenchurch blew on his drink. A scum had covered the surface, like a rank garden pond. 'Funny how every time I do talk to you, it ends up back with Abi.'

'Simon, you told me there are no secrets between you two these days.'

'There aren't.' Fenchurch touched his lips to the tea. Still far too hot. 'Doesn't mean I don't want the chance to tell her my secrets before you do.'

'Look, I'm sorry.' Temple patted Fenchurch's shoulder. 'She's just worried about you. Simon, you've got to stop putting up the Berlin Wall, okay? Talk to her. Share with her.'

Floodlights shone on the grey stone opposite, some London bastardisation of an Oxbridge quad. The hospital corridor was dim and dark. Didn't even have that cabbage smell, just cleaning fluids strong enough to burn your sinuses at a thousand paces.

'Just let me do it on my time, okay?'

'As long as you do it.'

The doctor appeared from the room two down, his designer stubble not quite obscuring a long scar running from his left ear. 'Sirs . . . My name's Dr Gold. I'm afraid to tell you that Mr Shelvey has just passed away.'

Fenchurch dumped his cup on the window ledge and shut his eyes. Another one lost to complacency and laziness . . . Stupidity and sloth . . . He reopened them, settling his focus on Temple, then shifted it to Gold. 'Was it poisoning?'

'Possibly.' Gold slid a hand through the rasping stubble. 'It's not my position to give a cause of death. I will comply with the pathologist—'

Fenchurch stepped closer, towering over the doctor. 'The duty doctor thought it might be poisoning.'

'And he should've known not to feed his suspicions to detectives.' Gold rested his hand on his chin, tapping two fingers and a thumb against it. 'I've arranged to transport the body to Lewisham for the autopsy. As it stands, I cannot comment on any of it.'

'Aren't you supposed to be a specialist in poisoning?'

'My specialism is none of your concern.' Gold ran his hands down his blue trousers. 'Due process dictates that I'm unable to give a cause of death.'

Fenchurch got in his face. 'This is a murder case. I need to know what's happened to him.'

'Then I suggest you contact the pathologist's office.' Gold turned on his heels and marched off, his white coat flapping behind him.

Fenchurch clenched his fists, tempted to give chase and force an answer out of him.

Temple blocked the way, like he was reading his violent thoughts. 'This isn't your fight, okay? You've caught a murderer. Take that as a victory, okay?'

'I can't just do that, Paul. That evil bastard dying in a holding cell isn't justice.'

Temple smiled at him. 'I know it's not, but it's not your fight any more.'

'You pig scumbag!' Barbara Shelvey was powering down the corridor, her brother and Anna Xiang trailing in her wake. 'You killed my boy!'

Give me strength . . . Fenchurch raised his hands up to placate her, his training kicking in. 'Mrs Shelvey, I'm very sorry for your loss.' Not as sorry as I am that he didn't get a trial and life in prison. 'I want to—'

'I'm going to get your bloody badge for this.' Mrs Shelvey stopped in front of him and prodded him in the chest. 'You killed my son!'

'Your son was in custody, and I assure you I had no access to—'

'You're lying!' She cracked her rings off Fenchurch's chest, digging into muscle and bone. 'You lying scumbag!'

'Come on, come on.' Pete Morris grabbed his sister's arms and tugged her back. 'This isn't the time or place, Barb. Okay? Come on.' She let him lead her down the corridor.

Fenchurch's shirt was torn where her gemstone had connected with him.

Xiang shook her head slightly. 'You better make sure you're clean, Fenchurch.'

'You care to repeat that?'

She held his gaze for a few seconds, then waltzed off down the corridor, heading for the lifts.

When she was out of sight, Fenchurch slumped back against the windowsill, almost knocking his discarded tea over. 'Remind me why I do this job again?'

'Because when you stop hitting your head against the brick wall, there's that surge of relief.' Temple smirked as his eyes rolled back in his head. 'My god.'

Fenchurch almost laughed.

His Airwave blared out. Reed.

'Kay, I could use some good news, if you've got any.'

'Not sure what it is, guv.' Reed paused on the line. 'Remember DS Grove from yesterday evening?'

'Feels like a few weeks ago, Kay.'

'Well, I put in a call with her. She's CO11, the Public Order Control lot. She's just got back to me. Turns out she managed the protest Shelvey got arrested at. Fancy a trip over there?'

Chapter Eleven

CO11 was near the top of New Scotland Yard, not quite at the Commissioner's level, but close. Not sure they'd get such a lofty position when they moved to the new building. London was waking up through the windows, the sun rising between buildings still glowing in the darkness.

Reed was waiting by an office, fiddling with her phone. She looked up at Fenchurch's approach, pocketing her mobile. A frosty glare on her face. 'Guv.' She held up the *Post*, the photo of Fenchurch beaming out. 'Take it this is what you were speaking to Liam about?'

Fenchurch ignored her flapping it at him. 'My bloody father.'

'You went along with it, though.'

Fenchurch snatched the paper from her. 'What if this is just for nothing?'

'You're a stupid bastard. Putting her through this.'

'Sergeant . . . It was my—'

'Guv, I'm talking to you as a friend.' She tucked the paper under her arm, shaking her head. 'Whether it was you or your father, you'd better help Abi, okay?'

'Of course I will.' Fenchurch tapped at the door, his gut feeling like it was a few storeys lower.

DS Michelle Grove sat in her thin office, just enough room for a desk and two chairs. She'd swapped the riot gear for a plain grey trouser suit and a pink blouse. Her dark hair was just a few shades lighter than the black frames of her glasses, offset with neon-lime flashes on the arms. She looked up and beckoned them in, standing to give Reed an air kiss. 'Kay, good to see you again.' She sat and yawned into a giant beaker of coffee. 'That was a shambles yesterday. We were there till *eleven*.'

Fenchurch took the right-hand chair. 'Heard they charged the attacker.'

'Not that the Met gets any credit for it.' Grove sipped from her cup and yawned again. 'Anyway. You said you wanted to know about the cabbies storming City Hall?' She chuckled, her fingers snaking around the cup. 'Our former mayor called them Luddites?'

'I remember.' Reed looked like she was hiding a smirk. 'So you arrested this Steve Shelvey?'

'That's right.' Another glug of coffee, leaving a ring of lipstick around the lid. 'The whole operation was a complete nightmare, I swear. One of those drop-your-drawers things. Everyone across London was there. I had nineteen in full riot gear, none of them trained and no time to knit them together. Meanwhile, a bunch of cabbies were kicking off by City Hall.' She bit her lip. 'Full-blown, hardcore EDL taxi drivers battering us. Batons out, tear gas, that kind of thing. They'd already blocked the streets surrounding City Hall, including Tower Bridge. Hundreds of them and not many of us. Nightmare, I tell you.'

Fenchurch unclenched his hands and feet. 'So you arrested this Shelvey guy . . . ?'

'Did we? Oh yeah, we did.' Grove slid her glasses down her nose and peered over them at Reed. 'Shelvey lamped a guard. We got it on three CCTV cameras and about ten Body-Worn Videos.' She pushed her specs back up. 'We caught him, locked him up and did him with a load of public-order offences. Assault, that kind of thing.'

Fenchurch raised his eyebrows. 'So why's he still not locked up then?'

Grove switched her gaze between them, her elbows grinding on the wood. 'What's your interest in this guy?'

Reed glanced at Fenchurch. 'We believe Mr Shelvey raped and murdered a woman.' She swallowed hard. 'Then he died in custody this morning . . .'

'Shit.' Grove rubbed her eyes. 'Shit.' She swivelled her chair round to face the window, arms folded. 'You didn't hear this from me, right?'

Reed did that zip-and-key move again. 'Lips are sealed, Michelle.'

'The reason Mr Shelvey isn't locked up is one of those borrowed cops took it upon himself to beat the shit out of him as he arrested him.'

Oh, shit . . . Fenchurch slouched back in his seat. 'How badly are we talking here?'

'Brutal. He saw Shelvey attack the guard and lashed out.' Grove drank some coffee, her hands shaking. 'We're trained to restrain people in a sensible manner, but he went right over the top. Battered the guy with his baton. Five strikes to the back of the neck. Almost broke his vertebrae.' She spun back round to face them again, her lips twitching. 'The IPCC were in quick as you like. I expected them to take months, but it was over in weeks. They sacked him.'

'You going to give us a name or keep teasing us?'

Grove laughed at him. 'He got a deal and didn't face any criminal charges. Left the job at Christmas, back in May.'

'He's back on the force?'

Grove twisted her coffee cup like an offender's neck. 'That's enough punishment, apparently.' She tore off her glasses and rested them on her desk. 'Works in this building, as it happens.'

Fenchurch raised his eyebrows, pleading with her. 'What's his name?'

———— ⌣ ————

A Toblerone-shaped piece of white paper printed with **DC Christopher Johnson** sat on top of a monitor. Fenchurch stopped by a desk. 'You're in early, Constable.'

DC Chris Johnson looked up from his computer, the double-width screen filled with a spreadsheet. He was cut from the same lump of granite as his mate, Clive Naismith, but his skinhead had grown out into a patchy middle parting. His shirt strained to contain the glamour muscles bulging on his upper arms and torso. 'Sorry, who are you?'

Fenchurch flashed his ID, the lanyard straining against his neck. 'DI Simon Fenchurch. And I still need that word.'

'Can't this wait? I've got to do the latest report before the eight o'clock command briefing.'

'That sounds very important.' Fenchurch propped himself down on the edge of the desk, folding his arms. 'But this can't wait. I need to ask a few questions about the demo in September.'

'I don't know anything about that.' Johnson went back to his computer. 'Now I need to get on with this.'

Uniformed officers sat around, phone headsets clamped to their skulls. A glass meeting room was in the middle, empty. 'I'm going into that room and if you don't follow me in, your bosses will hear all about this.'

Johnson let out a sigh but didn't budge.

Fenchurch walked over to the room and followed Reed in. He sat at the head of the table, crunching back in the sort of pink fluffy chair they were gradually replacing across the Met. 'Is he coming, Kay?'

'Still sitting there.'

'And the Custody Officer?'

Reed waved in a slightly different direction. 'Waiting by the stairs.' She patted Fenchurch on the arm and sat next to him. 'Here he comes.'

The door thunked shut and Johnson paced around the glass-walled meeting room like a caged lion, just a second or two away from lashing out. 'Being stuck in a room with you pair isn't helping me get that report to the Commissioner, you know?'

Fenchurch motioned at the table. 'Have a seat. Any of them.'

'I prefer to stand.'

'Suit yourself.' Fenchurch unlocked his Pronto and stabbed the stylus off the screen, creating a new note. 'Like I said, I need to ask a few questions about the demo in September.'

'What you talking about?' Johnson stopped his pacing. 'Sure it's me you're after?'

'You were there, sunshine.' Fenchurch adjusted himself in the chair. Hopefully they'd get replaced by the time they moved to the new HQ. He motioned at the seat opposite. 'We've spoken to the DS running the operation. Said you assaulted one of the protestors.'

'I didn't assault anyone.' Johnson shrugged. 'And besides, they was animals.'

'Still don't deserve to get their arms broken, though, do they?'

'Eh? Who had their arm broken?'

Fenchurch smiled. 'Steven Shelvey.'

'Don't know a Steve Shelvey.'

'Really? Cos he was the cabbie you decided to go all medieval on outside City Hall.' Fenchurch got out the bundle of paperwork on Shelvey and started flicking through. 'Thing is, he's just turned up as a murder suspect in a case of ours. Interesting thing about this one is that the geezer died in custody this morning.'

'What?'

Fenchurch flicked to another page. 'Did you kill him?'

Johnson finally sat down, lumbering into a chair at the far side of the table, nearer Reed than Fenchurch. 'I'm not answering that without a lawyer.'

'That never looks good, especially when a cop has to do it.'

'I've done *nothing*.'

'If you're playing that game, we might just have to pass it over to Professional Standards.'

'Eh?' Johnson glowered at both of them. 'Thought you *was* Professional Standards?'

'Major Investigation Team East, sunshine.' Fenchurch opened the glass door, waving at the lump of gristle by the stairwell. 'Come with me.'

'That's nothing to do with me! I was at my daughter's school play last night, I swear!'

Fenchurch stepped aside to let the Custody Officer get at Johnson. 'Take him over to Leman Street, okay?'

Johnson slumped behind the interview room table, blinking hard and fast. 'Someone's stitched me up.'

'Constable, just quit it.' Fenchurch tossed a paper file onto the table, the copy of Grove's report. 'The IPCC investigated your conduct.'

'So? Doesn't mean it was me. We was all covered in riot gear. Could've been anyone.'

'I know you're lying, son.' Fenchurch held up the report. 'Your helmet came off. Four officers identified you. So did six cabbies and a journalist. And it's all on video.'

Johnson shook his head. 'They were lying.'

'I'm more inclined to believe them than you.'

'Suit yourself.' Johnson splayed his hands on the table, his thumbs smoothing over the surface, and glanced over at his lawyer. 'Look, that Shelvey kid had his face covered in a hanky. He broke ranks and was about to throw something at the building. *City Hall.* What if it'd been a bomb?' He put his hands together, interlinking the fingers. 'The order came over the radio, so I took him down. Disabled him and took his weapon off him.'

Fenchurch scribbled it onto his Pronto. 'What was he carrying?'

'Hammer. A big one, too.' Johnson pulled his hands apart to about a foot's distance. 'Could do a lot of damage with one that size.'

Fenchurch doodled a picture. 'What happened next?'

'A couple of CO11 officers came over and took him off me. That's the last I saw of the geezer.' Johnson smoothed down his parting, not quite in the centre. 'When I let go of him, he was fine, just a scratch and a bruise.'

'You're saying someone assaulted Mr Shelvey?' Fenchurch left him a bit of space. Johnson didn't fill it. 'You're saying police officers assaulted him?'

'This is what I told the IPCC. Nothing to do with me.'

'But you were disciplined for the assault.'

'So why am I back on the force, then, eh?' Johnson flicked up an eyebrow and grinned at them. 'They offered me a decent little number if I fell on my sword.' He rubbed his slimy hands together. 'Shut the whole case out without going to court, make the cabbies think they've got justice.'

Fenchurch ran his hand across the report. 'Says here that five officers saw you lay into Mr Shelvey with your baton.'

Johnson waved his hands away from his body. 'I didn't beat anyone up.'

'You were seen.'

'My client isn't answering that question, Inspector.' The lawyer didn't even look up, just kept scribbling in his pad.

Reed cleared her throat and gave Johnson the once-over, a snarl on her face. 'You've got history with Frank Blunden, haven't you?'

'He's a source. That's all.' Johnson slumped back in his chair. 'This is you stitching me up now, ain't you?'

'We're not the dodgy ones here, Constable.' Reed unfolded a photocopied sheet, smiling coldly. 'You visited Leman Street at midnight last night, didn't you?'

'Eh? What you talking about?'

'This is the visitors' log.' Reed held up the page, scribbles and signatures filling the grid, one row highlighted in acid yellow. 'Correct me if I'm wrong, but that's your name and badge number there.'

Johnson smoothed down his hair again, then whispered into his lawyer's ear. His eyes wobbled about until he nodded. Johnson coughed, elbows on the table. 'Sergeant, I work in the Management Information department. I get stats for the bosses. They ask some difficult questions, so I have to dig behind it and see what's going on. That's why I was here.'

'That's a lot of digging, though.' Reed flicked through the rest of the sheets, at least one yellow line on each page. 'Five visits in the last week. Including last night. At midnight. Clocked out after the suspect died.'

'Yeah, so what? I popped in on my way home to speak to a couple of the AFOs.'

'Firearms officers?'

'Yeah, the geezers up on the fourth floor. Friendly lot. Not.' Johnson scratched at his chin. 'They ran an obbo on Mansell Street a couple of weeks back. Supposed to be off books, helping the Americans or something, but the stupid buggers put it through an official cost centre, so it showed up in the stats. The Commissioner spat out his tea when he saw it.'

Fenchurch leaned across the table, getting close to Johnson. 'You happened to be in the station at the time that suspect died. You expect us to believe you're not involved?'

'Speak to them!'

'We will, don't you worry.'

'So can I get back to my report?'

Fenchurch raised his eyebrows, grinning. 'Not for a very long time . . .'

Chapter Twelve

Fenchurch walked around the interview room, his knees grind-ing, little threads of gristle snapping with each step. 'Where the hell is he?'

Reed kept staring at her notebook. 'Chill, guv, okay?'

'If he's—'

The door ground open and Clive Naismith entered the room, running his tongue around his teeth, stretching out his lips. 'You called for me, guv?'

'Take a seat.' Fenchurch stayed standing.

'Don't know if I'm coming or going.' Naismith slumped into the chair. 'When can I get off home?'

'After we've asked you some questions, Constable.' Fenchurch kept eye contact with Naismith. 'Have you finished your statement?'

'DS Nelson's going through it just now.'

Fenchurch sat next to Reed, his keys digging into his thighs. He adjusted them and stretched forward, speaking in an undertone. 'I need to ask you about DC Chris Johnson.'

Naismith's mouth twisted into a scowl. 'What's he done now?'

'I want to know everything there is about Johnson.' Fenchurch jabbed a finger in the air. 'For starters, I don't like bent cops.'

'You think I'm bent?' Naismith laughed. 'Is that what this is? You keeping me close so you can keep an eye on me?'

Fenchurch held his gaze. 'You're providing key information to this case.'

'I'm not stupid.' Naismith raised a finger. 'And I'm not bent.'

'What about Johnson? Is he connected to Frank Blunden?'

'Blunden? He's just some git messing with us.' Naismith clasped his hands together, locking his thumbs in place. 'Me and Chris only got stuff about Shelvey. I know a few guys who got tipped off about drug deals. Another about some gang of black kids nicking mobile phones.'

Acid burnt at Fenchurch's gullet. 'Did either of you take money from him?'

'I never.'

'And Johnson?'

'You'll have to ask him.' He crunched back in his seat and started up the old thumb twiddling. Good enough to compete at Rio. 'Look, sir, I'll level with you here, okay? I worked with Chris Johnson for a few years. Always had to pull him back.'

'At City Hall?'

Naismith rolled his eyes. 'What Chris got up to at City Hall was—' He chuckled, cutting it off with a snort. 'We was working for some CO11 DS, Greaves or something. You spoken to her?'

'I believe you're referring to DS Michelle Grove.' Reed narrowed her eyes at him. 'We have spoken to her. It's our understanding that DC Johnson assaulted Mr Shelvey.'

'Right.'

'And did he?'

'It was all a blur.' Naismith ran a hand through the stubble on top of his head, making what was there stand on end. 'That kid came at us, all tooled up. Next thing I know, he's on the ground, Chris is kicking and punching him. But he's got that anger in him, yeah? He's gone over the top a few times. He lost his job because of it, you know?'

'Didn't stop him returning, though, did it?' Fenchurch rested against the desk, arms spread wide. 'You saw what happened down in the Custody Suite, didn't you?'

Naismith's eyes bulged. 'That was Shelvey?'

'Johnson was here last night. Could he have killed him?'

'What, some sort of revenge thing?' Naismith frowned. 'Maybe. Wouldn't put it past him. He's got a load of mates in here. He'll have heard Shelvey's been brought in. Doesn't take a lot to—' He drew a line with his finger across his throat. 'How did he die?'

One of those mates wouldn't be you, would it? 'We're still awaiting the post-mortem.'

'Right. Well, you've heard what I've got to say.' Naismith pushed his chair back and got to his feet. 'You need anything else from me?'

Fenchurch got a shrug off Reed. He checked his watch, just past half seven. 'I need you in at five p.m. for the back shift, okay?'

'What?' Naismith held his hands out wide. 'I'm supposed to be nights this week.'

'Constable, you're seconded to a murder case. End of.'

⌣

Fenchurch opened the office door and stepped inside. Absolutely starving. Need a cereal bar from my—

'The Scarlet Pimpernel returns.' DCI Alan Docherty was in DI Mulholland's chair, feet up on the desk, sitting at right angles to Fenchurch's, dowsed in street light. His suit hung lank off his skinny body, like a wraith. He sat upright as the lights flickered on. 'Well, I've just spent a couple of hours up at University College fighting off that kid's solicitor. Have we got any idea who killed him?'

Fenchurch perched on the edge of his desk. 'Maybe.' He shrugged off his jacket and slung it on the coat rack. 'DC Chris Johnson.' He tossed a paper file over at Docherty. 'Battered Shelvey at a protest. Lost his job. As happens all the time, he's back in over at the Yard.'

Docherty scanned across the file. 'How likely is he?'

'He was here last night. We should treat him as a suspect.' Fenchurch folded his arms. 'There's a possible connection to Blunden. Doubtful we could nail him, mind.'

Docherty dumped the file on Mulholland's desk. 'It was you who found Shelvey, right?'

'Martin did, boss.' Fenchurch unfolded his arms and stretched out. 'Shelvey's got form. We were going to try and force a confession.'

'What's this new information?'

'Possibly history of attempted sexual assault. Oh, and the murder weapon matched the victim.'

'That old chestnut.'

'Look, Johnson has a mate, Clive Naismith. Think they were partners before he got the old heave ho. They're a bit too close to Blunden. I want to second Naismith to the investigation.'

'Why?'

'Keep him close in case anything slips.' Fenchurch let his arms fall down to his sides. 'But he's the one giving us the background on Shelvey. I want that watertight.'

'Right. Fine. I'll raise it.'

Fenchurch waited for him to write something down. Nothing. 'He's based in Brick Lane.'

'And I said I'll raise it.' Docherty blew air up his face as he grabbed the file back. Then he dropped it with a smack. 'The Independent Police Complaints Commission are coming in to investigate the boy's death. This station'll become infested with the buggers, just you watch.' A finger pointed at Fenchurch. 'Better not be any skeletons in your closet.'

Cheeky bastard. Fenchurch held the glare. 'You know all of them, boss.'

'I better.' Docherty scribbled something on his notepad. 'DI Mulholland's in with Shelvey's mother. Not a very happy woman.'

'Why Mulholland?'

'Why not? She's got no connection to the case, Si. You do.'

'But I had nothing to do with the boy's death.'

'Then that's what the IPCC will find at the inquest.' Docherty scribbled another note and grimaced. 'I've got an appointment with the Commissioner and a shitload of senior officers at nine. That's not a good sign. You saw that guy dying in custody up in Fife last year?'

'I take it Fife's in Scotland, sir.'

'Of course it is. Christ.' Docherty dropped his pen on the desk. 'That Shelvey prick should be getting a grilling right now, but the focus will be on some vigilante taking out a suspect without due process. The press won't see it as us catching a young lawyer's killer.' He reached down and picked up a newspaper, dumping it on the desk. 'I see this has finally landed.'

Fenchurch didn't even need to see the paper's masthead. Blood flushed up his arms. 'You should be talking to my dad about it, boss.'

'Aye, I know. It's just . . . shite timing.' Docherty tapped at the page. 'Plus I didn't know it was going to be this in-depth. There are four photos in there of you and your old boy outside your house. Abi can't be happy with that.'

'It doesn't say we still live there.'

'Whatever. Now every idiot in London knows your face.' Docherty folded the paper in half. 'Christ.'

'There's nothing I can do about it, boss.'

'Aye, *now.*'

Fenchurch got to his feet, scraping the chair legs across the threadbare carpet. 'Thanks for the sympathy.'

Docherty swallowed, his Adam's apple bobbing up and down. 'This Liam boy's behind it, isn't he?'

'I kept warning him. Dad, too.' Fenchurch collapsed back into his seat. 'But you know what he's like.'

'Don't I just.' Docherty held up the paper. 'You sure this is the right thing to do? It's not got you anywhere in almost eleven years.'

'There's new stuff in there.' Blood boiled behind Fenchurch's ears. 'I remembered seeing a car.'

'*Remembered?*'

'I've . . .' Fenchurch coughed. 'I had regressive hypnosis last month. It made things a lot clearer.'

'Hang on a sec . . .' Docherty leafed through the paper, taking care to lick his fingers. 'Ah, here we go. Twelfth November is . . . Ah, yes, Scorpio. "You will meet a tall, dark stranger who kidnapped your daughter eleven years ago." Christ's sake, Si, sure it's not scrambled your brain?' He tossed the paper into the bin and got out his phone. 'Speaking of scrambled brains, I got a text from none other than Jason sodding Bell.'

Jesus Christ.

Docherty waved his mobile around. 'You know he's got a DCI gig?'

Fenchurch clenched his fists in his pockets, trying to hide his rage under the desk. 'Sir, Bell's—'

'Simon, this crap with him has to stop, okay?' Docherty got up from Mulholland's chair and sat on Fenchurch's desk. Close enough to grab. 'I'm not asking you, I'm telling you. Your childish games with him and Mulholland and anyone else I can name . . . It all needs to stop.'

The drums were back, thundering in Fenchurch's ears. 'Come on, boss—'

'Any dealings with Bell come through me, okay? You need to speak to either of his areas, you come through me.' Docherty snorted through his nostrils. 'Through. Me.'

'Look, whatever, you need to clear my team to access his CCTV. He's got the keys to the kingdom, and DS Reed's struggling to get anywhere.'

'Right. Well, I'll call Bell.'

'Cheers.' Fenchurch flashed him a smile. 'A standing order would help.'

'I'm not promising the Earth . . .' Docherty huffed out acid breath and screwed up his face, propping himself against Fenchurch's desk.

A rap on the door. Paul Temple stood there, grinning away. 'Am I interrupting something?'

'I'm just waiting for you, Paul.' Docherty stabbed a finger at Fenchurch. 'Mind what I'm saying now, aye?'

'Boss.' Fenchurch tried a smile at Temple, but there was too much poison in his veins. 'What are you still doing here?'

'A DCI Bell told me to advise on the prosecution of a Steven Shelvey.'

'Christ in a Volvo . . .' Fenchurch got up again and marched over to Docherty. 'You see what I'm up against here? Bell's pissing about playing politics, while we're investigating a murder.'

Docherty prodded Fenchurch in the chest. 'Right, I'll make sure Bell disappears in a puff of smoke.' He nodded at Temple. 'Come on, Paul. Let's have ourselves an adult chat.' He left the room, Temple pursing his lips at Fenchurch.

Fenchurch collapsed back into his chair, knackered. So bloody tired.

Another pile of Brownie points swallowed up by that dickhead Bell.

'Oy!' Docherty craned his neck around the door. 'Get your arse out of here, okay? Back in tonight, okay?'

'Boss.' Fenchurch got up again and paused by the door. 'You remember I've got a . . . dinner tomorrow night. Shit. Tonight.'

Docherty cocked his eyebrows. 'Sure this isn't you sneaking off to watch the France game?'

'What? No, of course it—'

'Shite.' Docherty winced. 'It's Chloe's thing.' He screwed his eyes up tight. 'Sorry, Si.'

'Sorry you forgot or sorry I can't go?'

'Si, I can't just let you—'

'Boss, this has been in the diary since April. Just because you've decided to change the shift pattern—'

Docherty huffed out a pathetic sigh. 'Okay, it's ten past six now. Get home, get some kip, then back for four p.m. I'll need you to make up the time on Saturday, okay?'

Chapter Thirteen

Still early, but the café was buzzing. Most of the customers sat in booths, hiding behind laptop lids, headphones on, clinking spoons at their granola or crunching into bagels. A waitress strolled around, dressed like she was in a diner on Route 66, pouring out fresh filter coffee for people.

Fenchurch bit into his fried-egg roll. Yolk dripped down his chin, splodging onto the plate. Beautiful. But lacking in something. He opened the hot-sauce bottle and tipped some in, then had another bite. That's it.

He sipped at his smoothie. Raspberry and nettle or something. Half decent. Then he got out his phone and checked for messages. Still nothing from—

'Thought you'd be a sausage guy.' Liam Sharpe stood over him, but only just. Guy wasn't much over five and a half foot, even with those platform boots on. His bright eyes hid behind a lumberjack beard, stretching scarf-like over his jacket. He sat opposite Fenchurch and dumped his record bag on the floor, sweeping a hand over his shaved head, his comb-forward consigned to history. 'Egg, right?'

'And habanero sauce.' Fenchurch mopped the yolk on his chin with a napkin. 'I stopped eating sausages when they said it caused cancer. Same with bacon.'

Liam adjusted his record bag, frowning. 'When was that?'

'November, I think.' Fenchurch dropped the napkin onto the table. 'You're the journalist.'

'I run a clickbait farm, mate.' Liam reached into his bag for a copy of the *Post*.

Fenchurch had lost count of how many he'd seen that day, and it wasn't even eight o'clock. 'I've read it.'

'And what did you think?'

Fenchurch took another bite of eggy mush, the fire building up. 'We'll see.'

'You don't think it's any good?'

'I'm not interested in the journalistic merits of the article. Just the outcome.'

'Very Machiavellian.'

'I was thinking Orwellian, but I'll let you have that.' Fenchurch finished his smoothie, sucking on the straw until it rattled. 'You going to order something?'

'Wish I had the time.' Liam picked up a menu and absently turned it over in his hands. 'Yvette is busting my balls at work, so I'll need to piss off soon.'

'Enjoying your new gig?'

'Beats writing twenty "You'll never believe what happened next!" articles a day.' Liam placed the menu back in the holder. 'Not sure I'm cut out for it.'

'You'll be fine.' Fenchurch nodded at the paper. 'That's a well-written article.'

'Thought you didn't assess the journalistic merits?' Liam grinned, then flagged down the passing waitress. 'Can I get a large latte to take away, please? Extra shot.' She scribbled on her pad and wandered off. Mischief twinkled in Liam's eyes. 'Your old man says "hi".'

Fenchurch dropped the last handful of roll. 'You shouldn't be involving him.'

'He's involved me.'

Fenchurch tore his roll in half and smeared his plate with the yellow mess. 'The sort of people you're investigating don't tend to take too kindly to people like you nosing around. Or my bloody father.'

'Suit yourself.' Liam smiled as the waitress handed him the coffee. He wrapped his hands around the cardboard sleeve. 'Do you mind paying for this?'

'So long as you keep my dad out of whatever you're up to.'

'It'd help if you listened to me. He's involving *me*.' Liam sucked coffee through the lid. 'Besides, anything we get will go straight to you.' He raised his cup, shaking his head. 'Cheers for this.'

'I'm serious.' Fenchurch grabbed Liam's wrists. 'This isn't a game, okay? You're not in that job two months. You don't know the rules. Remember what happened to your girlfriend. She was poking around where she shouldn't have been. Someone paid to have her killed.'

Liam pulled his hands away, bumping into the coffee and spilling some on the table. 'You think I can forget, do you?'

'Just make sure you're safe, okay?' Fenchurch bit into the roll. 'And keep my old man out of it.'

Liam got to his feet and wrapped his bag around his thick coat. 'I'll see you around.'

Fenchurch opened his flat door, clutching his mobile tight to his head.

The plummy voice rasped in his ear, 'We're sorry but . . .' Crackle, hiss. 'Em, eh, Ian Fenchurch.' Crackle. 'What's—' BEEP. 'This fu—' Hiss. '. . . is unable to take your call. Please leave a message after the tone.' BEEEEP!

Fenchurch sat at the kitchen table. 'Dad, it's Simon. Give me a bell. Oh, and change your voicemail answering message. Cheers.' He ended the call and dropped his phone onto the wood.

Just after nine. Back in for four. Still nowhere near enough—

The *Post* lay open at the photo of his father, filling most of a page. Classic tabloid shot: their block of flats behind him, his old man brooding at the camera, his stupid moustache ruining the effect.

Dots of moisture covered the paper. Tears. The picture of Chloe was almost smudged out, just a pink mush with pigtails.

Abi . . .

Fenchurch grabbed his phone and dialled Abi's number.

She answered before it even rang. 'Simon, where are you?'

'What?'

'We've got the baby's ultrasound now!'

———

Fenchurch sprinted down the corridor, his old man's knees twanging as he went, then cut round a tight bend.

'Watch it!' An orderly swerved the wheelchair out of his path, an old man muttering to himself.

'Sorry . . .' Fenchurch ran on, feet squeaking off the floor. He burst into the waiting room, the walls greener than a farm, and stopped at the counter, chest heaving. 'Got an . . . appointment . . . Fenchurch.'

The nurse flicked her glasses up and snorted at him. 'Like that station?' She tapped at her computer. 'You're with Mr Stephenson.' She waved an arm to a door in the corridor behind her. 'Through there.'

'Thanks.' Fenchurch marched over to the door and knocked. Felt like he'd popped the kneecap right off.

Something clattered behind the door, then it opened. A heavy man leered out, tall and hairy, wearing a designer suit smudged with egg yolk and red sauce. 'Yes?'

'Simon Fenchurch.' He peered behind the doctor, though he pretty much filled the doorway. 'Is Abi here?'

'I'm Mr Stephenson. Come on in.' He stood to the side and let Fenchurch past.

Abi was lying on the bed, her belly covered in gunk. A ringlet slipped from her ponytail, obscuring the dimple on her cheek. A greyscale image slithered slowly on the screen next to her. Then she noticed him. 'Simon.'

'Sorry, love. Been a hell of a day.' Fenchurch leaned over to kiss her. Her perfume smelled like walking through a Highland wood. He collapsed into a chair by the bed. Could do with lying down on that, just for a few minutes. 'I was in here a couple of hours ago.'

'What for?'

'Long story.' Fenchurch reached over and kissed her on the forehead. 'Have I missed anything?'

'Just about everything.'

Fenchurch smiled at the doctor. Lank grey hair, with a rash of grey stubble crawling over his grey skin, Stephenson was that John Major *Spitting Image* puppet. 'Can I get the highlights, then?'

Stephenson picked up a paddle and ran it over Abi's tummy. 'The good news, Mr Fenchurch, is baby is healthy.'

The grey dots on the screen coalesced into a king prawn, its tiny heartbeat squishing the gunk around it.

Fenchurch slumped back in the chair. The tiniest bump in the world on Abi's stomach.

His baby . . . Their baby . . . Living, its little heart pumping away. And healthy. Thank God.

Another chance to do it right.

He sat forward, rubbing his hands together. 'So what's the bad news?'

Stephenson glanced over at Abi. 'Mrs Fenchurch doesn't wish to know the gender.'

Abi shifted round, getting another view of the little monster bug. 'I don't know why you'd want to know before you give birth. It ruins the surprise.'

'It's a surprise whether we find out now or in seven months, love.' Fenchurch squeezed her hand. 'But it's your choice. We'll wait.'

'Thanks.' She returned the squeeze.

Stephenson put the paddle down. 'Well, that's us for now. We should do another test in a month's time.'

'It used to be at eighteen weeks.' Fenchurch frowned at him. 'Is that because of Abi's age?'

'It's best practice with older mothers, yes. Mrs Fenchurch will be forty by the time baby arrives, so I'd like to keep a close eye on—' Stephenson grinned. 'On *baby*. And on Mrs Fenchurch. As I'm sure you both know, there can be complications with mothers over the age of thirty-five. Over forty and the risk factors are a lot higher.' He stretched out and fiddled with his stethoscope. 'But there's nothing concrete to worry about at this stage, okay?'

'I know all that stuff.' Fenchurch tried to swallow the lump in his throat. 'Have you tested for Down's?'

'I've taken a sample, from which I shall perform what we call the combined test. It'll assess the risk levels for Down's, Edwards' or Patau's syndromes. The res—'

'What are those other two?'

'They're unfortunately fatal for most babies.'

Fenchurch stared at Abi, then at her exposed belly. 'So our child could die?'

'Mr Fenchurch, that's only possible if he or she is at risk.' Stephenson wrapped his stethoscope round his neck like a scarf. 'The results will take a couple of weeks, though we might be able to accelerate that using some new techniques.'

'I'd appreciate it.' Fenchurch winked at Abi. 'But other than that?'

'We'll just need to keep on top of it.' Stephenson tugged down the stethoscope like he was doing a lat pulldown. 'Now, if you could make a follow-up appointment with the nurse on your way out? I'll leave you to get changed.' He squelched across the floor to the door, his bright-green crocs clashing with his navy suit, and left them to it.

Fenchurch got up and handed Abi her trousers. 'Charming bastard.'

'At least *he* turned up on time.'

'You wouldn't believe the night shift I've just had, love.'

'I'll get it out of you later, Simon.' She wriggled off the bed. 'I've got to get to work.'

'Right.' Fenchurch swallowed hard, the lump forcing its way back up into his mouth. 'So we'll just wait, yeah?'

Abi shook out her trousers, dust flying around the room. 'Are you worried?'

Fenchurch's focus settled on her stomach as she pulled her trousers on. 'I know the risks but—'

'Having a doctor talk about it makes it real?'

Fenchurch collapsed onto the bed, the wheels squeaking against his weight. 'Our baby could have Down's.'

She grabbed his shoulder and pumped it. 'If it does, we'll love him or her just the same. Okay?'

'I know that. It's just . . .' Fenchurch let out his breath. 'At my age, it'll be extra hard.'

'You old bastard.' A smile flickered across her lips, swept away by the tide of a frown. 'I saw the paper.'

'I've been kicking arse about it, love. I'm really sorry for bringing this back up.'

Abi eased off her gown and picked up her blouse, just standing there in her bra and trousers. 'Your bloody father . . .' She wiped away a tear. 'But, if someone knows anything about what happened . . .'

Fenchurch pulled her close and kissed the top of her head. 'I'll have a stronger word with him.'

Fenchurch killed the Mondeo's engine and listened to it grind to a halt, the suspension slumping away. He picked up the Chilango's bag and slumped back in his seat.

Their flat was empty in the sunshine, just one of a long, squat row of brick tenements without a roof. Half of them were townhouses, the other half flats. Some worth millions, theirs much less.

Ahead, the pavement where Chloe . . .

Fenchurch swallowed the lump in his throat and got out of the car, zapping it as the door slammed. His stomach was growling, but the thought of food just . . .

Jesus, keep it together.

'Excuse me, mate.' A liveried delivery driver stood by a van, lugging a big package. 'You wouldn't happen to know an Abigail Fenchurch, would you? I've been buzzing but—'

'She's my wife.'

'Lifesaver.' The driver handed the box to Fenchurch. Weighed a ton. He had to stick it on the car roof. 'Can you sign this?'

Fenchurch snatched the digital device thing and scrawled something vaguely resembling his signature across it. 'That it?'

'Cheers, mate.' The driver strolled over to his van, whistling that new Stone Roses song. Or what could pass for it.

Fenchurch hefted up the box and walked it over to the building door, his burrito bag swinging underneath. He got out his keys and entered. Nobody on the stairs, thank God. He staggered up, dropping the bag just the once, and got inside the flat. The telltale click gave it away as he dumped the box down. Not another one . . .

He tore at the tape, pulling it from the cardboard in a single rip. An antique typewriter, the fifth that month. He carried it through to the spare room and put it with the others.

A row of the old keyboards sat on the dresser, various bits hanging off them. One was on the desk by the window, loaded with paper. Fenchurch hit a few keys, the hammers clacking as they spelled out C-H-L-O-E. He yanked the paper through the mechanism and twisted it into a ball.

Chloe's old room. No longer a museum to her, just full of the shit Abi had replaced her with.

Fenchurch shut the door and went back into the hall. He dumped his keys in the bowl and got out his mobile. Three missed calls, all from Dad. He took the burrito through to the bedroom, blinking in the bright sunlight. He rolled the blinds down and collapsed onto the bed, pulling off his shirt and dumping it on the floor.

Bloody hell, I am so tired . . .

He redialled Dad's number, and it rang and rang and rang. Here comes the voicemail.

'Simon?'

'Dad. Finally.'

'What's happened, son?'

'What?' Fenchurch tightened his grip on the phone. 'Nothing's happened, Dad. Why?'

'Oh.' Sounded like Dad was in a café. No doubt out at Lewisham, charming the canteen servers. 'What did you want, then?'

'I've seen this morning's paper.' Fenchurch kicked off his left shoe, getting a satisfying thunk on the floor. 'Then I had breakfast with Liam Sharpe.'

Dad gasped. 'Has someone got in touch?'

'Not yet.'

No response, just the clanking of cutlery.

'What've you been up to with him, Dad?'

'Nothing, son.'

'Sure about that?'

Dad let out a sigh. 'I met him for a coffee last week and we had a chat about this story going in the paper. I told him about all that private-detective shit I was doing when Chloe . . . When . . . You remember? Your mother went mental at me. Didn't achieve anything. He didn't even put it in the story.'

'There are two recent photos of you next to the story.' Fenchurch let the pillows snake round his neck. So easy to just let go . . . 'Liam seemed to be under the impression you were working with him.'

'Well, he's got the wrong end of the stick, son.' Dad cackled down the line. 'I'd not use that lad for changing a lightbulb. There's nothing going on.'

'Dad . . . If there is . . . Just be careful, okay?'

'Always am, son.' Dad left a pause, filled with background chatter. 'How's Abi?'

'She's pissed off with you. You really need to make it up to her.'

'Right, right. We still on for dinner tonight?'

'For now.' Fenchurch kicked the other shoe off. 'I've really got to get to sleep.'

'I'll see you later, then.'

'Just keep yourself out of trouble, Dad.' Fenchurch killed the call and lay back, his head on the tall pile of pillows. He untwisted the foil at the top of his burrito, his mouth watering, and reached over to set the alarm clock.

Six hours of sleep would have to be enough . . .

Day 2
Back Shift
Friday, 10th June 2016

Chapter Fourteen

*F*enchurch dipped his hands into the soapy water and picked up a slimy plate, the suds sliding off as he held it under the cold tap.

Blur's oiky noise faded out on the radio. 'Good afternoon. The news at two o'clock. The former Prime Minister, Ted Heath, has died at his home in—'

Fenchurch twisted the dial and cut the voice dead. He caught his reflection in the window. More than a flash of grey in his blond hair. Alan Docherty was right — the soul patch made him look like a twat.

Through the glass, Chloe was downstairs in her full England kit, the lilywhite glowing in the sun, the red offset St George's cross on her right shoulder. She skipped across the blue-chalk hopscotch grid on the opposite pavement and came to a halt, glancing up at the window and grinning at him, her mother's dimple in her cheek, her blonde pigtails dancing.

'Simon, have you seen this?' Abi marched into the kitchen, waving a sheet of paper in the air. 'Another bloody garage bill.'

'That was last week.' Fenchurch turned round and folded his wet arms. 'You know the ignition's been playing up, love.'

'That car's costing a fortune!'

'I'm a DI now. We'll manage.'

'I'm not sure—'

SCREEECH.

VRRRRRRRRRR.

Fenchurch swung round. The hopscotch grid was empty. Chloe wasn't there. 'Shit!'

'*What's up?*'

'*Chloe!*' *Fenchurch rushed through the flat and bounced down the stairs three at a time. His foot gave way halfway down. He caught himself on the banister and hauled himself up, then powered out of the front door onto the street.*

Spinning around.

Trying to see her.

Trying to spot her.

Trying to—

'*Mr Fenchurch?*'

He swung round. Amy was licking a red lolly, holding up another one. '*I got an ice cream for Chloe.*'

'*Where did she go?*'

'*She was waiting here for her lolly.*'

'*Have you seen anyone?*' *Liverpool Road was empty and quiet.* '*Anyone at all?*'

'*There was a car.*'

'*What kind?*'

'*I didn't see.*'

'*Stay there, Amy.*' *Fenchurch sprinted down to the end of the street. Nothing moving in either direction on Liverpool Road. He fished in his pocket for his mobile and dialled 999.* '*This is DI Simon Fenchurch, I need urgent assistance at—*'

A man stood at the end of the street beside a grey Volvo, or was it a Saab? He was over ten foot tall, holding Chloe up over his head, swinging her out like a kettle bell. '*Hey, little girl, do you want some sweets?*'

Chloe squealed out, laughing. '*Bye-bye, Daddy!*'

'—Chloe!' Fenchurch opened his eyes, his voice echoing round the empty room. His chest heaved, sweat all up his back, the bedsheet yanked out so he was lying on the bare mattress.

He lay back, eyes shut. Just a dream. His rubbed his eye sockets, encrusted with sleep. Just another dream. The same bloody one.

He reached over to his bedside table and wrote 'Volvo'. The fifth time it'd appeared now. Could he really remember it? Was it just wish fulfilment?

The clock radio clicked round to 15.00. '—continue the build-up to tonight's Euro 2016 opener at the Stade de France between the hosts and Romania. But first, the news with—'

Fenchurch snapped it off. A half-eaten burrito lay on the bedside table. No time for a workout today. He got up and padded towards the shower.

Chapter Fifteen

B loody sodding, buggering, bastarding hell.

Fenchurch pulled in next to the Bentley again and took another look at the space.

You've got Advanced Drivers' Training, you stupid git. You can get into that.

Fenchurch slid the Mondeo back and swung the wheel round, missing the Bentley's wing mirror by inches. Not lost my mojo after all. He got out of the car and trotted over the road, yawning as he entered the building. Another bloody day. Same as it ever was . . .

Fenchurch made for the security door and patted in his pockets for his ID.

'Si!'

Fenchurch swung round.

Steve, the Desk Sergeant, was sweating over by the front desk. A hulking brute with a skinhead, he was a good couple of stones heavier than he should be. 'Got a minute?'

Fenchurch trudged over, still yawning into his hand. 'What's up?'

Steve nodded over to the side. 'Geezer to see you.'

Lord Ingham hauled himself to his feet. Despite the twenty-odd-degree heat outside, he was wearing a long duster and a trilby. He grinned at Fenchurch like they were old roommates at Eton. 'Inspector, thanks for your efforts in apprehending my assailant yesterday afternoon.'

Fenchurch rubbed at his burning ears. 'All part of the job, sir.'

'Oh, poppycock. You saved my life.' Ingham handed him a designer paper bag, black with a logo embossed in black. 'A small token of my gratitude.'

Fenchurch peered inside the bag, heavier than it looked. A long black box sat at the bottom, some arcane lettering indented into the wood. Dunpender or something. Some stupid ornament . . . 'Well, I appreciate it.'

'I imagine you officers still enjoy a tipple.' Ingham winked like a grandfather handing over a bag of sherbet lemons. 'Or have things changed so much since my day, eh?'

Fenchurch checked the contents again. 'Sorry, what is this?'

'It's Scotch, my dear boy. Single malt.' Ingham clapped Fenchurch on the arm. 'And a jolly good one, too.'

Fenchurch tried to push the bag back. 'I can't accept this, sir.'

'Accept what?' Another wink. 'I shall be seeing you, Inspector.' Ingham marched past him and doffed his hat to Steve. 'Sergeant.'

Steve stepped over the tiles, eyes on Ingham through the window as he got into the waiting Bentley. 'That bloke used to be Foreign Secretary, didn't he?'

'Something like that.' Fenchurch swung the bag back and forth. 'What the hell do I do with this?'

'What is it?' Steve grabbed the bag and it rattled. 'Let me see . . .' He reached in and took out the box. Then he whistled. 'Lovely jubbly . . .' He couldn't keep his eyes from it. 'That's their centenary edition, you know? Bit of a story about it, as it happens. Not many got made at all. Worth a pretty penny.'

'Shit.' Fenchurch wrapped the bag around the box. 'I'll have to bloody log this, then.'

'Too right. If you fancy sharing, though . . .'

Fenchurch snuck another peek at the whisky container thing before wrapping the bag around it and dumping it in his bottom drawer.

Becoming a bloody cliché now. Just need some always-clean glasses in the desk drawer.

He unlocked his computer and typed DUNPENDER CENTENARY EDITION, then clicked enter. His eyes scanned down the search results. A few news stories about a dead body at the distillery, then some shopping listings, some images of the black box standing proud behind the amber spirit.

What. The. Hell?

Four grand for a bottle of bloody whisky?

Fenchurch picked up his tea mug and sipped, his hands shaking. Shit. That screamed bribe. And Steve wasn't exactly Secret Squirrel about these things.

What the hell was Ingham playing at? Four grand's worth of whisky to a cop. Maybe the toad-faced arse candle didn't know that was a month's salary to us mere mortals.

A knock on the door. Sounded like Thor's hammer striking the wood.

Just Docherty, his face like Thor had been at it with some clouds. 'Afternoon, Si. Nice of you to join us.' He stepped in and prowled around the office.

'Boss, I need to have a word.'

A young woman stood by the door, tall and waif-like, her hair dark enough to be delivered by a coal van.

'This is Zenna Abercrombie from the IPCC Commissioner's office.' Docherty flicked up his eyebrows and tucked his tongue into his cheek. He stayed by the door, like he didn't trust Fenchurch to leave the varnish off the truth.

'Good afternoon, Inspector.' Zenna Abercrombie gave a tight smile as she sat across from him, her eyes scanning up and down. Felt like she was monitoring his heart rate. She glanced over at the door. 'DCI Docherty said I could have some of your time?'

Docherty stepped into the room and tilted his head at Fenchurch. 'Si, can you—' His Airwave blared out. He reached into his pocket and checked the display. 'It's the boss. Give me a minute.' He stomped out into the corridor.

Fenchurch wished he could fire lasers into Docherty's arse. Or piles at the very least. He gave Zenna a tight smile. 'So?'

Zenna slumped down into a chair. 'So.'

Another glug of tea, his hand just about steady. 'Zenna, eh? Never heard that name before.'

'Mum was Greek.' She opened a leather document holder and got out some paperwork. 'It means "daughter of Zeus". He'd be preferable to my real father.'

'Tell me about it . . .'

She looked up, frowning. 'Excuse me?'

'Nothing. What can I help you with?'

'As I'm sure you're aware, we've been drafted in to investigate the death of Steven Robert Shelvey whilst in custody.' Zenna handed him a wad of paper, at least twenty sheets thick. Didn't even look padded. 'There will, of course, be an inquest. This is the draft Terms of Reference for my initial investigation leading up to the opening of the inquest.' She tapped the document. 'I require you to review it by close of business tonight.' She slid the pages over to him. 'I've sent you an invite for a meeting at five p.m. so we can go through the points in person.'

'That's an hour. I won't have time to do it justice.' Fenchurch squinted at the microscopic text, arching his eyebrow like that'd have any impact. He dumped the document into his drawer next to the whisky. Better not let her see that. 'I'll have a look when I get the chance.'

'It's critical.'

'Sure it is.' Fenchurch slammed the drawer. 'I've got a team to run and we need to close off all the actions relating to the murder of Victoria Brocklehurst.'

Zenna reached into her document holder and opened another copy. She tapped on a page halfway through. 'According to my TOR, that case falls within our purview.'

Still no sign of Docherty in the doorway. 'Does my boss think that?'

'He's got his opinion. I've got mine.'

'Then I'm afraid I'll have to defer to his judgement.'

'Very well, Inspector. I shall formally interview you at some point.' Zenna got to her feet and held out a hand, a business card tucked inside. 'Please make sure all documentation is up to date.' She smiled at Fenchurch. 'We need to establish a Chinese Wall around this. I can't have you tampering with any evidence.'

Fenchurch slumped back in his chair. 'Ms Abercrombie, if you're running this shitstorm, you—'

'That's not how I'd put it.'

'A man dying in custody is what the Germans would term "*ein riesen Shitstorm*".' Fenchurch held her gaze. 'Now, I've been trying to piece together that girl's murder. If it's in your remit, then you need to speak to her godfather. I promised to keep in touch with him. He deserves an update.'

Zenna stuck a hand on her hip. 'You haven't told him about Mr Shelvey's death, have you?'

Fenchurch winked at her. 'I'm not that stupid.'

'Simon, if I can call you that, you—'

'Let's just keep it as Inspector for now, yeah?' Fenchurch stuffed his hands in his pockets. 'Have you spoken to DC Chris Johnson yet?'

'Detectives from DI Mulholland's team have been taking his statement all morning, so I've not had the pleasure.'

'Might be worth getting in there before someone poisons him.'

Zenna's eyes tightened. 'We still haven't ascertained whether that's the cause of death.'

'Well, why don't you see if laughing boy downstairs got access to any thallium or whatever.'

'Thallium? How do you know it's that?'

'I don't. I'm just—'

The door burst open and Temple flew through. 'Si, I need a— Oh.' He smiled at Zenna. 'Sorry, am I interrupting something?'

'We're just about done. And your presence might be helpful.' Zenna switched her precision focus back to Fenchurch. She put her other hand on her hip, her mouth twitching back and forth. 'I'll be in touch, Inspector. In the meantime, I'd appreciate it if you could review my Terms of Reference and document your movements during the last shift.'

'Will do.' Fenchurch gave her a salute.

Temple smiled at her. 'I'll be with you in a minute.'

'We're in room three.' She stomped down the corridor, shaking her head.

Fenchurch collapsed back in his chair. 'You'd think I'd done something wrong here.'

Temple sat on Mulholland's desk and picked up a stray scarf from her seat. 'Did you kill Shelvey?'

'What?' Fenchurch burst to his feet. 'Of course I didn't.'

'Is anyone trying to frame you?'

'Not that I know of.'

Temple dumped the scarf and grinned. 'Then you're not in the shit.'

Fenchurch waved a hand at the open door. 'I thought they'd be kicking our arses over this.'

'That's not how they work. Very formal. Very slow. Just keep your nose clean, mate.'

'I don't need reminding, Paul. Do you think she'll charge Johnson?'

'Only a matter of time, amigo.' Temple sprang to his feet, like a small child getting off a trampoline. 'Now, if I were you, I'd get with the type-y type-y.'

Fenchurch battered the computer keys like they were parts of Docherty's anatomy. His fingertips hit the stained white plastic so hard that bits of bread and tortilla bounced out of the cracks, covering his desk in a fine dusting of crud. He lifted up the keyboard and wiped the spray into the bin.

'Guv?' Reed was in the doorway, her face like she'd just caught her brother masturbating. 'What on Earth are you doing?'

'They don't clean these things any more.' Fenchurch tipped up the keyboard and showered ex-food into the bin. 'Disgusting.' He thumped it from behind, another wave of crap falling out. 'How the hell am I supposed to write my report with this thing?'

'A bad workman blames his tools.' Reed's face twisted back into its resting position. 'IPCC got to you yet?'

'Still just about got all my teeth.' Fenchurch sat back in his office chair. 'You?'

'Me and Jon have already given our statements, guv. Naismith's speaking to them now. They're keeping Martin waiting.'

'You couldn't have been in that long.' Fenchurch adjusted his keyboard on the desk. He'd missed a few patches of crumbs. 'I don't want to know what they asked you, okay?'

'Wasn't going to tell you.' Reed shut the door and sat opposite, leaning forward, her head almost halfway across. 'Steve downstairs said some bloke gave you something.'

'Bloody hell.' Fenchurch scuttled the keyboard across the desk. 'Is nothing sacred in this place?'

'Nothing, guv.' She nibbled at her lip. 'What was it?'

Fenchurch sighed, then opened his drawer and got out the bag. 'It's a four-grand bottle of whisky.'

'Shit. You're serious?' Reed picked up the black box and ran it around her hands. 'What's this for?'

'Saving his life.'

She smirked. 'Could've spent some money on it, then, couldn't he?'

'I'm serious, Kay.' Fenchurch put the bag away. 'What the hell do I do with it?'

'Sticking it on eBay's out of the question.' Reed perched on the edge of his desk, arms crossed. 'Anyone you could just give it to?'

'My old man likes a tipple, but he's more of a meths kind of guy.' Fenchurch locked his drawer.

The door burst open again and Docherty appeared, running his tongue over his teeth. 'Have you lost our chum already?'

'She's speaking with Temple about Johnson.'

'Ah. Good.' Docherty folded his bony arms, like a skull and crossbones. 'Decent effort finding that guy, by the way. A bent cop is always a good deflection for us.' He raised his eyebrows. 'But you pair really do need to keep yourselves a million miles away from this Shelvey case, okay?'

Fenchurch saluted. 'I'll set my controls for the heart of the sun, boss.'

'Less of that Pink Floyd shite, Si. Bloody hell.'

Reed smirked at Fenchurch again. 'You're showing your age, guv.'

'I'm serious.' Docherty wagged his finger at them. 'I want you pair running everything past me.'

'Boss.' Fenchurch eyed his desk drawer. 'I need to have a word with you about something.'

'Is it urgent, Si?'

'Not very.' Fenchurch glanced at Reed. 'Just that Lord Ingham dropped off a bottle of whisky.'

'Nothing wrong with a wee dram, is there?' Docherty pointed at him. 'So long as you bloody log it.' He waited for a nod. 'In the meantime, I've got a bone for you, Si.'

'What?'

'That call was another case coming in. Get your arse out to Canning Town.'

Chapter Sixteen

Fenchurch powered up the road, glad to be driving rather than stuck in traffic. The Holiday Inn Express passed on the right, a huge complex surrounded by empty space, like it was waiting for the rest of the world to discover Canning Town as a thriving business hub. 'No, I don't think I'll mention how much the whisky cost.'

'You sure about that?' Reed looked over at him. 'What about if Steve mentions it?'

'I thought it was a ten-quid bottle.' Fenchurch slowed towards the lights. The DLR station and its conjoined bus interchange lurked over to the left.

A bulbous new block of flats rushed past, followed by the navy boards of the Canning Town Caravanserai, a community performance space. A last-ditch effort at some social cohesion in this hellhole before it all got gentrified. Blue light strobed from the right, brighter than the late-afternoon sun. A male uniformed officer pulled a roll of police tape across the side-street entrance, wrapping it around a tall sycamore.

Reed screwed her eyes up at the crime scene. 'Plausible deniability.'

The lights were still red, so Fenchurch pulled across the oncoming lane and bumped onto the pavement, coming to a halt behind a Lexus.

'Jon Nelson and his posh motors.' Fenchurch got out and charged over to the uniform, now taping up part of the Caravanserai's hoarding. 'Where's DS Nelson?'

'Over by the motor, sir.' The uniform let the tape hang and reached for a clipboard. 'Think you've got to sign in.'

'You think?' Fenchurch snatched it off him and autographed the page, before handing it to Reed. 'Make sure nobody even gets to this point without you knowing their inside-leg measurement, okay?'

'Sir.' He took the clipboard back from Reed, frowning like he needed a tape measure, wondering if the crime-scene tape would do.

Bloody useless.

Fenchurch set off down the side street towards the huddle of officers in white SOCO suits surrounding a red car, the Nissan logo glinting in the sun, a circle with a horizontal bar across it. One of those space-age Japanese things. Electric. Hybrid. Something like that. An answer to the Toyota Prius Shelvey drove for Travis.

A suited figure broke off and limped over to him, tearing his mask open as he reached the outer edge of the police tape. Nelson, out of breath. 'Guv. Kay.'

Fenchurch peered past him but couldn't get much of a view. 'What've we got?'

Nelson stepped over to their side of the tape and let his romper suit hang free behind him. Beads of sweat slid down his cheeks. Expensive aftershave rolled off him. He shifted to the side so they could get a better look at the car. The driver's window was down, the passenger side sprayed red. 'I'm thinking she pulled up, then . . .' He made his hand into a pistol, holding it side-on, gangster-style. 'BANG.'

Fenchurch shut his eyes. 'What's this bloody city coming to?'

'Two shots, guv.' Nelson tapped his neck. 'One in her throat, the other in her chest. Dead when we got here.'

Fenchurch opened his eyes again, the late-afternoon sunshine still blinding. 'Any good news?'

'Don't have the weapon yet, guv. But the paramedics have confirmed that there were only two gunshot wounds, and we've got both casings.' Nelson waved over at the car. 'Not got a time of death, but

three separate sources have reported two gunshots just after four p.m.'
He pointed over the road at the transport terminus. 'Got a team going
round the DLR station and the bus terminal for eyewitnesses or . . .'
He grinned. 'Earwitnesses.'

'Not now, Jon.'

The wide car park next to them was probably parking for the station
into the City. A grim set of houses sat in an L-shape behind, two-up
two-downs. New-build flats further over, at least eight storeys.

'Get people going through every single car there, okay? Someone
might've parked here just before it happened.' Which begged the question . . . 'Do we know who called it in?'

'Working on it, guv. Think it was a call box a few blocks away.'
Nelson thumbed back at the car. 'You want to have a look at the car?'

'I'll just get suited up.'

'Get out of the way.' Fenchurch brushed past the SOCO, his suit crinkling in the gentle breeze, his breath misting in the goggles. He followed Nelson down the side street towards the car, a slightly bulbous
red thing. If anything was a hybrid, this car was it. Like one of those
concept cars you used to get, now a reality.

The driver's window was down and a SOCO was dusting around it.
Fenchurch stopped beside them. 'Was it like this when you arrived?'

The SOCO nodded. 'Wound down on arrival. And, before you ask,
she was shot through this window.'

Fenchurch squatted down to peer inside. A young woman sat in the
driver's seat, hands on the wheel, staring straight ahead. Early twenties,
maybe. Tousled hair in ringlets. Still looked like she was driving, just the
two holes in her neck and chest giving any clue to her death.

The interior of the car was a mess. A mobile phone was mounted
in the middle, the system of cables linking it to the car stereo similar to

Fenchurch's. A fine spray of blood misted the passenger window and the other seat. Confirmed the shooting angle, if nothing else.

Sickening.

Fenchurch looked around the masked faces. 'Do we know who she is?'

They all shook their heads at different frequencies.

'We've got nothing?' Fenchurch stabbed a finger at the car. 'Nobody's run these plates?'

'I've just done it, guv.' Reed was over by the crime-scene tape, holding her Airwave Pronto. 'The owner's name is Cassie McBride.'

Fenchurch pointed back at the car. 'Do we know if this is her?'

'Not yet.' Reed waved her gloved hand at the brick terrace on the other side of the wide car park behind them. 'The address is one of those houses, though.'

'God, I hate those suits.' Fenchurch was still flapping his jacket, waiting on the doorbell. Felt like the SOCO suit was still clinging to him, squeezing him. 'That car . . . I don't like the implications of someone just shooting her on the street like that.' He stepped back onto the road.

A sixties terrace with tiny gardens, most of them filled with shiny new cars. Cassie McBride's address was pretty much the only one on the row that hadn't had a porch stuck on the front. Curtains drawn in both upstairs windows, the downstairs one too small to see in.

Fenchurch thumped the door. 'This is the police! Open up!'

A new block of flats overlooked the houses and the car park opposite.

'We got anyone going door-to-door up there?'

'Just a sec.' Reed stabbed something into her Pronto. 'Still not got enough officers.'

'I'll have a word with Docherty.' Fenchurch checked his watch. Ten seconds up. Still nothing. Then he kicked the bottom of the door and got a satisfying thunk in response. 'This is the police!'

Upstairs curtains twitched next door.

'Come on.' Fenchurch skipped along the pavement and crossed over the block-paved driveway past an old Vectra, glowing silver where it wasn't rusty. He knocked on the door and waited as Reed joined him.

The door opened to a crack and a middle-aged man stomped out, wearing a tartan dressing gown and monster-feet slippers. 'What?'

'I'm a police officer, sir.' Fenchurch flipped out his warrant card. 'We're looking to speak to your neighbours.'

'Pair of bloody *dykes*.' He snarled the words out. Stale BO wafted off him. 'I've written to their bloody landlord God knows how many times. It's not bloody natural. Should still be illegal, if you ask me.'

Nobody's asked you.

'When was the last time you saw either of them?'

'I *hear* them all the bloody time.' His lips twitched. 'Moaning and groaning in the middle of the night. *Pleasuring* each other. Dirty little bitches. I know sod all about them.'

'A young woman was shot about an hour ago.' Fenchurch pointed towards the crime scene. 'Just down the road there, sir. You didn't hear anything?'

'If it was one of them clam-jousters from next door, then good bloody riddance.' He slammed the door in their faces.

'Charming geezer.' Fenchurch checked out the other houses on the road. 'Worth trying any others?'

'Lesbians were never illegal, anyway.' Reed was still glaring at the door. 'I think we should do him, guv.'

'Kay, I don't think he knows anything, but we'll get a statement to be on the safe side.' Fenchurch trudged back towards the crime scene. 'Okay?'

'Maybe. Just . . .' Reed clicked her tongue. 'I don't know, guv. That sort of shit really gets my back up.'

'It's not just you.' Fenchurch stopped by the outer perimeter.

The crime scene had swollen with a squad of officers, both uniformed and plainclothes, taking in a good chunk of the main road, coated in red and white glow as rubberneckers slowed.

The arc lights bleached Cassie McBride's car, a pre-emptive measure against a long night. SOCOs combed the vehicle, inside and out.

By the blue hoarding, uniforms had paired off with members of the public, each cop furiously scribbling in their notebooks. Nelson was chatting to a female DC, his gaze scattering across the scene. She winked at him and walked off towards the mobile unit, a hulking van that'd be more at home in a static caravan park.

Fenchurch tapped Nelson on the shoulder, causing him to spin round. 'You getting anything, Jon?'

'Nothing much, guv.' Nelson put his vape stick away. 'Just backing up the story.' He waved over at the mobile unit. 'Clive's got a cut of the CCTV, though.'

'Naismith?' Fenchurch groaned. 'We should've sent him back to Brick Lane, Jon.'

'Nobody's shouting for him, guv. Decent cop, actually. Might want to think about keeping him on. Keep your enemies close and all that.'

'I'll think about it.' Fenchurch started off towards the crime van, Reed following. He knocked at the door as he entered.

The interior would be blinding if it wasn't so grubby. The white walls and furniture probably hadn't been cleaned since Thatcher had been in power. It stank of coffee whitener, a huge tub of it open to the elements, with three dirty spoons sticking out.

A tower of styrofoam cups arched over Clive Naismith's head as he worked at a laptop. He glanced round at them and sat up straight, clearing his throat. 'Sir.'

'No need to salute, I'm not the Queen.' Fenchurch pulled out a light-beige chair and scraped it over to sit next to him. 'How's it going?'

'Slowly, sir.' Naismith tapped at his laptop, which was showing a grainy shot of the street outside. 'Finally got the CCTV through. You might like to see this.' He jockeyed the footage back, switching to another view from over by the DLR station.

A man stood on the pavement, his face obscured by a hood. The red Nissan Leaf was dark grey in the monochrome image. The video rolled on and the car window wound down. The man stepped closer, reaching into his pocket. He aimed a gun through the window, maybe a metre from the victim's head. They stayed like that for a few seconds. Then gunfire bleached him white. Then again. Then he marched off, casual as you like.

'Well, that nails it, I suppose.' Fenchurch's lips bit together. 'See when he's pointing the gun at her? How long was it like that?'

'Twenty-two seconds.' Naismith tapped at a page in his notebook. 'They had a chat first.'

The man was blurry as hell, his hood pulled up. No chance they'd get anything from it.

'Still leaves a million and one questions.'

'Hopefully this can answer one of them.' Naismith clicked the mouse a couple of times, then tapped at the screen, focusing on the area at the top right, the part nearest the DLR.

By the lights, a cyclist stood on his pedals. The footage ran on and the shooter jogged towards the cyclist as he sped off past the Caravanserai.

Naismith wound it back and drew a circle around the cyclist with his finger. 'Whoever that is, sir, they saw what happened.'

Docherty stood in the mobile unit, jangling keys in his pocket as he sucked coffee from the styrofoam cup, the earthy reek of instant and curdling milk coming off him in waves. On the screen, the cyclist shot off again, followed by the shooter, but no bullets. 'So he doesn't shoot this boy?'

'No, boss.' Fenchurch was resting against the back of the grimy chair, careful not to put too much weight on it. 'The way I read it, he doesn't want to shoot anyone else.'

'You think this is an assassination?' Docherty grimaced at another sip. 'The girl pulls up at the lights, winds down the windows, he has a word with her, then shoots her.' Another slurp, then Docherty smacked his lips together. 'Any idea what this word's about?'

'None.'

'See, if it's an assassination, you'd just bang bang, then clear off, right?' Docherty waved his free hand at the monitor. 'Why talk to her?'

'Not sure, guv.' Fenchurch stood and stretched out his spine. That little nugget of connective tissue needed a bit of work before it popped. Crack. There we go. 'We don't know anything about this girl. It's possible he could be a known associate. He's probably giving her a death message.'

'Well, I'll get a press conference together, see if we can coax this cyclist out of hiding.' Docherty finished the coffee with a glower. 'I want you to thank Bell for this, okay?'

'Come on, boss.'

'Not often someone does us a favour, okay? Give him credit.'

'Fine.' Fenchurch clicked his teeth together and leaned in close. 'Did you get anywhere with Naismith's guv'nor?'

Docherty dumped the cup in a bin. 'You've got him till Tuesday, if you need him.'

'Cheers, boss.'

Fenchurch's Airwave blared out. Nelson. 'Guv, we've got an incident over at the girl's house.'

Fenchurch's knees clicked as he jogged through the car park towards the house, sending some gravel pinging off a pair of Fords.

Cassie McBride's neighbour was outside the house, partially obscured by two uniformed officers, his face twisted into disgust. His tartan dressing gown flapped open to show a stained white T-shirt, a V of sweat at the neck and a muffin-top of flab wobbling over the matching pyjama bottoms. He jabbed a finger in the air, aiming at his target. 'You sicken me. You and your bloody dyke bitch girlfriend!'

'Oh yeah?' A woman stepped forward, going head to head with him. 'What about the shit we hear coming through the walls at night from your house, you filthy pervert? You should be locked up!'

Nelson grabbed hold of her arm. 'Madam, can you—'

'*I* should be locked up?' The neighbour let out a belly laugh. 'You and your girlfriend—'

'Sir!'

'She's *not* my—'

'—filthy bitches!'

Fenchurch stepped between them and pushed them apart. 'Sir, I need you to back off.' He grabbed the neighbour by the shoulder and walked him away. 'Sir, can you give my colleague here a full statement?' Then he whispered in the uniform's ear. 'Go door to door and see if he's done anything physical to them, okay?'

The uniform scowled at him. 'Fine.'

Fenchurch narrowed his eyes, making sure the punk got the message. 'Am I clear?'

'Sir.' The uniform led the neighbour away.

'Filthy bloody dykes! Hey! My oven's on! I need to get in there!'

Fenchurch returned to the target of his abuse. 'I'm sorry about that.'

The girl tucked her arms tight around her torso. 'Nothing I haven't heard a hundred times from him.' Her skin was mid-tone, her chin rounded. As tall as Reed, even in flat shoes. 'He's a filthy pervert. Watching all sorts of dirty shit on his computer, loud as you like.'

'Have you reported him to the police?'

Her eyes followed the uniform leading the neighbour into his house. 'Is that what this is about?'

Fenchurch shook his head. Couldn't keep eye contact. 'What's your name?'

'Rebecca. Rebecca Thurston. I've just got back from work. What's going on?'

'Okay, Rebecca. Do you know a Cassie McBride?'

'She's my— What?' Rebecca looked over to the crime scene. 'What's going on?'

Fenchurch gestured at the house. 'Let's do this inside, Ms Thurston.'

Her gaze switched back to Fenchurch. 'Has something happened to Cassie?'

'We should do this inside.'

Rebecca shoved him backwards and he fell on his arse. She broke into a run, her shoes splashing across the car park towards the glowing crime scene.

Fenchurch clambered to his feet and set off after her, his knee twanging as he ran. 'Rebecca!'

A uniform sprinted after her. She feinted left and darted round a parked Focus, then sped up, losing him.

Fenchurch followed her and spotted a shortcut as she cut round an Astra to avoid another uniform.

He crouched down behind a Porsche SUV and listened as she hurtled towards him. Then he burst out and grabbed hold of her, clutching his hands around her waist.

'No!'

'Rebecca, it's okay.'

'Let me go!' She struggled for a few seconds, then her body went limp. 'What happened to her?'

Fenchurch grabbed her shoulders and restrained her against the Porsche. 'Cassie was shot.'

'Over there?'

Fenchurch nodded.

'I want to see her.'

'Trust me, you don't.'

'Jesus . . .' She slumped forward, Fenchurch's grip the only thing holding her up. 'What've they done?'

'Who? What've who done?'

She screwed her eyes tight and covered her ears.

'Rebecca, who?'

Fenchurch kneaded his brow as she nibbled at her lip. 'Rebecca, do you have any idea who could've killed her?'

Her nostrils flared, mouth closed. 'Cassie . . .'

⌣

Fenchurch let the female uniformed officer take Rebecca away, back towards her house. 'Stay with her, okay?'

'Sir.' She led Rebecca off, still mute.

Was it just the murder of her friend?

Fenchurch stomped across the car park towards the crime scene, his left hand clasped around his keys.

The engine of a squad Astra growled into life, the neighbour in the back seat, shouting and screaming silent curses at the cops in the front.

Fenchurch stopped by Docherty. 'Boss.'

Docherty glanced up from his Pronto and waved over at the departing car. 'That your doing?'

'It's someone we can do on some homophobic hate crimes.'

'That's mightily impressive for the stats, but has it got anything to do with this case?'

'No, boss.'

'Christ with a harpoon gun.'

Fenchurch pointed at Rebecca, struggling with the uniform outside her house. 'I've got an FLO heading to sit with the housemate.

She'll maybe coax her into speaking. Once we get the girl's body out to Lewisham, we'll do a full ID.'

'You don't think it's her?'

'No, I think it's her. Her DVLA photo matches the body.' Flashes of light cannoned off the inside of the car, dancing across the car park. 'I'm just thrown by this.' Rebecca dipped her head and nodded, letting the uniform drag her into the house. 'We need a squad car stationed outside her house in case Rebecca's next.'

'Simon, do you honestly think someone will go after her?'

'She clammed up after she said, "What have they done?" Didn't say who.'

'Fenchurch!' A smurf was walking towards them, waving. He tore the mask away. Clooney's face bulged out. 'Get over here.'

Fenchurch stormed over. 'What's up?'

Clooney pointed over at Cassie's car. 'Might have something. Did you see that phone mounted on the dashboard?'

'What about it, Mick?'

'Well, the screen keeps lighting up.' Clooney held up a bagged Sony smartphone, black body. The display was filled with text over a topless photo of David Beckham. 'It's got a ton of notifications from the Travis app . . .' He tossed it over. 'I think she might be a driver.'

Chapter Seventeen

Fenchurch couldn't even look at Bell, but Pavel Udzinski's shades mirrored two copies of the smug wanker. Standing in the open-plan office space, his shirt failing to halt the spillage of guts. Could even see Reed's eyes rolling in the reflection. 'I just need to know more about this girl.'

Udzinski sat back in his leather chair and steepled his fingers. 'Okay, I hear you, but the answer's still no.'

'Listen, it's possible this was a random attack, but . . .' Fenchurch crouched down in front of Udzinski. 'Someone put two bullets in her. Point-blank range.' He tried to peer over the shades. 'I need to know about Cassie McBride.'

'I keep telling you . . .' Udzinski tore off his shades and dumped them on his desk. Dark pools where his eyes should be, the whites more red than white, like he hadn't slept in months. 'I can't give out that information.'

'You gave us it last night for another of your drivers.'

'*Co-signs.*' Udzinski rubbed the skin under his eyes, pulling the bottom half of his lids out. 'It's very important you use the correct terminology. Our co-signs are our partners in the business. They're equally liable should anything happen.'

'I just need to know about this driver. Cassie McBride.'

'I can't tell you that.' Udzinski picked up his shades and blew on the lenses. 'From what I'm hearing, this sounds like an attack on Travis as a corporate entity.'

'What? No—'

'Simon, let me.' Bell perched on the edge of Udzinski's desk and flashed a grin, his belly rolling over the top of his trousers. 'Pavel, mate, this is all covered under our standard warrant. Just give DI Fenchurch the information and we'll be on our merry way.'

'That warrant covers crimes committed by our co-signs, not our co-signs as victims.'

Fenchurch nearly reached out to grab Udzinski's throat, but just about kept his hands by his sides. 'So you're not going to help us?'

'Inspector.' Bell's glare shifted to a smile at Udzinski. 'Pavel, this girl was murdered this afternoon. Shot dead. You don't want me to go to the press with a story about how Travis refused to help us now, do you?'

'You're playing the same game as last night, yes?'

'This is serious. You can't just operate unilaterally in this city. You need to work with us.'

'And I can't just decide to do this *unilaterally*. This is a corporate policy.' Udzinski waved his hand away. 'Not part of my remit.'

Bell gripped Udzinski's shoulder and squeezed hard. 'So run it up the flagpole.'

'Run . . . What?'

'Go and call your boss.'

'Stay here.' Udzinski locked his computer and marched off, sticking his phone to his ear.

The floor was quieter than the other night, clearly in some sort of lull between shifts.

'Think these would suit me?' Bell picked up the mirror shades and gave them a thorough investigation. 'We're taking the kids to Florida next summer. Costs a—'

'Jason, I need that—'

'Simon, I'm telling you to butt out. Be thankful I don't ask you to leave.'

I'll knock you into the middle of next week.

Bell tried on the sunglasses. 'They're really comfortable, though. You can see why—'

'Put them down!' Udzinski yanked the glasses out of Bell's podgy grasp. 'I leave you for just one minute . . .' He shook the shades around. 'These are private property. Maybe I will report you to the police, eh?'

'Hey, do I know you?' An American accent. John Gomez stood there grinning, tanned and muscular. Black Levi's and a crisp white shirt. He clicked his fingers a few times, trying to jog his memory, then pointed at Fenchurch, pistol-like. 'I've got it. You were guarding that . . . guy at that panel I did yesterday.' He held out a hand. 'John Q. Gomez, CEO of Travis Cars, Inc.'

'It's a pleasure to meet you, sir.' Bell shook his hand like he was meeting the Prime Minister, only letting go after a good few healthy pumps. 'The name's DCI Jason Bell.'

Fenchurch waved to the side. 'This is DS Kay Reed.'

Two heavies pushed past Gomez, both with an air of Israeli Defence Force about them. He raised a hand. 'We're cool, guys. These are the police.'

They relaxed and separated.

Bell waved over at Fenchurch. 'My colleagues are assisting me with an investigation.'

Lying bastard.

Fenchurch kept his peace.

'You're lucky to be able to speak to me.' Gomez flashed his perfect American teeth, white pillars which no doubt required a good salary to fix. 'I fly back to SD tonight. I'm over here fixing out the teething problems with our UK operation, then things blow up back in the States.' He pulled up the seat next to Udzinski and sat down. 'So how can we help you, dude?'

'We need to obtain some information on one of your dri—' Bell caught himself with a grin. 'One of your co-signs.' His expression darkened as he swallowed the smile. 'A Cassie McBride. She was murdered today.'

'Shit.' Gomez gritted his teeth. 'Have the press got hold of this?'

'Not yet.' Bell's mouth twitched, switching between a smile and a grimace. 'We desperately need any information you can give us.'

'You're talking about something very sensitive. I can't just—'

'Mr Gomez, sir. This is a shooting on a London street. We don't get a lot of them.'

Gomez raised his hands. 'The answer's no.'

'I've got a good friend at the *Post*.' Fenchurch got out his mobile and held it out. 'Shall I give him a ring and tell him about what Mr Shelvey was up to?'

'What?' Gomez stepped forward, the goons shadowing his movement. 'Are you threatening me?'

'Sir, we need that information.'

'Can't do it.'

Fenchurch hit dial and put the phone to his ear. Let it ring a few times.

Sounded like Liam was at the gym. Machines whirred and house music thumped in the background. 'Yo?'

'Got a story for you, Liam.'

'I'm all ears.'

'Okay, okay.' Gomez sighed. 'What do you want to know?'

'Catch you later, Liam.' Fenchurch killed the call. 'Mr Udzinski here knows.'

Gomez clicked his fingers at his security goons. 'Get Kim to change my flight, would you? I'll be here for a few more days.' The left gorilla goose-stepped across the open-plan office. Gomez smiled at Udzinski. 'Now, Paul, I need you to—'

'I know.' Udzinski unlocked his machine and started beating the shit out of the keyboard. 'It's Pavel.'

Gomez doubled over in mock laughter. 'I love this dude.'

'Glad to hear it.' Udzinski put his shades back on. 'Are you ready?'

'When you are.' Bell clapped his back as he perched on the desk again. 'What've you got?'

Udzinski reached over to the droning printer and grabbed a sheet of paper. Bell scanned it and handed it over to Fenchurch.

Blonde hair in a ponytail, hanging over her shoulder. No expression on her face, just catwalk ice. Cassie McBride was beautiful, even in a poorly lit passport shot printed on a crappy desktop printer. At least a stone underweight, though. Like something plagued her, eating away at her soul.

Fenchurch handed the page to Reed and whispered, 'This is her, right?'

'Could be, guv. I didn't get a look, remember.'

'We'll need to back this up, but I'm afraid that I believe this is our victim.'

Gomez snatched Udzinski's shades from his hand and put them on. 'This isn't good.'

Fenchurch stared at him, just getting his own face reflected back. 'It's a tragedy, sir.'

'No, you don't get it.' Gomez ran a hand across his designer stubble. 'We've been in beta in this city since December and now we're into our official launch. This is the *worst* possible time for this. The *worst*.'

'I'll pass your regards on to Ms McBride's family, sir.'

Gomez tore off the shades and threw them at Udzinski's desk, the left lens snapping out and skidding over the floor. 'Jesus Christ! You don't get it, do you?'

Udzinski reached over for the glasses, his chest rising and falling slowly. He snapped the lens back into the frame and put them back on, the lens slightly wonky. No idea what the eyes were doing, but they were probably glaring at Gomez. 'What else do you need to know?'

'Was she working today?'

Udzinski ran a finger along a line of data on his screen. 'Ms McBride logged on at three fifty-eight.'

Fenchurch raised his eyebrows at Reed. 'So she'd only just gone out on her rounds?'

'Given she was shot near her house, that make sense.'

'Ms McBride accepted a Travis Go at three fifty-nine.' Udzinski glanced round at Gomez, busy tapping at his mobile. 'The collect location was two hundred metres from her home. She responded to it and sat for forty-eight seconds waiting for the passenger.'

Shit.

Fenchurch stood and folded his arms. 'Can you give us anything about this passenger?'

'Mr Gomez?'

Gomez looked up at the ceiling, clicking his tongue. 'I'll need to consult my General Counsel on that matter.'

Fenchurch paced over to him, raising up his phone to Gomez's eye line. 'This is a murder, sir.'

'And this is a legal precedent.' Gomez stabbed his finger at Udzinski's screen. 'This passenger could have nothing to do with it. It could be a neighbour who shot her, could just be some random. I'm not giving you that info until I've run this past a lawyer.'

Fenchurch tapped his foot a couple of times. 'Just don't take too long.'

'Are you threatening me again?'

'Nothing of the sort, sir.' The remaining suited goon stepped towards Fenchurch, his right hand reaching into his jacket pocket. 'What else can you tell us about her?'

'We've got nothing else on her.' Udzinski locked his machine again. 'Just what your colleague has on that page.'

'This is one of your employees and you've got that little on her?' Fenchurch rattled the sheet Reed was looking at. 'That's not—'

'Guv . . .' Reed passed it to him. 'Her reference is Howard Savage.'

Chapter Eighteen

Fenchurch stormed down the corridor in Leman Street, his footsteps in serious danger of dislodging floorboards.

Reed jogged to catch up with him, just as he pushed open the office door.

Docherty was standing over by his shrine to Rangers tat, while Temple sat on the desk, huffing and puffing. 'I've told you to knock, Fenchurch. We could've had our cocks out.'

DCI Howard Savage was silhouetted in the evening light softened by the filthy windows. He'd finally seen sense and trimmed the combover down to a rough suedehead. Took years off. He marched over, his right hand outstretched, the left inside his blazer, like a minor royal at a tennis tournament. 'Simon, it's been a while.'

'Just a couple of months . . .' Fenchurch gripped the hand tight, resisting the urge to throw in a little masonic flourish to mess with him. 'Your secretary said you'd be here, sir.'

'Ah, yes.' Savage frowned. 'We're just discussing prosecution strategy for those chaps we arrested in December, as it happens.' His frown deepened, sending diagonal ridges out of his forehead. 'What's the matter?'

'How come *you've* got a secretary? I actually need one.' Looked like Docherty'd been on the strong coffee again. The room stank of it.

Fenchurch shot him a shut-up glare and closed in on Savage, passing him the sheet of paper. 'Do you want to tell me what's going on with this girl?'

'You'll need to slow down.' Savage checked the page, swigging at his coffee. His expression was unreadable.

Fenchurch had no idea how he'd ever made it as a copper. Probably an ex-army officer, shunted up the ranks. Not a bloody clue what he's doing.

Fenchurch got closer to him, could almost taste the second-hand coffee fumes. 'DS Reed and I just visited Travis cars.'

'Wait a minute.' Docherty got between them, gripping Fenchurch's shoulder tight. 'That wee IPCC lassie told you to keep clear of the Shelvey case.'

'We are, boss.' Fenchurch brushed off Docherty's grip. 'This is about that shooting in Canning Town.'

Docherty dug his finger into Fenchurch's chest, like he was breaking soil with a spade. 'Did you—'

'Relax, boss. You won't be getting any calls from Bell.' Fenchurch raised his eyebrows at Savage and stepped closer. 'You know a Cassie McBride?'

Savage passed the paper back. 'Ah.'

'Ah? That's all I get?' Fenchurch clicked his fingers in front of his face. 'She's *dead*, Howard.'

Savage shut his eyes. 'Oh dear God.' He collapsed against the wall, huffing out breath. 'It's definitely her?'

'I don't bloody know, Howard, because you're keeping shit from us!' Fenchurch grabbed him under the armpits and pulled him to his feet. 'Cut this *Fight Club* bollocks out, please. First rule of Trafficking and Prostitution Unit is there's no such—'

'*Simon.*' Savage's eyes opened again, filled with menace. 'Get to the point, Inspector.'

'You are Cassie McBride's reference at Travis. Her next of kin needs to identify her body out at Lewisham. ASAP.'

'There is no next of kin. She's . . .' Savage licked his lips, slowly. What the hell was he holding back? 'It's complicated.'

'Try me.'

Savage glanced over at Docherty, then at Temple. Reed didn't even warrant a look. 'I can't tell you. Any of you.'

Fenchurch snarled at him, teeth bared. 'Howard, I'm this close to tossing you out of that window.'

'She's under witness protection.' Savage swallowed hard, trying to regain his composure. 'Young Cassie's starting a new life driving that car. I told her it didn't pay well, but she's a stubborn one. Tunnel vision.' He put a hand to his head, scrabbling at where the comb-over used to be. 'And there's no next of kin.'

Fenchurch put his hands on his hips. 'Can *you* ID the body?'

'I'll have to.' Savage slumped into a chair. 'Do you know who did it?'

'We've just found her. Still early days.' Fenchurch stood over him. 'She was shot in cold blood, Howard. A public execution.'

Savage ran his hand across his bald head but kept quiet.

'Funny thing is . . .' Fenchurch squatted in front of him, his thighs burning. 'It was very much like they were sending a message. So if someone had found out about Cassie and her new life, who and how?'

Savage's skin had lost all of its summer tan, just blotchy pink.

'Now, we were speaking to Rebecca Thur—'

'Okay.' Savage stood and cracked his knuckles. 'Take me to Cassie, please.'

⌣

Rebecca Thurston cowered in the corner of Fenchurch's office, wiping at her cheeks. 'She can't be dead. She just can't.'

Savage crouched in front of her, looking like he wanted to hug her tight. 'I've . . . I've just been out to Lewisham, where we . . .' He coughed. 'I saw her there, Rebecca. Cassie. She's dead.'

'How?' Rebecca gasped. 'Shot? How? How can that happen?' She twirled her hair round, fury twisting it tight. 'Will you find who did this, Howard?'

'We're going to try.' Savage pecked her on the forehead, like a seedy stepfather. 'First things first, we need to understand if anyone knew about you and Cassie.'

Rebecca exhaled slowly, shaking her head. 'Not that I can think of.' A frown dented her forehead. 'Wait. Cassie mentioned something about a bloke last night.' She twisted her hair tighter. 'Lurking out the back of our house, I think.'

'Rebecca, you're supposed to call in anything like that.' Savage rubbed his face. 'Anything.'

'Okay, so did she?' Fenchurch left him a space. 'Howard?'

'Not to me.'

'Right, so a suspicious man was lurking in the street behind her house last night and you've done nothing about it?'

'The standing order for our girls is to call either myself or DI Gill.' Savage scratched the top of his head. 'I can check with him, if you want?'

'Go on.' Fenchurch waited until Savage got out his mobile, an old Nokia job. 'Kay, can you see if Control got anything on this?'

'Guv.' She left the room.

Savage spoke into his phone, his free arm windmilling. 'Jerry, hi, it's Howard. Have you heard anything from the canaries?' His arm flopped to his side. 'No? Nothing last night? Okay. Thanks.' He killed the call and glowered at Fenchurch. 'Nothing.'

'Bloody hell.'

'Guv.' Reed entered the room. 'Just checked with Control. No reports of suspicious activity in that location for the last month.'

'Okay.' Savage winced. 'Leave this with me.' He led Rebecca out into the corridor.

'Leave it with him . . .' Fenchurch slammed his office door and leaned back against it. 'He'll just sit on it, form a committee and escalate some shit to the Commissioner.'

Reed twisted a chair round and sat. 'So what do we do, guv?'

The wall was blank except for next season's West Ham season ticket pinned to his day planner. What can we do?

Waiting for Savage didn't seem like an option. Go back to the crime scene, maybe. Call up Bell and hope he doesn't grass to teacher.

'I don't bloody know, Kay.' Fenchurch perched on Mulholland's desk. 'Everything we've got on this so far doesn't feel like a random attack.'

'Of course it's not random. Someone must've found out about them, put a hit out.'

'Who and what are they covering up?' Fenchurch stepped away from the door and jabbed his thumb at it as it swung open. 'Of course, Savage is playing secret bloody squirrel with the why and the who.'

Docherty peered through the doorway. 'Who's playing secret squirrel?'

'Nobody.'

'Aye, right. Never is with you.' Docherty rapped his knuckles on the door frame. 'By the way, the assorted ghouls and demons from the press are waiting for us.'

The TV lights were so hot it felt like they could brand your skin. So bright they obscured the crowd of reporters. Craven arseholes scribbling in their notebooks, typing on their laptops. Just waiting to bite. The room stank of air freshener, not quite overpowering the stale-sweat smell.

Fenchurch shuffled the papers on his desk like he was a newsreader. Stop doing that. He checked his watch just as it ticked to 19.30 and cleared his throat. 'So, to reiterate, we appreciate you all coming here at such a late hour, but we hope this can still make the front page or the nightly news. Any coverage we get can only help.' He raised a shot of the car, the shooter starting to run away. 'We are looking to speak to the man in your press packs, but also the cyclist spotted here.' He held up an enlarged A3 photo of the cyclist, even vaguer and murkier than the other. 'We believe he may have seen something which could lead to us identifying this killer.'

'Thanks, Simon.' Docherty shifted his gaze round the audience, grinning wide. 'Now, any questions?'

A sea of hands raised up, partially eclipsing the lights.

Docherty pointed to the nearest, a young woman holding out her mobile. 'Aye?'

'Kat Fletcher, *Post*. Who's the victim in this shooting?'

Docherty smiled. 'We're unable to give out that information at this time.'

'But you've got a press release covering her death?'

'Aye.' Docherty pointed at an older woman peering over her laptop. 'Your question, madam?'

'Christine Spencer, *Daily Mail*. DI Fenchurch, does this seem connected to the disappearance of your daughter?'

Bloody hell . . .

Docherty folded his arms. 'Why would you think that?'

'Well, there's this.' She held up a copy of that morning's *Post*. 'And having DI Fenchurch on the case. What is it they say, "A coincidence is like Jesus winking at you"?'

Docherty turned his head round to Fenchurch, eyes like laser beams. 'Do you want to take that?'

Fenchurch focused on the reporter, her eyes burrowing into his skull. Or at least trying to. 'Of course I don't believe this is connected.'

His focus swept through the hands and he pointed at a male reporter holding up an old-school notepad. 'Next, you.'

'Ian Mowat, *Express*. Have you had any responses from the public relating to the article in the *Post* this morning?'

Docherty tapped the microphone. 'Ladies and gentlemen, we're here to discuss this murder. Please can we stick to that?'

———

'Christ on the cross.' Docherty slammed his office door so hard it bounced back to fully open. He booted it shut and swung round, hands on hips. 'What part of "stick to Cassie McBride" do those arseholes not understand?' He thundered over to his desk and collapsed into his seat, arms folded. 'Complete waste of time.'

Fenchurch kept a room's width away from Docherty. 'If it's any consolation, boss, you handled it well.'

'I shouldn't have to *handle* anything but the case at hand, you idiot.' Docherty picked up his TV remote and switched on the set in the corner, a small LCD he'd bought to watch the Euros out of hours.

BBC News showed the two of them, their clown make-up barely hiding their bad skin.

Police Officer's Missing Daughter: Connection to Current
Case Denied

'Oh, for crying out loud!' Docherty picked up his Rangers mug and threw it against the wall, spraying dark brown liquid across the magnolia paint. 'You really chose the worst possible time to run this story. You happy with this?'

'Do I look happy?' The coffee dribbled down the wall towards the shattered mug. Stale-coffee smell mixed with the rotting-banana stench coming from the bin. 'This is my dad's doing, not mine.'

'Think the Commissioner's going to care, eh?' Spit flobbed onto Docherty's chin. 'You happy that your missing daughter is overshadowing a dead girl?'

Fenchurch smoothed down his tie, his jaw clenched tight. 'You want to take that back?'

'You're a cheeky bastard, Simon. Did you plan this?'

'What, shooting a cabbie so my story got a little bit of traction? Piss off.' Fenchurch opened the door. 'My personal tragedy might help this case.'

Docherty got up from his desk and crouched by the wall. He pieced together bits of Rangers blue. 'God save us, Si. God save us.'

Fenchurch left him to the ruins of his mug and turned his mobile back on. Fifteen missed calls. Shit.

Could someone have seen the news?

A shiver shot up his spine. No voicemail. What the hell did—

His phone rang. Unknown caller. He stabbed the button to answer it. 'Fenchurch.'

A rasping, distorted robot voice blasted out, 'Slacken off your hunt or your loved ones will suffer.'

Chapter Nineteen

'Cheers, Mick.' Fenchurch stood in the corridor outside Docherty's office, his shaking fingers fumbling through the menus on his mobile. Who designs these things? There we go . . . He hit 'Abi' and it switched to the phone app. He put it to his skull and listened to the ringing tone burning his eardrum.

Come on, come on.

'Hello?'

'Thank God, Abi.' Fenchurch let out his breath. 'Where are you?'

'I'm at home, getting ready.' She paused. 'Where you should be.'

'What?'

'You're late again.' Her voice echoed around the room. Sounded like she was in the kitchen. 'Your dad's already at the restaurant. I've got a hundred missed calls from him. Twice as many as I've got from you.'

'I had my phone off. I was on the telly.'

'What?'

'Never mind.' Fenchurch slumped back against the wall. 'Has anyone been by the house? Anyone called? Anything like that?'

'What? No, why?'

'Nothing. Just . . . I'll be home soon.'

'You've not got the time, Simon. I'll meet you at the restaurant.'

'Where is it again?'

She sighed. 'The Broken Bridge, just off Shoreditch High Street.'

'Got you. See you soon.' Fenchurch ended the call, his gut aching.

Temple squeezed past Fenchurch into Docherty's office. 'Is this because of the TV?'

Fenchurch came back into the room, willing his phone to ring again. 'Sky and the BBC both broadcast it.'

Temple crossed his legs. 'That article was a stupid idea.'

The coffee stain still dribbled down the wall, but most of the royal-blue crockery had been tidied away, just a few shards on the carpet.

'It's just unfortunate timing.' Fenchurch's phone rang again. His heart just about exploded. Clooney. His fingers slicked off the case as he answered it. 'Mick, are you getting anywhere with that call?'

'Hold your horses, Simon. You know how many cases you've got me working just now?'

'This is the priority.'

'Just as well I've done it then, isn't it?' Clooney left a pause which Fenchurch wasn't going to fill. 'It's a burner, Si. Call was made out in Greenwich.'

'A burner? Shit. Any chance—'

'I suspect the phone's at the bottom of the Thames now. Switched it off after the call.'

'Right, cheers. Let me know if it goes back on.'

'Will do.'

Fenchurch pocketed his phone. 'Take it you got the gist of that?'

'Some prick pranking you, no doubt, Si.' Docherty picked up a chunk of his coffee mug and dumped it in his bin. 'Happens to the best of us.'

'Boss, I need to get home.'

'Right, aye.' Docherty pinched his nose, his head low. 'Back in for day shift tomorrow, okay?' He grabbed Fenchurch's arm as he set off. 'And don't get too blootered tonight.'

Fenchurch traipsed off. 'Like that's on the cards.'

Temple got up and hauled his coat on. 'Any chance I could get a lift off you, Simon?'

'What's up with your beautiful Audi?'

'She's in the garage.'

'"She"?' Fenchurch winked at him. 'Well, as it happens, I'm heading to Shoreditch.'

———⌣———

Fenchurch pulled up on Shoreditch High Street, the street buzzing with Friday-night action. The restaurant was just down a side street. Charring steak seeped in through the air conditioning. 'You sure this is fine?'

'I'm sure.' Temple let his seat belt whizz up. 'The walk'll help me clear my head.'

'But on a Friday night?'

'I'm just short.' Temple grinned at him. 'I'm not a dwarf, okay? And I'm a black belt. I'll be fine.'

'Well, if you insist.' Fenchurch killed the engine. Chased a kid on a bike down there a couple of months back. Little shit.

'—that phone call.'

Fenchurch glanced over at him. 'Sorry, I was miles away.'

'I said, I'm here if you want to talk about that phone call.'

'It's not the first time some little scrotum has called me like that.'

'They went to some effort to disguise their voice, though.' Temple had his hand on the door handle. 'That's got to count for something.'

'You trying to frighten me or something? I'm not a black belt.'

Temple shook his head. 'Simon, I'm just watching out for you, mate. Okay?'

'Didn't know I needed a guardian angel.'

'Everyone does. Trust me.' Temple pointed out of the windscreen at a cab. Abi was leaning into the front, handing over some cash. 'There's your date.' He got out onto the pavement and marched over to Abi, who was still glowering at her phone.

Looks a million dollars, dressed to kill. Her frosty expression looks like she's ready to . . .

Fenchurch reached into the glovebox and checked the box was still intact inside. He got out and locked the car.

Temple pulled Abi into a hug and stepped back, staring at her midriff. 'You're starting to show, princess.'

Abi covered her tummy with her hands. 'Shit, am I?'

'Not at all.' Temple winked at her. 'You are pregnant, though, right?'

'Oh, crap.' Abi shut her eyes and gritted her teeth. 'Keep this a secret, Paul. Okay?'

'You aren't showing, by the way. I was just chancing my arm.' Temple grinned at Fenchurch. 'Good to see Simon's still got lead in his pencil.'

'This is a secret, Paul. Okay?'

'Safe with me.' Temple zipped up his coat. 'How far gone are you?'

'Eight weeks, so keep it quiet. We had our ultrasound this morning and everything's looking good.'

Fenchurch's gut jolted at the thought of those tests.

Temple clapped Fenchurch on the arm. 'There's no hanging around with you two. Some couples take months to conceive. Years, even.'

'It was a lot harder the first time.' Abi shot Fenchurch a frosty glare. Definitely not in her good books. 'Come on, Simon, we're late.'

———

'I'll just show you to your table now, sir. Madam.' The maître d' sashayed over to the far end of the restaurant, a world away from the bright soft-play café it used to be. Candlelight flickered in the gloom, the dark-red paint now stripped back to brick and stone. The steak smell was stronger inside, merging with garlic and butter. He stopped and waved them into a long table in the corner.

Fenchurch's dad cackled as he got to his feet, holding out his liver-spotted hands. He winked at Fenchurch and rubbed at his thick moustache, in bad need of a trim. 'Abi, you look fabulous.' He grabbed his son in a bear hug. 'Simon!'

Fenchurch took the seat opposite his father. Three empty beer bottles sat in front of him. At least they weren't pints, but they were Italian. And bloody strong. He passed the bag over the table. 'Have a look at this.'

Dad peered inside and his eyes bulged. 'Did you buy this?'

'I got given it.'

'This is good stuff, son.' Dad took another look, like he feared it might change into supermarket own-brand. Schrödinger's whisky. 'Did you get a bung from those lads who did Hatton Garden, or something?'

'I did someone a favour.'

Abi held up the box, the black sucking in what little light there was. 'You're not drinking this now, are you?'

'Hardly.' Fenchurch shrugged. 'It's not for drinking, Ab. I'm saving it as an investment.'

Dad winked at him. 'What sort of whisky isn't for drinking?'

'The sort that's worth a fortune.'

Abi handed the box back to Dad and folded her arms. 'Who gave you that?'

'That toff I was guarding yesterday.' Fenchurch frowned. 'Was it yesterday?'

'I used to get that fog when I was switching shifts.' Dad cackled again. 'Never stops, does it?'

'Wish it did, Dad. Wish it bloody did.' Fenchurch grabbed a menu from the stack. Burgers, burgers and more burgers. Not a burrito in sight. The Chilli Destroyer, though . . .

'How's it going, son?'

'Same as it ever is, Dad.' Maybe the You're Habanero Laugh . . . 'Murders happen too often in the summer, if you ask me.'

'Happen too often, full stop.'

'Well, there is that.' Fenchurch put the menu back, still undecided, and smiled at his father. 'What've you been up to?'

'Oh, you know. Car chases, sex with dangerous women, locking dwarves in suitcases.'

'The usual, then?'

'I do get bored, son.' Dad drank some beer and smacked his lips. Foam covered his moustache. 'Nice place, this.'

'It's not bad.' Abi stifled a yawn, her nostrils curling up. 'Sorry, been a hell of a week.' Her gaze drifted around the place. 'It's quite a change.'

'Bet they make a lot more dough out of this.' Dad clicked his fingers at a passing waiter. Got ignored. 'Bloody hell.' He grunted. 'Anyway, what's your news, Ab?'

'My news?' Her eyes went wide, shooting across the whole room. 'What news?'

Dad raised his shoulders, cupping hands like a footballer pleading innocence. 'Anything new with you, I think that's what it means?'

'Oh, right.' She tried to swallow down her blush. 'You know me, Ian, I'm just gearing up for summer. Not long now.' She grabbed a menu from the middle of the table. 'Seven weeks of nothing . . .'

Fenchurch waited until Abi started inspecting the menu. 'Dad, has anyone funny been hanging around you, anything like that?'

'That James Corden was out at Lewisham doing his karaoke.'

'I said funny.'

'Right, son.' Dad cackled again. 'What do you mean?'

'I'm being serious. Anyone, you know . . .'

'Not that I've noticed, son, and I'm a copper: it's the sort of thing I notice.' Dad sipped at his beer, soaking his moustache. 'Why do you ask?'

'No reason.'

'Bollocks there isn't.'

Fenchurch snorted. 'I had a call from someone. Warning me.'

'Used to get five of them a week back in the day. Much easier to hide it then, mind.' Dad's eyes moistened around the edges. 'Some nutcase who'd just got out calling from a call box in Soho after a skinful. Your mother used to go bloody potty.'

Fenchurch waited until Dad looked at him. 'This was a burner in Greenwich.'

'Just a 2016 version of my Soho nutter.'

The maître d' appeared with a wide smile, arms splayed to point at their table.

Abi grinned at him. 'Sorry, I've not finished with the menu yet.'

'Oh, I won't be taking your order, madam.' He pointed at the other two chairs. 'Sir, madam?'

Rosie emerged from behind him, pearl necklace and twinset like she was off to the Tory party conference in Harrogate or wherever. Blonde hair, straight as when Princess Di wore it.

What was the sharp-elbowed cow doing here?

'Simon!' She reached over and pecked Fenchurch on the cheek, a blast of perfume and champagne hitting his nose. 'How's my big brother?'

Peter Barnes appeared next to her, still had the smell of the farm about him. Hadn't aged well, looked about twenty years older than Rosie. He clasped a meaty hand on Abi's shoulder. 'Been too long, Abs.' The smooth git held out a hand to Dad. 'Ian, thanks for inviting us along.'

Fenchurch whisper-shouted at his old man, 'You could've warned us.'

⌣

Rosie drained her wine glass and got to her feet. 'I need to go to the toilet.' She raised her eyebrows at Abi and set off.

'Okay.' Abi touched her glass to her lips, but it still looked full. She followed Rosie, head bowed.

'I don't get why women have to go to the toilet in packs.' Peter let out a roar of braying laughter. *Hwa, hwa, hwa.* He drained his glass of sparkling white and scowled around the place. 'The service in here is *shocking*. I'll go and chivvy up *garçon* and get him to do his ruddy job.' He dumped his napkin on the table and marched off, the bottom of his sports jacket folded up.

Fenchurch drank some beer, the pint tasting exactly like he'd stretched it out over an hour. 'Why the hell did you have to invite him?'

'Sorry, son. I thought it'd be fun to have us all together for once.'

Fenchurch downed the rest of his beer. 'Well, I'd hate to see your idea of torture.'

'He's not that bad, is he?'

'Maybe not, but the pair of them are.' Beer suds slid down the side of Fenchurch's glass. 'There's a reason I haven't seen her in two years. She's a complete arsehole.'

Dad took a big drink of his seventh beer. 'That's your sister you're talking about.'

'My sister who didn't bother helping me when Chloe went missing. Just one afternoon of talking would've done the world of good to me. Instead, she's chatting up that boorish twat.' Fenchurch almost jabbed his finger at Peter, resting on the bar as he tried to attract someone's attention, ever more disgusted with the world's lack of recognition of his majesty.

Fenchurch reached over the table for Abi's wine glass, completely untouched except for a few lipstick marks. Dad didn't seem to notice. *She can drive us home.* He had a sip of the red. Spoiled a bit, but decent. 'Dad, that voice said something about my loved ones.'

'And?' Dad looked into Fenchurch's glass, like he was about to pick it up and drink it himself. 'Simon, I've not lost it.'

Fenchurch grabbed his arm, trying to make him just see sense. 'I'm worried about you.'

'You bloody shouldn't be.' Dad downed his drink. 'You should be worried about yourself, the number of stupid things you do on the job. Putting yourself on the line like that. Never seen a DI do what you do. Chasing people on train tracks.'

'The Met would be a better place if they all did.' More wine, burning his throat. 'Just promise me you'll take care of yourself.'

'I've been kicking the shit out of punks since long before you were born.' Dad got to his feet with a moan and shook off his son's grip. 'If you think I'm incapable of looking after myself, then you can piss off, okay?'

'Dad, you're digging around places you shouldn't.'

'So you want me to piss off? Fine.' Dad grabbed the whisky bag and stormed off through the restaurant, almost bumping into Abi and Rosie as they left the ladies.

'Dad? What's going on?' Rosie tottered off across the tiles towards him. 'Dad!'

'Oh, Gordon Bennett.' Peter abandoned his quest at the bar and left the restaurant, following them out into the Shoreditch evening.

Abi sat down again. 'Something you said?'

Fenchurch slouched in his chair and finished the glass, his fingers coiled round it. 'I'm just watching out for him.'

'He knows that, Simon.'

'Got a funny way of showing it.'

A sigh escaped through her nostrils. 'Think they'll be back?'

'Doubt it. More Fenchurch family melodrama, I swear. What the hell was he doing inviting *them*?'

'Simon, that's your bloody sister. Maybe he's trying to do the right thing?'

Fenchurch nudged the glass back over to her side of the table. 'What, pissing me off so much that I piss him off enough for him to piss off?'

She groaned. 'I can't follow that.'

Fenchurch reached over for the bottle of red and splashed some into his glass. 'You okay to drive?'

'I'm a bit tired, but it's not exactly far, is it?'

'Thanks, love.' Another sip. Much better. Fenchurch fished out his mobile and dialled Dad's number. Bloody thing ran through to voice-mail. 'He's not answering his phone now.'

Abi waved hers in the air. 'Rosie's just texted me. They're taking him home. Said we'll have to rearrange.' She put it down and reached over for the water jug, the ice all melted. 'Let's have our meal and see how the night plays out, shall we?'

Fenchurch looked around at the empty place settings. 'Going to need a doggy bag for all this food . . .'

Abi frowned. 'Where's your whisky bottle?'

'Ah, shit.' Fenchurch slapped his forehead. 'He better not bloody drink that.' He glanced at Abi's stomach. 'I was saving it for junior.'

The waiter appeared, a plate in each hand, another one nestling in his elbow. 'I've got a Chilli Destroyer?'

⌣

Abi stirred her peppermint tea, the steam billowing up between them. The kitchen lights blazed away, the rest of the flat in darkness. 'Do you want to talk about it?'

'The stupid old goat will be fine, Ab.' Fenchurch blew on the top of his tea, waves rippling across the murky surface like an uncharted sea. 'You know what he's like.'

'You still think he's looking for Chloe?'

'Of course he bloody is. Probably the only thing keeping him going.' Fenchurch drank some tea. Felt like he'd swallowed a lump of burning coal. He let it burn his tongue, trying to feel something. Tastes like gnat's piss. Should've used a fresh kettle of water . . .

'You okay, love?'

'Usual shit. Bloody night shift drives me crazy. Nothing happens. My in-tray and email are close to zero. Then it blows up.' Fenchurch wrapped his fingers around the teacup. 'Maybe you're right. We should move out of this city.'

'You change like the weather, Simon.'

'Sorry. I'm just . . .' Fenchurch lifted his shoulders. A burp forced itself up, acid wine burning at his throat. Another sip of tea swallowed it back down. 'How was your day?'

'Work was the usual shit. Can't wait for the summer break.'

'You sitting around moping all day? Great . . .' Fenchurch set his cup down again. 'Speaking of which, another typewriter turned up. It's in Chloe's room.'

'Thanks, love.' She sat on his lap, running a hand through his hair, catching a kink.

He brushed a loose frond away. 'You talk to your shrink about them?'

'No.' She tucked the hair back into her ponytail. 'They help. You know that. Repairing something. Putting it all back together, refurbishing it. Letting someone use something that's been broken.'

'Nobody uses typewriters these days, do they?'

'Enough people do, Simon.' Her whole body tensed up. Felt like she was floating above him. 'I wish you'd stop enabling this shit with your father.'

Another sip of burning tea. 'What if he finds something? There's people out there who might know more.' Fenchurch hugged her tight, wrapping his arms around her light frame. 'She might be out there.'

Abi gazed off into the middle distance.

'This morning, I dreamed about her again. The same one. The usual one. Her outside. Everything's so crystal clear, like it's a memory. You complaining about the garage bill.'

'And yet being in your memory palace can't piece it all together.' She pecked him on the forehead.

He pulled away. 'I'm being serious here.'

'And so am I.' She got her kiss in. 'There's no way you can piece it all together. It was eleven years ago.' She wrapped her arms around him. 'Have you spoken to *your* shrink about it, Simon?'

'I feel enough like Tony Soprano as it is . . .'

'You know I didn't watch that shit.'

'It's not shit, love. Come on . . .'

She touched her forehead against his. 'Have you spoken to him?'

'I'll speak to him, okay?' Fenchurch adjusted her on his lap, so she didn't fall off. 'I need to talk about it. I don't like to be constantly dreaming about it, you know?'

'Welcome to my life, Simon.'

Day 3
Day Shift
Saturday, 11th June 2016

Chapter Twenty

Fenchurch rolled over again, but that didn't empty his bladder. A flicker of sunlight caught between the curtains, glowing in the early-morning air.

Buggeration.

He heaved himself up. The other side of the bed was empty.

Where was she?

He got up and padded through the flat, his bladder burning.

Abi sat by the living-room window, a cup of tea resting in her hands, the steam billowing up into her face. A shiver pushed her shoulders up.

Dancing was the only thing stopping him peeing there and then. 'Hey, you okay, love?'

She shrugged and sipped at her tea.

'Are you okay?' Fenchurch huffed out a breath. 'I really need to go to the toilet.'

Another shrug. 'Have your pee, Simon.'

Fenchurch dashed to the toilet, grabbing his phone on the way. He sat down and let go, checking his messages.

Bliss.

Still nothing from his old man.

Fenchurch got up and flushed. He washed his hands, the acrid stink of that natural soap hitting his nostrils, and headed back through, dumping his mobile by the key bowl. 'Hey.' He stood behind Abi and rubbed her shoulder, cold as ice.

'Your hands are wet.'

'Sorry.' Fenchurch dried his hands on his thighs. 'What's up?'

'Just thinking about that call.' She wiped a hand across her cheek, smearing a tear. 'Is that the first one you've had?'

'It's not the first idiot trying to wind me up, but it's the first one with that robot voice.' He rubbed her shoulders again. The red bricks opposite glowed, a shiver of wind hitting the trees. 'There's nobody out there, love. Those calls are probably nothing, Ab.'

'"Probably" isn't good enough for me.' She reached over to the side table for a hanky and dabbed at her cheek. 'Someone saw you on the telly, right? All those questions the journalists were asking . . .' She blew her nose and balled up the tissue. 'Could it be about Chloe?'

'I don't see how.' Fenchurch put an arm around her and tried to hug her tight. 'It's probably this case I'm working, love.'

She pushed away from his hug. 'I'm fed up with being collateral damage.'

'Nobody's going to harm you. Not while I've got any say in it.'

Abi finished her tea and put the cup down on the coffee table. 'You're working today, though, aren't you?'

'Got to make up time for last night.'

She nodded slowly, hiding some intricate calculus behind her eyes. 'Right, you can squeeze in a workout if you head off now.'

Fenchurch frowned. 'I'm not going anywhere while you're like this . . .'

'I'm fine, Simon. Thought I could go shopping, get some maternity clothes.'

Fenchurch picked up his cup from the desk at the front of the Incident Room and had another look at the whiteboard, trying to stretch out his shoulders. Really overdone it with the weights this morning . . .

'So this cyclist still hasn't come forward. Great.' Thirty-two officers in attendance. Fenchurch settled on Reed. 'Kay, can you take a lead in sifting through the calls?'

'Already on it, guv. Got half the uniforms in the station working it. One hundred and fifty-seven calls in overnight, three hundred emails and the Met's Facebook wall is toppling over.'

Fenchurch let her have her moment of laughter. 'And anything in the rubble?'

'Just the usual nutters. We're bringing a few in, just in case.'

Fenchurch stabbed a finger on the stills on the whiteboard. 'That footage showed an assassination. By all means speak to them, but it's probably more a case of verifying if they've seen anything on their way between braziers.'

'Guv.'

Fenchurch looked around for Clooney. A female officer was almost sitting on Nelson's lap over on the far side of the room. Clooney wasn't here. 'Does anyone know if Clooney got anything on the weapon yet?'

'Sorry, guv.' Nelson focused on his Pronto. 'Uniform are looking for the weapon, but usual rules apply. That gun's probably dumped down a drain or in the Thames.'

Like that phone . . .

'Well, let's not give up yet. Someone might've been stupid.' Fenchurch left a few seconds' space, hoping the message got into the skulls. 'Jon, the post-mortem on Cassie McBride starts at eight. Can you take that for me?'

Nelson covered his disappointment with a glug from his posey coffee cup. 'But, guv, I've—' He scowled through the forest of uniforms. 'Fine.'

'Okay, then.' Another sip of tea, scalding Fenchurch's tongue. At least one officer needed a wash with Dettol. 'I know you've got a heavy caseload already, but you'll have seen the press conference last night. DCI Docherty is giving the Commissioner hourly updates. Our priority remains finding this shooter.'

Naismith raised his hand, an impish grin on his face. 'Sir, what about the Victoria Brocklehurst case?'

'As you all should be aware, the IPCC are running the Victoria Brocklehurst case. DI Mulholland's team are supporting.'

Naismith jotted something on his Pronto. 'So we think Steve Shelvey killed her?'

'That's with DI Mulholland and the IPCC investigators.' Fenchurch gave the room another sweep. 'Okay, guys. We will catch this killer. Our duty is to take him off the streets before he can do it again. Go to it.'

The room exploded into a wall of noise, ripping across him like a wave. Fenchurch caught a glare from Nelson as he approached, quickly shifting to a grin.

Nelson smacked Fenchurch on the shoulder, his free hand clutching a poser's coffee. 'Your lad Payet did well for France last night. Be lucky to keep him next season.'

'Like I've had the chance to watch the bloody football.'

'Right.' Another sip of coffee. 'Well, I'd better get out to Lewisham.'

'I take it you're not happy going to the PM?'

'Not my place to say, guv.'

'It'll be good for your CV, Jon.'

'Yeah, the fiftieth autopsy I've attended . . .' Nelson wandered off, reaching into his pocket for that infernal vape stick.

Reed approached the desk and sat next to Fenchurch. 'Congrats, guv.'

'What for?'

'Your baby.'

Fenchurch almost spat tea across the floor.

'Well, yours and Abi's.' Reed gripped his arm tight. 'You really expect Paul Temple to be able to keep a secret like that?'

'That little . . .'

'How are you feeling about it, guv?'

'It's the one good thing in my life, Kay.' Fenchurch finished the tea and set the cup down. Could do with another five. 'What time did you knock off last night?'

'Back of three.' Reed yawned into her fist. 'Why?'

'Anything happen while I was away?'

'Precious little. Just the fallout from your press conference.' She flicked her hair behind her ear. 'Nothing new about Chloe?'

'Nothing, no.' Fenchurch got up and took in the whiteboard. Bloody thing was a desert. Just a victim, a missing witness and a connection to a case they weren't allowed to know anything about.

Reed joined him. 'I saw Savage before I left. Said he's still running with it.'

'Bollocks to that.' Fenchurch jotted "DCI SAVAGE" in giant letters in the top-left corner of the whiteboard. 'We're burning a lot of money on this, so I'm not waiting for Savage to finish playing with himself before I act.' He blew air up his face. Separate lines joined Cassie McBride's photo to Travis and Savage. 'What's he keeping from us?'

'I don't know, guv. You think it's connected to those girls we found at Christmas?'

'I hope not. But I wouldn't put anything past Savage.' Fenchurch picked up his cup and sifted the dregs around the bottom, as if he'd get a view of the future from it. 'The other possibility—'

Fenchurch's Airwave blasted out. Steve on the front desk. 'What's up?'

'Got somebody here to see you. Something Ogden?'

Fenchurch opened his office door and checked it was empty. He smiled at Ogden. 'In here, sir.'

Ogden powered past and took one of the chairs in front of Fenchurch's desk. His blond hair was damp and a muddy brown, though it hadn't been raining. He folded his arms. 'Thank you for making time to see me.'

Fenchurch lowered himself into his office chair, his knee cracking as he sat. 'That's not a problem, sir, though—'

'I've been trying to find someone to give me an update on Victoria's case, but I can't get anyone to answer the phone.'

'I'm sorry, sir, I can only—'

'It's not your fault, Fenchurch. I just need to get Victoria's body. Put her to rest.'

'I'm afraid that won't happen for a long time, sir.' Fenchurch propped himself up against the back of his seat. 'As much as I'd like to help, we can't release it until the investigation into her death is closed.' Cover the lies with process. 'When we get a suspect, his defence team will—'

'I thought you had a suspect?'

Fenchurch swallowed hard. Careful . . . 'The suspect's defence team will want to perform their own autopsy, usually months from now. As part of that process, the body can't be released until after any appeals.'

Ogden tilted his head to the side. 'Are you winding me up?'

'Put yourself in their position, sir. If you'd been accused of murder, wouldn't you want to perform your own autopsy?'

'Yes, yes. But . . .' Ogden made claws out of his hands, bear-like. 'I thought—'

The door opened behind Ogden, and Zenna Abercrombie appeared, clutching a folder in front of her like she was guarding it with her life. A young man in a suit waited behind her. 'Inspector?'

'Ah, Ms Abercrombie. Allow me to introduce Gerald Ogden.'

She flashed a frown at Fenchurch. 'What's . . . ?'

'Mr Ogden is Victoria Brocklehurst's next of kin.'

'Oh. Oh, I see.' She smiled at Ogden as he stood, hand in his jacket pocket. 'Zenna Abercrombie.' She put the folder on Fenchurch's desk and held out her hand. 'I'm leading the investigation into your daughter's death.'

'Goddaughter.'

'Of course.' She peeled off a business card from her wallet and handed him one. 'You can give me a call any—'

'I just want to know when I'll get her body back.' Ogden jabbed a thumb at Fenchurch. 'This one's telling me it'll be *months*.'

'That's correct, sir. Most likely eighteen months.' Zenna patted the colleague behind her on the shoulder. 'Lenny here is leading that part of the case for me. Can I ask you to accompany him? He'll be able to answer all of your questions and put a timetable in place.'

'Thank you.' Ogden's quick glower hit Fenchurch. 'I'm glad someone's taking this seriously.'

'If you'll just follow me?' Lenny held out a hand and waited for Ogden. He flashed his eyebrows at Zenna and shut the door.

Fenchurch let out a deep breath. 'Well, that's saved me a load of grief.'

Zenna smiled. 'Grief's what he should be going through now.'

'I take it you're not here just to save my bacon?'

Zenna slapped a hand on her paperwork. 'I need some of your support.'

Fenchurch reached into his desk. 'If it's about that Terms of Reference . . .'

'No, it's not.' She hefted up her stack of papers. 'I need you to accompany me out to Lewisham for your formal interview.'

Chapter Twenty-One

Fenchurch walked along the narrow walkway, overgrown by weeds on either side, nettles and thistles where they should've grown bushes. A lone honeysuckle spewed out its sweet scent, reminding him of summer nights when he was at school, hanging out in the park.

The Lewisham Police Support Centre loomed above him, gleaming in the sun. A pair of jet streams crossed over each other in the blue sky. He charged up towards the front door.

Zenna was already inside, handing off her evidence pile to an underling.

How the hell did she get here so fast?

'Simon?'

Fenchurch swung round.

Liam Sharpe stood behind him, wearing a grin and a brown leather jacket. '*Knew* I'd bump into you.'

'Liam.' Fenchurch tapped at his watch. 'Bit early for you, isn't it?'

'Late, more like.' Liam's hand was lost under his hipster beard. 'Still up from yesterday.'

'You here to see me?' Something pierced Fenchurch in the heart. Drums skittered in his ears. 'Is this about Chloe?'

'Shit, sorry. I didn't think.' Liam raised his hands. 'No, I've not had anything yet.'

'So you're here to see my old man?'

He looked away. 'Maybe.'

'I told you to keep away from him.'

'That's why I'm here, okay? I'm going to stop him calling me.' Liam grinned. 'Some big cop warned me off.'

'Well, when you speak to him, get him to call me.' Fenchurch marched up the steps into the building.

Clooney was just hurrying inside, his tablet covered with as many stickers as his arm had tattoos. He tried to duck away from Fenchurch.

'Thanks for coming to the briefing, Mick.'

'What?' Clooney's forehead twisted into a satanic ridge. Then it slackened off and he laughed, his eyes shut. 'Right. Look, mate, I've been in since five. And I was in till midnight.'

'Doing what?'

'A million and one things.' Clooney hugged his tablet tight to his chest. 'That girl driving the Travis car. Cassie McThingy.'

'McBride.'

'Right.' Clooney unlocked his tablet and rolled his finger down the screen. 'Her PM's just about to start, so I had to do a lot of work for his nibs. Pratt.' He jabbed at the tablet. 'Anyway . . . It's a straight shooting, no messing about. Two bullets: pop, pop.' He tapped Fenchurch on the neck and the chest. Then he flashed the tablet, the display filled with a shot of the crime scene. Still turned Fenchurch's stomach. 'The casings your team got are with my ballistics expert now, but we're still missing the weapon.'

'That's all you've got?'

Clooney stepped away. 'It's always the same with you.' He glanced up at Fenchurch, then back at the tablet. 'My guy checked the shells. From the dent marks on the casing, he reckons it's a Baikal.'

'A what?'

'Baikals are Russian self-defence pistols, Simon. Supposed to fire CS gas. Eight mil chamber. You can buy them in Germany, but you can take the . . .' Clooney squinted at his tablet, then pinched and zoomed. 'You can take the partially blocked barrel, whatever that is, and swap it out for a rifled barrel. A few other little tweaks and it can fire nine-mil bullets. Also takes a silencer.'

'Our guy didn't use one.' Fenchurch sniffed the morning air, getting a whiff of cigarette smoke. He pushed open the front door and entered. 'How come I've never heard of them?'

'No idea, Si. Must be losing your touch. Streets are flooded with them. Firearms call them a "hitman kit". Some little punk running a street corner fancies some steel, all he needs is a grand. Grand and a half, if he's a bit cheeky.' Clooney walked over to the lifts. 'You coming to the PM?'

'Nelson's attending.'

'Right.' Clooney hit the down button. 'You cast your beady little eyes over the report I sent on Shelvey?'

'No.'

'PM's after this McThingy girl's. We're just going through the motions, right? Open.' Clooney snapped his tablet's lid. 'Shut.'

'What happened?'

The lift dinged open, but Clooney didn't seem in a hurry to enter. 'You really want to know?'

'It's important to me.'

'Right. Well.' Clooney opened his tablet again and prodded the screen a few times. The lift doors shut again. 'Pratt had a sneaky peek inside the lad first thing.' He flashed up a photo that belonged in an abattoir. 'Judging from the severe damage to his stomach lining and the fatty deposits in the liver, kidneys and heart, he reckons Shelvey died from acute arsenic poisoning.'

'Arsenic?' Fenchurch waited for Clooney to burst out laughing. Instead, he got a shrug. 'Jesus. Thought that went out with the horse and cart.'

'Happens more often than you'd think. Pratt's seen a lot of accidental or natural water contamination cases. And I'm running some jobs just now to confirm. Hang on . . .' Clooney fondled the tablet's screen. 'Nah, still not finished. Anyway, that investigator girl, Zara?'

'Zenna.'

'Right. Well, she's been chasing me up to tell her when the poison was administered.'

'And?'

'Hard to tell. The damage is severe. Really severe. Most of the stuff I've found is, like I say, contamination, so I had to dig to find the useful stuff about homicidal poisoning.' Clooney tilted his head from side to side. 'I'd say it's possibly prior to arrest. With the dose I'm thinking he's had, the symptoms start kicking in about thirty minutes after the poison is administered.'

Fenchurch twisted his brain around the intricate algebra of the timeline. 'Garlic breath?'

'Wait, what? How do you know that?'

'I noticed it. And Shelvey became delirious as we went on.'

'Shit . . . When was this?'

'During the interview, Mick. You should watch it.'

'Right, right.' Clooney locked his tablet again and thumped the down button again. 'That secures it, then.' He winked. 'And we didn't have this chat.'

'What chat?'

———⁀———

'Let me think.' Fenchurch balled up the tinfoil from his breakfast burrito, the leftover liquid from the salsa raining down, pitter-pattering onto the polystyrene takeaway box.

Arsenic.

Thirty minutes to kick in.

Piecing it together hurt. Fenchurch got out his Pronto and flipped back a few pages.

Thirty minutes before the time of death was—

No. The symptoms only started thirty minutes after. So . . . The interview started at 02.08 on Friday morning. Got a waft of garlic from Shelvey then.

Okay, so 01.38.

Picked him up just before half one. Took him straight to Leman Street.

Bollocks. Could've been poisoned before, during or after his arrest.

He put his Pronto down and cleared his throat. 'Mr Shelvey wasn't very well in the interview we had with him. It was late, ten past two. Towards the end, he was acting all woozy. At the time, I thought it was a ploy or maybe just exhaustion. I sniffed his breath and got a whiff of garlic. Maybe a dodgy pizza or maybe he was on something.'

Zenna looked up from her notebook. 'Are you suggesting he was drunk?'

'I'd have smelled it.' Fenchurch shut the container. 'It's possible that, in hindsight, he could've been under the influence of any of the drugs we found in his house, though that's not my department. The blood toxicology should show it one way or another.'

'I'd rather you didn't try to infer cause.' Zenna finished scribbling it all down. 'But we'll take it from here.'

'We're done?'

'That's correct.' Zenna gathered up her notes and zipped up her document holder. 'Well, for now. We've still to identify the cause of death and will indubitably have additional questions.'

Fenchurch raised his hands. 'Whenever you need me.'

'Don't forget that I'm still waiting on your review of my Terms of Reference. Until then.' She sashayed out of the room.

Fenchurch tossed his breakfast into the recycling and wedged the container into the top.

Treating me like a criminal. That kid probably raped and almost certainly killed that girl. A watertight case, but someone decided frontier justice was the way to go . . .

Fenchurch huffed to his feet, feeling like an old man. Christ knows what it'll feel like chasing after a three-year-old in the park.

'Inspector.' Zenna was back by the door. 'I'm a man short. Lenny's had to dash off home. Is there any chance I could borrow you for an interview?'

'Depends on who it is.'

⌣

'What?' Chris Johnson sat back in the chair, stale BO wafting off him. His sleeves were rolled up, a long Celtic tattoo running down his left arm, the right covered in thick hair. 'I can't tell you it again, sweetheart. I had nothing to do with that geezer's death. Okay?' He ran a hand through his hair, soaked with sweat, and groaned. 'Wasn't even here when he was killed.'

Fenchurch was opposite, still unsure why the bloody hell he was there.

Temple was loitering by the door, giving him a wink. Just play along and look threatening.

Zenna stared hard at Johnson, then down at her notebook. 'But you can't provide a solid alibi.'

'I shouldn't have to tell you where I was.' Johnson massaged his arm. 'I'm a serving officer, darling. You should trust me.'

'If only it was all based on trust.' Zenna gave a warm smile, letting Johnson fill the space. He didn't.

Temple walked over and leaned against the table, his head a good few inches shorter than Johnson sitting down. 'Constable, in your inter-views you stated that you were in this very station visiting firearms officers at the time in question. We've checked and they confirm that chain of events.' He smiled wide, like a snake about to devour its prey. 'That places you inside this station when Mr Shelvey was murdered.'

'Look, mate, I didn't do *nothing*.'

185

Temple nodded at him, like he was thinking it over. 'Okay. I'm satisfied.'

'Excellent.' Zenna got to her feet and smoothed down her suit jacket. She adjusted the order of her files, sticking the thickest document on the top, and cradled the pile in her arms like it was a baby. 'This paperwork is for the murder of one William Picard.' She leaned forward. 'Christopher Johnson, I'm arresting you for the murder of Steven Robert Shelvey.'

'*What?* You've got nothing on me!' Johnson pleaded with Fenchurch. 'This . . . this is bullshit!'

'You and DC Clive Naismith were lead investigators on that case. Mr Picard was poisoned by his son-in-law.' Zenna licked a finger and started rifling through the pages. 'Arsenic, as it happens.'

Johnson thudded his fist off the table. 'I've not done—'

Zenna smiled at him. 'Mr Johnson, while the conviction was successful, you do remember the matter of a small amount of evidence going missing in that case?'

'What?' Johnson rubbed at his untattooed arm, smoothing down the hair like he was grooming a horse. 'That was nothing—'

'You stole a sample of arsenic from the suspect's home, which you used to poison Steven Shelvey.' Zenna waved her hand at the Custody Officer. 'Constable, can you escort Mr Johnson downstairs and charge him, please?'

'Ma'am.' The lump of gristle and standard-issue jumper hauled Johnson to his feet. 'Come on, sir.'

Johnson tried to wriggle free, just managing to secure getting his face mashed into the table. 'This is a mistake!'

Zenna and Temple both stepped away from the table, letting the CO drag Johnson out of the room. He left the door open.

Fenchurch crunched back in the chair. 'How did you find that other case?'

'DC Clive Naismith.' Zenna patted her evidence pile. 'We've got enough here. It's solid.'

'And then some.' Temple sat in Johnson's vacant chair and tossed his phone in the air. 'Well, I've got us a slot at Westminster Magistrates Court at eleven. He'll be in Belmarsh by lunchtime.'

Zenna beamed at him. 'Thanks, Paul.'

Good luck getting any of that past a judge. Fenchurch stretched out his spine. 'Got time for a coffee, Paul?'

Fenchurch's phone blasted out 'Kashmir' again. Getting fed up with it. Reed. He held it up to Temple. 'Better take this, Paul.'

Temple shot him a wink. 'Say hi to Kayleigh.' He trotted off out of the room.

Fenchurch slumped forward in his chair. 'What's up, Kay?'

'That cyclist has come forward.'

Chapter Twenty-Two

Fenchurch stopped outside the interview-room door and sucked in air, trying to calm his breathing. He tugged at his shirt, separating the soaked cotton from his damp skin with a *shlup*. 'Is he definitely our guy?'

'Tom Lynch.' Reed held up her Pronto. 'I've asked him a few questions and he seems legit. Wanted to wait till you got here, guv. I know how much you like to blunder in, regardless.'

'Charming.' Fenchurch grinned at her, then pushed at the door. He sat next to Reed, across from Tom Lynch. 'My name is DI Simon Fenchurch and I'm the Deputy Senior Investigating Officer on this case. Thanks for coming forward, sir.'

'Right.' Lynch peered up from a sheet of paper, his eyes darting around the room, like he wasn't in a safe place. Skinny, like a sixty-mile ride was a warm-up. While he was clearly on a day off, he still dressed like a cyclist. Acid-yellow chevrons dug into the black of his tight-fitting jacket, a navy cycling shirt poking through the gap. A tiny bag sat at his feet, his trainers looking like they'd attach to pedals. 'Doesn't that just make you an Investigating Officer?'

'Excuse me?'

'You know, the Deputy cancels out the Senior?'

Just put it down to nerves.

Fenchurch covered the car in the photo in front of Lynch with his finger. 'What kind of car is it?'

'A Nissan.'

'Definitely?'

'I saw the badge. Think it was one of those electric ones.'

Fenchurch ringed the shooter in the photo. 'You saw this guy, yes?'

Lynch tugged at the zip on his jacket. He prodded a finger at the A3 blow-up of the CCTV footage in front of Reed. 'This guy you're looking for. The one on Sky News.' It was like his eyes were stuck to the page. 'He got into a car and tried to run me off the road.'

Fenchurch snatched the sheet back and drew the shooter's eyeline with his finger, like he was analysing football on Sky Sports on those stupid big iPads. 'Did you get a good look at him?'

'Very good. That's why he came after me.' Lynch wasn't taking his eyes off the page, no matter how much Fenchurch moved it around.

'But he didn't try to shoot you?'

'Would I be here if he did?' Lynch hugged his arms around his shoulders. 'He shouted after me. "Get back here!" — that sort of thing.'

'What accent did he have?'

'London, maybe.' Lynch was transfixed by the photo. 'Wasn't foreign.'

Fenchurch glanced over at Reed, then back at Lynch. 'Okay, so take us through what you think you saw. Wind back to the start of your journey.'

Lynch steepled his fingers on the sheet of A3 and shut his eyes. 'I work in the City and live in Woolwich. If I can get on the DLR at Tower Gateway by four, they let me take my bike on.'

Fenchurch tilted his head. 'Hang on, you work in the City and you left the office at four o'clock?'

'I get in early. Usually at my desk before seven, washed and changed.' Lynch pushed the page away, like he was now disgusted by the image. 'My wife gave birth to our daughter four weeks ago, and my boss is happy with that arrangement until Beth's back at work. I mean, I log in at night to go through emails and I've got a BlackBerry . . .'

'Okay, so I buy your story for now. Continue.'

'What can I say?' Lynch seemed to shiver all over his body. He tapped at the picture again. 'This guy just walked up to that car. The driver wound the window down and they had a little chat. I don't know what it was about.' Cough. 'Anyway, he shot the driver.'

'This took a while to unfold.' Fenchurch held up the image of Lynch standing on his bike pedals, holding himself steady. 'You didn't think to cycle off when you saw someone with a gun?'

'I was stopped at the lights.' Lynch gulped, his blinking turning frantic. 'When I spotted the gun, I just froze. This is London, you know?'

Don't I just?

'So what happened next?'

'I shot off. The lights weren't green, but I just pedalled like the devil was after me.' Lynch ran his nail along the far left of the image, the blue of the Caravanserai's boards just visible in the grey. 'I usually take the path up the back of those flats to get home. But I obviously couldn't today, so I kept on the main road and powered on. I heard the car coming up behind me and I panicked. There's a turning on the left, so I hid in this yard. It was a carwash, I think. You know, one of the manual ones?'

Fenchurch pulled up a map on his Pronto. Looked like a carwash just off the road. 'Did the car follow you in?'

'I heard it drive off.'

'But you didn't see it?'

'No. That's when I called you guys.'

'Anonymously.'

'I . . .' Lynch sighed. 'I watch a lot of American TV. Corrupt cops everywhere. How was I to know I'd not get, you know . . .?' He put a gun to his head.

'So you did half of your civic duty.'

'"Half"? What?' Lynch looked away, scratching his neck. 'I'm here, right?' He tapped at the figure on the page. 'That image is better than I can remember.' He squinted at it. 'His car's not on here.'

'What kind was it?'

'Dark grey. German, I think.' Lynch's face pinched tight. 'I'm not a car guy.'

Drums thundered in Fenchurch's ears, hard but out of time, out of control. We're losing this . . .

He tapped Cassie's car. 'But you recognised the Nissan?'

'We've got a Nissan at home. Big enough for a football team . . .' Lynch reached down and hefted up his bag. 'Hang on a sec . . .' He rummaged around and pulled out a little black box, rounded corners and a glassy front. 'This might help. This is my GoPro. I mount it on my handlebars. Records everything that happens.'

Reed grabbed it off him. 'One of those camera things?'

Lynch bared his teeth. 'Too many cyclists getting run over these days.'

———

Fenchurch paced around Leman Street's CCTV room, trying to stop his muscles seizing up. Place was bitterly cold despite the roaring heat outside. Stank of polystyrene and brown sauce. Not so much as a crack of light around the door, let alone a window. 'How you getting on?'

'He must've dropped it, sir.' Reed was wrestling with the GoPro, trying to get the cable in. 'Bloody lead doesn't fit.'

Fenchurch marched over. 'You're saying it's broken?'

'Sorry.' Reed waggled the lead but it wasn't going in. 'Bollocks.'

Fenchurch picked it up. Thing could've dropped off an alien space-ship or something. He turned it over and checked the back, completely lost. Even worse than that infernal Blu-Ray thing Abi had bought. 'What else can we try?'

Reed's lips twitched.

'Want me to get Clooney in here?'

'No. I can do this. I just . . .' Reed grabbed the box from him and spun it round a few times. She squinted at it, her tongue sticking out of the side of her mouth, then burst into a grin. 'Here we bloody go . . .' She unclipped a catch. A little memory card nestled in there, white and grey plastic with red lettering. 'Got you, you little bugger.' She wiggled it out and slid it into a device hanging out of the side of the laptop. 'Give me a sec, guv.' She winked at Fenchurch. 'Better hope he's only been using this for cycling . . .'

'What's that supposed to— Oh. Right.'

The big screen filled with the display from Reed's laptop, lighting up the whole room. Reed double-clicked something and it spun to life.

The point-of-view footage was at handlebar height and slightly disconcerting.

Reed smirked. 'Must be how Paul Temple sees the world.'

Lynch's gloved hands lugged the bike down from Canning Town station, his feet clacking off the steps, then onto the lower concourse for the Jubilee line.

'Wind it on, Kay.'

'Sure thing.'

The footage skipped forward to the road, Lynch resting his bike on the edge of the pavement as the cars droned around him.

'Bloody hell . . . Sorry, guv, but it's facing forward. We're not going to see— Oh here we go . . .'

The handlebars swivelled to the left, taking the camera with it, the view panning from the main road to the side street. The shooter fired, then again, echoing the other footage they had.

'Shit!' Lynch lurched the handlebars round and pedalled through the traffic, sprinting fast. Someone was shouting after him, but it was muffled. Lynch passed the Canning Town Caravanserai and took the first left. Then he cut into the carwash, pulling in behind a grimy white van, the camera focusing on penises drawn in the stuck-on dirt. The bike poked out the side, pointing back at the road. A German car whizzed past.

'Wind it back!'

'Guv.'

The video rattled back to the knob-joke van.

'Now, forward slowly . . .'

The footage jerked a few frames at a time, like a football action replay from the seventies, clicking forward as the bike sneaked round the side of the van. The grey car juddered past the entrance to the carwash.

'Looks like a Merc to me, guv.'

'Great.' Fenchurch slumped into a chair. 'We've got nothing.'

'No, that's a shitload.' Reed hammered at the laptop's trackpad and pulled up the street CCTV. 'Now we've got that, we can use this a bit better.' She pointed at the screen, filled with CCTV footage from further down, nearer to Cassie McBride's house. 'See all those cars? I gave a list of these to uniform to hunt down.'

Fenchurch counted about fifteen with legible licence plates. 'Have they got anywhere?'

'DI Mulholland put that to the bottom of the priority list last night.'

Fenchurch thumped a fist off the table. 'Did she?'

'Said anyone who saw anything should've called in.'

'Sometimes they need their bloody memory jogged.' Fenchurch stood and cracked his spine. 'So is it on there or not?'

Reed got up and tapped the giant screen. 'That's it there, I think.' Hard to make out, just a fuzzy grey blob. 'I've got a licence plate, though.'

'From that?'

'Hardly.' Reed laughed at him as she sat down again. 'One of those ones that take a high-resolution shot every ten frames or so.' She hit play and three of the cars disappeared, leaving a Smart car and a Ford. 'Now we know which one the shooter got in . . .' She tapped at the keyboard and groaned. The screen filled with the image of a Mercedes. 'That car belongs to Frank Blunden.'

Chapter Twenty-Three

Fenchurch stomped down the corridor, carrying a wad of paper evidence. His phone blasted out 'Kashmir'. He answered it and kept walking. 'Dad, I'm kind of—'

'S-s-s-shit.'

Fenchurch stopped dead, his fingers tightening around the handset. 'Dad, what's going on?'

Loud music played in the background, sounded like bloody Weather Report. Must be at his flat. 'S-s-sex. Se-se-sex.'

Fenchurch checked his watch. Quarter to eleven and he was out of the box.

'Look, I've been trying to call you about what happened last night. I need that whisky—'

'RING! Fu-fu-fu—' Beeeeep.

Shit. Fenchurch hit redial, but it went to voicemail. 'Dad, it's Simon. Call me.' He set off again, letting his phone dial again. Voicemail again. 'Dad. This is important, okay? Call me.'

Fenchurch pocketed the mobile.

Just my old man out of his tree. Nothing to worry about.

He opened Docherty's office door and entered. 'Boss, I need—'

'Wait your turn.' Docherty was behind his desk, tearing apart a pain au chocolat with his fingers like some fifteenth-century peasant who'd not eaten in days.

Temple was sitting opposite Docherty, slurping from a coffee. He gave a brief nod, but he seemed irritated by something.

Fenchurch rested against the back of the other chair. 'Boss, this is urgent.'

'Jesus Christ.' Docherty slammed his pastry on the table, sending shards of it everywhere. 'What isn't with you?'

'The cyclist came forward.' Fenchurch waved the photo in the air. 'Whoever shot Cassie tried to run this guy over.' Then he showed him the PNC print. 'Problem is, he's in one of Flick Knife's cabs.'

Docherty picked up a crumb and put it in his mouth slowly, his forehead creasing. 'And you want a word with Blunden?'

'If I just wanted a word, boss, I'd be in Mile End by now. I want to raid his office.'

'Christ on a scooter.'

'And his house, if necessary.'

'Sodding hell.' Docherty glugged some coffee and dabbed up the pastry with his fingers. 'Paul, can you get us a warrant?'

Temple got up and crushed his cup. 'How soon do you need it?'

Fenchurch winked at him. 'How soon is now?'

———————

Fenchurch clutched his Airwave. 'Right, let's take this slowly.'

Down the road, a DLR train rumbled by overhead, mostly empty. The street was quiet in both directions. That Smiths song rattled round his head, 'How Soon Is Now?' *Serves me bloody right for joking . . .*

'Serial Alpha, are you in position?'

He got a wave from Naismith down towards Mile End Road. 'Confirmed. Over.'

'Serial Bravo?'

Up the street, Nelson waved out at him. 'In position, guv. Over.'

'Serial Charlie?'

'In position, sir.'

Fenchurch couldn't see them, but if they said they were blocking the rear entrance . . . He looked round at Reed. 'Ready?'

She huffed out breath. 'Ready, guv.'

'Come on, then.' Fenchurch set off, Airwave to his mouth. 'We are go. Hold position. Repeat, hold position.'

'Don't you think this is overkill, guv?'

'What?' Fenchurch entered the courtyard and strode over to Frank's Cabs, the office basking in the mid-morning sun. 'Whoever shot Cassie McBride was in one of Flick Knife's cabs. He's got one gun. How many more can he have?' He knocked on the door and waited. 'Come on, come on, come on . . .'

Another knock and he stepped back, peering through the window. Couldn't see anything. Nobody working, that's for sure.

The courtyard was filled with empty black cabs.

'Think he's bolted, guv?'

'Don't say that, Kay.'

'What about the cancer? Think he's . . . ?'

Noise came from inside, shouting.

'Oh, shit . . .' Fenchurch snapped out his baton with his free hand. 'We are entering the building. Everybody stay ready.' He reached for the handle and twisted it open, standing there, watching and listening.

Voices boomed out from the back. Quite a heated argument.

Fenchurch held up a finger, stopping anyone else advancing. He entered, taking it slowly. He stopped by Blunden's office door, baton raised, and stepped back. A drunken Scotsman and a Scouser.

He twisted the handle and pulled the door open.

Blunden sat in his chair, slumped forward into a crimson pool covering his desk, dripping onto the floor, *pat, pat, pat*. Blood dribbled from a cut on his throat, soaking his white shirt.

Fenchurch raced in, shouting into the Airwave, 'Urgent medical assistance needed! Repeat, urgent medical assistance is required!' He felt Blunden's neck for a pulse. Still warm, but definitely dead.

'And here's Alan Thomson with the news.' A bloody radio.

'Sex!'

Fenchurch lurched back. The shout came from the far side of the room.

His dad sat wedged into the corner, clutching a white bread knife in both hands, the blade covered in blood. Rocking forward, eyes closed. 'Sex!'

Chapter Twenty-Four

B loody, bloody hell!' Fenchurch wheeled around the quadrangle, fists clenched. 'What is he doing here?'

'Guv.' Reed pressed a hand into his chest, stopping his movement. 'You need to calm down.'

'"Calm down"?' Fenchurch glared at her. 'How the hell am I supposed to react?'

She tilted her head to the side. 'Talk about it, maybe?'

'You're not my shrink, Kay.'

'I'm glad of that.'

Fenchurch stopped dead, clenching his fists tighter. 'What's that supposed to mean?'

'Nothing. Just . . .' She pursed her lips, her forehead creasing up. 'I'm sorry, guv. I don't understand what's happened.'

'Oh, I'll tell you what's bloody happened.' Fenchurch pointed at the office. 'My father's gone off on a vigilante crusade. Killing Flick Knife before . . .'

'Before what, guv?'

Fenchurch sighed. 'I don't know, Kay.'

'What's getting to you is you don't know what he's been up to and you don't know why he's done this.'

'You're . . .' Fenchurch shook his head at her. 'Bloody hell.'

Nelson emerged from Frank's Cabs and tore off his SOCO suit. Another ripped off his mask — Naismith, leading two officers as they helped Dad out, handcuffed and wobbling all over the place.

Fenchurch stepped towards them. 'Jon!'

Nelson held out his free hand, the other carrying a bag with the knife — keep away from us . . .

They disappeared through the gap out to the street, the waiting meat wagon rumbling, its diesel stink filling the courtyard.

'Guv, your dad's a decent bloke.' Reed's face settled back to its resting position. 'Why's he here, though? Has he talked to you about Flick Knife?'

Fenchurch shrugged. 'Not for a while.'

'You think this is something to do with the newspaper?'

'Maybe. Look, we just don't know, Kay.'

Reed smoothed a hand down his arm. 'He can't actually have done this, can he?'

'Maybe.'

'Guv, really?'

'You don't know what he was like when me and Rosie were growing up.' Fenchurch pinched the bridge of his nose, eyes shut, trying to blot it all out. 'Had a bloody temper on him. Every little scrote that got away from him, he'd take it out on us. Not physical.' A shard of glass dug into his gut. 'Well, only when I really took the piss. But he'd shout. A lot.'

'You really think he could do this, though? At his age?'

SOCOs milled around the open door.

Just through there. Christ.

'He was right there, Kay, knife in his bloody hand.'

Dr Pratt staggered out of the door, his monstrous beard catching the light breeze. He glanced at Fenchurch and marched away, head down.

'William.' Fenchurch jogged after him. 'Come on, mate. What's happened?'

Pratt kept on walking. 'I'm not sure I should even be *looking* at you, Simon.'

Fenchurch got in front of him and stopped him in his tracks. Still didn't get any eye contact. 'Come on, William, I need to know what's going on here.'

'I'm under strict instructions not to speak to you or any of your close team.'

'Come on, you owe me.'

'I owe you nothing, Simon.'

'Just . . . When did it happen?'

Pratt glowered at him. 'Listen, if I give you that, will you let me go?'

'I never heard it from you.'

Pratt finally made brief eye contact. 'Mr Blunden's time of death was just before eleven a.m. this morning.'

Fenchurch ran his hands through his damp hair. 'We just bloody missed it.'

'I'm sorry, I—'

'Oy! Get away from him!' Docherty was sprinting over the tarmac towards them. He grabbed Fenchurch's arm and pulled him away from Pratt. 'William, get the hell out of here.'

Pratt slunk off. Fenchurch wanted to grab him and pull him back for more questions.

Docherty waved a hand at Reed. 'You too, Sergeant!'

Fenchurch watched her follow Pratt, then switched to Docherty. 'Guv, I need to—'

'Shut it!' Docherty shook him like he was a misbehaving child. 'Do you honestly think I'll let you investigate a case where your father is the prime suspect? Eh?' Another shake. 'It's not even "Ooh, he might get off with a decent lawyer." You caught him red-handed!'

Fenchurch broke free of him and stepped back, getting away from the coffee breath. The squad car finally powered off, Dad slouched over in the back seat.

Looks every inch the guilty party.

Maybe he did do it. His brain crumbling with all the pressure he put himself under. What didn't help anyone was ambiguity. Confusion. Uncertainty.

'If he killed him, boss, I don't get it.'

'Aye, neither do I.' Docherty walked him away from the queue of SOCOs heading into the building. 'But you need to get your arse out of here, okay? I'm not warning you, I'm telling you. Your old man's gone all Wild West here, and you need to distance yourself from it if you still want a career after the dust settles.'

'You can't expect me—'

'I *expect* you to act like a professional.' Docherty jabbed a finger into Fenchurch's chest. It actually hurt. '*Like* a professional. I know you have difficulty with authority at times, but you need to back off, okay? Keep a million miles away from this.'

Fenchurch stuck his hands on his hips. 'Or what?'

'What?' Docherty's eyes inflated like air balloons. 'Or I'll send you out to Adrian Farrell in Middlesex. He's down a DI.'

'Let me think on that . . .'

'Like you've got a choice.' Docherty winked at Temple as he strolled over. 'DI Mulholland is investigating this case for me, okay?'

Not her. Anyone but her . . .

'Boss, look, it's possible he didn't do this.'

'What?' Docherty screwed his face up. 'You honestly—'

'Guys, guys.' Temple got between them, smiling at Fenchurch, then at Docherty. 'Al, do you want to give us a minute?'

Docherty stared hard at Fenchurch, his nostrils flaring. Then he nodded with a final snort. 'I'd better inspect the disaster zone, I suppose.' He wandered over to Frank's Cabs, shaking his head.

Temple exhaled slowly, watching him go, then he attached a smile to Fenchurch. 'Simon, I'm really sorry about this.'

'Paul, you need to help me.'

Temple's mouth seemed undecided on whether it should smile or grimace, twitching between the two. 'The Director of Public Prosecutions just called me. Told me to work with the IPCC and the Met's Professional Standards.' He settled for the grimace. 'Unfortunately, we have to prosecute your father. A serving officer going all vigilante isn't good for anyone. Worst case, it'll undermine faith in the criminal justice system and cause more riots.'

Fenchurch slumped back against a wall, knocking off a chunk of roughcast. 'You're talking shit.'

'Am I? Simon, your father's been carrying out clandestine investigations on Met time for years. We've turned a blind eye to it, because of your situation, but this has to stop.'

'Dad's put away hundreds of stabbings over his career. If he killed Blunden, why was he still there?' Fenchurch dug the heels of his hands into his eyeballs, trying to drive some pain into his skull. 'Why didn't he run off?'

'Because your father's off his face.' Temple walked away, shaking his head. 'You of all people should know how irrational drunk people are.'

'What's that supposed to bloody mean?'

'It means all those times you called Abi up out of the blue when you were off your tits, Simon.' Temple spun round on his heels. 'You think that was easy for her? Listening to you dribbling down the line, swearing, talking nonsense?'

Fenchurch swallowed. 'I can't believe she told you.'

'What do you expect, you idiot? We're best friends. Who do you think she talked to? Kay's too close to you.' Temple looked him up and down, sneering like a public-school headmaster. 'You're lucky she didn't report you.'

Fenchurch watched him go, his heart thudding even harder, drums pounding like they were being hit with mallets.

Good to know who your friends are . . .

Speak of the devil.

DI Dawn Mulholland appeared under the overhanging building, tightening her black scarf to reveal just enough skin to show it hadn't had a chance to burn in the sun yet. She was pouting like the cat who'd broken into the dairy and found the cream. 'Simon. There you are. I need to take your statement now.'

'Now's not a good—'

Fenchurch's phone blasted out 'Kashmir'. Zenna Abercrombie.

Mulholland raised an eyebrow.

Which was the lesser evil?

———

Fenchurch sat on the wrong side of the table in the interview room. So this is how it feels.

Opposite, Mulholland and Nelson pouted and grinned. Interviewing him when . . .

When what?

When his old man had killed a known underworld ganglord?

When his old man had killed the racist scumbag who ran black prostitutes because he didn't want white girls out on the streets?

When his old man had killed the scumbag who used his cabs as a front for God knows what. Drugs, off-street prostitution . . .

Couldn't really blame his target, but . . . why? Why do it now? What the hell was going through his mind? Other than whisky.

Maybe he did do it. Maybe he just snapped and decided to take Blunden's death away from cancer's icy grip. Ten minutes bleeding to death versus six months rotting away, the morphine masking the pain until it ate him whole. Six months of putting his affairs in order, ensuring the misery he'd inflicted on east London kept on into the next generation.

'—your father?' Nelson's eyebrows were standing to attention. 'Guv?'

'Sorry, I was miles away.' Fenchurch rested his elbows on the table and rubbed his hands together. 'What was the question?'

'I asked you what your father said when—?'

'I'm not giving you the story backwards.' Fenchurch waited until Nelson looked away. 'You've got your statement. Happy to spell out anything you don't get, but you're not interrogating me, okay?'

Mulholland looked up from her notebook, pouting. 'Simon, I do need to clarify a few points.'

'Then send me the rough draft and I'll fix anything either of you have failed to capture correctly.'

Mulholland ran her tongue round her lips, slowly. She tightened her scarf. 'Very well, I shall arrange for a paper copy. Mark that up, please.'

Fenchurch held her gaze. 'I'd just like to speak to my father.'

'That's not going to happen.' Mulholland gave him a wide smile. 'Given the state he's in, the duty doctor tells me his blood-alcohol level is consistent with drinking half a bottle of whisky.'

Jesus, Dad. Fenchurch deflated as he tumbled back into his seat. He cleared his throat. 'Have you got the shooter yet?'

Mulholland was standing by the door now, like she'd just transported there. 'Excuse me?'

'The whole reason we went round was to find out who Blunden had sent to shoot Cassie McBride. Have you got someone going through the records to find out who was driving the Mercedes?'

'We'll arrange for that.' Mulholland opened the door and let Nelson out first. She gave Fenchurch an icy smile. 'I'm truly sorry about this, Simon, but I am just doing my job.'

Like hell you are. You're enjoying every second of this.

Fenchurch waited for them to leave him alone. He sat there, like some chav from the arse end of Hackney who'd stabbed a mate in the pub for a dare.

Treating him like a criminal. Like he'd stuck the knife into Blunden himself. Like he was the one dribbling in a cell, shouting, 'Sex!'

What was up with that, anyway?

Maybe Dad has finally cracked, his mind crumbling after too much stress, too much booze, too much life. All the work he was doing looking for Chloe . . .

Fenchurch fished his phone out of his pocket and hit dial.

'Simon?' Sounded like Abi was out and about. 'What's up?'

'I just don't know, Abi.' Fenchurch pulled up on the street, Maida Vale sprawling around them, the long row of magnolia-painted Georgian terraces disrupted by a sixties block replacing a wartime bombsite. 'What makes it harder is I just don't know what he was up to.'

A deep frown creased Abi's forehead. 'Did you put him up to it?'

'What? Of course I bloody didn't.' He hit the steering wheel. 'How can you think that?'

'Sorry. I don't know what I'm saying. This is a shock.' She reached over to play with the hair on the back of his neck. 'Could you have said anything that sparked off one of his flights of fancy?'

'Chance'd be a fine thing. He wasn't answering my calls after he stormed off last night.' Fenchurch switched off the engine and nudged his door open. 'He's not mentioned anything to you?'

'I try to have as little to do with him as possible.'

'Right.' Fenchurch got out onto the pavement, his whole soul feeling emptied. The sun beat down on his neck, fresh grass cuttings hit his nose. 'How do you even begin to think about this?'

'In tiny steps. Come on.' Abi grabbed his hand and led him across the road and up the path. She rang the bell and leaned over to peck his cheek. 'Be strong.'

The door pulled open a crack and Rosie looked out. 'Simon? Abi?' She opened it wide and stepped out, grabbing Abi in a hug. 'I can't believe it.'

Fenchurch made eye contact, but his training failed him. The path was mossed up between the slabs. 'Take it you heard about Dad, then?'

Rosie dried her hands on her apron. 'I just got a call from a DI Mullarkey.'

'Mulholland.'

'Whatever. Is it true?'

Some grass crept up between another two slabs. 'I found him, Rosie . . .'

'Shit.' Rosie nibbled at her lips. 'Look.' She rubbed her face. 'Look, Peter's out with the kids. Usual Saturday-afternoon craziness. Becca and Ollie are both at football.' She tore at her apron, tears streaming down her face. 'Look at the state of me.'

Abi wrapped her in a hug. 'Come on, love.' She led her inside.

Fenchurch followed them in, stepping over a fire engine and a spray of Lego as he navigated into the living room.

Abi helped Rosie to an armchair, then perched on the mushroom sofa by the fireplace — dotted with photos of their childhood. Hugging each other as kids. Them as teenagers, more distant, him with a Madchester bowl cut, her in Nirvana grunge. Behind, a row of black-and-white shots showing Mum as a schoolgirl, Dad joining the force, thumbs up and grinning in his uniform.

Fenchurch sat next to Abi and smiled at his sister. 'How you doing, sis?'

'I can't believe what's happened.' Her west London accent was slipping a few miles in the opposite direction. 'He's really killed someone?'

Fenchurch let breath slither out. 'If it's any consolation, the guy's a nasty piece of work.'

'Simon, what the hell?' Rosie got up, clasping a hand to her forehead. 'What am I going to tell Ollie and Becca? How do you tell children their grandfather's a murderer?' She stared at Fenchurch, then shook herself. 'Where are my manners?' She clapped her hands together. 'Tea? Coffee?'

Fenchurch slouched back in the sofa. 'Tea, if you're making some.'

Abi got up and patted Rosie's arm. 'I'll make the tea.'

'Thanks. Do you need any—'

'I'm sure I'll find the kettle, teabags and milk.'

'Well, it's leaf tea and—'

'Rosie, I'll be fine.' Abi left them to it, shutting the door behind her.

The living room was very different to the last time Fenchurch'd been there. Had a wall been knocked through?

'Is he going to be okay, Simon?'

Fenchurch stroked Rosie's arm as she sat next to him, just how she used to like it when Dad had blown a gasket at them. 'He was there with the murder weapon, Rosie. Off his bloody trolley. Christ knows why he did it.'

'I've been worried about him.' Rosie picked at the stitches on her cardigan, just like she did as a kid. 'You know that Alzheimer's is in our family?' She pushed the cardigan away, smoothing it down.

'They brought him back as a civilian after his retirement. They wouldn't let him back if his brain was rotting.'

'He's killed someone, Simon. If that doesn't mean his brain's rotting . . .'

But had he killed Blunden? Had he really?

Why didn't he run? Well, half a bottle of whisky and he'd be on the bloody floor. But that phone call . . .

Fenchurch got up and started pacing around the room. 'He can't have killed him. It's not in his nature. He just can't have.'

'That DI Mullarkey told me the knife was definitely used to kill him.'

Might as well have stuck the knife into Fenchurch's heart.

He huffed out air. 'I can't just sit around drinking tea. I've got to go and do something.'

Chapter Twenty-Five

Fenchurch parked on Dad's street and got out. A fat tabby lay on its back on the pavement outside the flat, basking in the morning sun, oblivious to the world. No sign of the rickety old Saab. He got out his Airwave and tapped a message to Reed: 'Can you get someone to check round there for Dad's Saab? It's my old one.'

He put the Airwave away and knocked on Dad's door. It just swung open.

Jesus, Dad.

Fenchurch entered, fists clenched. The lights were blazing away, same as it ever was. Jazz blared from inside, definitely Weather Report. 'Birdland', the musicians sounding like they were fighting each other. A North Face jacket was heaped on the floor. House keys rattled on the rug. No sign of his car keys.

Fenchurch listened hard. Sounds empty. Can never be too careful, though. He snapped on some gloves and crept through to the living room. Stank like an old pub, a cigarette burnt to a stub in the ashtray. A wooden table was smashed against the wall, just a pile of kindling. All four legs of a dining chair dug into the wall, stuck into the plaster. A family photo of Dad with his parents lay there, the glass like cracked ice. All that ivory shit had been swept off the dresser, scattered around the room. A well-used tumbler covered in ghostly fingerprints cuddled up to the half-empty bottle of Dunpender.

Bloody hell. Four grand down the toilet. Plus eighteen years of investment return . . .

Fenchurch sat on the sofa and pinched the bridge of his nose. He sucked in the stale air and tried to piece it all together.

Dad's shaking hand pouring out the nectar, sucking it down, not even tasting it. Pouring another. Then another.

Why, though?

Dad must've found something. Something new. Came back here, got hammered on expensive whisky. Can't have been good.

What did he find out? And then what did he do?

That call. What the hell was that all about?

Sex?

Ring?

Sex ring? What the bloody hell was he on about? Blunden running a sex ring?

Fenchurch got out his mobile and called Reed.

'Guv, thought you were off the reservation?'

'Not in so many words . . .'

'Mulholland's been looking for you.' The background chatter sounded more like a football match. 'I'm still stuck up at Blunden's office. She's got me managing the crime scene, can you believe it?'

'Bet she has.'

'Just got your text. Not found your dad's motor yet, but we'll keep looking.'

'I appreciate it.' Fenchurch stood, unable to stay seated. 'Kay, has anyone been round to my old man's flat yet?'

'Don't think so.'

'Get a team round here.' Fenchurch coughed. 'Sorry, to Dad's flat.'

'You're there, right?'

'Right. Either someone's been in here or he's smashed the place up in a drunken rage.'

'Oh, shit, guv.'

'He called me, Kay.' Fenchurch stretched back on the sofa. 'About half ten, quarter to eleven. Sounded drunk, didn't make any sense. He might've said something about a sex ring.'

'Mean anything to you?'

'Well, I don't think Dad was in one.' Fenchurch walked through to the kitchen. The trail of destruction stopped here. 'Must be about Flick Knife. I'm wondering, what if someone's taken him? Picked him up here, driven him to Mile End and killed Blunden. Then—'

The big knife block, the one he'd got Dad from Aldi at Christmas two years ago. All those white Japanese cooking knives.

The bread knife was gone.

'Guv?'

It didn't prove anything. Whoever framed him took the knife, killed Blunden, made it look like Dad.

What to do with it, though? Leave the block for the SOCOs or . . . ?

'Guv, you still there?'

Fenchurch walked back to the living room. 'Sorry.'

'Right. Who would do it, though? Who'd want to frame him?'

Fenchurch sniffed the whisky. Four grand bought a rancid spirit. 'I don't know.'

'I'm drawing a blank, guv.'

Fenchurch sat forward. 'Anything happening up there?'

'Well, other than Mulholland thinking I know where you are. They're accelerating Blunden's post-mortem. It's on now.'

'Bloody hell. That witch can't wait to put my old man away, can she?'

'Guv.'

'Have they found that Merc yet?'

'Naismith's still working on it.' Reed paused, sounded like she'd covered her hand over the mouthpiece. 'Sorry, I've got to go, okay?'

'Just send some of Clooney's lot round here.' Fenchurch ended the call and put his phone away, unsure how much of that she'd got.

Better get out of here before they pitch up. If they do.

Liam . . .

Liam bloody Sharpe. What was that little punk up to at Lewisham?

Fenchurch checked through the notes on his Pronto. That was just before eight. Quarter to, maybe.

Three hours later, Dad slotted Flick Knife. What the hell was he doing there?

He looked around the scuffed carpet at the tiny elephant figures. Drums thwacked as he picked up his phone and dialled Liam's number.

'Sorry, but I'm probably asleep or drunk in a hedge. Leave a message and I'll get back to you!' BEEEEP!

'Liam, it's Simon. I need a word with you. And if you don't call me back, I'll come round your flat, okay?'

Fenchurch stood in the corridor in the basement and waited. Sounded like old music hall coming through the door.

A cleaner squeaked behind him, his bucket and mop rattling as he trudged. Stank of bleach.

Fenchurch called Liam again. Straight to voicemail. He swallowed hard and finally rapped on the door.

It opened and Bert McArthur stood there. Dad's mate and partner in crime, at least in investigating old ones. Wiry, like a ferret. Hair far too dark for his pale skin. He tilted his head to the side. 'Simon.'

'Take it you've heard?'

'Stupid, stupid bastard.' Bert nodded, puffing out his cheeks. 'Come on in.'

Fenchurch followed him inside and shut the door behind him. The place was even more chaotic than the last time he'd visited. Floor-to-ceiling shelves, rammed with files and boxes, covering all four walls. Even had a little document rack set into the back of the door.

Bert slumped in a chair by a little alcove sculpted out of the mess. An old computer sat there, the sort that could only log on to the PNC. No emails or internet. He gave a sly wink. 'You're probably not supposed to be here, are you?'

'True.'

'Have you spoken to him?'

'Not been allowed to.' Fenchurch stayed standing, not that he had much choice. 'I was the one who found him, Bert. Just sitting there, red-handed, out of his skull.'

'Stupid old goat.'

Going through those files would take weeks. Months, maybe. 'What's he been working on?'

'Search me.' Bert waved his hands around the room. 'While this place is a bit of a dump, it's an organised one. More archaeology, I'll grant you.'

'So you don't know what he was looking into?' Getting worse, not better . . . 'But you both worked on that case at Christmas, didn't you?'

'That's only because I found a case that looked funny.' Bert slurped at some tea from an old mug that belonged in a skip. 'Your old man did the rest, linking it with that Bishopsgate fish-gutter.' He picked up a yellow Post-it and crumpled it into a ball. 'Your dad's been losing it, Simon. His obsessions have been worse than ever.'

Fenchurch shut his eyes. 'What do you mean?'

'You know how secretive he can be. He's been beavering away at that . . . *stuff* full-time.' Another drink of tea, followed by a grimace. 'Your old man got a bollocking from our gaffer the other day.' He pointed at a stack on the edge of his desk. 'He'd been requesting old case files from 2008 and 2009.'

That didn't make any sense. Chloe's file was 2005. There were those kids from the last two or three years, admittedly, but everything else had been eighties and nineties.

Fenchurch picked up the top file. A missing persons from 2009. A young girl. 'You've no idea what he's working on?'

'Nothing. Sorry, son.'

'Who's it for? Savage?'

'Big posh sod? Works for the Trafficking and Prostitution Unit?' Bert glugged at his tea, puckering up his nose. 'Not him, no. And I've no idea who, before you ask.'

'Right.' Fenchurch put the file back. 'When did you last see him?'

'Last night. Wasn't he heading out with you and Abi?'

'We had a meal together, yeah.' Fenchurch frowned. 'You know a Liam Sharpe?'

'Yeah, journalist, right?'

'I was here first thing this morning on another matter. Liam was coming in to see Dad.'

'Always in early is Ian. He loves this job.' Bert set the cup down. Thing was more encrusted tea than porcelain. 'Anyway, I got here about ten, think he'd been here a while. No sign of your father or this Liam chap.'

'He'd left or not been here?'

'Hard to say.' Bert waved around the chaos, chuckling away.

'Well, thanks for your help, Bert.' Fenchurch passed him a business card. 'If anything comes up, give us a bell, yeah?'

⌣

The door to the flat opened and Liam Sharpe took one look at Fenchurch and gave a sigh. Dressed like he'd just woken up and hadn't had time to put on the full hipster uniform. Trackies and a ripped T-shirt. 'Right. Simon.'

'I need a word with you.'

Liam wasn't himself. No eye contact, no grin. Even worse than when— 'Look, just leave me alone.'

'Liam, I've tried calling you.'

'Yeah, I know.'

'Are you okay?'

Liam stepped back, his shoulders slumped. 'No, I'm not.'

'What's happened?'

'Nothing. It's cool.'

'Liam, I need—'

'Goodbye.'

Fenchurch pushed at the door, barging through into the hall. He grabbed Liam's T-shirt, bunching it up around his fists. 'It looks like my old man's just murdered someone.'

'I know.' Liam backed against the wall, like he was trying to go through it. 'Frank Blunden. Flick Knife. He stabbed him.' He slumped back, sliding down. 'All my fault.'

Fenchurch's grip stopped him hitting the floor. 'What've you done?'

'I shouldn't have . . .'

Fenchurch pulled him close. 'Liam, what the hell have you done?'

Liam clumsily pushed himself up and pointed to the open door. 'You should leave. I've had enough of putting my neck on the line for you.'

'I'm not going anywhere until I get answers.' Fenchurch let go of Liam. 'The only thing keeping my father from remand in a prison is he's too late for a Saturday court. Now, you're going to talk to me.'

Liam swallowed hard, rubbing his arms. 'You can't just—'

Fenchurch shut the flat door and barged in, his heart thudding. He rested against the kitchen wall, inches from a massive Batman poster. A pale-blue coffee cup steamed on the counter. 'Did you meet him this morning?'

'First thing.' Liam propped himself up on the counter. His cat was on her haunches next to him, cracking at biscuits in a bowl with the Batman logo, the one from the old Michael Keaton film that looked like teeth if you stared at it too long. 'We might've had a breakthrough.'

Fenchurch's gut plunged below his feet. 'With Chloe?'

Liam shook some more biscuits into the cat bowl.

Fenchurch grabbed his wrist and stopped him pouring. 'Is that why you were at Lewisham this morning?'

Liam dropped the pack on the counter, a couple of biscuits spilling out. 'I found an old driver, used to work for Flick Knife.'

'What's his name?'

'I can't tell you.' Liam wrapped his arms tight around his torso. 'My source is a secretive type, so we met him at your old man's flat. He told us Blunden had them picking up kids.'

The drums rattled. 'Like my daughter?'

'He didn't name her. But he'd seen the story in the paper. Said she might've been part of that whole thing.'

Fenchurch launched himself across the kitchen towards Liam, getting right in his face. 'Why didn't you take this source in to the police?'

'Er, your dad's a cop?'

'You should've come to me, Liam.' Hackney loomed around them, just blocks and blocks of flats. That article had forced one of them out into the open. 'When did you leave?'

'Just before nine.' Liam hefted the cat up and put her down on the floor, then stroked her back as she licked her lips. He sat on the kitchen counter, his legs swaying. 'Had to come back here to file some copy.'

Fenchurch pinched his nose. 'I got a phone call last night. Told me to stop what I was doing.' He shut his eyes, breath emptying from his lungs. 'A robotic voice, warning harm would come to my loved ones.'

'But you said your dad murdered someone.'

Fenchurch got up and folded his arms. 'So, between nine and eleven, my father's managed to get blind drunk and kill Blunden.' He narrowed his eyes at Liam. 'Did this source leave with you?'

'He stayed with your old man to give a statement.'

'You stupid bastard.' Fenchurch lurched across the kitchen and grabbed his T-shirt again, pressing his head to Liam's. 'That guy's framed him.'

'Come on, it's not like that.' Liam tried to wriggle away. 'Can't be . . .'

'I need to know who he is.'

'I can't give you his name.'

Fenchurch let him go. 'It won't have come from you, okay?'

Liam dug the heels of his palms into his eye sockets. 'If anything happens to him . . .'

'Nothing's going to happen.' Fenchurch took a few steps back. Could still feel the fabric around his fingertips. 'What exactly did he tell you?'

'He might've said something about Chloe.'

'"Might have"?' Fenchurch raised his eyebrows. 'Christ, Liam.'

'He saw the stuff on the news last night. He read the story again and called me up.' Liam clapped him on the shoulder. 'I'm sorry, mate. He thinks she might've been involved.'

'Just tell me this guy's name.'

Chapter Twenty-Six

The Golden Lane Estate swamped Fenchurch, a huge chunk of the Barbican that hadn't succumbed to gentrification, a feral housing development just spitting distance from the City and Shoreditch. A couple of kids glared at him for having the temerity to park on their patch. Better put out the 'ON POLICE BUSINESS' sign.

He got out of his car and powered across the road. 'Kashmir' yanked him from his reverie. He fished out his phone. Zenna Abercrombie added another to her five missed calls.

Fenchurch pocketed the mobile and bumped between the kids, getting a high-pitched 'Oy' in response. He entered the external stair-well and climbed. Three storeys of concrete and misery, someone's idea of social housing. He strolled along the corridor. At the back, bare slabs surrounding a token tree were dusted with smashed lager bottles.

Number eighteen's door was battered and broken, the paint peeling off, 'CONNOLLY' handwritten above the one and the eight, hanging loose.

Fenchurch knocked and stepped back.

No answer.

Another knock and the neighbouring door opened. A black woman who looked to be in her sixties looked out. 'Can I help you, boy?' Thick Jamaican accent, like she was still on the island.

Fenchurch held his warrant card close enough for her to inspect. 'DI Simon Fenchurch. I'm looking for a Daniel Connolly.'

'Who?'

He thumbed at the door. 'Your neighbour?'

'He not in. I never spoke to him but I hear him. All the time. Not been back today, boy.'

'Okay, thanks.' One last look inside the door window and Fenchurch marched off towards the stairwell, getting his mobile out and dialling. 'Kay, it's Simon. How's it going?'

'Shit.' From the grinding and shouting in the background it sounded like Reed was in a mine somewhere. 'I'm still at Frank's Cabs. Mulholland's using this as an opportunity to take most of Blunden's fleet apart.'

'Good luck with that.' Fenchurch danced down the stairs, his knee clicking with each step. 'Got a hold of the Merc yet?'

'Not that I've heard, guv. How you doing?'

'Coping. Just.' Fenchurch stopped at the bottom of the stairs. The kids were still scoping out his motor. He whistled and they cleared off, hands deep in pockets. 'Wonder if you could do me a favour?'

'Depends on what it is.'

'I need you to get a lookout for one Daniel Connolly.'

'Who's he?'

'At this point, it's better you don't know.'

'Jesus, Simon.' Temple sat back in the meeting-room chair and brushed a hand through his hair. 'Have you told anyone about this?'

'Just Kay.' Fenchurch was lurking by the door, keeping an ear out for passing feet. Could recognise Docherty's gait a mile off in about five types of shoes. Always like he was marching across a glen to war with a rival clan. 'I doubt they'll believe me.'

'All that shit I said back at the crime scene? Forget it.' Temple smoothed down his trouser legs. 'It was an act for Docherty and the others there. I meant it when I said I'm your guardian angel.'

'Feels like we could do this another time.' Click, clack in the corridor. Not Docherty. 'This isn't—'

'Simon, I want to help, okay? It just needs to be subtle.'

'I can do subtle.'

'Believe that when I see it.' Temple sat back in his seat and crossed one leg over the other. 'You think this Connolly guy will close the gap in your timeline?'

Fenchurch nodded slowly. 'I hope so.'

'Leave it with me.' Temple jotted something in his notebook. 'I'll raise it with DI Mulholland.'

'She's still out at Lewisham?'

'At the PM, yeah. They kicked me out after Blunden's. The IPCC have made it abundantly clear that the Brocklehurst–Shelvey case is no longer part of my remit.'

The familiar burn hit Fenchurch's gut. 'For my sanity, was it just drink in Dad's system?'

'I haven't seen the blood toxicology yet, but I did have a word on the QT with the duty doctor.' Temple sighed. 'Just booze. No drugs.'

And the scale tips back . . .

Fenchurch drummed his fingers on the door. 'Look, given Mulholland's away, is there any chance I can speak to my old man?'

'You're pushing it, Simon. What happened to subtle?'

'I just need to know what happened between Liam leaving Dad's flat and me turning up in Mile End.' Fenchurch tried to get some moisture back into his tongue. 'I don't care if it helps with prosecuting him. Right now, I just need closure.'

Temple snapped his notebook shut and got up. 'Let's see what we can do.'

'Give me a call, yeah?' Temple sloped off down the corridor away from the Custody Suite.

Martin took yet another look back towards the front desk, then at Fenchurch. He swallowed hard, shaking his head. 'This is a favour, okay?' His voice was a hiss. 'They're still ramming a red-hot poker up my hoop every five minutes as it is.'

'I appreciate it.' Fenchurch locked eyes with him. 'I really do.'

Martin raised up his pile of keys and opened the lock. 'Here you go.'

Dad lay on the bed, barely looking up. Bleary-eyed and stinking like a tramp. 'Simon? What— Where am I?'

'You're in Leman Street, Dad.'

'Piss off.' Dad rolled to the side and toppled over, landing on the concrete floor with a crunch.

'Shit!' Fenchurch darted over and crouched next to him. 'Is your hip okay?'

'Ah, you bastard.' Dad hauled himself up, wincing at the pain. 'I'll live. What's going on? Why are you here?'

'Dad, I—'

In the corridor, Martin's hands were in the air, waving away. 'Shit! Get out!'

Fenchurch leaned closer. 'Dad, I need to speak to Daniel Connolly.'

Dad grimaced. 'Don't talk to me about him.'

'What did he tell you?'

Dad stared at him with mad eyes. 'He took Chloe!'

'Who did? Connolly?'

'No, Flick Knife! Blunden took her, son!'

'Simon!' Mulholland stormed into the cell and pulled Fenchurch away. 'What the hell are you doing in here?'

'Speaking to my father!'

'Only under *my* supervision.' She pointed a finger at Martin. 'Did you know about this?'

'Ma'am, he's an Inspector. I couldn't—'

'You should've called me.' She hauled Fenchurch out into the corridor. 'Listen to me, Simon, this behaviour has to stop. Your father's under investigation for murder. You need to back off.'

'Have you found Daniel Connolly yet?'

'Daniel who?'

'Connolly. He's . . .' Fenchurch shrugged off her grip. 'You need to speak to him. He was with Dad before he—'

'Right. Okay.' Mulholland gripped his arm by the elbow. 'Alan Docherty's searching for you. Do I need to get someone to escort you upstairs?'

Fenchurch stormed into Docherty's office and slammed the door behind him. 'Boss.'

'Here he is.' Docherty picked up a Scotland football mug, navy blue with a yellow lion rampant, and slurped, like he was trying to be as irritating as possible. 'Dawn just called me. What are you playing at?'

Fenchurch collapsed into a chair. Felt like he'd fallen through it. 'Boss, I—'

'You need to get out of here, you daft bastard.' Docherty set the mug down, his eyebrows shrouding his eyes. 'And the last thing you should be doing is sneaking around behind anyone's back, you arsehead.'

Fenchurch ran his hand over his face. 'My old man's being framed, boss.'

'I worked for and with your old boy for years.' Docherty hunched his shoulders. 'I know him. But, Simon, you saw it with your own

221

eyes. Him sitting there with that knife. He's as guilty as Gary Glitter in an orphanage.'

Fenchurch sprang to his feet, fists clenched. 'Come on, boss. You need to—'

'Get out of here.' Docherty pointed at the door. '*Now*. No second chances this time. As of Monday, you're out in Middlesex.'

Fenchurch stomped down the corridor, hands thrust deep into his pockets. Past open meeting-room doors. Past the Incident Room, buzzing at this time, the new shift swelling the numbers and giving a bit more enthusiasm for the task at hand.

Bloody Docherty.

Bloody Mulholland.

Middlesex? Bloody hell.

Fenchurch opened the stair door and clattered down the steps, the sound of his feet ricocheting round the tight space like fireworks.

Destroying that bottle of whisky can't have been the only option Dad had when he found out—

Fenchurch slipped on the stairs, stumbling a few steps. He caught hold of the handrail and pulled himself up. Chest heaving, a jolt of adrenaline firing through his veins.

Bloody hell.

He sat on the step, sucking in air, trying to calm his breathing. A downstairs door opened.

Think it through, slowly. Connolly told Dad what happened to Chloe, then he got blind drunk and killed Blunden.

How did he get to Mile End? It was about half an hour's walk up from Dad's flat in Limehouse, maybe ten minutes' drive if you went round the houses. Dad's driving was terrible at the best of times, and with a half-bottle of whisky in his guts?

No chance.

He definitely had help getting there.

His car was gone, meaning he probably didn't get a cab up there. The amount of whisky in his system meant he couldn't have driven up there without getting pulled over.

Meaning Daniel Connolly. And where the—

'Guv?' Reed was climbing the stairs, frowning at him over the banister. 'You frightened the life out of me.'

'Kay.' Fenchurch hauled himself to his feet and slouched past her. 'I'll see you later.'

She grabbed his wrist, her fingers digging deep. 'Not so fast. You okay, guv?'

'Not really, Kay.' Fenchurch stepped back from her, the buzz from the trip still surging through his system. 'Docherty's . . .' He huffed out and shook her off. 'You got anything from the taxi office?'

'If we did, I can't tell you.'

Fenchurch winked at her, but he couldn't put much effort in. 'So can you tell me?'

'Very good. I can't tell you if there wasn't anything, either. Still nothing on your APB.' She glanced upstairs at an opening door, footsteps thundering up, away from them. 'Found your old man's motor three streets away.'

'Oh shit.'

Fenchurch's phone blasted out 'Kashmir'. Unknown caller. Could be anyone. His heart thudded again. 'Better take this.' He stabbed the call button and sloped back, though Reed still had her eyes on him. 'Fenchurch.'

'We told you to stop. You didn't.' The same robotic voice, hissing and distorted. 'Who's next, Simon?' Click, and it was gone.

Fenchurch swallowed as he turned away from Reed. 'Okay, well, I'll . . . I'll see you there.'

'Quit it with the act, guv.' Reed snatched his mobile from his hands. 'Was that another call?'

Fenchurch couldn't look at her. 'They said someone's next.'

'You?'

'Shit, not me.' Fenchurch grabbed the phone from her and dialled. He listened to the ringing tone, then the voicemail kicked in.

'We're sorry but . . .' Click. 'Abi Fenchurch.' Click. '. . . isn't available to take your call right now. Please—'

Chapter Twenty-Seven

S ame story as last time, Si.' Clooney's voice was almost drowned out by the roar of the engine as Fenchurch pulled off the Westway and descended the ramp. 'Call was made in the Isle of Dogs this time. Another burner — on, then switched off after the call. Suspect this one's in the Thames as well.'

Fenchurch took a quick right, then a left. 'So there's nothing at all?'

'Just that your guy likes east London.'

'Cheers, Mick.' Fenchurch killed the call and hit dial again as he roared over cobbles, the whole car rattling.

'We're sorry but . . .' Click. 'Abi Fenchurch.' Click. '. . . isn't—'

He stabbed the screen and pressed another button, just before a sharp right chicane by a modern church.

'Simon?' Temple's voice dominated the car, even drowning out the rattle from the cobbles. 'What's up?'

'Where are you?'

'At Leman Street. Mulholland's asked me to supervise the prosecution of your father. I told her I can't, but—'

'Have you heard from Abi?'

'Abi? Not since last night. Why?'

'Get her to call me if you hear from her, okay?' Fenchurch killed the call and screeched to a halt, tearing off his seat belt as he tugged at the door. He grabbed his keys and bolted out of the double-parked car, rushing in front of a silver Škoda as it powered towards him.

Too close . . .

He sprinted up the path and hammered on the door, panting already. 'Rosie!' He thumped on her door again, the din echoing down the street.

The door slid open and Rosie stood there, her arms folded across her chest, glowering at him. Bacon smells accompanied her. 'Simon, have you got him off?'

'What? No. Is Ab—'

'What's happened? Is he—' She put a hand to her mouth.

'Where's Abi?' Fenchurch got a slapped arm for his troubles.

'You said you were going to—' Rosie's accent slipped right back from Maida Vale to Limehouse. 'Oh my god, he did it. He killed him!'

'Rosie, listen to me. I've just not got him off yet, okay?' Fenchurch danced around, like a naughty little boy not getting let in. 'Is Abi still here?'

'I am.' She was in the hall, head tilted to the side, arms folded like his sister. 'What's happened?'

'I had a phone call. Another warning one.'

'You thought someone had taken me?'

Fenchurch huffed out air. 'They said someone else close to me was next. I thought it'd be you. I couldn't get hold of you . . .'

'My phone's been in my purse on silent.' Abi reached down onto the hall parquet and picked up her bag. She checked her phone and her eyes bulged. 'Simon, if you can't get hold of someone, calling them *twenty-six* times isn't going to get them any quicker.'

'I need to feel I'm doing something.' Fenchurch collapsed against the railings separating the two houses, his lungs deflating like a burst beach ball. The street was deadly quiet, just parked cars and an elderly couple walking some poodle chimera thing. 'You've seen nothing?'

Abi padded over the slabs and hugged Fenchurch, her perfume snaking over him. Calming him. 'We've just been catching up, Simon.'

She grinned, her cheek dimpling. 'Wouldn't be the first time you were being paranoid.'

'No, it wouldn't . . .' Fenchurch smiled at Rosie. 'Thanks for looking after her.'

'Erm, Simon, it's more the other way round?'

'Right, right.'

A silver Škoda trundled past, going as slowly as a funeral procession. Same one as before . . .

'Shit.' Fenchurch stormed down the path, then onto the road. He waved the Škoda to a halt, then thrust his warrant card at the lowering window. 'Step out of the car, please, sir.'

The driver was a pimply oik, all tracksuit and limbs, shrouded in the vinegary tang of takeaway pizza competing with Lynx. 'Ain't doing nothing, mate.'

'I need you to step out of the car, sir.'

'You ain't got any probable cause, mate.' He hit the window button and it started grinding back up. He reached over for the central locking.

Fenchurch tore open the door and grabbed two handfuls of T-shirt. He picked him up like a small child, kicking and screaming, and dumped him on the road. 'Oh, I've got probable cause, son.' He flipped the wriggling kid onto his front and pinned his arm behind his back. 'Who was your target, son? Eh? My wife?'

'"Target"?' Pimples' cheek was flat against the bitumen, his mouth sticking out to the side. 'What are you talking about?'

'Quit it with the shit, okay?' Fenchurch ratcheted the arm up the kid's back. 'You were sent to kill someone, weren't you? Maybe abduct them?'

'I wasn't!'

Another notch on the ratchet. 'Who was it?'

'I'm delivering pizza!'

What?

'You're lying!' Fenchurch let the arm go a touch. 'Who are you targeting? My wife?'

'I'm not targeting— Check in the—'

'Simon!' Abi held up a giant leather pouch, unzipped slightly to show five huge pizza boxes. 'Let him go.'

Fenchurch released his grip and stepped away. 'Sorry, son.'

'I'm going to get your badge for this, mate.' The kid snarled at him as he got up, shaking his head slowly and rubbing his puny arm. 'Bloody police state.'

'I'm truly sorry, sir.'

'Yeah, bullshit you are. You fascist wanker!' He tore the pizza bag from Abi's hands and got in the car. Then he fiddled with his phone and the Škoda screeched off.

That'll come back to haunt me.

'Uncle Simon! That was so cool!' Footsteps pounded towards them. Becca and Ollie came to a halt next to their mother, both dressed in Chelsea strips, the bright blue catching in the sun. That fresh grass smell. 'Did you see that, Mummy? He just took him down!'

Peter caught up with his kids and grabbed their shoulders. 'Let's get you two inside, okay?'

'Daddy!'

'Your uncle will be in soon, won't he?'

Fenchurch crouched down, his knees grinding a little bit. 'I'll be in soon, just do as your old man says.'

Ollie grinned at him. 'What's an old man?'

'That'll be me.' Peter glared at Fenchurch, like the lord of the manor to one of his lowest servants. 'Now, it's time for your baths. Who's first?'

Abi watched Peter lead the kids inside. 'They've grown.'

'What?' Fenchurch's brows twitched. 'How have you seen them?'

'Simon, when you and I were separated, Rosie and I met up. A few times.'

Fenchurch scowled at his sister. 'Nobody told me.'

'No.' Abi thumbed the way the Škoda had gone. 'You see what happens to people who annoy you?'

The blue sky above was burnt white with vapour trails.

Rosie pecked Fenchurch on the cheek. 'Come on inside, love. I've got some bacon under the gri— Shit!' She ran across the road towards the house.

Abi gripped his shoulder and hugged him tight, cloaking him in her perfume. 'Simon, you need to chill out, okay?'

'I need to get out there, Ab.' Eyes darting around the quiet street, seeking out new threats. 'I need to sort this shit out.'

'No.' Abi prodded him in the chest. 'You're taking a break.' She grabbed his hand and led him over the road.

———

'I need to go to the little girl's room.' Abi got up and walked off, leaving Fenchurch with Rosie. The extractor still whirred away on a high setting. As the door opened, Peter's voice boomed down from upstairs, something about baths and whose turn it was . . . The sickly-sweet bubble-bath smell fought a brief battle with the burnt bacon.

Fenchurch sipped some tea and wobbled about on the stool, elbows almost scoring the breakfast bar's granite. 'You still make a good cup of tea, sis.'

'Well I never.' Rosie stuffed the grill pan in the Miele dishwasher and hit the button, starting it hissing. 'A compliment from my big brother.'

'I'm not that bad, am I?'

'I'll let you think on that one.' Rosie picked up her mug and blew on it, even though it must have been stone cold by now. 'What's going to happen to Dad?'

'I think they're going to prosecute.' Fenchurch dabbed at some crumbs covered in brown sauce. 'I need to know what happened, even if it means finding out that he's guilty.'

Rosie slurped at her tea, grimacing. She ran a hand across her forehead.

'I spoke to Dad's mate Bert.' Fenchurch wrapped his fingers around the warm mug. 'Dad's been doing all this secret shit. I was just keeping an eye on what was happening to Chloe's file . . . Him . . . He was . . . running down these back channels, trying to find these little angles.' Another sip. 'Couple of months ago, I caught him speaking to some cops up in Walthamstow about missing black kids. It's gone way beyond obsession.'

'And you never fed it, I suppose?'

'I told him to stop, Rosie. These are people you keep away from.' Fenchurch finished his tea. 'Not that he listened to me.'

'You don't have to tell me what Dad's like, Simon. I had to put up with him as well.'

'He's not that bad.'

'No, but he's not that good.' The cut-glass ripped through her East End accent. 'Do you honestly think he's killed this man?'

'I'm eighty per cent sure he didn't.'

'Just eighty?'

The remaining twenty ate at his guts. Fenchurch pushed his mug away. 'Look, sis, I'm sorry I've been distant.'

'Distant. Right. That's how you describe not seeing me for years despite living in the same city?'

'It's not like that. I've been busy.'

'I know. Looking for your daughter.' She gripped his wrist. 'Simon, I wish you'd let me help.'

'The time you could've helped was when she went missing.'

She let go of his wrist and backed off, running a cloth along the edge of the worktop. 'Simon, I had a lot going on.'

'Come on, Rosie.' Fenchurch left her a gap. The dishwasher hissed and the extractor groaned. 'I needed you and it felt like you just abandoned us.'

She collected up a sweep of crumbs in her hand and kicked the bin out. 'Keep telling yourself that.'

'What was going on that was so important?'

Rosie tossed the cloth in the sink and leaned forward onto the counter, sucking in breath. 'I got raped.'

'What?'

'A week before Chloe disappeared.' She twisted round and shut her eyes. 'I was out with some girls from work. Someone stuck a Mickey Finn in my wine glass, and the next thing I know I wake up beside these bins at the back of a nightclub. Felt like someone had scooped out my insides.'

'Rosie . . .' Fenchurch walked over and pulled her close. He held her there for a few seconds. 'Why didn't you tell me?'

'Because I felt so ashamed.'

He hugged her tighter. 'I could've helped.'

She cried into his chest, quivering with each sob. 'Simon, I wish I'd been there, but I couldn't help anyone. I couldn't even speak to Mum or Dad.'

Fenchurch pulled her tight again, resting his head on his shoulder. Just like when they were kids. Before all this shit, when the world made sense. 'I'm so sorry, love. I can't believe it.'

'Peter helped me get over it. He's a rock.' She broke off from his hug. 'Do you want any more tea?'

Fenchurch ran a hand down his face. 'I'm sorry, okay? What can I—'

His phone blasted out 'Kashmir' again. He checked the display. Reed. He answered it, smiling at Rosie. 'Kay, it's cool. I've found Abi.'

'Good news, then.' Sounded like Reed was in a bathroom somewhere, her voice echoing round a small space. 'That's not why I'm calling, though. We've just got a sighting on Daniel Connolly.'

Fenchurch got out of the car and walked over. Back at the glorious Golden Lane Estate, the three tower blocks backlit by the evening sun. The block Connolly lived in was quiet, the locals probably building up to England's first match in the Euros, against Russia. If it wasn't a walkover, this place would explode with drunken violence. Probably would anyway.

Not that he'd get time to even hear the score . . .

Reed was resting against a van, talking into her Airwave, accompanied by two plainclothes officers he didn't recognise. She whispered into her handset, 'Serial Bravo, that's us all in place. Good to go in sixty seconds.' She waved the handset over towards the ramshackle terrace. 'Got a unit on the far side of the concourse, guv. Still no movement from Connolly's flat.'

Fenchurch scanned the front of the building, not quite sure which one was Connolly's. 'You're sure it's him?'

'Bell sent his file, guv. It's him.' Reed put the Airwave to her lips again. 'That's us heading in now.'

Fenchurch followed her across the road. The foyer stank even worse than at lunchtime, like someone had freshly pissed against a wall. He motioned for the two DCs to wait and trotted up the staircase behind Reed. Two other officers stood on the concrete quad, guarding that exit.

Reed opened the door at the top of the first flight of stairs and walked through. She stopped dead.

A man loomed over her. Lad must've cleared six foot six. Had the bulk to back up any threat as well. A long scar rose from his left eyebrow, disappearing into the thin fingers of hair crawling down his forehead. 'Excuse me, love, I need to get past.'

'Are you Daniel Connolly?'

He gave her a cheeky wink. 'Depends who's asking.'

Reed reached into her pocket for her warrant card. 'Police.'

Connolly pushed her shoulders, sending her toppling into Fenchurch. He stumbled backwards and landed on the top stair. Then started rolling down.

Connolly vaulted over them and disappeared down the stairwell.

'Get up!' Reed hauled herself to her feet and grabbed Fenchurch by the wrist, wrenching him up. 'Come on!' She bombed down the stairs, snapping out her baton as she went.

The two DCs lay on their backs in the foyer, one cupping his balls, the other face down, out cold.

Reed grabbed her Airwave as she ran onto the road. 'Serial Bravo, requesting urgent assistance out front!'

'We're in pursuit, Sarge. He took a left outside the—'

'Shit.' Reed raced off, still clutching her Airwave.

Fenchurch outpaced her and sprinted down the street, heading towards a ragtag bunch of brick buildings. Just beyond, a man lay on the ground. Another of Reed's DCs, blood seeping out of his forehead. Still breathing, just unconscious.

A less feral tower block loomed to the right, a row of hipster scooters in front partially obscuring Connolly as he approached a grey Mercedes.

The car Cassie McBride's killer got into.

Reed sprinted across the cobbles into a private parking area, making a beeline for the Merc.

'Kay! Stop!' Fenchurch darted after her, but he was too slow.

Connolly spotted Reed's approach and squatted down, reaching inside the car. He reappeared seconds later, holding out a gun.

Reed dived sideways, putting the car between her and Connolly. BANG.

A bullet fizzed into the Merc.

Fenchurch curved his run through the car park and swung past a row of lock-ups, trying to keep Connolly ignorant of his approach. He crouched behind a green Renault.

Connolly was rounding the back of the car, the gun trained on Reed's location. 'Come on, darling, out you come.'

Fenchurch set off across the tarmac, waiting to time the jump to—

Connolly swung round and aimed the pistol at him. 'Slow down, chief.'

Fenchurch skidded to a halt. 'Daniel Connolly, my name is DI Simon Fenchurch.' No sign of Reed. 'I need to speak to you in connection—'

'Shut up!' Connolly stepped forward, pushing the gun into Fenchurch's chest. 'Now, you're getting in the motor with me and we're going for a little drive.'

'Please. We need to speak to you about—'

Connolly pulled the weapon back, the barrel pointing at Fenchurch's thudding heart. 'We'll do all the—'

CRACK.

Connolly tumbled to the ground, the back half of Reed's Airwave landing at his feet.

Reed kicked the gun away, then held up her cracked radio, the screen splintering into shards. 'Think you'd better call this in, guv.'

Chapter Twenty-Eight

Fenchurch unlocked the back door and pushed Connolly into the station. He weighed a ton. 'Get through there!'

Connolly stopped dead, pushing his giant frame against Fenchurch's hands. 'This is harassment!'

'You pointed a gun at me!' Fenchurch twisted Connolly's arm round behind his back. 'Now, if you want my advice, the sensible move here is to keep your mouth shut and get charged.'

'But I've not done anything!'

Fenchurch nudged him forward, keeping the grip on his sweaty wrist. 'Back to that, is it?'

'This is police brutality!'

'Shut up.' Fenchurch flagged down a passing Custody Officer, the same hulking brute in charge of Johnson that morning. Probably the only one big enough to handle Connolly. 'Can you process this guy and put him in an interview room?'

'Bloody hell.' The CO gripped a giant fist around Connolly's upper arm and led him into the Custody Suite.

The back door rattled open and Reed entered. 'Fancy a cup of tea before we haul him over the coals, guv?'

'Why not?'

Reed led through to the front foyer, brushing her fingers through her hair, looking like it had turned itself inside out. 'Hate this cut.'

'It suits you.'

'Yeah, you try wearing it when someone's pointing a gun at you and it's bloody dancing everywhere.' She held the door for him. 'How's Abi?'

'Looking after my sister.' Fenchurch ran his fingers across his palms. 'I can't sit still. God knows how they can.'

Reed set off towards the front door. 'It's called not being an idiot, guv.'

Fenchurch laughed. He pulled off his lanyard and stuffed it in his pocket. 'So you happy to lead the—'

'Simon!' Steve was over by his desk. 'You not answering your phone?'

'I've been a bit busy. Sorry.'

'Got a fella here for you.' Steve thumbed to the side.

Lord Ingham sat on a chair, his toad face lit up by the screen of his tablet. His tongue swept from side to side as his frown deepened.

Fenchurch smiled at Reed as he handed her a fiver. 'I'll pay if you fetch.'

'Guv.' She scowled as she snatched the money and pushed through the front door.

Fenchurch waited until Ingham looked up, his piggy little eyes focusing on him. 'I gather you wanted to see me, sir.'

Ingham locked his tablet and stuffed it inside a purple sleeve. 'Is there somewhere private we could . . . ?'

'Here's fine.' Fenchurch stood over him, his arms folded. 'What can I help with?'

'Just, eh, wondering if you'd sampled the whisky?' Ingham's tongue rolled around his lips again, like he was going to catch a fly. 'It's a delightful wee dram.' Pathetic Scottish accent.

A stab of pain shot through Fenchurch's gut. 'I've, eh, not had the chance, but thanks for the kind gift.'

'I saw the press conference on the television last night.' Ingham reached out a shaking hand and rested it on Fenchurch's shoulder. 'I'd no idea what you'd been through. Your daughter . . . It must be . . .' He blew out a puff of air, smelling of mints and cigars. 'Well.'

Fenchurch looked away. 'Thanks for the sympathy, sir.'

Ingham inched closer and whispered, 'I heard about your father's situation.' Another lick of the lips, his eyes checking out Steve. 'I have *contacts* in the judiciary, you know.'

Fenchurch stepped back and brushed his hand off. 'Listen, if my father killed that man, then he deserves to face the full force of the law, okay?'

Ingham gave a warm smile, his lips puckering. 'Well, I am still grateful for you saving me the other day.' He stuffed the tablet under his arm. 'Did you hear they've charged the man who attacked me? Some filthy vagrant.'

'I'm pleased to hear it, sir.' Fenchurch smiled and swiped his card through the security system, only exhaling when he was through.

Bloody hell. A corrupt judge is the last thing I need.

Someone was thundering down the stairs. 'Heard you were in the station again.' Docherty appeared at the bottom, his eyebrows raised. 'My office, now.'

—◡—

'Simon, I swear I'm going to wring your neck!' Docherty held his new Scotland mug out like he was going to smash it off another wall in his office. 'What the hell are you up to?'

Fenchurch dipped his chin, avoided any and all eye contact. 'Boss, I'm just doing my job.'

'Your *job*?' Docherty's head was shaking with rage. 'You want me to stick you on suspension, is that it?' He glugged his coffee and slammed the mug on the desk. 'You are a cheeky, cheeky bastard.'

'Boss, we need to get to the bottom of this. I've got a lead, and—'

'Let me tell you what's going on here.' Docherty slurped from his mug. 'First, I've got a rogue officer who keeps getting stuck into things I've explicitly told him not to. Second, said rogue officer's old man has killed someone. Third, said rogue officer is trying to clear said old man's name with a load of cowboy antics.'

Fenchurch gripped his thighs, tight enough to clot the blood. 'It's hardly "cowboy antics", Al. I'm—'

'Don't you "Al" me, okay? You've stepped way over the line on this, you stupid bastard.'

'I could've taken Connolly elsewhere.' Fenchurch let his thighs go again. 'I brought him here, put it on the books.' He flicked through his Pronto. 'This is a timeline of my father's movements from leaving his house through to allegedly killing Frank Blunden.'

'He killed him, Simon. You were there!'

'Boss, whatever.' Fenchurch tossed his Pronto on the desk. 'With the amount of booze in his system, my father was in no fit state to get from his house up to Mile End and then kill Blunden.' He held up his Pronto. 'There's a gap of two hours from Dad leaving Lewisham to me turning up at Frank's Cabs. Liam Sharpe left him at nine, after Connolly told Dad Flick Knife had abducted Chloe.'

Docherty slurped his coffee. 'Well, that explains why he's slotted Blunden, then.'

'But that's the thing, boss. Connolly shot Cassie McBride, yeah? We've got his motor there. What I'm thinking is he killed Flick Knife and made it appear like Dad did it. Stole the knife from his flat.'

'Why, though?'

Fenchurch huffed and tried to force his logic through closed synapses. 'I want to speak to Connolly.'

Docherty clunked his mug on the table and got up. 'You're not speaking to anyone but your wife and your sister.'

'Al, I just need five minutes with him. Please.'

⌣‿⌣

'No comment.'

Docherty tapped at his watch and raised his eyebrows.

Just a few more minutes . . . Fenchurch held up five fingers, pleading with Docherty until he looked away, nodding. He scowled at Connolly, the giant looking like he was sitting in a schoolkid's chair, squashed in there. 'You shot at a car, then shot at me.'

Connolly just shrugged, still wearing a blank expression. Bloodshot eyes, thin stubble around his mouth, but patchy like he'd had a few too many flaming sambucas. The interview-room recorder thrummed next to him, giving off that new computer smell. 'Did nothing of the sort.'

Finally getting a reaction . . .

Fenchurch held up the bagged handgun, keeping up the eye contact. 'This is the weapon you pointed at me, loaded. After you shot the car.' He prodded at the barrel through the plastic. 'We call it a Hitman Kit. Someone's had a little fiddle with it, so it now fires bullets.'

Connolly nibbled at his bottom lip, pulling the flesh up. He couldn't take his eyes off the gun.

Fenchurch picked up another bag, containing two casings. 'These were found in the street where one Cassie McBride was shot yesterday evening.' Another bag, this one with a spent slug. 'This was in her car's driver-side door. It slowed down a lot when it passed through her neck.' He ran a hand across his own neck, then raised a final bag, another slug rattling around inside. 'This was retrieved from Miss McBride's ribcage.' He left a pause.

Connolly tore off a chunk of skin from his lip and swallowed it down. 'I'm saying nothing.'

'The smart move would've been to dump the gun in the Thames, along with those burner phones.'

Connolly scratched at his cheek. 'What phones?'

'You haven't made any calls on a burner?'

'No.' Connolly dabbed a finger at the fresh cut on his lip. 'Suggest you move on, mate. Wouldn't mind catching the football tonight.'

'Mr Connolly, what's your connection to Frank Blunden?'

'I work for him. That Merc's his.' Connolly smoothed down the shards of gelled hair leaking onto his forehead and nibbled at his cheek. 'Lovely motor.'

'When was the last time you saw Mr Blunden?'

Connolly rested his hands behind his neck and yawned. 'Last night.'

Docherty tapped his watch again and held up a finger.

'That car was seen by a shooting out east last night. You kill for him, don't you?' Fenchurch produced a CCTV still of the Mercedes by the crime scene. 'Where were you at four o'clock yesterday afternoon?'

Connolly stared at the sheet of paper for a good while, then pushed it away. 'I'm not answering that.'

'I've got a witness saying you were speaking to an Ian Fenchurch at an address in Limehouse this morning.'

Connolly barked out a laugh and scratched at the scar on his eyebrow. 'That little hipster? Glen? Len?'

'Liam.' Fenchurch sat forward, his leg jiggling. 'What happened after he left?'

'That old geezer's cracked.' Connolly twirled a finger round his temple and whistled. 'You might want to take him to the doctor's.' His forehead pulsed a couple of times. 'I left ten minutes later. Went home for a kip.'

Docherty gripped Fenchurch's bicep and whispered into his ear, 'Time's up, okay?'

'Just another minute.'

'A deal's a deal.' Docherty got to his feet and smiled at Connolly. 'Thanks for your time, sir. The Custody Officer will take you downstairs for processing.'

Connolly smacked a giant fist off the table. 'What?'

Docherty snatched up the bag containing the gun. 'You pointed this at two of my officers and assaulted a further three. What did you expect to happen?' He thunked the pistol down on the desk. Thank God it wasn't loaded.

Connolly frowned at Fenchurch. 'Wait a sec, you're Ian's son, right?'

'Didn't the name give it away?'

'That was you in the paper, right?' Connolly nodded slowly. 'That means it's your daughter who went missing, right?'

Fenchurch's breath raced away. He had to keep his hands by his sides. Keith Moon thumped at the drums. 'Won't Get Fooled Again' . . . 'Did you abduct her?'

Connolly inspected his nails, the forefinger of his left hand longer than the rest. Giveaway coke nail. He ran a hand across his nose. 'I want my lawyer in here. I'm saying nothing till then.'

'If you're after a deal or something, we need to know what you've got to offer.' Fenchurch's elbows pressed into the wood. 'As it stands, we've got you for Cassie McBride's death. You assaulted multiple police officers and fired an illegal firearm at us. All your lawyer's going to say is don't speak to us. Which means we can't offer you a deal.'

Connolly's mouth twitched, hard and fast, every other twitch distorting his nose.

'Right, come on.' Docherty grabbed Connolly's arm and pulled him to his feet.

Connolly let Docherty take him towards the door. He stopped by the doorway and stared at the floor. 'Look, a few blokes in Blunden's crew . . . They used to . . . kidnap kids off the street.'

'They were definitely Blunden's boys?'

'Hundred per cent. His cab drivers.' Connolly nudged Docherty away and stepped closer to Fenchurch, propping himself up on the back of a chair. 'They'd drive around, looking for kids playing on their own. Grab them and stick them in their motors. They'd hand them off between them, so if someone saw a motor driving away, by the time you lot caught up with it . . . well, the kid wasn't there. We'd broken the chain.'

'What's your involvement in this?'

Connolly's fingers tightened around the chair back.

'You don't feel anything about this, do you? You destroyed families and created misery.'

'I've done so many bad things over the years, I can't sleep at night.' Connolly held Fenchurch's gaze, his red eyes glistening with tears. 'You got any idea what that's like?'

'You just lie there, staring at the ceiling. All night. Then you give up, get out of bed. Drink coffee. Eat sugary shit.'

'Right.' Connolly parted his hair again, smoothing down both greasy halves. 'When I get drunk enough to drift away, when my eyes shut, I see the kids. I see their faces, feel them kicking.'

'So why's this the first time you're speaking to us?'

'Because I see a way out of this for me.' Connolly's lip curled up. 'The number of times I've thought about killing myself . . . I came close a couple of weeks ago. Really thought about it. Had it all planned out. Then Blunden guessed what I was up to.' He collapsed into the chair. 'Had someone go and have a word with my mother.' He stared into space, his pupils losing all focus, his shoulders deflating like a bouncy castle full of drunk dads. 'They threatened my mother and my sisters. Anything I tell you . . .' He drew a line across his throat. Then he leaned back and exhaled. 'But then I saw that story in the paper yesterday morning. Made me think if I can do something here, maybe your old man can sort me out.'

Docherty sat next to him, flashing a smile at Fenchurch. 'We're listening.'

'I remember that girl, Chloe. Islington, right? Blonde hair. England kit.'

That wasn't in the paper . . .

Fenchurch's sinuses burned like someone was holding a lighter to his nose. 'You took her?'

'I didn't take her, I swear.' Connolly squeaked out an 'A . . .', then shut up. He looked around the room, then opened his mouth again. 'Like I said, we used to pass these kids around between us. This time, I was the second driver. Most times, we had three. This woman got in the back with her. Changed her clothes, cut her hair. Supposed to pretend to be the girl's mother, say she got sick, something like that.'

'Where was Blunden taking them?'

'It was for some gang. Never met any of them. Blunden spoke to them. We were just air cover for the people who took them. Our motors were driving around all the time, innocent as you like. Easy to explain away.'

Fenchurch tugged at his nose, trying to stop the burning. 'Who took her?'

'I've no idea. Never met him in my life.' Connolly shook his head at the table top. Then up at Fenchurch. 'I passed her off to this big fella. Think he was a cop. Called himself Johnson or something.'

The flames licked up into Fenchurch's brain. 'Chris Johnson?'

'Mean something to you?'

Chapter Twenty-Nine

'So what are you saying?' Fenchurch took the turning marked BELMARSH & COURTS and trundled to a halt by the lights. 'Should I have just smashed his face off the table?'

'Thankfully you've moved past those days . . .' Docherty gripped the 'oh shit' handle above the door like they were going into orbit. 'So what now?'

Fenchurch tightened his grip on the wheel, like it was Johnson's lying serpent throat. 'I don't know.' He drove off and stopped by the security barrier, winding the window down. A plane droned overhead, probably coming in to land at City Airport.

The guard appeared and Fenchurch held out his warrant card. He frowned at his clipboard. 'You're not on my list for today, sir.'

'I'm meeting someone here.' Fenchurch grabbed his ID back. 'Paul Temple. He's a CPS barrister.'

The guard checked his clipboard again. 'Okay, sir.' He clicked a button and the barrier started grinding up, wobbling like it'd drunk eighteen pints of craft beer. 'If you're not gone in ten minutes, I'll be calling it in. Okay?'

Jobsworth wanker.

'Cheers.' Fenchurch drove on and pulled in next to a turquoise Audi soft-top with '16 plates. In a prison car park. Like that didn't scream 'DRUG DEALER' in six-foot-high letters. Or screw on the take.

Docherty let go of the handle and rubbed his forehead. 'Can you see him?'

'Nah. Come on.' Fenchurch got out and stretched his back, his vertebrae snapping back into almost the right place.

The fruit trees flanking the prison hid the orange-brick bulk and its turret-like rounded entranceway. Grey walls surrounded it on both sides, big enough for a stupid-haired American dictator to keep the Mexicans out.

'Simon!' The Audi's door opened wide and Temple got out, his head barely up to the top of the door. 'You got my message, then?'

Fenchurch held up his phone. 'You managed to knock back Johnson's bail?'

Temple joined them as Docherty got out of the Mondeo. 'So you think he's going to talk this time?'

'Hope so.'

'Hope, eh?' Temple winked at him. 'That bastard.'

Another sting of pain hit Fenchurch's gut. 'Not that I've got much left.'

Temple stuffed his document pouch under his left arm and started off across the tarmac, the clicking of his heeled shoes drowned out by the drone of another landing plane. 'Come on, gentlemen, time and tide waits for no man. I've had to call in some favours to get a few minutes with him on a Saturday.'

'You know I'll wash your car forever.'

'The soft-top needs special attention, Simon.' Temple winked. 'But I'll just settle for seeing you smile again.'

'In here, sirs.' The prison officer led them into the room and waited by the door. Place stank of bleach, like they'd tried to scour it of all DNA traces. Six tables were arranged in a two by three formation, the barred windows letting shafts of light advance across the red lino flooring. 'I'll just be a second.'

Docherty sat at the table nearest the door. 'Right, Si, against my better judgement, you're running this, okay?'

'Boss.' Fenchurch rested against another table, letting his suit jacket hang open by his sides. 'I'm calm, I promise.'

Temple was talking on his phone out in the hallway, facing away. Behind him, the white-walled prison corridor stretched off to infinity. DC Chris Johnson lumbered down it, flanked by two officers who looked like American wrestlers. The guards yanked him into the room, followed by Temple.

Johnson slouched down opposite Fenchurch, running his tongue along his teeth, a sneer on his face. His curtains hair was all messed up.

'I'm going to cut to the chase.' Fenchurch cracked his knuckles, enjoying the cartilage popping. 'We know you worked for Frank Blunden.'

Johnson tried to smooth his hair into the curtains. The left side jutted up like the hull of a boat. He licked his finger and tried again.

'Okay, so that's the game you're playing, is it?' Fenchurch cracked his knuckles again, the only thing he could do to stop himself from diving across the room and smashing Johnson's face into the wall. The drums thundered like rapids. 'You abducted kids for Blunden. You took my daughter.'

Johnson stopped fussing with his hair and smoothing down his stubble. 'I know the rules here, okay? All I want to know is, what's this worth?'

Fenchurch looked at Temple, pleading with him like he was a dog in the kennels.

Temple cleared his throat. 'Mr Johnson, as I'm sure you'll understand, this whole thing depends on what you've got to offer.' He unzipped his document holder and sifted through papers. 'At the present time, though no official date has been set, you're pencilled in to stand trial in mid-April for the death of Steven Shelvey. If you bring in someone else, we might cancel the charges levelled against you.'

'That so?' Johnson picked at his teeth. 'How do I know this is on the level?'

'Because it's over for you.' Fenchurch battled the urge to reach for his throat and just squeeze. 'There's two things you can do to help yourself here. Face trial, or tell us everything you know.' He crouched down next to him. 'It's over, Chris. Your rank, your pension. The money you've been taking for what you've been doing. We'll get all of that. And I reckon you'll get at least thirty years.'

'I want a deal.'

'Everyone does.' Fenchurch stood and put his hands in his pockets. 'Was Blunden in charge?'

'I dealt with Frank. That's it. If he had bosses, I never met them.'

'And Mr Blunden's dead. Convenient.' Fenchurch folded his arms. 'Who did the order to murder Steven Shelvey come from?'

Johnson clacked his teeth together for a few seconds. 'Came from Blunden.'

'So you killed Shelvey?'

Johnson nodded. 'Sod it.' He crumbled, almost disappearing into his seat. 'What you said is true. I was working with this gang Blunden knew. I helped them make sure the law didn't interfere. They used to move packages around. Drugs, guns. Other things.'

'People?'

Johnson swallowed a nod. 'This one day, we was supposed to be shifting some prostitutes, taking them from Blunden's brothel in Hackney to his new place south of the river. Then I got a call from this bloke. Daniel Connolly. You might want a word with him.'

Fenchurch winked at Temple, hiding it from Johnson. 'And what did Connolly tell you?'

'Said the plan's changed. He pulled up in this street in Camden, right next to me. Had a little girl in the back seat, asleep. Then this woman got out of the back, supposed to be her mother.' Johnson sucked in a breath and let it out in one long sigh. 'I remember her clear as day. Cute girl. Always find it funny when girls wear football kits.'

That one detail, the thing they'd kept from the press all those years. Connolly and Johnson both knew it. The bloody pair of them, they had to be playing us . . .

'Next thing I know, a call came in on my radio. Said an officer's girl had gone missing near Angel. Now, I had a bag with a load of blonde hair and an England kit, and a sleeping girl in my boot. Didn't take two and two to—'

'What did you do with her?'

'You think I killed her, don't you?' Johnson's grin slipped away. 'You should wish I killed her. Let's just say that some people were going to have a little bit of fun with her.'

Fenchurch reached over and grabbed hold of his shirt, damp and stinking. 'It's either I smash your brains out now or some big bastard in here does when the doors are left unlocked at night. Your choice. What happened to her?'

'Let go!'

Fenchurch grabbed Johnson by the throat and choked him, squeezing his fingers around his prickly flesh. 'What happened to her?'

Johnson's nails scratched into Fenchurch's hands, like a feral cat. 'Let go of me!'

Fenchurch glanced over at Docherty, who sat arms folded, and loosened his grip. He stalked around the room, prowling round Johnson, and spoke through a lump in his throat. 'You were the end of the chain. What happened to her?'

Johnson massaged his throat, then smoothed apart his curtains, a red weal covering his neck. 'I drove her to Blunden.'

'Frank's Cabs?'

Johnson shook his head, his expression darkening, the act slipping from the actor's face, revealing the terror below. 'His brothel.' He swallowed hard. 'When I got there, Blunden was spitting teeth about who she was.'

'What was Blunden going to do with her?'

Johnson pulled at his shirt. 'What I've heard, they keep them for about six months. They drug them while they're . . . You know. At it with them.'

Ice chilled Fenchurch's veins. Felt like someone was stabbing a cigarette out on his eyes. 'Blunden was?'

'Probably.' Johnson folded his arms. 'They treated them like little princes and princesses, until they got fed up of them. Then we disappeared them.'

Cigarettes stabbed Fenchurch's eyes. 'You killed her?'

'Aren't you listening to me? We *disappeared* her.'

Fenchurch's gut flew up, hope raising its bastard head through the burning acid. 'What do you mean, you disappeared her?'

'The way this whole scheme works, right, Blunden didn't want to leave a trail of dead kids once . . . You know. Once they'd finished with them. So Blunden ran a fake adoption agency.'

Fenchurch swallowed bile. 'He what?'

'You heard. We give these kids to desperate parents at the other end of the country. These people had been rejected from the system for one reason or another. Desperate people, one step away from getting a Romanian or a Chink. Nowhere near London. And they were told never to bring them here.'

'So you gave them children who'd been abused?'

'Not me. Blunden.' Johnson snarled, pointing out of the room. 'The adoptive parents wouldn't know. The kids were drugged when it was going on. We told them their birth parents were dead. Sometimes gave them a little bit of a helping hand. Made sure they'd never visit London again, and if they did, the kids wouldn't look anything like the parents remembered. There was no risk. It was a lot more effective than killing them. Questions weren't asked.'

I should just kill you now, you dirty, filthy pervert.

Smash your brains in, kick your guts all over the floor.

Stamp on your heart and your bollocks.

Fenchurch sat down next to Docherty. 'How can you live with yourself?'

'What makes you think I can?' Johnson pushed his chair back and started pacing around the room. 'Nature's red in tooth and claw and all that. This civilisation bollocks, that's just so people can control us. It's still a wild world. I've seen the darkness and, believe me, these are people you do not want to mess with. I did, and I'm paying the price.'

'How did you mess with them?'

'I never used to be like this.' Johnson swallowed, his Adam's apple bobbing up and down. 'Back then, I was a good cop. Decent conviction rate, played by the rules. Then one day, I was investigating this kidnapping.' He shut his eyes. 'I brought this geezer into the station. You know what he said to me? He said, speak to your wife.' He wiped at his cheek. 'I got out of there and I called her, called her mother, called her mates. Nobody'd seen her.' He opened his eyes, deep holes without any emotion left. 'They've got my wife and my son. I get to see them once a month. I'm so far in the shit, right? I've had enough of this. This constant struggle. This worry. If you catch them, then . . . Maybe . . .'

Docherty held up a hand, stopping Fenchurch from continuing. 'Did you kill Steven Shelvey?'

'I'm not answering that.'

Fenchurch butted in. 'Where is my daughter?'

'She was rehomed, mate, but I don't know where. The agency is in Hammersmith.'

Fenchurch gripped Johnson's shirt tight again. 'What's the address?'

'Not so fast.' Johnson brushed him off. 'I can take you there. Get you inside. Show you how it all works.'

Chapter Thirty

Fenchurch drove through the night-time traffic, taking a right past the Hammersmith Apollo. He switched his rear-view from the trailing squad car and focused it on Johnson in the back, pondering his own mortality.

Nothing worse than a dirty cop.

Especially one who'd . . .

Why not just drive into the Berkshire countryside and smash his brains out with a tyre iron? Drive down to Brighton and dump his body in the sea? Drive up to Scotland and dig a shallow grave somewhere. Enough cans of Red Bull and you were there in eight hours. Yorkshire, Wales or Cornwall, even less time and just as barren.

'—along, guv?'

Fenchurch pulled onto King Street and caught Reed's glower from the passenger seat. 'What?'

'You've gone all quiet, guv. I'm getting a little bit worried.'

'Sorry.'

'I was asking why you brought me along.'

Fenchurch checked Johnson wasn't listening and spoke in an undertone. 'Because you're the only one I can trust. Well, you and Paul Temple.'

'He's a good guy.' She glanced behind them. 'Unlike our chum there.'

Johnson's cuffed hands rattled between the seats. 'It's just up ahead. On the right.'

Fenchurch cut across a black cab and took the side street.

The cuffs jangled as Johnson pointed to the left. 'There.'

Fenchurch parked between a Saab and a Fiat. 'This us?'

'This is us.' Johnson waved his hands at a shop on the left, stuck between a Polish supermarket and an upmarket café. Dark-grey frontage, heavy oak door, **Fresh Start** daubed in a tasteful font, with two stick-figure adults holding hands with a child and waving.

'Come on, then.' Fenchurch caught a whiff of hash from somewhere. No sign where. The squad car double-parked up ahead, the uniforms staying inside.

A tropical bird flapped between two trees, squawking loud enough to draw in the neighbourhood's cats. Yellow and blue feathers dusted the pavement.

'That's not a Kingston parakeet, guv.' Reed already had her Airwave out. 'I'll call the RSPCA.'

Fenchurch helped Johnson out of the car. 'Right, no funny business here, okay?'

'I'm a desperate man in a desperate situation.' Johnson stepped across the pavement and flipped down a security panel by the door. He tapped in a code and smiled at Fenchurch. 'Keys?'

The street was empty apart from the now-wild bird. 'Fine.' Fenchurch rummaged in his pocket and got out Johnson's keys, all neat and tidy, not even a supermarket trolley token.

Johnson caught them and unlocked the shutter. 'Going to need a hand here.'

Fenchurch crouched down and helped haul up the metal gate.

Johnson put another key in the door, his eyes dancing up and down the street as he twisted it in the lock.

Inside, it was more like a funeral home than an adoption agency, whatever one of them should look like. Flowers and cartoons of smiling children, maybe. Not dark panelling and the sort of paintings that'd give you a hefty shrink's bill.

Johnson hefted up a partition in the middle of the long bench and sat behind a computer, shaking the mouse to wake it. 'Okay, this should be quick.'

Fenchurch joined him behind the partition, making sure there wasn't any funny business going on. 'What's the password?'

Johnson hammered the keyboard. 'What's going to happen to me?'

'I'll owe you a massive favour.'

'You still going to prosecute me?'

'Not my remit.' Fenchurch rested against the counter. 'If things go well, we might get your wife and son back to you. You won't keep your job, not this time. But you might just get a short prison sentence.' He clapped him on the back, hard enough to pass on the threat. 'Now, what's the password?'

'Right. It's "Bubbles" with a capital "B" and a zero instead of the "u".' Johnson typed it in slowly. It opened to a web browser, the Fresh Start logo above a few buttons. He entered 'July 2005' and hit return. The screen switched to show a list of names and dates. He ran his finger down the monitor and tapped at one. 'There you go.'

Fenchurch frowned at it. Couldn't make it out. 'What?'

Johnson clicked on a name. 'Your daughter came in under the name Chloe Holland.'

Fenchurch sucked in a deep breath. 'Why Holland?'

'They keep the first name because the kids answer to it. But they change the surname to hide the truth.' Johnson switched to another tab on the screen. 'She was adopted by a couple in early August 2005.'

Fenchurch swallowed hard, hope burning at the acid in his gut, pushing up to his chest. 'Is she still alive?'

'You'll have to find out for yourself.' The laser printer next to Johnson rumbled and he grabbed the sheet of paper it spat out. 'This is their address.'

The one thing I've been after for so long . . . Now it was finally here?

Can't even look at it.

Fenchurch folded it in half and put it in his pocket. 'Come on, I've got to get you back to safety.'

'Right.' Johnson stared at the floor. 'I thought—'

'You didn't expect me to just let you go, did you?'

'No.' Johnson huffed to his feet and led Fenchurch through the partition and out into the street.

Reed was putting her Airwave away, a motorbike engine droning in the distance, the bird still squawking. 'Guv?'

Fenchurch just nodded at her, unable to get any words out of—

BANG.

A motorbike revved past as Johnson toppled over.

Reed dived at Fenchurch, pushing him back against the door.

BANG.

The door frame splintered with a gunshot. The squad car's siren screeched out as it revved off after the bike.

Reed rolled off Fenchurch and sat up in a squat. 'You okay, guv?'

'I'll live.' Fenchurch eased himself up, panting. 'Oh, shit.'

Johnson lay on his side, a pool of blood leaking out of his skull onto the pavement, forming a speech bubble on the slabs.

The crime scene was a mess of police tape and an RSPCA van trying to rescue the bird of paradise.

Fenchurch unfolded the paper and read it for the first time.

CHILD:	CHLOE HOLLAND
ADOPTION:	**03/08/2005**

ADOPTERS:	LAWRENCE SIMON
	CHERYL SIMON
ADDRESS:	27 REMPSTONE ROAD
	SWANAGE
	DORSET
	BH19 1DW

Dorset . . . Bloody miles away. Hundred and twenty, maybe more. Other side of the bloody country.

He got out his Airwave Pronto and put the names into the PNC. A drink-driving charge on the father. Nothing on the mother. Looked like they'd moved in August 2005, not long after they'd adopted Chloe. Then again a few years later. And again. Current address was some place called Poundbury in Dorchester.

The Airwave blared out. 'Control to DI Fenchurch.'

'Receiving.'

'Sir, all three units in pursuit of the motorcycle are reporting they've lost it somewhere between the South Circular and Richmond Park.'

Somewhere between . . . Got to love the precision.

'Thanks.' Fenchurch killed the call and closed his eyes, shaking his head.

Reed was over the road, briefing the two SOCOs who'd turned up.

Docherty's car pulled in and he got out, leaving his door open. He clocked Fenchurch and made a beeline for him. 'Si . . . What the bloody hell is going on?'

'We've lost Johnson, boss. The shooter . . .'

'Aye, so it goes.' Docherty did up his tie, almost choking himself. 'Well, I've grabbed this case with both hands. Or rather, had it shat on my head.' He slackened the tie off. 'You okay?'

Over the road, Reed was waving her hands in the air as she spoke. 'If Kay hadn't pushed me to the ground . . .'

'What?'

'This was an assassination, boss.' Fenchurch pointed at the splintered door frame, a SOCO photographing the wood. 'That bullet had my name on it.'

'Well, it's better wedged in a door than in some nutter's gun.' Docherty waved over at Fresh Start, tape flapping in the breeze, the blood dialogue balloon now a flat paddling pool. 'Did you get anything?'

Fenchurch handed him the sheet of paper, waited while he scanned it. 'Boss, I want to—'

'Go.' Docherty returned him the page. 'Get to the bottom of this.'

Fenchurch waited for Rosie's door to clunk open. Heart thudding, eyes shut, ears almost bleeding with the cacophony of drums. He expected bedlam inside, kids running up and down the stairs, shouting at each other, but it was as quiet as a funeral.

Another knock.

The evening breeze rustled the hedge lining the road and rippled his jacket like a corner flag at Upton Park.

Dorchester. A hundred and thirty miles away. Far enough to hide her from them in plain sight. Far enough to let her start a new life with new parents.

Rosie opened the door and tucked her arms around herself. 'You're back, then. Thought you'd call before—'

'Is Abi still here?'

'We're in the kitchen.' Rosie stepped out into the night. 'I sent Peter out with the kids to give us some space. They're—'

'Thanks.' Fenchurch barged past her into the house, storming through the hall into the kitchen at the back.

Abi was waiting for the kettle to boil, picking at her nails. A football goal dominated the floodlit lawn, a punctured ball lying in the net. She turned to him and frowned. 'Simon?'

Fenchurch tried to get the words out but nothing happened. 'Ehm.'

Rosie entered the room, arms still folded. 'Abi, I think there's enough milk for—'

Fenchurch twisted round to smile at her, but he was struggling to get his mouth to move. Christ knows what it looked like . . . 'Can you give us a minute, sis?'

'Okay.' Rosie backed out of the room, shutting the door behind her. No doubt standing with her ear to the stripped wood, a cup placed against it.

Abi came over to him and brushed her hand up and down his arm. 'Simon, what's up? You look . . . odd.'

'I feel it.' Fenchurch rubbed a hand across his face. 'Chloe . . .' He shut his eyes and tried to swallow down the bitter tears. 'She's . . .' He broke off, his throat like sandpaper. 'There's a possibility she's alive.'

Abi's lips formed a horizontal line as her eyes shifted around. Then her face twisted up. 'What? What are you talking about?'

'Chloe.' Fenchurch reached into his jacket pocket for the tear-stained print and handed it to her, like it was the golden ticket. 'They took her, Ab. Gave her a new name.'

Abi snatched it off him and scanned down the page, her frown deepening. She looked up at him, tears welling in her eyes. 'Chloe Holland?'

⌣

'Can't find anything here.' Fenchurch piled along a road in Dorchester, no vanishing points or landmarks to navigate by, just posh new houses, like a Cotswold village stretched out of all recognition. Nowhere near enough lighting, either. He finished the second can of Red Bull, the caffeine just about holding him together. 'Never even heard of Poundbury.'

'I thought about moving here a few years ago, when . . .' Abi broke off. 'Don't you think it's lovely?'

'I think it's a maze.'

'It's supposed to be. It's meant to make it more welcoming. If you'd switch that satnav on . . .' Abi stabbed at her phone, then pointed to the right. 'Just down there.'

'There?' Fenchurch squinted down the lane, dark and menacing. Looked like a building site at the other end. Reed's red Fiat was parked halfway down, the cabin lit up in the night-time gloom. He set off again. 'I'm wondering where the bloody werewolves are.'

'Simon, do you think this is funny? Because I'm not laughing.'

'Force of habit, love. Sorry.' Fenchurch's hands were clammy on the wheel. Sweat trickled down his back. He trundled along the lane and pulled up outside a stone cottage that wouldn't have looked out of place in a small Yorkshire village. No lights on, clear rear exits, too.

Abi opened her door and made eye contact. 'Now . . . Jesus Christ.' She swallowed and got out onto the street, covering her face.

Reed got out of her Fiat and jogged over, speaking into her Airwave. She grabbed Abi in a hug. 'How you doing?'

'How do you bloody think?' Abi glared at the house. 'I just want to see my daughter.'

Squad cars pulled down the lane from both directions, trapping them in.

'Got the place surrounded, guv.' Reed waved at the cottage. 'Been here an hour. There's people inside. Don't know who, but nobody's entered or left in that time. Thought you'd appreciate it if I left the approach to you guys.'

'Thanks, Kay . . .' Fenchurch joined Abi at the front door. Waiting . . . The rage building up. He reached out and held his hand over the door knocker, breathing hard and deep.

The moment it all becomes real, all of Chloe's many possible pasts coalescing into a single present. Reality. What happened to her. What they did to her. Who she is now. Everything.

Sounds came from inside. Music and chatter. Laughter.

Fenchurch cracked the brass knocker off the plate. A stab of pain sliced through his gut.

Footsteps thumped through the hall. An eye appeared at the window, peering out. Then nothing.

A pause for what felt like days, weeks. Abi tugged her hair behind her ear.

The door flew open and a red-faced man scowled out. Tall, bald and silver-haired, mid-sixties, but like those years had taken a toll. His gaze swept over Fenchurch and Abi, then Reed behind them. 'Can I help?'

'Mr Simon?'

'That's correct. My friends call me Larry.' His smile fizzed to a grimace and back again. 'It's quite late. What's this about?'

Fenchurch flashed his warrant card. 'DI Simon Fenchurch. I need you to answer a few questions about a case dating back to 2005.'

Larry blinked hard and slow. 'I'm sorry, what?'

'Are you the . . .' Fenchurch put his warrant card away, his heart like a pneumatic drill tearing into his ribs. 'Are you the father of Chloe Holland?'

'Chloe?' Larry swallowed. 'Good heavens.'

Fenchurch gritted his teeth. 'Are you her father?'

The door creaked open and a woman appeared next to Larry. Looked about twenty years younger than him. Could've been his daughter. Her face was pinched tight, like Fenchurch and Abi were trying to steal from her. Lines spidered around her eyes, a few silver threads in her dark hair. 'What's this about?'

Larry stepped to the side. 'Cheryl, they wanted to ask us about Chloe.'

Cheryl eyed them suspiciously. 'Why?'

'Are you her father, Mr Simon?'

'I am. Well, I was.'

Fenchurch's breathing sped up. 'What do you mean, was?'

'Can't this wait until the morning?'

Fenchurch grabbed fistfuls of his shirt. 'What do you mean, was?'

Cheryl bit at her lip. 'Not long after we took her in. She was hit by a bus. She died.'

What? She . . . Dead?

Chapter Thirty-One

F enchurch pulled off the roundabout, then drove down the long road lined with tall stone buildings. 'Do you want to talk, love?'

'I want to know what the hell happened, Simon.' Abi was leaning back in her seat, one arm folded across her chest, the other guarding her belly. 'I need to know what happened to my baby girl.'

Fenchurch pulled into the police station's car park, less than half the size of Leman Street, even though it seemed to be the divisional HQ. He turned off the engine and ran a hand through his hair, damp with sweat. 'This is probably going to be very difficult to process, love. There's . . .' He brushed tears from his eyes. 'There's going to be—'

Water welled around Abi's eyes. A tear slid down her cheek, soon turning into a torrent. 'Let's get this over with, okay?' She tugged her door open and got out.

Fenchurch sat there, watching her step over the wet tarmac to the side entrance.

Maybe Chloe had walked along this street during her short second life, holding hands with her new parents, skipping, running off.

How could they let her die? After the pain and torment the girl had been through. Just months after he and Abi had lost her.

Reed's car pulled in behind him, flanked by the squad car. Two local uniforms raced through the rain from the station. Larry Simon stepped out of the first car, his head bowed.

Fenchurch ground his teeth together as he trudged up the steps in the glow of the dim streetlights. He opened the security door and entered, his leaden shoes filled with concrete.

Abi paced towards an open door and knocked on the wood. 'PC Marks?'

'I take it you're Mrs Fenchurch?' An old copper looked out of the door, his uniform needing a good pressing. 'Call me Glyn.'

Abi reached for Fenchurch's hand as he arrived. 'This is my husband.'

He flashed his ID at Marks. 'DI Simon Fenchurch.'

'Right, sir.' Marks's eyes almost bulged. 'Met, eh? Come on in.' He held the door open and let them into the room.

Fenchurch nudged the door shut behind him and stayed by it. Force of habit.

Abi sat down in a cream armchair and fiddled with her handbag. 'I want to know everything about Chloe Holland.' Her voice was breaking. 'You might know her as Chloe Simon.'

Marks collapsed into another armchair and picked up a paper file from the side table. 'Sorry, I didn't investigate this case. That was . . .' He flicked through the file. 'Keith Holliday.' He glanced over at the door, as if he'd suddenly appear through it. 'He's a DI in Bristol now. I checked with them and he's in the Algarve on a golfing weekend or something.'

'Tell us what happened.'

Marks flicked through the thin file, like he was refreshing himself with the loose details. 'The girl was shopping in town with her mother and sister. Stepped out in front of a bus. That's it. The poor driver . . .'

Abi reached over for a tissue, but just held it in her fingers. 'Did she die on impact?'

Marks winced at a page of the report, his skin losing a bit of tone.

Fenchurch tore the file from Marks's hands. He flicked through, immediately regretting it. The photos were brutal, like something you'd see in an abattoir. A polka-dot school dress with a navy cardigan in among all that crimson. Couldn't even look at the rest. He flipped back to the start.

A photo of a girl was pinned to the front page, the blonde hair she'd inherited from him cut short. The same school uniform as in the crime-scene photos. She wasn't smiling, but there was a slight dimple on her cheek.

It was her.

Chloe.

Two months from them taking her and she was dead. Why rehome her just for her to die? Why?

Fenchurch stood and handed the file back. 'Was there an autopsy?'

'She got run over, sir.' Marks tossed the file onto the table. 'This is the file. End of story, far as I'm concerned.'

Fenchurch frowned at Abi. 'You said "sister".'

'Again . . .' Marks tapped a finger of the file. 'Just what I read in here.' His eyes danced between them, narrowing. 'What's your interest in this case?'

Abi took a long, deep breath. 'That girl was our daughter.'

Marks closed the file and sat back, sniffing. 'I'm not following you.'

Fenchurch paced over and stroked her arm. 'We believe that Chloe Holland is our daughter.'

Abi pushed his hand away. 'We don't believe it, Simon. She is. *Was.*' Fire burned in her eyes. 'Chloe was our daughter. She was kidnapped. We've . . .' She cleared her throat. 'We've recently discovered what happened.' She broke off, prodding her eyes.

Marks screwed up his face. 'What?'

'Like Abi said, Chloe was abducted from outside our house.' Fenchurch took the report back and jabbed a finger at the door. 'The Simons adopted her from the people who kidnapped her.'

'What, you think they knew about this? You *really* think they're involved in child abduction?'

Fenchurch walked over to the door. 'That's what I'm about to find out.'

———— ————

Instead of a kitted-out Observation Suite, Dorchester station had a tiny cupboard with a folding plastic chair and a two-way mirror. The room stank of rusting cleaning buckets and stale sweat. Through the smudged glass, Larry Simon was deep in conversation with his lawyer.

'Five minutes with him, Ab. That's all I need. Five minutes and I'll boot the truth out of him.'

'The truth you want to hear isn't the same as the truth you need to hear.' Abi adjusted her seat on the fold-up chair. 'He's an old man, Simon.'

Fenchurch sipped at his tea, more sugar than liquid. He wagged a finger at the mirror. 'How much does he know?'

Abi set her cup down. 'You think he's involved in the cover-up?'

'A girl like that doesn't just fall off the back of a bloody lorry.' Fenchurch finished the tea, already dizzy from the Red Bull. 'He must've known. If something's too good to be true, it usually is. You've got to check the gift horse's teeth.'

'Simon, I know you're angry, but just find out the truth, okay?' She grabbed his arm. 'I mean it.'

Fenchurch crushed his cup and tossed it in the overflowing bin, which reeked of stale yoghurt and rotting apple cores. 'You don't have to watch this.'

'I need to.'

'Do you want me to send Kay in?'

'Won't she be better in the room with you?'

'She'll keep me calm, I suppose.' Fenchurch went out into the corridor and rested his head against the wall, eyes shut.

Keep calm and don't kill anyone.

'Simon?' Howard Savage was waiting in the corridor by a notice-board, frowning at him. 'Alan Docherty called me. Are you okay?'

Fenchurch stood up straight. 'We found her, Howard. Chloe . . .'

'So I gather.' Savage tried a smile. 'Have you managed to get anywhere?'

Fenchurch snorted. 'I want to kill someone, Howard.' He ran his tongue round his teeth. 'But I'll settle for finding out what happened to my daughter.'

'Listen, from what Al Docherty told me, it really feels like there's a correlation between this case and my strategic work. It'll certainly fall into my lap at a later date, so I'd rather get in on the ground floor, if that's all the same?'

Fenchurch put his hand on the door handle, the brass warm. 'You're welcome to sit in.'

'It's the other way round, Simon. You're sitting in on my interview.'

Fire burnt in Fenchurch's gut. Then it flickered out, leaving just a flare of acid reflux. 'You know what? Normally I'd pin you to the wall and shout and scream and . . .' He let his shoulders sag. 'But right now, I just want to know what happened to my daughter and find out who I have to throw off Tower Bridge.'

'I'll ignore the allusion to vigilantism, Inspector.' Savage barged past him into the interview room and sat opposite Larry Simon. 'Sorry for keeping you, sir. My name is Howard Savage and I lead the Met's Trafficking and Prostitution Unit.'

'Whoa, whoa.' Larry's lawyer had his hands in the air. A tall rod of a man, his bald dome poking through a crown of red hair turning to rust. 'My client does not consent to answer questions relating to matters other than the fate of his late daughter.'

'Then your client will be arrested on conspiracy charges.' Savage got out a Moleskine notebook and opened it to a fresh page, pulling out an A4 sheet. 'Mr Simon has played a key part in the abduction of a child, hiding her from the law and, more importantly, her parents.'

'No. No, no, no.' Larry's tongue hovered between his lips, darting from side to side. 'This is *preposterous*. My wife and I adopted this child in good faith. Her parents were dead! We gave her a loving home and treated her like she was our own!'

'But she wasn't yours.' Fenchurch was resting against the door, hands clasping the handle tight. 'She was my daughter.'

'Chloe's been dead a long time.' Larry held out his hands, like he could ward off evil spirits. Or big cops. 'You can't just come in here and bring this all back up again. My wife and I had months of counselling to—'

'She was *my* daughter!' Fenchurch dug a finger into his chest. 'She was kidnapped from outside our home!'

The lawyer flashed him a toothy smile. 'And what proof do you have of my client's involvement?'

Fenchurch just about kept his voice level. 'Your client engaged a criminal enterprise and took our daughter off their hands.'

'I asked what proof you had of my client's involvement. Seems like it's none. Now, are we done here?'

Fenchurch held the lawyer's gaze. 'Chloe wasn't the first and she wasn't the last. But she was the first they took whose father was a serving officer. Me. I knocked on every door in north London looking for her!'

The lawyer was shaking his head, like that could change the past, change the truth. 'My clients adopted her from a legitimate agency.'

'Fresh Start?' Fenchurch stepped away from the door. 'Let me tell you a little story about where Fresh Start get their orphans from, shall I?'

Larry pounded his fist into the table. 'They're a legitimate business!'

'They kidnapped my little girl from outside our house in London.' Fenchurch held Larry's gaze until he looked away, his face flushing red. Shame or just anger? 'The first guy drugged her and passed her to another guy. Her hair was cut and her clothes changed. Then she was passed on to someone else. But this third bloke was a cop, you see? He found out a cop's daughter had gone missing. Didn't take a lot of calculus to work out he had her in the back of his car.' He left a pause. Larry just licked his lips. Over and over again, wetting and licking. 'She ends up here, in the arse end of middle England.'

'They're a legitimate business.'

Savage cleared his throat. 'We believe they may not be.'

'What? They . . . We didn't know. I swear, we'd been looking for . . .'

Savage coughed again. 'Mr Simon, you need to start talking.'

Larry looked at his lawyer, who flashed his eyebrows. He pinched his nose. 'We'd just lost our own daughter. Amanda died of leukaemia. In 2002. She was seven. A year before, I'd been in an accident and . . . well, my wife and I can't have children. Those are the cards we were dealt and this was the option we went with.' His face twisted into a snarl. 'It took us a year to get to the point of wanting to have another child. Then another two years to get through all the red tape. Then the system rejected us. This was our last hope in this country.' He wiped at his eyes. 'I just wanted my daughter back.'

'So you took mine.'

'I didn't take anybody's!' Larry slammed his fist on the table. 'They gave Chloe to us. They told us she'd had a difficult life. That she was traumatised. They told us she was broken apart by what happened to her parents.'

Acid spat in Fenchurch's gut. 'What did she think happened to us?'

'That her parents died in a car crash.'

'And you believed them?'

'We had no reason to doubt it. They had police reports and everything.'

Fenchurch snarled at Larry, 'You ever heard the phrase "Looking a gift horse in the mouth"?'

Chapter Thirty-Two

What, you still don't believe us?' Cheryl's jaw slackened, like she'd lost all motor control. 'They fooled us. If Chloe was . . . taken from you . . . We didn't know. I swear.'

Savage sat opposite Cheryl Simon and the Simons' lawyer. 'That all tallies with what your husband told us.'

Fenchurch pushed away from the door and walked over to her, standing too close probably, but he was past caring. 'How did you get in touch with Fresh Start in the first place?'

'An advert in the *Mail*. It took me a week to pluck up the courage to call the number.' She brushed her hair out of her eyes. 'They had an office in Poole and we visited them a couple of days after I phoned. They were very helpful, very thorough. They warned us we might not . . . might not get picked, but we did.'

Fenchurch sweated. Abi was just on the other side of the two-way mirror.

Cheryl swivelled round to glare at Fenchurch. 'When you lost your daughter, what did you and your wife do? Did you consider adoption? Did you?' Her lip curled up, twitching slightly. 'Do you know what it feels like to watch your flesh and blood rot away to nothing? Amanda went from a healthy girl to skin and bones in weeks. We tried everything but we couldn't save her.'

Another glance over at the two-way. 'That doesn't excuse this.'

'We needed to fill up a deep void in our lives. Fresh Start offered us the chance.' Cheryl's nostrils flared at Fenchurch. 'I'll ask you again, didn't you and your wife think about adoption?'

Fenchurch swallowed hard. 'It's a long story.'

'If you're telling me this lot aren't on the level . . .' Cheryl gasped. 'Jennifer, our daughter . . . We got her from the same agency we got Chloe. After . . . after what happened.' She composed herself, her lips pressed tight together. 'Jennifer's just finished her first year at university. Finishing up for summer, though her exams were over a long time ago.'

Savage gave a polite smile. 'Mrs Simon, we'll need to speak to your daughter in connection with this investigation.'

'Of course.' She looked round at Fenchurch. 'Inspector, if someone gave you a chance to wind the clock back, wouldn't you have taken it?'

'I . . .'

The door juddered open and Abi entered, standing beside Fenchurch, arms folded, face like thunder. 'I believe you.'

Cheryl gasped and covered her mouth, tears splashing down her face.

Savage nodded at Fenchurch. Abi could stay.

Cheryl wiped her cheeks. 'You would've done the same?'

Abi reached across the table to grab Cheryl's hands. 'When . . . when we lost Chloe, Simon and I split up. There was too much to deal with.'

'You're not still together?'

'We are. It took a long time, but we . . .' Abi pulsed her grip on Cheryl's hands. 'We came to an understanding.'

'Here . . .' Cheryl reached into her bag and pulled out an old photo album covered in dust. She rifled through it and handed it to Abi. 'This is Chloe.' She stabbed her finger on the page. 'There's not a lot. We thought we'd get more time with her.'

Fenchurch sat down and looked through with Abi. Like the photo on the case file, Chloe's hair had been cut into a short bob, still blonde. She didn't smile in any of the photos, but it was definitely her. Hit him like a knife in the gut. He stroked a finger on the pictures and whispered, 'My little angel.'

Abi flicked over. Another six of Chloe, including one with a smile, her cheek dimpling. Her mother's dimple. Definitely her, no question. 'Jesus, Simon.'

'It's okay.' Fenchurch ran his fingers over the photos again, as if that could give some contact with their lost daughter.

Abi got up, tears sliding down her face.

Cheryl reached over and clasped her wrist. 'If Chloe was your daughter . . . she . . . she was a lovely girl. Lovely. But . . . difficult. She had a darkness. The death of her parents had hit her hard.'

Abi's yelp punctured the silence. 'Christ!' She joined Fenchurch by the wall, folding herself into his embrace. 'Tell me what happened the day she died.'

'I'm not sure I can—'

'Tell me.'

Cheryl shut her eyes and exhaled softly, like a monk about to start chanting. 'She was always running off from me, very impulsive girl like that, but this day . . . This day, we were shopping in town. Chloe didn't look both ways. It was a bus. She didn't stand a chance.'

Fenchurch hugged Abi tight, pulling her close. Felt like he could break her, but he didn't want to let her go. Didn't want anyone to take her away from him.

Cheryl held up the photo album. 'I could have copies of these made, if you'd like?'

Abi broke off from Fenchurch and blew her nose. 'I'd really like that.'

⌣

Savage clapped Fenchurch on the back and leaned against the door Larry Simon was behind. 'I can't even think what's going through your head, Simon, but I think it's in our best interests if you leave now.'

'But we're—'

'You've got your answers. My team will validate these stories, okay?' Savage stood and buttoned up his blazer. 'As it stands, we're proving exactly what we knew. These poor people have been duped. The story DC Johnson told you about your daughter's abduction . . . Well, it is panning out.'

'I need to see this through.'

'You need to be with your wife, Simon.'

Fenchurch wanted to just punch through the wood and then punch and kick and scratch and bite and . . .

He shook his head, trying to throw the rage off. 'Are you going to catch the bastards who took her?'

'I listened to the interview with DC Johnson on my drive over here. It's a crying shame he's . . . well . . .' Savage wet his lips with his tongue, his brows creasing in. 'The tale he told, however, *precisely* matches what happened to Cassie McBride.'

'What?' Fenchurch frowned, his gut climbing up to his teeth. 'So these people shot her and Johnson?'

'It appears that way, yes.' Savage got a handkerchief out of his top pocket and wiped the sweat from his brow. 'Cassie was abducted from her home, aged nine. A year later, a random stop and search found her in the boot of a taxi, asleep and with another girl. Their hair had been cut short. You know the second girl as Rebecca Thurston.'

'When was this?'

'2006.' More dabbing, like Savage was waiting for Fenchurch to butt in. 'Sadly, Cassie's parents had passed away in the meantime. Cancer and . . .' He shook out the hankie, dust motes dancing about in the strip lighting. 'Suicide. Her father threw himself in front of a train.'

'I know the feeling.'

'Rebecca and Cassie went through a lot of counselling. Together. They remained close friends, struggling to get over their ordeal, not that they could ever recover fully, of course. When they were both six-teen, they moved into a shared house.' Savage stuffed the hankie away. 'Cassie's birth name is Melanie Edwards, but we obviously renamed her during the witness-protection process.'

'Protection from who? Who did you prosecute?'

Savage's upper lip trembled.

Fenchurch gripped his arm. 'You had suspects, right?'

'Oh, we've had a couple. Problem is, they just disappeared.' Savage clicked his fingers in the air. 'Poof, like that. They're either dead or hidden away somewhere.'

'I hope you strung up the car's owner.'

'Paul Temple and I prosecuted the driver of the taxi Cassie and Rebecca were in.' Savage sighed. 'But, as is so often the case, he didn't give up his accomplices. He got out of Belmarsh last year and moved to Greece. We couldn't link the money he retired on to anything illegal. Neither girl knew where they'd been kept. We never found the place.'

'And Blunden's lot were behind this?'

'We didn't know it was him.'

'Jesus.' Fenchurch rubbed the heels of his hands into his eye sockets. Wanted to squash his brain. 'That's what Chloe went through?'

'If it's any consolation, given the timelines, it appears she didn't suffer the same . . . abuse the other girls did. Cassie and Rebecca . . . well, you couldn't touch them without getting your eyes gouged out.'

'Thought they were drugging them while they . . . ?'

'Of course, but they told them their parents were dead and kept them hidden in a dungeon. They'd been in there a year, and they must've finished with them.'

'So why shoot her, Howard? Why now?'

'Someone must've spotted her. Wanted to close the door.' Savage bared his teeth. 'You know what these people are like. They treat these children like sex toys. Discard them when they're done with them. They needed to close the door in case it ever opened again.'

Fenchurch dug his hands into his skull again. 'We need to find these people, Howard.'

'And I'm doing my best, Simon.' Savage jerked his head around. 'It's not all bad news. We picked up another girl in March. Same circumstances as Cassie. We found her parents and reunited them.'

'But you didn't find these bastards?' Fenchurch clenched his fists, the acid burning at his gut again, and he got in Savage's face. 'You're nowhere near finding them, are you?'

'Not nowhere, just . . .' Savage smoothed his bald head, like his comb-over was still there. 'That man in there, he's our great hope. The first we've had in years. We've got access to the Fresh Start database, thanks to you. We will close in on them.'

'Let me help. I want to do my job.'

'I'm sorry, but I can't let you get in the way of a prosecution on this scale.' Savage patted Fenchurch's arm. 'There are other parents out there who've suffered the trauma you and Abigail have. But you need to be with her.'

⌣

Dorchester slept around the dark graveyard. Not even the thud of a nearby club or the reek of smoke from a taxi rank. Yew trees sucked in the glow of the street lights, leaving a thin shaft of light creeping over from the church's uplighters to illuminate a handful of graves.

Fenchurch ran his fingers across 'Chloe Katherine Simon', the words etched into a plain grey stone, worn by almost eleven years of English weather. 'We should get the name changed. Christ.'

Abi got up from her crouch and tossed the petrol-station flowers on the grass in front. She ran her hand over the stone. 'My daughter deserves better than these.'

'She'll get the best, love.' Fenchurch kissed her cheek. 'The very best.'

Fenchurch sipped at the Rioja, smooth and clean. Barely tasted of anything. He stared out of the kitchen window, his hip still burning from the long drive back. Red Bull still battered his guts, throbbed in his brain. He sat at the table and reached over to grasp Abi's hand. 'How you doing?'

'I'm okay. I think.' She blew on her peppermint tea and took a dainty sip. 'It's over. All those years, Simon. All that time.' She tightened her grip on his hand.

'It's all . . .' Fenchurch let the tears on his cheeks sit there. 'All that time, she was in bloody Dorchester. *Dorchester.*'

'We know what happened to her, Simon. It sounds like she was happy in her . . . her final few days.'

'She should've been here, Abi. Should've been playing with her friends. Going to your school, being embarrassed to have her mum as a teacher. She should've . . .' Fenchurch broke off and gulped wine like it'd dowse the flame in his guts. 'Howard said they're still doing it, Ab. These people. They're still out there, taking kids. People like us are still suffering.'

'Simon, you need to let this go.'

Fenchurch drank again, starting to taste the dark wine. Starting to dowse the fire. He wiped a droplet threading its way down the side of the glass. 'How could they not know?'

'They didn't, Simon. They lost a daughter.' She held his hand. 'After that, they just wanted to move on. It sounds like it was hell for them getting through the adoption process . . . We've been through what they went through without getting anything in return.'

'They shouldn't have done it with someone else's kid.'

'Simon.'

'Come on, love. They're as much to blame as the barbarians who took her.'

'They're not. After we lost Chloe, I thought about us adopting.' She gripped his hand tight. 'You wouldn't speak, so . . . We were in their situation. If someone had given me the chance with someone else . . . Look, I don't blame them.'

Fenchurch had a big gulp of wine, draining his glass. He got up and kissed her on the forehead. Then patted her stomach. 'We've got that chance now.'

Day 4
Day Shift
Sunday, 12th June 2016

Chapter Thirty-Three

*F*enchurch picked up Chloe and put her on the bench. 'There you go, petal . . .' He sat next to her and opened a bag of sweets, offering them to her. 'Your favourites.'

She grinned at him, her cheek dimpling. 'I'll not tell Mummy.'

Fenchurch stroked a hand through her hair. 'Good girl.' He took a wine gum from the packet.

'They're mine, Daddy!'

'Sorry, love. Can't I just have one?'

'Maybe one . . .' She wagged a finger at him, like a referee admonishing a naughty player. 'But that's it.'

Fenchurch popped the wine gum in his mouth and chewed, the sweet sticking to his teeth. Lovely. He sat back on the bench and wrapped his arm around his daughter, like she'd be there forever.

Some rotting Victorian buildings surrounded the open park on one side, sixties towers on the other. Bit of a disappointment, but then most inner-city parks were. A group of black kids played basketball, spinning and swivelling like they were on their way to the NBA.

Fenchurch waved over at them. 'You know what that is, pet?'

'Basketball, Daddy. Mylo did his show-and-tell on it last week.'

Show-and-tell? Bloody Americanisation . . .

Fenchurch clasped her tiny hand in his lumps of meat. 'What did I ask you to remember?'

'Our phone number?' Chloe's cheek dimpled. 'Can I get another sweetie if I get it right?'

'I think that's fair enough.' Fenchurch tightened his grip on her hands, like it would keep her with him. Like it would stop what's going to happen. Tears streamed down his face, dripping onto the tarmac at his feet like a heavy nosebleed.

'Daddy? What's up?' Chloe's smooth forehead puckered in the middle. 'Are you okay?'

'You knew our number, Chloe.' Fenchurch rubbed at his eyes, but he couldn't stop the tears. 'Why didn't you call?'

'Daddy . . . That's sore.'

Fenchurch let go and sucked in deep breaths. Couldn't smell her, couldn't . . . 'Chloe, you knew our number, I made you recite it all the time. Why didn't you call?'

'They said that you, Mummy, Grandpa and Granny were all dead.' Chloe's face collapsed in on itself, her eyes closing as her lips quivered. 'I didn't have Mumpy and Grumpy's number.'

Pain lanced Fenchurch's chest. Mumpy and Grumpy . . . Abi's bloody parents. How could I forget that?

'Why didn't you just call?'

'Maybe they didn't let me near the phone, Daddy. Did you ever think of that?'

The basketballers hit their moves on the court, a white kid slaloming through the tight defence. His slam dunk was about a foot short, barely touching the swaying tendrils of the net.

'Here they are!' Dad dumped himself in the seat next to Chloe and grabbed her cheek between thumb and forefinger. 'How's my favourite girl?'

'Grandad!' Chloe squealed. She hugged Dad tight, nestling into his chest. Then she peeked out. 'If I'm your favourite girl, you better not tell Auntie Rosie.'

'I'll tell her what I like, sweetheart. You're my favourite.' Dad winked at Fenchurch. 'Your mother's on her way over, son. How's my boy?'

'I'm fine, Dad. For once.' Fenchurch floated up off the bench, a good inch between his trousers and the wood. 'It's over.'

'What is?'

Fenchurch reached over and hefted Chloe up onto his lap, tears streaming down his cheeks. She didn't weigh anything. He kept floating in mid-air. 'I know what happened to her.'

'Is it really over, though?' Dad blew out a kiss at Chloe. 'I'll be in court tomorrow morning. Stabbing Flick Knife . . . What was I thinking?'

Over at the basketball court, one of the kids broke off on his own and jumped on a racer. Fenchurch glanced away, and when he looked back it had turned into a Volvo.

A man sat behind the wheel, face in shadow, his evil eyes trained on Chloe. 'Hey, little girl, do you want some sweets from me?'

'Go away, you stinky idiot!' Chloe snatched the bag off Fenchurch and raised it up, shaking it in the air. 'My Daddy already gave me some!'

Fenchurch got up and shooed him away. 'It's over.'

'We've won, Fenchurch . . . Your old man's still inside.' The car sped off across the grass.

Fenchurch looked over at his dad. 'I'll get you out of there.'

'Thanks, boy.' Dad ruffled Chloe's hair, just like he'd done. 'Your mother says she'll look after Chloe for us, okay?'

'Thanks.' Fenchurch lifted Chloe up in the air, making her squeal. 'Tell Granny that I miss her and I'm sorry I didn't get to say good—'

'. . . single by Richard Ashcroft. A real return to form, that record.' The DJ cut back to the music, a thumping disco beat and strings. 'Anyway, it's coming up to six o'clock and here's the news and sport with Jitinder.'

Fenchurch reached over to the clock radio, his hand hovering over the sleep button. Just give it a few seconds.

'Trouble between English and Russian fans erupted in Marseilles last night following the last-minute equaliser by Russia in the one-all draw in the teams' opening match of Euro 2016. UEFA have opened disciplinary proceedings against—'

He stabbed the button, killing the sound.

Bloody idiots. A little drop of foreign beer and you start smashing the place up.

He lay back on the bed, the matt flatness of the ceiling above. His back had straightened out after the drive back from Dorchester, each vertebra back in the right place. Just about. Then he let his eyes shut again.

Peace.

Relief.

It's over.

So why does it still sting?

Dad . . . Rotting in the cell in Leman Street, waiting for his day in court. Not a chance he'll get bail, with what he's supposed to have done.

CRASH.

Fenchurch opened his eyes, head thumping, the daylight burning through the curtains.

What the hell was that?

He put his foot down on the cool wooden floor, then eased himself over to the corner, avoiding the floorboard he'd spent an afternoon failing to fix. He hefted up the baseball bat and nudged the door open. The hall was empty. He stepped out and raised the bat to shoulder height.

THUD.

Nothing in the lounge. He crept over to the kitchen.

Abi was by the sink, sipping from a teacup, her lined eyes focusing on the past. Her left hand absently stroked her belly. She noticed him and stood, smiling. 'Morning.'

'Shit.' Fenchurch lowered the bat and let out a breath. 'It's just you.'

Her smile swapped to a frown. 'Who did you expect?'

'I heard a crash and thought . . .' Fenchurch shut his eyes. 'I thought someone had broken in.'

'I dropped a typewriter. It took one of those mugs with it.' The typewriter looked even more damaged than before. She held up some cracked cream pottery, the weird bird-like creature sliced down the middle. 'One of the ones we got in Scotland when we renewed our vows?'

'I liked them.' Fenchurch put the bat on the table and leaned over to kiss her. 'You okay?'

'I didn't sleep at all last night.' Fresh dark rings had puffed up around her eyes. She wiped the tears on her cheeks. 'You were right to keep looking.'

Fenchurch clutched her hand. 'Trying to make me stop was right. I should've grieved back then. You got it out of your system.'

'If you hadn't kept this up, we wouldn't know what happened to her . . .' She smeared the tears across her cheek. 'You had something to cling to. I had nothing. Just pushing you away, being a selfish cow.'

'You're the least selfish person I know.' Fenchurch crouched down to kiss her belly. 'We've got something else to worry about now.'

'Christ . . . How can we . . . ?'

'Because we have to.' Fenchurch brushed the fresh tears from her cheeks. 'Listen, I think we need to get out of the house. How about we drive out to Greenwich and walk around the park, maybe get something to eat in one of them lovely pubs over there? Maybe get a boat along the Thames?'

Abi gave a half-hearted shrug.

Fenchurch's shoulders fell. 'I take it that's a no?'

'Simon, I just don't know what I want.'

Fenchurch shut his eyes. 'Look, I should tell Dad about Chloe.' Disappointment leached off Abi's tiny nod. 'He's spent as long as I have searching for her. He deserves to know.'

She pecked his cheek. 'Go on, then.'

'Then we'll do something, okay?'

'That'd be nice.'

'I'll pick up some breakfast on the way back.'

——— ———

'Did you see the match, guv?' Steve sat behind his partition, the Leman Street entry area quiet as the grave, despite it being a Sunday morning. No sign yet of the exodus of drunks having slept it off. 'Thought I was having a low-level heart attack throughout that match, I swear. And that was a right kick in the bollocks at the end.' His lips pinched together. 'I mean—'

'Didn't see it. Sorry.' Fenchurch swiped his card through the reader. A red cross flashed up. He tried again. Red cross again. 'Steve?'

'Been doing that all morning. With that chump Martin letting that geezer die on his watch, that Abercrombie bird's made me update the whole database.'

Fenchurch swiped his card again, really ramming it into the slot. 'I should still be on the database.'

'Yeah, you might just need a new card, though.' The scanner hit green and Steve gave a thumbs-up. 'There you are. I swear, Roy Hodgson still hasn't got a—'

'Cheers.' Fenchurch pushed through the door and stomped down the corridor. He entered the stairwell and draped his lanyard around his neck.

Martin was in the entrance to the Custody Suite, looking like someone had dug him up from a shallow grave. The skin under his eyes had the texture of golf balls.

Daniel Connolly stood in front of the desk, head bowed. His giant body slumped, looked like he'd lost six inches.

Fenchurch kept his distance, just listening.

Martin spotted Fenchurch and held up a set of cuffs, the metal clanking. 'I am arresting you for the murder of Cassandra McBride. You do not have to say anything, but it may harm your defence if you do not mention, when questioned, something which you later rely on in court. Anything you do say may be given in evidence. Do you understand?'

Connolly curled his lips, baring his savage teeth at Fenchurch. Eyes screwed tight, a purple ring around the left. His expression said, You betrayed me. I gave you that information and you're letting me rot in here. He nodded at Martin. 'I understand.'

Martin gripped his shoulder and led him through the Custody Suite towards the cells.

Fenchurch climbed the stairs, shaking his head.

Did I betray him? What he told me started me off on the track that led to the truth about Chloe. Still, you don't shoot someone in cold blood and get away with it.

A voice bounced off the stark walls from above. Male, deep. Whisper-shouting. '—don't think we should, but okay.' Paul Temple was on the first-floor landing, speaking on the phone. 'I'll press for it.' He ended the call and gave Fenchurch a kind smile. 'Simon, I heard what happened. You okay?'

'Just want to put it behind us, Paul.' Fenchurch turned to the side, struggling to keep his voice steady and hide the tears. 'You know how it is.'

'I do, I do. Come here.' Temple grabbed Fenchurch into a tight hug, arms wrapped round his waist. 'I mean it, mate, I really can't imagine what you're going through.'

Fenchurch broke off and pointed back down the stairs. 'I see you got your man?'

'What?'

'Daniel Connolly?'

'Ah, right. Yes.' Temple's eyebrows danced up. 'Well, DI Mulholland and I agree that Daniel Connolly is responsible for the murder of Cassie

McBride on Friday evening. Thanks to your efforts bringing him into custody yesterday. Must've been tempting to keep him away from official channels?'

Fenchurch winked. 'Don't know what you mean.' He flashed his eyebrows. 'How's it going with my—'

Temple put a finger to Fenchurch's lips. 'You know I can't talk about your father's case.'

'So you're on that full-time?'

'Zenna Abercrombie shifted me from the Shelvey case, so yes, I'm afraid so.' Temple leaned against the banister. 'Ms Abercrombie passed Gerald Ogden on to me. Supposed to be the liaison, but it's like babysitting. He wants us to release young Victoria's body.'

'I already gave him the script.' Fenchurch shook his head. 'You know him, don't you?'

'As he keeps reminding me.' Temple waved up the stairs. 'Your boss isn't in a good mood.'

'He's usually in a shit one, so that's an improvement.'

Temple bellowed with laughter, the *hwa* bouncing off the walls. His brow creased. 'How you coping, mate?'

'It's over. I've finally stopped bashing my head against the wall.' Fenchurch gripped the banister tight and rested against it. 'Part of me is glad, but the rest of me . . .' He let out a deep sigh. 'The rest of me isn't finished with these bastards. Not by a long shot.'

'I thought you'd give up.'

'They're still at it, Paul. Howard Savage said they found a girl in March?'

'Right.' Temple's nod disagreed with his grimace. 'Howard shouldn't be talking about that, Simon. We're nowhere near a prosecution.'

'Well, I'm not giving up. These bastards still have a lot to answer for. I'm going to get them, Paul. Every last one of them. Be lucky if there's anything left for you to prosecute.'

'Well, anything I can do, mate.' Temple squeezed his shoulder. 'I've got to get back to Rose Court. No rest for the wicked, even on a Sunday morning.'

'See you around.' Fenchurch climbed the stairs two at a time, the metal ringing out, and pushed into the corridor.

The Incident Room door was open. The squad must've doubled overnight. Two shootings in two days. Amazing how the budget flew out of the window just like that. Didn't matter that they'd died, just how they went.

Fenchurch crept in at the back, lurking between Nelson and Naismith, but getting recognition from neither. Naismith had a scowl on his face like he'd eaten an off curry.

'—secured.' Mulholland stood at the front, flanked by Docherty. She swept her gaze around the room, adding a grin. 'Okay, so I need you all to document your findings. DS Ashkani has a list of open actions and will be coming around to allocate them. Okay? Thanks for your efforts here. It's not often we get to celebrate a victory like this.' She grinned around the room again. 'Drinks in the Conquest at five. Make sure you're there.'

Fenchurch stood back as the crowd dispersed. Nelson winked and sauntered off to his laptop at the far side of the room.

Docherty strolled over, deep in conversation with Mulholland, then stopped. 'Oh.'

Mulholland tightened her scarf. 'Simon, you shouldn't be here.'

Fenchurch ignored her. 'Boss, I need a word.'

'I need a coffee.' Docherty brushed Mulholland away and held the door. 'Walk with me.'

Fenchurch was half aware of Mulholland's glower burning into his back as he left the room. 'Boss, I take it you heard?'

'Sodding Dorchester. Never even heard of the place.'

'I need to speak to my father.'

Docherty stopped by the stairs and let out the mother of all groans. 'Simon, Dawn and DS Nelson interviewed him first thing. Paul's approved us charging him.'

'What? Boss, he was blind drunk. He shouldn't—'

'The duty doctor passed him fit for interview. Look, his motor was right next to Blunden's place.' Docherty screwed his face tight and groaned again. 'The murder weapon came from a set we found in his kitchen. It all fits into place.'

'This is—'

'That's him until his court appearance on Monday morning. Leave it.'

Fenchurch huffed out a sigh. Wrong attack. Switch it up. 'He needs to know what happened.'

'Christ.' Docherty stepped out of the way of a couple of uniforms skipping up the steps. 'Fine. You can go speak to your old boy.' He grabbed Fenchurch's arm, steel fingertips digging into soft flesh. 'But only about Chloe, okay?'

Chapter Thirty-Four

Martin gave Fenchurch a thumbs-up as he left the interview room and locked it behind him. Guy looked ready to reanimate as a zombie.

Docherty stayed by the door, giving him all ten fingers. Ten minutes.

Fenchurch grabbed his dad's hands, cold and clammy. He got a slight glance, then Dad's eyes were away again. 'How are they treating you?'

'I've been better, son.' Dad let go and sat back in his chair. 'Been a lot better.'

'I've got something to tell you.'

Hope glinted in Dad's eyes. Maybe that was just the strip lights. 'I'm getting out?'

'I wish.' Fenchurch sucked in breath like it was courage. He filled his lungs, but it seeped away. 'That Connolly guy you spoke to . . . he was working for Flick Knife. They were picking up kids. He told us they picked up Chloe.'

'I know, son. He told me.'

'It's not just that . . .' Fenchurch broke off, panting, the drums beating hard. He got his breathing under control, but they kept on pounding. 'They found out who I was and it spooked them. So they moved her on, gave her to an adoption agency.'

The whites of Dad's eyes lost some yellow in among the red veins. 'They didn't kill her?'

'They didn't kill any of them, Dad.' Fenchurch gripped the edge of the table tight. 'When they were done with them, they moved them on to this agency. Lied to them. Made sure the adopters kept them away from London and their past.'

'What?' Dad tried to lock eyes with Fenchurch, like when he told him about the birds and the bees. 'Chloe's alive?'

'A couple in Dorchester adopted her.' Fenchurch scraped at the tabletop, letting the tears slide down his cheeks. 'Dad, she died not long after they took her in. She was run over by a bus.'

'She's dead? Really?' Water filled Dad's eyes, his focus unwavering. 'Jesus Christ. All that wasted effort.'

'You were right to keep looking.' Fenchurch clasped his father's hands again. 'We know what happened to her.'

'That's enough for you, is it?'

'No, Dad, it's not.' Fenchurch folded his arms. 'But it's a start. We've spent eleven years looking for our keys in the place where the light is, not where we dropped them. She was in Dorchester, not London. Okay? We've got leads. Howard Savage is working it.'

Dad slumped back in his seat and smoothed down his moustache. His face was a lawn of salt-and-pepper stubble, blending into the thick brush. 'Oh.'

'What happened yesterday, Dad?' Fenchurch got no reaction from Docherty. No sign of him trying to shut him up.

'I don't remember, son.'

Docherty sat down next to Fenchurch. 'Ian, you need to tell us what happened yesterday.'

'When?'

'When do you bloody think? When you killed Flick Knife, you daft sod.'

Dad's nose wrinkled up. 'Doc, I didn't kill anyone.'

'So take us through what happened, then.'

Dad looked away. 'I "no commented" my statement, Doc.' Dad scratched at his moustache like it had fleas. 'Didn't want to incriminate myself.'

'You're as much of an idiot as your son.' Docherty thumbed at Fenchurch. 'Just take us through what happened.'

'I was at work, right?' Dad rasped a hand over his stubble. 'Got in early, like most Saturdays. Had the place to myself.' He scratched the sandpaper on his chin. 'I got a call from the front desk, so I went upstairs. Liam Sharpe was there. The journalist who did that piece.' More scratching at the stubble. 'We'd been working together, but it'd been on the QT, so I was a bit puzzled at him coming to the station. Anyway, he said some geezer had come forward.'

Docherty nodded. 'Daniel Connolly?'

'He'd seen the telly thing. The story in the *Post*. He was shitting himself, didn't want to be out in public, so we went to my flat.' Dad blinked slow and hard. 'He told us that Blunden led a child sex ring, kidnapping kids off the street.' He snarled at Docherty. 'And he told me what they were doing with those kids.' His gaze just passed over Fenchurch. 'He said they took Chloe.' He thumped the table. 'I saw red. He left, and I had a drink. That nice Scottish stuff you gave me.'

The stuff you bloody nicked.

'Dad, you should've come to me.'

Dad smoothed down his greasy hair. 'Do you think I don't realise that?' He huffed out a groan. 'But you and me, son, we're cut from the same cloth.'

Fenchurch settled back in his seat, arms folded. 'Dad, you—'

Docherty grabbed Fenchurch's arm and shut him up. 'Ian, do you remember anything after you started drinking?'

Dad smoothed down his moustache. 'When Connolly told me what he'd done I smashed the place up.'

Fenchurch grimaced. 'I saw.'

Docherty shook his head at Fenchurch. 'Then what?'

'Next thing I remember is being round there.' Dad rubbed at the back of his head. 'Someone hit me from behind, knocked me clean out. Next thing I know, Simon was tearing into the cab office like a raging bull.'

'You don't remember how you got there?'

'Sorry.' Dad's lips twitched slowly. 'Blunden was behind it all. He was the boss.' His crazed eyes blinked furiously. 'Connolly told me.'

'Did Blunden tell you himself when you stabbed him?'

'I didn't—' Dad's eyes flickered shut. 'If I stabbed him, I don't remember.' He grimaced and opened his eyes. 'I've no idea what happened.' He leaned across the table. 'I wish I could help, son.'

'Is there anything you remember? Anything at all?'

'It's just . . . gone.'

Docherty grabbed Fenchurch by the arm and led him away.

'Boss, I need to—'

'Simon.' Docherty ran his tongue through his teeth. 'I need you to back off. You need to keep yourself a good distance away from this, okay?'

Fenchurch stared around the corridor, looking for anything he could use. Leverage. A baseball bat. Anything. 'You should be letting Dad help, not locking him up.'

'Give me a break, Si.' Docherty gripped him by the shoulder. 'You've had some traumatic news. Go home and spend time with your wife. Try and cope like you didn't ten years ago.'

'Eleven.'

'Just. Go.'

Fenchurch turned into Barford Street and parked behind a Toyota SUV, the skinhead driver scowling at him. Tosser.

Bloody Docherty. Using him to get that information out of Dad.

Fenchurch put the paper bag on the roof and grabbed the coffee tray from the passenger seat, resting it alongside, the bitter aroma escaping the baking car.

Across the street, the patch of pavement where Chloe had been playing . . . Eleven years of misery and questions and confusion and hatred and break-up and resolution and . . .

Fenchurch wiped the tears from his cheeks and grabbed the coffee and pastries.

Whatever happened, happened. Time to move on.

He entered the building and climbed the stairs.

Whistling cannoned around the stairwell, some jaunty classical piece by Mozart or whatever, accompanied by the thunder of feet. His neighbour Quentin was jogging down. He inclined his shaved head at Fenchurch and bounced across the floor tiles. 'It's a glorious day, isn't it?'

Fenchurch smiled as he passed. 'I'll give you that cheque for the acid-cleaning deposit tonight.'

'Sure thing.' Quentin jogged on the spot. 'There's no hurry. They won't be in until November.'

'Okay, then. See you around.' Fenchurch trundled up the stairs, bathed in morning sunlight, careful not to spill any coffee. He put the breakfast on their welcome mat as he unlocked the door. It wasn't locked.

What the hell? Had I left it open this morning?

He opened the door and stumbled through. 'Abi?'

Silence.

He walked through to the kitchen and put the coffee and pastries down on the table. 'Abi? You in?'

Silence.

The *Post on Sunday* was all over the kitchen table. His press conference had been relegated to a distant memory now, though Liam had a story on the front about an ISIS cell in Clapham.

Chloe's room was empty, just a typewriter graveyard. 'Abi?'

In the bathroom, a trail of shampoo suds dowsed in puddles led from the shower cubicle.

Why wouldn't she have dried herself off? Why didn't she wash out the soap?

Fenchurch fumbled his phone from his pocket and dialled her number. The ringtone blasted out 'Human' by The Killers. Sounded like it was in the living room. Not like her to leave her mobile . . .

He walked into the hall, drums thundering in his ears. Her purse was on the chest of drawers. No sign of her keys.

Shit.

A muffled squeak came from behind him.

Fenchurch paced over to the bedroom door. He nudged it and it swung wide open. 'Abi?'

The same squeak, louder.

Fenchurch stepped in. 'You here, love?'

She was by the bed, a towel loosely tied round her, soap suds stuck to her upper arms, her hair white with shampoo.

A masked man held her in a sleeper hold, his gloved hand covering her mouth.

'Let her go!'

'You're still messing about, Fenchurch.' He spoke with the same robot voice as the phone calls. 'See what you've made us do now?'

Fenchurch couldn't breathe. 'I'm giving you one last—'

Crack. Something hit him from behind and Fenchurch tumbled forward.

Chapter Thirty-Five

Cold against his cheek. Wood. Creak. The floorboard, the broken one.

Head on fire. Feels like someone's clawed my skull apart.

Fenchurch opened his eyes and eased up onto all fours. The bedroom swam beneath him as he struggled to focus. A trail of water ran across the laminate to the doorway.

Shit. Abi!

He pushed himself up to standing. Then slipped back down to a crouch.

Jesus.

The baseball bat was on the floor, rolling around his feet. He picked it up and used it to push himself all the way up.

'Abi!'

Fenchurch stepped over to the door, woozy and dizzy. He used the bat as a crutch and staggered out into the hall. 'Abi!'

Silence.

His keys and phone were still there. He grabbed them.

The front door was hanging open. Fenchurch pulled it all the way and walked out into the stairwell. 'Abi!'

His voice echoed round. No other sounds joined it. No whispers of footsteps.

Dots of moisture lined the route down.

He set off down the steps, his right hand gripping the smooth wood of the rail as he descended, his left keeping the bat from clunking off the steps. At the bottom, the street door was wedged open. He stepped out into the bright morning and spun around.

A car screeched off at the far end of the street, heading right.

Fenchurch jogged off, stabbing at the screen on his phone.

'Guv?' Reed sounded like she was in a café. 'What's going on?'

'Kay, can you get hold of the CCTV for my street?'

Fenchurch rattled along the long Camden street, not stopping for the couple trying to cross the pedestrian crossing, and held up the Airwave. 'Kay, I'm at the end of Offord Road. I think. Which way do I go?'

Sounded like Reed was driving now. 'Hang on a sec.' Someone put her phone underwater.

Then a man cleared his throat. 'Sir, it's DC Naismith. DS Reed's on her way over. Take a right.'

Fenchurch hauled the wheel round and cut up a Merc on the mini-roundabout. He squinted up ahead. 'I'm heading to Pentonville, is that right?'

'Yeah, just before you get there, you should see a little industrial estate on the left. And I mean little.'

'Got it.' Fenchurch's tyres squealed as he pulled in through black bars. 'Sure it's here?'

'That's where the Toyota went.'

Fenchurch stopped the car and got out. He wheeled around, scanning the cars and mini-factories. Nothing looked like—

Wait.

A Toyota RAV4 sat behind a Mitsubishi van, the doors open.

Fenchurch jogged over. 'I've got it.' The keys jangled as he leaned in. Empty. He checked the boot, getting a click as it opened. An empty shopping bag. 'There's nobody here.' He stood up and looked around.

Could go through every motor there, but what would that give me? Nobody will have seen anything, they'll have just—

He swallowed.

Break the chain. They'll have transferred Abi to another car.

Bloody hell.

'Sorry, sir, but—'

'They've swapped cars.' Two CCTV cameras pointed across the car park, avoiding this spot. 'Clive, can you get the cameras here?'

'I'm doing my best here, sir. It's blocked. Hang on. There we go. I can see you. Give us a—'

Fenchurch waved at the camera.

'Got you.'

'Wind it back until the RAV4 arrives!'

'Right.'

'Do any other cars leave just after?'

'No.' He paused. 'There, gotcha.'

⌣

'Can you see the Morrisons yet?' Naismith sighed down the line. 'You should be right by it!'

'No.' Fenchurch piled along the road, the old train tracks running on the right, opposite beige-brick flats. He pulled towards a roundabout and the low-slung supermarket came into view. 'Right, got it now.' He swerved into the car park. 'At the back, you say?'

'Yeah, by the lorry entrance. It's a Lexus. Hang on, I've got a call coming in from DS Reed. Sorry.'

Fenchurch branched off into the layby on the right and dumped the Airwave on the seat.

A blue Lexus hugged the supermarket's walls, the engine still running.

Fenchurch got out of his car and shot off towards it.

A heavy man in a yellow vest blocked his path, hands raised. 'Can't come in here, mate.'

Fenchurch flashed his warrant card. 'Police. I'm looking for a—'

BOOM.

The Lexus erupted in a bright explosion.

Fenchurch hit the deck, hauling the guard down.

Flames climbed ten feet high, licking at the store's brick wall.

Abi . . . No . . .

Fenchurch rolled over, getting to his feet with a scraped knuckle. He darted over to the car. The air was on fire, felt like it could melt his skin. He tried to peer inside the car, the flames singeing his eyebrows and hair.

Bloody thing was empty.

He shrugged off his jacket and covered his hand, then opened the door. At least the central locking was off. Definitely nobody inside, front or back.

He jogged round to the boot. A good kick and it bounced open. He flicked it up with his covered hand and the mechanism winched it open fully.

Empty.

He staggered back away from the nuclear heat and sucked in smoke, coughing hard.

Abi wasn't in there.

One last look and Fenchurch jogged back to his car. He reached in and grabbed his Airwave.

'—there, sir?'

'The car's gone, Clive.' Fenchurch rested against the roof, still tasting soot. 'They must've shifted to another car here. Can you get anything?'

'This isn't *24*, sir. I can't access satellites. I'm trying to get the CCTV, but it's just the live feed.'

'Call DCI Bell.'

'Tried that. He's not talking to me.'

'Get Docherty to call him.'

'Right. I'll need to find him first.'

'Bloody find him!'

A car screeched to a halt behind him and footsteps rattled across the pavement.

Fenchurch swung round, raising the baton, ready to lash out. Docherty's Audi, Reed jumping out of the passenger side before it fully stopped.

She grabbed him in a hug. 'You okay, guv?'

Fenchurch collapsed into her arms. 'Someone's got her, Kay. I should've protected her.'

'What happened?'

'It's those warning calls. They framed Dad, and now they've got Abi.'

'It's okay, guv.' Reed let him go. 'We'll get her.'

Docherty was resting against the car, giving Fenchurch the up and down. The guard was scooshing a fire extinguisher at it. Like pissing in the Thames. 'I don't know what to say.'

Fenchurch's mouth was dry, felt like he could drink the North Sea. His Airwave chimed from his car. He reached in and answered it. 'Fenchurch.'

'Yeah, it's Clive Naismith again. Got some bad news, sir. I've lost the motor they transferred your wife into.'

'What was it?'

'That's the thing, it's just out of sight of the camera. And there's too many motors leaving the car park.'

'Right.' Fenchurch ended the call and glared at Docherty. 'This is the same MO as Chloe and Cassie. Swap the cars. Maybe they burnt

299

them out back in the day.' The flames were even higher now. He clicked his fingers. 'Connolly . . . He knows who did this, boss.'

Docherty shook his head. 'We can't have you in there speaking to him. The CPS will go ballistic.'

'Al, just give me ten minutes in there. I need to speak to him.'

'Si . . .'

'They've got Abi.'

'Bloody hell. Right, come on.'

Daniel Connolly rolled up his shirt sleeve to show a welt of bruises. His eye had developed into a proper shiner. 'Bet you hear this a lot, but this is police brutality.'

Docherty's mouth twitched. 'What happened?'

'You lot keep kicking the shit out of me, don't you?' Connolly drew a ring around his eye. 'See this? Got booted there by a big strapping lad. Must've been the same size as me.'

'What was his name?'

'Didn't even see him.' Connolly prodded the bruise again. 'The lights were out.'

Docherty rolled his eyes. 'So if the lights were out, how did you see he was a big strapping lad?'

'Because he picked me up off the bed in that cell and chucked me on the floor. You know how much I weigh?' Connolly pressed the flesh around the bruises, yellowing the purple. 'He'd have killed me if I hadn't caught him square in the knackers. You going to do anything about it?'

Docherty kept his focus on Connolly. 'That's not why we're here.'

'My life's in danger!' Connolly ran his hand down his arm, puckering the flesh. 'You need to protect me!'

Fenchurch made eye contact with Connolly, trying hard to smile. 'We need to ask you some questions.'

'About me getting a shoeing?'

'No, about your somewhat chequered employment history, you filthy little mongrel.' Docherty thumbed at Fenchurch. 'My colleague offered you a deal. You didn't take it. Why?'

'Why do you think, you bald arsehole?'

'Here's the deal, okay?' Docherty let the insult slide. 'You give up your paymasters and you walk. If we get your bosses, you walk. Even with the murder of Cassie McBride. No matter what else you've done.' He kept his focus on Connolly. 'New ID. New life. All you need to do is tell us exactly what's happened, who your bosses are and where they've taken these girls.'

Connolly rested his hands on his neck. 'What choice have I got?'

'None.' Docherty folded his arms, a smirk dancing across his lips. 'Son, we know you killed Cassie McBride. Marched up and shot her. You're going to prison for a very long time.'

'Look, I can't.'

Docherty reached across the table and grabbed a fistful of his shirt. He pulled Connolly towards him, yanking his gut into the table edge. 'What have they got on you, son?'

'What haven't they got on me?' Connolly choked as he jerked free. 'There's stuff that . . . Well, your immunity won't cut it.'

'Just tell us. Whatever it is, you walk. If it's good enough, you'll get a new life.'

Connolly smoothed out his shirt collar. 'I only ever dealt with Blunden.'

'Blunden told you to shoot Cassie McBride?'

'He'd got wind of her being back in London, wanted rid of her. I drove to near the girl's house, called a Travis car on this phone he gave me. She pulls up, I walk over and shoot her.' Connolly looked over at Fenchurch. 'Happy now?'

'I'm very far from happy.' Fenchurch narrowed his eyes at Connolly. 'Where are they taking people?'

Connolly jammed his hands into his armpits and lowered his head. 'A few years ago, I tried to run away. There's this service, yeah? You pay them half a million quid and you get a new ID, new passport and they take you away somewhere hot and cheap to live.' He swallowed hard. 'But Blunden caught me, took all the cash I'd saved up, then showed me what they had on me.'

'They?'

'The people Blunden was working with. I don't think he was in charge.'

Fenchurch narrowed his eyes further. 'Tell us where they take people and you can walk away. No strings.'

Connolly pointed around the walls of the interview room. 'I heard about that one that got shot last night. Johnson. That's because I put you onto him, right? You think whoever did that won't do it to me? You think whoever was in my cell last night won't try again?'

Docherty nodded at Fenchurch, then at Connolly. 'What are you saying?'

'I need to know you're serious. They'll kill me for this.'

'So tell us where it is they take people.'

'I'm not telling you, mate.' Connolly untucked his hands from his armpits and rested them on the table. 'But I will show you.'

Chapter Thirty-Six

Fenchurch kept his gaze on the road as he hit dial on his Airwave. 'I need an update on the whereabouts of Abigail Fenchurch.'

'Just checking, sir.' The line was filled with background chatter and typing. 'Sorry, no update, I'm afraid. There are units out across north London.'

'Thanks.' He sniffed. 'Fenchurch to DS Nelson. Where now?'

'Guv.' Nelson drove the squad car behind them. He waved his hand at Connolly in the middle of the back seat, leaning forward. 'Left here.'

Fenchurch turned off the Old Kent Road onto a Peckham street still stuck in the Del Trotter era. 'Then where?'

'He says it's just round the bend, guv. Only going to tell us when we get near.'

'Charming.' Fenchurch drove on with a deep sigh. 'Heard anything?'

Reed was in the passenger seat, texting away. 'Nobody's heard from her, guv.'

Fenchurch slumped back in his chair, tried to ease out his thighs. So much driving . . .

The Airwave buzzed again. 'Left here, guv.'

'Here?' A lane running between a low blue office block and a sprawling Royal Mail depot. 'Looks like a rat run, Jon.'

'Says it's not far, guv. Left at the end.'

Fenchurch took the turning and trundled down the road, eyes peeled for any suspicious activity. He stopped and indicated left, waiting for Nelson's car to join them. 'What do you make of this geezer, Kay?'

'I'm always suspicious of Greeks bearing gifts.'

Fenchurch pulled left onto the main road. 'Well, he's driving me around the bend.'

'Says it's a right now, guv.'

Fenchurch drove through an ancient part of London, Victorian brick mills and factories on the left now restored to flats, across from some post-war factory units still in service. 'How much further?'

'Pull in here.'

Fenchurch stopped opposite a lock-up, wedging his Mondeo between a Porsche Cayenne SUV and a black cab. He spoke into his Airwave. 'Serial Bravo, converge on my location on Curtis Street. Do not follow or enter any properties without my express permission. And for God's sake, keep yourselves out of sight.'

'Loud and clear.'

Fenchurch stuffed the Airwave into his jacket pocket.

Just up the road, Nelson hopped out of the squad car and stretched, before opening the back door.

Connolly squinted into the morning sunlight, hunched over on the back seat. 'I ain't getting out until I know it's safe.'

Fenchurch led Reed over to them. 'It's clear.'

'How do I know that?'

'You've been warned about any funny business, sunshine.' Fenchurch hauled him out of the car and spun him around. 'See?'

'Right.' Connolly lowered his shoulders and swallowed. He tugged his hair down his forehead. 'You sure it's safe?'

Give me bloody strength. Fenchurch thumbed behind him. 'Why did we snake around back there?'

'Because we might've been followed.' Connolly was paying particular attention to the bare wall of the mill towering above, just one window overlooking them. 'And I don't know who might be here already.'

'Let's just get this over with, shall we?'

Connolly slouched across the road, his cuffs dangling in front of him, and paced through the factory car park, cast in shadow and still damp from overnight rain. He stopped outside the fifth door along. The windows were painted black, the door covered with the sort of mechanical security a medium-scale drug dealer would install. He licked his lips as he gave the area another once-over. 'Doesn't look like this place has been used for a few months.' He swallowed and glanced at Nelson. 'Keys.'

Nelson held up a keyring, jammed with about twenty keys. 'Take your pick.'

Connolly grabbed it from Nelson and started unbolting the doors, his cuffs rattling. 'We lost a girl on her way to Fresh Start, back in March. You lot picked her up.' He undid another bolt. 'Blunden closed this place down, told us to keep clear of here.'

Still quiet, just the usual traffic noise from the main road.

Connolly glanced up at the brick tower, still visible from the yard. 'Course, I've stayed away, but you never know who's watching, though.'

'They haven't changed the locks.'

'Don't want to draw any attention to themselves.' Connolly undid the large horizontal bolt. 'The good news, though, is there's no CCTV. For obvious reasons.' He crouched down to undo a padlock, dropping it on the pavement. 'That's us.' He hauled the door open and reached inside.

Lights flickered on, subtle downlighters illuminating antique furnishing, like a West End designer-kitchen showroom. Four large cots lined the far wall, next to a bookshelf full of Harry Potter books and kids' DVDs.

Bitter saliva crawled down Fenchurch's throat.

The sort of place you'd keep children for six months to a year before sending them out to their eventual destination. The sort of place you'd keep children while you—

'Cost a pretty penny to do up, I can tell you.' Connolly waved a hand around. 'No expense spared . . .'

Fenchurch pointed at a staircase leading into a basement area, shining mirrors and fairy lights lining the way. 'What's down there?'

'Place is a lot bigger than you think.' Connolly thumped at the floor. 'Must be under all of the units—'

BANG.

Connolly toppled backwards, clutching his shoulder. He hit the door, blood pouring out of an open wound on his neck.

A motorbike droned off.

Chapter Thirty-Seven

Not this bloody time!

Fenchurch sprinted towards the road, Airwave to his mouth. 'Serial Bravo, shooter is on a red Honda motorbike. Repeat: a red Honda motorbike!'

Over to the left, the bike was closing on the junction with the main road, swerving out into the traffic and nearly hitting a white van. Blue lights throbbed from the opposite direction.

Fenchurch battered down the pavement and skidded to a halt at the junction. The motorbike swerved to the right, heading the way they'd driven. Another siren blasted out from behind him.

There.

A path ran between the Royal Mail yard and an office block. He bombed down, his feet splashing in the puddles, legs burning.

Not again. Not another stupid death. Not the only lead we've got.

He cut out onto the main road. The bike was at the junction, pulling a tight three-pointer, boots kicking up spray from the road. Looked male under the leathers. Big, too.

The squad car flashed towards it, siren wailing.

Fenchurch darted after the bike, baton out. He swung at the motorcyclist's helmet, cracking the baton off the plastic. The rider tumbled to the ground, the bike toppling in the opposite direction.

Fenchurch stepped forward and swung out again. Just missed.

In a flash, the rider was on his feet, reaching into his pocket.

Fenchurch lashed out and caught the cyclist under the helmet, sending him back down again. He vaulted over the prone motorbike, which was growling in the morning air, and landed knee first on the attacker's back. He grabbed his wrist and twisted it round, pushing it into his coccyx. He cracked the helmet off the tarmac.

Fenchurch got up and pulled the choking motorcyclist to his feet. He hauled off the helmet.

DC Clive Naismith, bruised and bloody.

Fenchurch almost let go. 'You?'

'You're a bit slow on the uptake, Fenchurch.' Naismith's fingers were reaching for his pocket.

Fenchurch lashed out with the baton. 'No, you don't.'

Naismith yanked his hand away.

Fenchurch raised the baton. 'Any more of that and you know what to expect, okay?' He reached with his left hand and tore open the pocket. A pistol poked out, the same German thing Clooney had shown him, altered beyond recognition, the exact same model that Connolly had tried to shoot him with. He grabbed Naismith by the lapels. 'Where the hell is my wife?'

Naismith gobbed at him, warm spit splattering his cheek.

Fenchurch swiped Naismith's legs and pushed him onto the ground. 'Where is she?'

'Piss off.'

Fenchurch smashed Naismith's head on the concrete, the blue lights bouncing off everything.

Feet thumped over the pavement and hands hauled Fenchurch back, digging into his armpits. 'Easy, easy. We'll take him from here.'

'Get him back to Leman Street, okay? Now.'

***

Fenchurch sprinted up the street and veered to the right, his knee just about giving way as he passed the front of the warehouses.

Reed was on her knees, trying to keep Connolly alive. Blood plastered her cream blouse, soaking into her trousers. 'Come on, Jon. Start it!'

Fenchurch stopped beside them. 'What's going on?'

Nelson held Connolly from behind, his giant Samsung mobile in front of the giant's lips. 'Trying to get a dying declaration from him.'

Fenchurch sucked in breath. 'Shit, it's that bad?'

'It's not good.' Reed cradled Connolly's head. 'Daniel, I need you to tell us it again.'

Connolly spluttered blood down his chin. He rubbed his bloody gums, like a boxer without a mouth guard. 'Who . . . who did this?'

'Clive Naismith.'

'Naismith? What?' Connolly coughed again. 'I told you we should be careful . . .'

Nelson put the phone in front of him. 'Tell him what you just told us.'

'My name is Daniel Connolly and this is my dying declaration. Clive Naismith . . . killed Frank Blunden. I was there. We were told to frame Ian Fenchurch. There is a video recording on my phone. The passcode is four, two, three, one.'

'Why did you kill Blunden?'

'He's not got long to live. That cancer.' Connolly gasped in some air, his mouth twisted into a grimace. 'Loose lips sink ships and all that. But we could frame your father at the same time.'

'Jesus . . .' Fenchurch leaned back against the cold brick and felt his breath escape. 'Thought you only dealt with Blunden?'

'I lied. I regret that now.' Connolly waved a faltering hand at the building. 'Inside.' A glob of blood landed on his cheek. 'Behind a radiator downstairs. Near the bathroom. There's . . . there's some video.' His head lolled into Nelson's lap.

'Keep him alive, Jon!' Fenchurch sprang forward and raced over to the building.

'Forensics, guv!'

Bugger forensics.

Fenchurch clomped over the floor, snapping on a pair of gloves as he thumped down the stairs, Reed's footsteps behind him, heels digging into the wood. He burst out into a corridor stretching another thirty metres or so, lined with mirrored doors like a really long changing room. 'Where's the bathroom, Kay?'

'I don't know.' Reed tried a door. A six-foot bed lay in the middle of a small room, clean black sheets and duvet covered with a thin layer of dust. 'Oh, Jesus Christ. What is this place?'

Fenchurch tried the next door. Black toilet and basin, a shower in the corner. Like something in a Wall Street film. 'Well, here's the bathroom . . .'

The light in the corridor was poor. Fenchurch squinted. The walls were painted grey, radiators in the same colour every few doors.

Wait, what's that?

Fenchurch crouched down and scrabbled away at the wall behind a radiator, about halfway between the two rooms. He got out his phone and switched the torch on, shining it down the back. A panel wedged next to the metal brackets. He flicked at it with his baton. The front tumbled to the floor, along with some bits of plastic. 'What the hell's that?'

Reed reached down beneath the radiator and picked them up. 'SD cards, guv.'

'Shit. We need to get Mick Clooney out—'

'Just a sec, guv.' Reed fiddled with the back of her mobile and stuck the first card in. The screen lit up her face. 'There's a lot of files on here.' She tapped at the screen, then held it up side-on so they could both see. 'Video files, guv.'

Looked like the room they'd just been in. Still footage, like it was on a tripod. A girl lay on the bed, eyes closed, legs wide. Naked. She couldn't have been any more than eight or nine. A man thrust away at her, greying hair on his muscled torso, his head just out of sight.

Fenchurch covered his mouth as sick climbed up from his gut. 'Jesus Christ . . .'

Reed slid the footage further on, the pace ramped up and harder. The man's head rolled forward.

'Pause it!' Fenchurch snatched the phone from Reed and stabbed at the screen. The image froze, the man mid-thrust at the child, his face in the shot a mixture of ecstasy and pain.

Gerald Ogden.

Chapter Thirty-Eight

Fenchurch stood on Austin Friars, the City lane Sunday quiet. Not a soul around, not even a banker or lawyer earning a few extra quid. The Ogden & Makepeace sign still glowed in the shaft of morning sun crawling down the lane. He held up his Airwave. 'Fenchurch to Nelson. Any movement at his house?'

'Receiving, guv. There are people living here, right?'

Fenchurch groaned. 'I'm taking that as a negative.' He put the Airwave down.

Which means Ogden's here.

Or he's disappeared.

Half a million quid and he's off to Connolly's hot and cheap place, new identity.

Reed wandered over, sipping from a Pret tea. 'What's the plan?'

'We wait on Clarke. It's his patch.'

'Guv.'

A silver Audi pulled up and DI Clarke got out, his tan looking fake in the bright morning. 'We meet again.'

'You want to lead in here?' Fenchurch shook his hand. 'It's your patch, after all.'

'Let's not get into that sort of rubbish.' Clarke stuck a hand on his shoulder. 'I can't imagine what you're going through.'

Fenchurch brushed his hand away. 'Forget it.'

'I'm here to support, okay?' Clarke pulsed his grip, an earnest grin spreading across his face. He put his hands in his pockets. 'So what's the plan?'

'We've got him surrounded.' Fenchurch looked around the area. 'Four officers over here. Two round the back on Old Broad Street. Squad cars on Bishopsgate and Moorgate.'

'Should be enough.' Clarke flashed a grin. 'Failing that, we could instigate the ring of steel.'

'That's overkill.'

'What you talking about?' Reed sipped her tea, eyes like piss holes in the snow. 'Ring of what?'

'DI Clarke's lot can lock the City down, if they want. Stop anyone getting in or out.' Fenchurch spoke into the Airwave again. 'Serial Bravo, are you in position?'

'Sir, Old Broad Street is secured.'

'All units in Austin Friars. We are going in now.' Fenchurch let Reed go first.

She put her empty cup on a squad car's roof and marched down the ancient street, past the praying monk and round the bend. Over in the courtyard, a group of workers stood on steps, sucking on cigarettes, breaking off eye contact as soon as it was made.

Reed thumped on the front door and clenched her jaw. 'Those videos . . . First gig I had as a DC, we raided this paedo's house out in Southend. His computer was full of that sort of shit. Hundreds of thousands of pictures, thousands of videos. Would've taken him a hundred years to look through them all, let alone . . . you know.' She gave a wanker gesture. 'None of them with him in it, mind.'

'You had to look through them, right?'

'Standard procedure. Twenty of us spent twelve weeks, guv. These people. I swear . . .'

'You're after me in the queue, okay?'

The door flew open. Gerald Ogden stood there, dressed like he was running a start-up — jeans, brogues and a shirt under a jumper. A frown twitched across his forehead. 'Officers . . . What are you doing here on a Sunday?'

'I was going to ask you the same thing.' Reed raised her warrant card and stepped inside the building. 'My name is Detective Sergeant Kay Reed of the Metropolitan Police Service. Gerald Ogden, I request your presence at a police station to answer some questions—'

'What? This isn't about Victoria's body?' Ogden's gaze strayed over to Fenchurch. 'What the hell's going on?'

Reed grabbed his forearm. 'Down the station, sir.'

'I want my lawyer!' Ogden's shoulders slouched and he let Reed lead him off. He stopped at the door. 'Look, I'm the only one here. I need to lock up.'

'On you go, sir.'

Ogden stepped over to the door and reached in, rustling a set of keys.

The officers were still in place down the street. Fenchurch beckoned them over.

'Shit!' Reed shouted.

The door was shut and Ogden missing. Reed was hauling at the handle. It didn't budge. 'He got in and closed the door, guv.'

'Bollocks!' Fenchurch spun back round.

'That backs onto Old Broad Street?' Clarke pointed the way they'd come. 'Follow me!'

Fenchurch set off, keeping pace with Clarke as he hopped up onto the pavement, and screamed into his Airwave, 'Serial Bravo, we have lost the suspect! Rendezvous on Old Broad Street! Over!'

Clarke raced ahead of him, his stride at least half as long again. 'Left at the end.'

Fenchurch swung out onto Old Broad Street and turned towards the heart of the City, passing an almost-empty Tesco Express and a vacant new-build office block.

A revolving door spun slowly to a halt. Clarke stood next to it, wheeling around. 'He's come this way . . .'

Two red-faced uniforms jogged up, holding their hats flat to their skulls. 'Sorry, sir, we were up the other end.'

Fenchurch gripped the Airwave. 'Control, send a unit into the entrance two on from the Tesco Express on Old Broad Street. Urgently.'

'Will do.'

Fenchurch put the handset away. Clarke was jogging down the street, the uniforms following.

Ogden can't have gone the way they'd come. So where was he?

A tall tower climbed into the sky over the road, reflecting the dark clouds. Didn't even know which bloody one it was, there were so many now. A couple were arguing, the woman jabbing a finger at the man. Just behind, a figure was darting down a lane.

'Got him!' Fenchurch burst off, sprinting hard, shouting into his Airwave, 'He's gone down the lane opposite my last location!' He followed the lane's curve round to a crossroads, the path heading onwards.

Which way now?

Fenchurch looked down the other lane running from Old Broad Street. Empty. Footsteps pounded behind him, heading the other way.

Fenchurch spun round and took Ogden's only path, bursting out onto Bishopsgate, thick with taxis and buses. Roadworks, old buildings and new skyscrapers.

Left, right or straight on?

There! Ogden was getting into a cab, just a few metres away.

Fenchurch sprinted over and grabbed the door. He pulled it open and reached a hand in, grabbing Ogden's cheek. Got a kick in the shin. He grasped at Ogden's throat and hauled him out of the cab, throwing him down onto the pavement. 'You filthy animal! You're nicked—'

A boot up the arse sent Fenchurch flying, tumbling over Ogden. Pain burned through his knees as they clunked onto the slabs. Fenchurch swung round, fingers reaching for Ogden. He caught fresh air.

Ogden was up and away, running north towards Shoreditch. Fenchurch got up.

An angry cabbie blocked his path. 'What the hell are you—'

'I'm police!'

The taxi driver spat in his face. 'Dirty scum bastard!'

Fenchurch barged him out of the way and ran off after Ogden. 'All units, I'm on Bishopsgate, following the suspect towards Shoreditch.' He wiped his cheek mostly free of second-hand saliva. 'Can any units in the vicinity please arrest the cab driver with his door open?'

Up ahead, Ogden was cutting across diagonally, heading for the base of the Heron tower, the bulbous mass of the Gherkin reflected in the glass.

Fenchurch crossed early at the black 100 Bishopsgate hoardings, still no sign of the tower breaking ground level yet.

If Ogden was staying on Bishopsgate, where the hell was he going? The pavement opened out on the left, a few people bursting out of Liverpool Street station.

Shit.

Fenchurch gasped into his Airwave, 'Suspect is heading for Liverpool Street. All units.'

'Want us to follow or take this cabbie back, guv?' Reed, out of breath.

'Take him to the station, Kay. If there's any cars, the suspect is on foot. He's just passed the Heron tower now.' Fenchurch crossed the road and cut along the shadow of the tower block, sprinting past the square pillars.

Ogden snaked to the left, just out of eyesight.

The Airwave crackled. 'Guv, we're in a squad car, heading to your location.' Reed again.

'Good.' Fenchurch sped up, taking the slight left incline and barrelling on.

Shit. No sign of Ogden.

He stopped opposite Liverpool Street, the escalators whirring and spitting out the underground's sweet-sweat smell. Maybe he'd taken the back entrance into the station. Fenchurch crouched low and peered in. Just a stag party weaving their way out, a dwarf handcuffed to a man dressed as Snow White.

Ahead, Bishopsgate opened out, a raised pavement to the left of it. No sign of him. Which meant . . .

Fenchurch turned right. Devonshire Row crept away, a narrow lane between two old blocks.

'—you friggin' maniac!' an Australian voice cannoned out.

Fenchurch crossed the road and sprinted down the street, his feet clacking off the double yellows marked onto the cobbles.

A squat man with a rugby-playing physique stood in the lane, glaring behind him.

Fenchurch caught his attention, huffing in breath. 'Police. Did a man in his fifties come this way?'

'Just about pushed me over, mate.' The Aussie thumbed further down the lane. 'Headed that way.'

Fenchurch set off again, his legs like concrete.

Ogden squeezed past some Japanese tourists, sending a huge camera and its owner tumbling over with a smash.

Fenchurch sprinted over and burst out into Devonshire Square, four sides of brick buildings with a road in on the far side. Old mills or something, now turned into organic cafés.

An engine thrummed behind a latticework of trees, their leaves obscuring the view.

Fenchurch clambered through just in time to see Ogden getting into a Range Rover. The car shot off out of the square. He screamed into his Airwave, 'Suspect's in a car leaving Devonshire Square!'

'Get down to Cutler Street, guv! We'll pick you up there!'

'I'm dead on my feet, Kay.'

'Wait, we've got—' CRASH. 'Guv—'

Fenchurch set off again, the fire in his legs climbing up his hips and back. His kneecap felt like it'd fallen off. He hobbled past a long row of pleached trees, their branches flattened out. The brick mills and seventies office blocks merged into the last ungentrified area in the City. Blue lights flashed at the base of a primeval tower hugging a newer Travelodge.

Fenchurch found another inch of energy and raced over.

The front of the Range Rover was mangled into a silver Passat, which hadn't taken too much of a battering.

Reed got out of the Passat, rubbing at her head, her hair matted with blood. She leaned against the side of the car, like she was going to topple over at any minute. She blinked at Fenchurch. 'Ambulance is on its way, guv.'

'Stay there, okay?'

A squad Mondeo pulled up, light dancing, and two burly officers tore out. Fenchurch joined them by the Range Rover. The driver was unmoving, his head stuck to the steering wheel. The nearest officer felt for a pulse and gave Fenchurch a shake of the head.

Fenchurch opened the back door.

Ogden's head between his knees, his chest heaving.

Fenchurch grabbed his right arm and hauled him out of the car. He pushed him face down on the tarmac and got out his cuffs. 'Where's my wife?'

'I've no idea what you're talking about!'

Fenchurch waved at the second officer to cuff Ogden. The back seat was empty. He reached into the driver's side and snatched the keys, then hobbled round and unlocked the boot, thunking it open.

Empty.

Bloody hell.

Fenchurch called Clarke. 'Have you been through the office yet?'

'Two employees here, that's it. They say they were working with Ogden and he just ran off.'

'Cheers.' Fenchurch dialled Nelson's number. 'Have you found her?'

'We've been through the whole house, guv. Completely spotless. Not even a hidden panic room.'

'. . . that you've found.' Fenchurch pocketed the device and grabbed Ogden by his shirt, hauling him to his feet. Another squad car pulled up and spilled out two officers. 'Get him back to Leman Street, now.'

'Sir.' The first one stuck Ogden in the back, behind the driver's seat.

Fenchurch got in next to Ogden. 'You're going to help me find my wife, okay?'

'I've no idea what you're talking about.'

'You'll be singing by the time I'm finished with you, you dirty pervert.'

The front doors shut and Fenchurch whizzed on his seat belt. The car shot forward and bundled along the side street. They pulled up at the end, indicating right. The car turned onto Middlesex Street. Could just about see the station from here.

Two white vans were coming down the opposite street, the front one not looking like it was going to stop.

Fenchurch grabbed the door handle. 'Shiiiit!'

CRASH.

The van battered into the side of the car, sending Fenchurch flying, the seat belt digging into his shoulder.

The van's driver got out and opened Ogden's door. He helped him towards the second van. Ogden tripped halfway over. The masked driver pulled him to his feet.

Fenchurch tried to move but the seat-belt mechanism was locked. The door was bent in on itself.

The driver tore open the second van's side door. A foot lashed out, cracking into his chest. He grabbed the leg and pulled someone out.

Abi, wriggling and kicking.

Fenchurch pushed against the mangled door, broken fists cracking off the glass. Still not shifting.

The driver pulled out a gun and pointed it at Abi. She raised her hands and got back into the van. Ogden and the driver followed her inside and it screeched off.

Chapter Thirty-Nine

Hold still!' The paramedic reached across from the far side and cut away at the seat belt with some brutal scissors. 'These aren't designed for this sort of work.'

Snip. Fenchurch struggled to stay still. Snip. Snip. He hauled at the seat belt and pulled the top half through the catch, slackening it off and squeezing out. He followed the paramedic onto the pavement and leaned against the squad car, as battered and broken as he felt. His body screamed like he'd been in a car crash.

Oh.

Back down the street, another paramedic tended to Reed. An Audi pulled in between them.

'Si?' Docherty got out and jogged over. 'Jesus, are you okay?'

Fenchurch looked down at his clothes. Didn't look too bad. He put a hand to his face. Covered in blood. 'I almost had her, boss!'

'Abi?'

'She was in that van. Ogden's lot have definitely got her!'

Docherty got out his Airwave. 'Jason? It's Alan Docherty. I need an urgent feed of CCTV from the corner of Middlesex Street and . . .' He swung round. 'Cobb Street.' He shook his head. 'For the whole city, you tube! And now! No, not to him!' He killed the call. 'Swear that fat bastard gets worse.'

Down Middlesex Street, the tall Bank of America building drowned out the surrounding council blocks.

'I almost had her, boss . . . That bloody seat belt . . .'

'That seat belt saved your life, you tit.' Docherty grabbed his arm. 'Let's get you patched up back at the ranch, okay?'

My jaw shouldn't click like that . . .

Fenchurch rested against the back of the chair in the Leman Street CCTV suite. His thighs and calves burned, his skin aching where the stitches pierced it. 'Is Bell still playing silly beggars?'

'No, guv. Here we go.' Reed pulled up the footage on the giant screen, a greyscale rendering of the quiet City back street. She paused it and drew a box around the licence plate on the van that drove off. 'I can run this against the Auto Number Plate Recognition system.'

'Go for it.'

Reed motioned over the big screen, filled with a map, a crooked red line leading east from the City. 'That line joins the ANPR hits we've got.'

'Is that live?'

'It is, but . . .' Her forehead crumpled like the car. 'Sorry, guv. The last hit is twenty minutes ago.'

Fenchurch slouched forward, his hands gripping the chair back. 'So we've lost it in bloody Millwall.' He sighed. 'Okay, Kay. See what else you can dig up.'

An almighty din droned through the glass. *The party's already started.* Fenchurch pushed into the meeting room, the door juddering open.

Docherty was hovering by the whiteboard, pen in hand. He put the cap back on and tossed it in the air. 'Any update on the CCTV?'

Clarke fiddled with his mobile, lips pinched tight. Savage stood behind, fidgeting with his jacket buttons. The table was covered in papers and takeaway coffee cups.

Fenchurch sat next to Clarke. 'We lost him at Millwall, boss.'

'So we've just lost this dude?' Docherty perched on the end chair, side on. 'No idea who else was in the van?'

Fenchurch grimaced. 'My wife.'

'Right. Aye.' Docherty picked up a cup and sipped through the lid. 'Buggeration.'

Fenchurch narrowed his eyes at Docherty. 'Have you been through Connolly's mobile yet?'

'It's with Michael Clooney. Don't worry.' Docherty put his feet up on the table and waved his hand around the room, settling his finger on Savage. 'Anyway, DCI Savage has been helping us go through the files you found.'

'Why? I don't think that's the priority here.'

'Si, just let him speak, okay?'

'Inspector, you've unearthed something quite, quite barbaric.' Savage flipped open a document. 'This evidence confirms our belief that Mr Ogden's in a fairly senior position in this group.' He rifled through the pages. 'These horrific photographs show him up to no good. Child abuse. Everything I've briefed you on over the last couple of days.' He held up some stills from the cache of SD cards. 'We have enough to put Ogden away for at least one life stretch, if Paul Temple does his job right. All those conspiracy charges, bribing police officers, that will only compound it.'

'Howard, do you know where he is?'

Savage smoothed his non-existent comb-over. 'Not as yet.'

'But Ogden is the big daddy?'

'We don't believe Ogden's at the pinnacle, no.' Savage let his words resonate around the room as he unbuttoned his blazer. 'This group are the worst London's ever seen, the worst western Europe's seen. They make Rochdale look like . . . Well, they're very bad.'

'If Ogden's not in charge, then who is?'

For once, Savage was lost for words. He sat there, tugging at his wild eyebrows.

'Howard, I'm not in the mood. Out with it or I swear I'll knock your bloody block off.' Fenchurch gritted his teeth. 'These bastards have my wife and I'm done playing silly buggers.'

'Howard's right.' Clarke got up and marched over to Fenchurch. 'Ogden isn't number one. We've had our eye on him in the City police. He's high up, probably number two.'

'So who's number one? And where have they taken my wife?'

'I've been through the footage.' Clarke tossed some stills over to Fenchurch and Savage. 'This is the guy we think is in charge. We've found similar images over the years, but his identity always remains hidden.' He flipped through another set. 'But we did get this.'

That same room, this time a different man with a black boy. The shot was from behind, showing a masked man wearing a towel around his hips, thrusting away. The next photo showed the towel slipping away.

With his finger, Clarke circled a large purple area that covered the small of the man's back. 'This is a somewhat distinct birthmark and it belongs to the man who we believe to be the leader of this gang.'

'Who the hell is it?'

'That's the thing.' Clarke shuffled his papers. 'We just don't know.'

Savage kept his gaze on the page. 'But you've got supporting evidence?'

'We've seen a few shots of this guy.' Clarke rubbed his smooth chin. 'Doesn't match any known perpetrator on any UK or European databases. Whoever it is is very good at covering their tracks.'

'So we need someone on the inside, correct?' Savage dropped the photos onto the desk in front of Docherty. 'Alan, when you were briefing me, you mentioned Daniel Connolly's sudden change of heart. Would he do?'

'You're in the wrong place, Howard. He's in King's College Hospital.'

Savage's eyes bulged. 'What?'

'He got shot.' Docherty rifled through the photographs, his lip curling up the further he went. 'Last I heard, it's not looking good.'

'Christ.' Savage's lips twitched. 'Did you—'

'It was a cop.' Docherty threw the photos back at Clarke. 'DC Clive Naismith.'

'*He's* working for them?'

Fenchurch nodded. 'Whoever *they* are. We believe he shot another witness: Chris Johnson.'

Savage got to his feet. 'I need to speak to him.'

———

'I'm not saying anything.' Naismith slouched back in his chair, his head covered in thick bandages. 'I've been a DC for thirteen years. I know the rules. I know the games you'll play.' He burped into his hand. 'How's about I just see you in court and we save each other a lot of time and effort, yeah?'

Fenchurch was standing by the door. Acid burned his knees and backside. Felt like he needed a hip replacement. 'You tried to beat up Daniel Connolly, didn't you?'

'Who?'

'In his cell last night.' Fenchurch flicked through a page of the entry log. 'You were in the station at that time. We had another CCTV blackout.'

'Whatever.'

Games, games, games. Time to play a different one.

Fenchurch tossed the paper file onto the desk and crouched next to Naismith. 'You killed someone, Constable.'

'Did I?' Naismith glared at him. 'You saw *me* shoot someone?'

'I was there. You shot Daniel Connolly in cold blood. He's fighting for his life just now.' Fenchurch sat opposite Naismith, spinning the paper file round on the desk. 'It's only a matter of time before we match your gun, your clothes, your motorbike's plates, anything you own, to the slaying of DC Chris Johnson last night in Hammersmith.'

'No comment.'

'That's it?' Fenchurch raised his eyebrows. 'You shot two people from a moving vehicle and you don't want to boast about it? That's very skilful, that. Must take a lot of practice.'

'I said, no comment.'

'We know you're small fry in this organisation.' Fenchurch waited until he had eye contact. 'Being a cop in prison won't be much fun. It'll be—'

Naismith smirked. 'Weren't you listening when I said I knew all about your tricks?'

'I know you're bent. You know you're bent.' Fenchurch stood and clicked his jaw again. Felt like a bloody tooth was going to pop out. 'The best thing for you is to tell us who you were working for.'

'No comment.'

'Was it Gerald Ogden?'

Naismith looked up. 'What? Who?'

'So you were working for him?'

Eyes back down. 'No comment.'

Got you, you idiot. Ogden's your boss.

Fenchurch smiled at him. 'We'll dig into your relationship with Mr Ogden in due course. We'll find the patterns. Now we know there's a link, we'll connect you to him.'

'No comment.'

'We've got a SOCO team combing that unit in Peckham.' Fenchurch watched Naismith's Adam's apple bob up and down. 'How much of your DNA will we find there? Or have you scrubbed the place?'

'No comment.'

Fenchurch left a few seconds, just long enough for Naismith to look up. 'Can't have done that good a job cleaning it, because we found a load of video files.'

Naismith dabbed at a cut on his forehead.

'I've seen what they do to the children they take.' Fenchurch swallowed the bile down, but it caught in his throat. Almost made him gag. 'I've seen Gerald Ogden on video.'

Naismith's eyes bulged. 'What?'

'If I keep searching, am I going to see you having sex with a child?'

'What?' Naismith pushed a fist against his lips and puffed out his cheeks. 'Of course not . . . Christ . . .'

Fenchurch paced around the room, waiting for Naismith's eyes to follow him round. 'This gang kidnapped my daughter eleven years ago. They killed her. They might as well have been driving the bus.'

'Did they?' Naismith stayed focused on the table, smirking. His cheeks widened. 'Who says they weren't?'

Fenchurch stopped dead, his heart skipping a beat. He swallowed hard. 'Tell us what you know.'

'What do you want to know?'

'They've abducted my wife.' Fenchurch let the words echo round the room. 'Where have they taken her?'

'That's very careless of you. Letting *them* frame your father, then losing your wife . . .' Naismith wagged his finger in the air. 'Tut tut.'

'We know it was you who killed Frank Blunden.' Fenchurch snarled at him. 'You framed my father for his murder.'

'No comment.'

Back to that.

'We've got a video file from Daniel Connolly.'

Naismith's eyes bulged. 'No. No comment.'

'You killing Frank Blunden. Framing my father.'

'I said, no comment.'

'Did you take her?'

'No.'

Savage cleared his throat and put a hand on Fenchurch's back. 'Constable, we're prepared to offer you a deal in exchange for the testimony against Gerald Ogden and—'

'Oh yeah?' Naismith grinned. 'What kind of thing? Reduce my sentence?'

'I'll eliminate all charges if you give us this man.' Savage slid a photograph across the table. 'You see this?' He circled the birthmark. 'Who is it?'

Naismith shut his eyes. 'Even if I wanted to, I couldn't tell you.'

'Why?'

'No comment.'

'This is your only chance, Constable. You clearly know who is in the photo.' Savage tapped the image again. 'We can stop them.'

'Can you?' Naismith chewed his nail.

Savage reached over and spoke into the microphone. 'Interview terminated at ten twenty-three a.m.' He got up and led Fenchurch out into the corridor. 'This whole police force is a nest of vipers.' He waved the photo around in the air. 'He knows who this is. That bent cop is covering for . . .'

'Give me a second. Alone.' Fenchurch grabbed the photo and pushed into the room, sitting next to Naismith. He waited until the door swung shut and it was just them. Naismith's stale sweat overpowered the musty-room smell. 'Didn't fancy bringing a lawyer in, did you?'

'Don't trust them.'

'Howard's right, you know? We can protect you and your family.'

'You can't even protect your own.'

Fenchurch put the photo down and smoothed it out. 'You know who this is.'

'I can't tell you.'

'Clive.' Fenchurch pushed the sheet across the table. 'Over the years, this man has abducted children, including my daughter. They took your mate Chris Johnson's wife and kid. Still have them somewhere. Who knows what they'll do to them now you've bumped him off. Kill them and chuck them in the North Sea. Now, what've they got on you?'

'It's complicated.'

Fenchurch patted the picture. 'Is it something like this?'

'Like I said, it's complicated.'

'It's just you and me in here, okay?' Fenchurch waved around the room. He tapped the recorder. 'This isn't doing anything. The video feed is off.'

'What are you saying?'

'I'm letting you hedge your bets. You know I'm not bent, right?'

'Because they've got your wife?'

'And I'm not bowing down to them. If you tell me, nobody else will know. If we catch this geezer, you get your deal.'

'And if not?'

Fenchurch smiled. 'This chat never happened.'

Naismith picked at his fingernails. 'You've no idea what they'll do to me. To my sister and her kids. My poor old mum.'

'I've got a good idea, Clive.' Fenchurch held up the page. 'It's something like this, isn't it?'

Naismith pointed at the birthmark on the photo. 'I guarded these blokes while they were doing this, you know?'

'How did that make you feel?'

Naismith stroked his throat, his nose wrinkling. 'You really want to know who this is?'

'I *need* to know.'

'Fine.' Naismith flipped the paper over and slapped it onto the desk. 'It's Lord Ingham.'

Chapter Forty

An elderly couple strolled down the quiet street, walking away from Fenchurch. 'Steve, you had me guard him the other day.'

Clarke was staring at the wall hiding Ingham's Hampstead mansion. He turned round, frowning. 'So?'

'Bit of a coincidence, isn't it?'

Clarke looked away, shaking his head.

'Steve, you knew he was behind this, didn't you?'

Clarke shrugged. 'I wanted you to get the measure of the man.'

'Would've been useful to know that at the time. I stopped someone killing him.' Fenchurch slammed his fist against the car, getting a dull crunch in return. 'If you're working—'

'Whoa, whoa.' Clarke raised his hands. 'Listen, I'm not involved. We've got three open cases against that lot. Kidnapped some kids from round the Barbican. Look, I gave you that evidence, Fenchurch. That's led us to this.'

'But you bloody knew it was him.'

'Remember that protestor?' Clarke scowled at him. 'The one who was spouting all that anti-Semitic shit? After you went, he told us Ingham was up to this. I just needed someone on the inside to confirm it.'

'If this goes tits up, I swear I'll—'

'If this goes tits up, I'll jump off Tower Bridge.' Clarke swallowed and held up his Airwave. 'All units, we are go!' He pushed open the gate and led the team up the drive towards Ingham's mansion.

Fenchurch kept near the back, searching around for threats, not seeing any. He stayed by the Bentley and let the others approach the house.

Clarke and Reed got on either side of the door, with two black-clad cops taking up the rear, their batons clinking slightly. One of them was lugging the big red Enforcer battering ram. Hopefully it wouldn't be needed . . .

Reed cupped her hands round her mouth. 'Mr Ingham, it's the police! We have a search warrant and are entering your premises!'

Upstairs looked quiet, not even a rustling curtain to disrupt the stillness. The house next door was barely visible over the wall, just some brick and slate peeking over. Silent as the grave.

Fenchurch put his Airwave to his mouth. 'Any movement out the back, Jon?'

'Negative, guv.' Nelson was out of breath. 'Place is dead.'

'Right. Keep on the line.' Fenchurch jogged over to the house and got between Reed and Clarke. 'The place is empty.'

'That's my assessment, too.' Clarke thumped on the oak again. No response. He unfolded the pages in his pocket. 'Let's get in there.'

Fenchurch spoke into the Airwave again. 'All units, we are go!' He stepped back and got out of the way.

The uniformed officer rested the Big Key against the door and swung it back. It dumped against the wood, barely marking it. Another go and it cracked the door handle. He tossed the Enforcer aside and yanked at the brass. 'Give us a minute . . .' He shoved his shoulder at the timber and it stuttered open. 'Sometimes, all it needs is a little bit of—'

'Stay there!' Fenchurch barged past him, Reed and Clarke following. His shoes clicked off a long parquet hallway, which looked like it ran to the back of the house. Several gleaming white doors led off, cut into the cream paintwork. A staircase towered up to the first floor.

Fenchurch waved at the officers following them in. 'Get in each and every door.' He grabbed the Airwave again. 'Jon, any movement out back yet?'

'Still negative, guv.'

Acid-yellow tangled with black as the officers opened the doors and entered in pairs. Six officers broke off and headed upstairs. 'Thoughts, Kay?'

'Let this play out, guv.'

'There's nobody here. Where the hell—'

BANG.

'Shit!' Fenchurch pushed Reed to the floor, rolling into a heap. 'Was that a gunshot?'

'Sounded like it.' Reed craned her neck round, facing towards a door in the left wall. 'Came from through there.'

BANG.

BANG.

'Shots fired! Repeat, shots fired!' Fenchurch got up to a crouch and spidered over to the wall, listening hard. No more gunfire, just raised voices. Reed was on the other side of the door. 'There's someone here after all.'

'What's the plan, guv?' She was trying to peer in. 'Wait for the ARU?'

'There are officers at risk. We've not got time.' Fenchurch crept round the edge of the doorway. Another hall, leading deep into one of the house's wings. Two doors hung open halfway down, a bathroom on the left and a closet on the right. At the end, it widened out into a living room. A tight black jacket sleeve, holding out a pistol.

'I'm going.' Fenchurch pushed himself to his feet and extended his baton, quietly and slowly. He stepped forward and put his back to the right-hand wall, the side the shooter was on. He inched along the hallway and made it to the closet. He rested behind the open door, listening.

'Stay where you are!' Foreign accents. Eastern, maybe Russian. Could be Israeli.

'No further movement!' Another voice, definitely Israeli.

Meant they were pros. Israeli Defence Force. Shit.

Maybe waiting for the ARU was the best plan after all . . .

Sod it. I haven't got the time.

Fenchurch sucked in breath and squeezed round the door, pushing back against the wall.

In the room, a head bobbed up behind a leather sofa. The shooter pointed his pistol straight at him. 'Stay there.'

On the sofa, a male officer lay back, a tight grip on his thigh, teeth clenched. Blood was dripping onto the cream carpet, clumping like spilled red wine.

Shit.

Another few steps forward and Fenchurch was by the open entrance. The gun was still aimed at the injured officer on the sofa and his colleague hiding behind.

Fenchurch licked at his dry lips and raised up his baton. Here we go. He slashed out with the weapon, cracking it off the gunman's wrist. The pistol fell to the floor, thunking off the carpet.

Fenchurch swiped his baton again, his right hand cradling his left wrist. He cracked the gunman in the throat and sent him flying backwards. Then he dived low and grabbed the pistol.

BANG.

The carpet next to him exploded. The second shooter was on him, his baggy beige suit smeared with blood, gun pointed at Fenchurch.

Fenchurch aimed the weapon at him. 'Stop! You are surrounded!'

The gunman took one look out of the front of the house and tossed the pistol. He put his hands behind his head and went down on both knees, like he'd done this many, many times before.

Fenchurch got up slowly and waved into the corridor, beckoning Reed along.

The officer behind the sofa burst out and patted his fallen comrade on the chest, then the cheek. 'Come on, Keith, mate . . .'

Fenchurch darted over to beige suit and kicked his gun away. He pinned him down with his baton. 'How many more are there?'

'Just us.'

'You're lying.'

'I'm not! It's just us!'

The room was bigger than Fenchurch's flat. Bigger than both his and Abi's and the rental job out in the Isle of Dogs. A grand piano sat in the corner, opposite a pair of heavy oak bookcases, holding first-edition copies of the Bible, by the look of things. The back garden was empty, just a sprawling lawn. 'Where is Ingham?'

'He's left.'

Fenchurch slapped his cuffs on beige suit's wrists and rolled him onto his back. Leave him there. He sucked in breath. 'Where the bloody hell is he? Where's my wife?'

'I'm not speaking.'

Nelson burst into the room, Airwave to his lips. '—urgent attention. Repeat: urgent attention.'

Fenchurch's Airwave crackled. Reed. 'Guv, you might want to have a look at this. Out the back.'

Fenchurch stormed down the hall into the entranceway. The back door led out across the garden. He trotted over to it and scanned around.

Reed was over to the right, by a small courtyard of outbuildings. She beckoned Fenchurch over. 'Guv.' One of the doors was wide open. 'None of our lot have been in there. There's a staircase, guv. And an old one at that.'

Fenchurch raised up his baton. 'We should really wait for the ARU, Kay. These lot are pros. We don't know how many are down there.'

Reed reached into her jacket pocket and pulled out a black Glock, barely glinting in the light. 'This do?'

'Jesus, Kay. Where did you get that?'

'I signed it out, guv.' She slid a bullet into the chamber. 'After what happened on Middlesex Street, I'm taking no chances.'

'You should've bloody said . . .' Fenchurch's eyes were adjusting to the darkness. 'Right, well, let's be careful, okay?'

Nelson was in the living-room window, looking out. Fenchurch pointed at the building, making it clear they were heading in. Nelson gave a thumbs-up and turned away.

Reed sucked in a deep breath and entered the staircase, aiming the weapon at the ground. One short step, then another, then she waved Fenchurch in.

He followed her down. The stairs led deep, probably under the house, worn into a groove by thousands of footsteps. Fenchurch stepped out into a vaulted area.

Metal pressed into his temple. 'Stop right there.' A shaft of light caught Ogden, his face as tight as it could get.

Another gunman was pointing a pistol at Reed's head, his face shrouded in darkness. 'You too, princess.'

Reed palmed her pistol, sticking the barrel up her sleeve.

Fenchurch dropped his baton and raised his hands. 'You're surrounded.'

Ogden pushed the barrel into Fenchurch's skin. 'Well, we've got two hostages who can help us get away.'

'There are thirty officers up there.' Fenchurch ran his foot over the baton and kept it where he wanted it. 'An Armed Response Unit, too. You're not getting away.'

'We are, and you are our insurance policy.' Ogden prodded the barrel into his neck.

Fenchurch stayed calm despite the blood thundering in his ears. 'Where's my wife?'

'Interesting question.' The second figure stepped out of the shadows. Lord Ingham, his face even more toad-like in the dim light. 'Now we have you, we can dispense with her.'

'Where is she?!' Fenchurch's voice cannoned around the space, echoing like it was an ancient monastery. 'Abi!?'

A whimper came from somewhere nearby.

'Abi, it's going to be—'

The barrel cracked into his forehead and Fenchurch stumbled forward, his knees cracking off stone. 'Shit.' The pistol dug into the back of his skull. 'You're not getting out of here.'

Fenchurch rested on all fours and snarled up at Ogden. 'I know what you've been doing. The pair of you. Kidnapping children. Raping them. Disposing of them. We know all about Fresh Start.'

'What?' Ingham's voice.

'You're surprised? You stupid bastard. You took—'

A boot between his shoulder blades pushed Fenchurch over, the flagstone scraping his cheek. 'You took my daughter. You killed her!'

'And now I'll kill you.' The gun pressed into his crown. 'Or shall we kill Mrs Fenchurch first?'

Fenchurch reached over to the left, his fingers scrabbling over the rough stone. 'Why did you do it?'

'Because we could.' Why not just bloody shoot? 'Because nobody could stop us.'

Cold metal. The baton . . . Fenchurch curled his fingers around it. Only got one go at this.

'Get up.'

'Shoot me now.'

'You're not listening to us, are you?' The gun pulled back, breaking skin contact. 'You're our insurance policy. Two serving officers make for a much better route out of here than a pregnant teacher.'

'What?'

'We know all about Mrs Fenchurch.' Fingers gripped his jacket and hoisted him up. 'Now get up!'

Fenchurch pushed himself up with his right hand, careful to keep the baton within arm's reach.

Ogden's teeth caught in the light, betraying his smile. 'Gilbert, let's get—'

Fenchurch swung out with the baton, aiming for the glint. CRACK. And again. THUD.

'My teese!' The gun clattered onto the floor.

BANG.

A gunshot whizzed through the air, just missing Fenchurch. The flash lit up Ingham's tweeds as he chambered another round.

Fenchurch lashed out with his baton, the metal rattling as it hit the pistol. He didn't stop, just stepped forward again, swiping the baton, crunching into Ingham's arms. Then lower, battering his legs, his torso. He pushed him over and kicked out. Cracking his kneecap, smashing his thighs, pounding into his balls. 'You killed my daughter! You killed my daughter!' Boot, boot, boot. Swipe, splat. Boot. Swipe, splat.

'Guv!' Reed grabbed his arms and jerked him backwards. 'Stop!'

Fenchurch hefted the baton up again, then stared at the floor. 'Right.'

Reed's grip slackened off. A muffled sound came from behind them.

Fenchurch got his phone out of his pocket and fumbled on the torch. Blinding light shot out, bouncing off ancient stone walls. In the corner, Abi lay in a ball, tied up and gagged. 'Jesus . . .'

Reed got out her Airwave. 'Need urgent assistance now!'

Fenchurch stomped over and tore off the gag.

She gasped out a breath. 'Simon!'

'It's okay, love. You're safe.' Fenchurch crouched down to tug at the rope binding her wrists then her legs. Her grey T-shirt was stained red. Drums thudded in his ears. 'What did they do to you?'

'Simon, I'm okay.'

'The baby . . .' Fenchurch darted back over to Ingham, who was coughing in the middle of the chamber. 'You filthy animal!' He thwacked him on the back with the baton. Again. And again.

Arms wrapped around him from behind, perfumed air floating over him like he was back in the tropical forest. 'Stop . . .' Abi, kissing his neck. 'Simon, you need to stop!'

The baton clattered to the ground. Fenchurch grabbed Abi in his arms and pulled her tight. 'I thought I'd lost you.'

'Simon . . .' She hugged him tighter. 'They were going to run away with new IDs. They were going to take me with them, in case . . . In case.'

'Shh. It's over, love.' Fenchurch kissed her on the top of her head. 'The only place they're running is away from bigger rapists in the prison shower.'

Chapter Forty-One

Fenchurch stood in the hot sun that was burning off the Sunday rain clouds, the breeze whipping the trees.

A paramedic was trying to help Abi into the back of the ambulance. 'I can bloody walk.' She slapped the male paramedic's hand and stepped into the ambulance, both hands covering her belly.

Fenchurch grabbed the paramedic's arm and stopped him going. 'Is she going to be okay?'

'Initial analysis is yes.' He folded up a gurney, the mechanism rattling. 'Trouble is, I'm a jack of all trades, so I need a master to give her the once over.'

'I need a minute with her.'

'That's the limit, okay?' Snap, crunk, and the gurney was flat. 'You're welcome to ride with us.' He hefted it up into the ambulance. 'I'm taking her to University College.'

'Seem to be spending half of my life there.' Fenchurch pulled himself up into the ambulance. 'Hey.'

Abi was sitting on the bed, feet kinked together. 'Simon.' She tried a smile but it slipped away. 'Will you get them for me?'

'Don't worry on that score. I'll smash them into little pieces.'

She stroked his arm as he sat next to her. 'Don't do anything stupid.'

Fenchurch hugged her tight. 'Did you see who took you?'

'No.'

'Was it Ogden?'

'No, it was a big guy.' She sighed. 'Looked like he'd been in the army.'

'You didn't see his face?'

'I don't know what happened.' Abi rested her head on his shoulder. 'Someone came in when I was in the shower. I thought it was you, forgetting your phone again. I had shampoo in my hair and I couldn't see. They pulled the cubicle open and grabbed me.'

'Jesus . . . I got back with coffee and pastries and they knocked me out.' Fenchurch showed her the cuts on his head.

She kissed his forehead, right over the plaster. 'Simon, this isn't your fault.'

'I'm doing this for Chloe.' The ambulance started up, vibrating through the floor. 'I need to see what's going on.' Fenchurch got up and kissed her. 'I'll join you soon.'

'Simon . . .'

'I'll be an hour at most.' Fenchurch jumped down and waved the ambulance off. It trundled down the lane, a blast of siren clearing a clump of uniformed officers chatting by the entrance.

'How's Abi?' Reed, brandishing her Airwave.

'I almost lost her, Kay.'

'You didn't, guv.' She brushed a hand down his arm. 'You saved her.'

'*We* did. Us storming in there like Butch and Sundance . . .' Fenchurch bit at his lip, drawing blood. 'They had guns pointed at us. The pair of them. We shouldn't have gone down there.'

'What if we hadn't?'

'You're right.' A van spewed out another load of officers.

'—and I want three guards on those pricks at all times.' Docherty burst through the wall of uniforms, face like he was going to murder someone. 'That's three guards *each*. No questions, okay?'

Mulholland was following, her scarf trailing along the ground. 'Sir.'

Docherty stopped to scowl at Fenchurch. 'I thought you'd be heading up to the hospital with Abi?'

Fenchurch glanced at Reed. 'Boss, I need to see those two scumbags taken down for this.'

'After you smashed the shite out of Ingham? No chance that's happening.'

'He had a gun on me, boss.'

'Aye, and you took it off him and his mate, then decided to go all medieval on him. Christ, I've seen better depictions of the plague than how he looks right now.'

'I want to interview them.'

Docherty picked at his teeth, screwing his face up tight. 'You can watch.'

Didn't know how bloody hungry I was . . .

Fenchurch walked along the Leman Street corridor, couldn't eat the burrito quickly enough. A quick drive-by job, not enough time to customise it properly. He bit another mouthful, then pulled the foil over, pretty much exactly halfway.

He entered the Observation Suite and blanked Mulholland as he perched next to her. On the screen, Nelson sat in the interview room with Ogden and a heavy man in a suit, his white hair plastered with sweat. 'Who's the lawyer?'

'Simon, I am genuinely sorry about what happened.' Mulholland's scarf flashed over like a flapping crow as she tied it back. 'I know we don't see eye to eye a lot of the time, but this is truly horrible. I can't even—'

'Who's the lawyer?' Fenchurch put the half-burrito down and waved a hand at the monitor.

Mulholland's lips twitched between pursed and a smile. 'Brian Makepeace, the other name partner in Ogden's firm.'

'They're a City firm.' Fenchurch frowned. 'That's all contract law and the dark arts of international law. Why's he defending him?'

'Before they started the firm, he had a background in criminal defence.'

'He must be very rusty.'

'Simon . . .' She smiled at him, her forehead creasing. 'I can't imagine what you must be going through.'

'Right. Thanks.' Still not looking at her.

On-screen, Nelson passed a sheet across the desk. 'Care to comment on this, sir?'

'No comment.' Ogden rubbed at his teeth, eyes screwed shut. 'I really need to see a dentist.'

Mulholland waved a hand at the monitor. 'Rusty or not, he's got Ogden well drilled. It's been like this all the way through.'

The door thudded open and Docherty stormed in, one hand in his pocket. 'Si . . . How's this going?'

Mulholland took off her scarf and started bunching it up, but it looked like it would take longer than forever. 'It's . . . well, it's going nowhere. And not particularly quickly, either.'

'Any sign Makepeace is involved or knows about what Ogden's . . . been up to?'

'Not yet, sir.'

Another screen flashed into action. The door opened and Martin led Ingham in. Looked like he'd been through a combine harvester backwards. His toad eyes were both swollen, his nose a black-and-red mess, blood spilling down his shirt, crusted around his cheeks. He spoke, but the speakers were muted.

'Righty-ho.' Docherty opened the door again. 'I'd better find Savage.'

Fenchurch grabbed Docherty's arm. 'Boss.' He glanced over at Mulholland. 'I want to speak to Ingham.'

'This is my case.' Docherty stabbed a finger into his own chest, a wad of spit dribbling down his chin. 'Howard and I are interviewing him. You're keeping out. End of.'

The door slammed in Fenchurch's face. Bloody, bloody hell.

'Simon . . .'

Fenchurch ignored Mulholland as he sat back down. Blood burning in his veins. Drums pounding in his ears.

Sitting here, watching those idiots make a dog's breakfast of the interview.

Maybe I should be with Abi right now.

Fenchurch risked a look at Mulholland. She had to be here to witness it. She had to watch the moment of bitter defeat, abject humiliation, something she'd savour for a long time.

The trees in the park rustled around them. Chloe nibbled at the wine gum, biting away at the rhombus bit by bit until she was halfway. 'How's your sweetie, Daddy?'

Fenchurch leaned back on the bench and chewed at his own wine gum. 'It's good.'

'Granny says hi.'

Fenchurch brushed a tear from his eye, then ruffled Chloe's hair. 'Your mother's in hospital now and they're fixing her up.'

'What was wrong with her?' Just a little red triangle left now.

'Some bad men took her from me, sweetheart. I got them.'

'Is it the same bad men who took me, Daddy?'

Fenchurch nodded as he swallowed the sweet, the bloody thing catching in his throat. He coughed it down. 'Same men.'

'And are you going to get them for me, Daddy?'

'I've been told to . . .'

'Daddy, they took me.' Chloe nestled in close. 'Are you saying Doc and Savage can do your job better than you?'

'Simon . . .'

'Chloe . . .'

'*Daddy, they killed me.*' Chloe pouted up at him, angel eyes dazzling in the light. '*Why don't you kill them?*'

'Simon . . .'

Fenchurch jerked awake. He looked around the room, his eyes thick and heavy. He yawned, felt like he'd never stop. 'Sorry, I must've drifted off.'

'You were snoring.'

'Sorry.' Fenchurch brushed away the sleep from his eyes and focused on the monitor. Ingham was on his own on the opposite side of the table. 'He's not got a lawyer?'

'Defending himself.'

'—basement under your house.'

'No comment.'

On-screen, Docherty got up and paced the room, one hand in his pockets, the jangling keys distorting the microphone. 'I asked why the wife of one of my officers was in a basement under your house.'

'No comment.'

'Mr Ingham, the constant no—'

'*Lord* Ingham. I am a peer of the realm and I deserve to be treated as such.'

'You know they'll strip you of your title.' Docherty stopped jangling, a smirk on his face. 'This isn't Jeffrey Archer perjuring himself. This is worse than Fred Goodwin, and look what happened to him.'

Ingham ran his tongue along his top lip. 'No comment.'

'The constant no commenting isn't helping your case, especially with the wealth of evidence against you.'

'Listen, you Scottish fool.' Ingham brushed his hands across his face, the monitor rendering it dark grey rather than purple. 'That officer beat me black and blue in my own home. Are you condoning that sort of behaviour?'

'This wasn't during a dinner party.' Docherty sat down again and folded his arms, head tilted to the side. 'This was part of an official police action, sanctioned by the courts and the Crown Prosecution Service. You had kidnapped that officer's wife and were holding her against her will.'

'I will get out of here.' Ingham rapped his fingers on the table. 'Mark my words.'

'We've got strong evidence against you.'

'And good luck getting that admissible in court.' Ingham's turn to grin. 'You're struggling for witnesses, aren't you?'

Yeah, because you've bloody killed them all . . .

Ingham turned his smile to the camera, his lips split in at least four different places.

Smug prick. Sitting there, laughing this off like it's nothing. Catch him red-handed, threatens me with a gun . . . Kidnapped Abi . . .

Right, sod it.

Fenchurch marched over to the door.

'Where are you going?' Mulholland grabbed hold of his jacket.

'I'm going to sort this out.' Fenchurch pushed her hand away and stormed down the corridor. He tore open the door.

Docherty and Savage wore frowns on their foreheads.

Ingham puckered his lips. 'Here he is.' He smoothed a hand over his bruised face. Looked ten times worse in the flesh, like he was a prime cut in the butcher's. 'Have you come to finish the job, eh?'

Fenchurch walked over to him and shrugged off Docherty's grip. He whispered into Ingham's ear, 'You took my daughter, all those years ago.'

Ingham glanced round at him. 'If you say so.'

Fenchurch pointed at his own heart. 'You took my daughter and you killed her.'

'If you say so.' Ingham laughed, braying, guffawing. *Hwa, hwa, hwa.* 'Who are we talking about?'

'Chloe Fenchurch. That might be where you knew my name from when I saved your life a few days ago.' Fenchurch rocked forward, so their foreheads almost touched. 'Your people kidnapped my daughter off the street, took her somewhere, then gave her to new parents. She died not long after.'

'I honestly don't know what you're talking about.' Ingham tried to pull away from Fenchurch, folding his arms. 'I swear I know nothing about what happened to your daughter.'

'I've seen what you do to kids.' Fenchurch snatched up a sheet of paper and held it in front of Ingham's face. 'You might know her as Chloe Holland.'

Ingham's nonce eyes bulged, even bigger than a toad's for once. He swallowed. 'The name means nothing to—'

'What did you do to her?'

'That's . . . that's . . .' Ingham gasped for air. 'That's . . . that's not me!'

'We know it is!' Fenchurch grabbed Ingham's throat and squeezed. 'What did you do with her?'

'Enough!' Docherty slammed his finger on the recorder and switched off the camera.

Fenchurch tightened his grip. 'What. Did. You. Do?'

'I don't—'

'I will kill you right now.' Fenchurch dug into the blubber with his other hand. 'I'll finish the job!'

Ingham coughed as Fenchurch let the pressure go. 'I remember her now. Young Chloe.' He laughed as his face turned purple. 'She was a porcelain goddess.' He flashed a smile at him, then licked his lips. 'We all took turns with her. It was *exquisite*.'

Fenchurch punched Ingham, cracking his knuckles off his jaw. He clutched the thin hair at the back of his head and launched Ingham's face into the desk. He toppled over onto his side, landing on the floor, prone.

Docherty tore Fenchurch off from behind. 'Easy, easy.' He pulled him into the corridor and jabbed a finger into his ribs. 'That's enough, okay? You see the state of him? Looks like he's gone twelve rounds with Muhammad Ali, God rest his soul.' He stepped back. 'You should be with Abi.'

———

A nurse was just emerging from a room, muttering to herself. She looked up at Fenchurch, eyes wide. 'Can I help?'

'Where's Abi Fenchurch?'

'Right.' The nurse pointed at an open door. 'She's in there.'

'How is she?'

'Your wife's fine.'

Butterflies fluttered in Fenchurch's gut. 'And the baby?'

'Mr Stephenson has just seen her.' The nurse waved into the room. 'There's no visible injury to her or baby. And he's happy with the progress.'

'So she's ready to go home?'

'Mr Stephenson is awaiting some final blood tests.'

'Can I go in?'

She stepped out of the way.

'Thanks.' Fenchurch gave her the best smile he could muster and entered the room.

Abi was lying back, cradling a paper cup. She looked over at Fenchurch, woozy and struggling to focus. 'Simon. Have you got them yet?'

'Almost.' Fenchurch perched on the edge of the bed, gripping her hand. 'You okay, love?'

She shut her eyes, her breath coming in fits and starts. 'I'll live.'

'The nurse said the baby's fine.'

Abi's eyes were still locked shut. 'She told me.'

Fenchurch let his breath calm down. 'How are you feeling?'

'I don't know, Simon.' She sipped from the coffee cup. 'The way you attacked him . . .'

'I'll pay for that, don't worry.'

'I didn't like what I saw.'

'I didn't like what you saw, either.' Fenchurch scratched at his stubble. 'I lost it. All this shit, years of it. Face to face with . . . with the man who took Chloe. That's all I could do.'

'You almost killed him.'

'I wanted to.' Fenchurch ran a guilty hand across his forehead. The hand that could've strangled Ingham. That should've . . . 'You stopped me.'

'You'd have stopped yourself.'

Fenchurch bunched up the bedsheets in his hands and pinched the bridge of his nose. 'Maybe.'

'Simon.'

The door opened, a wall of air brushing through Fenchurch's hair.

'Abi, they've not got any copies of—' Paul Temple stopped in the doorway. 'Sorry. I'll leave you guys to it.'

'No, it's fine.' Abi took another sip and smiled at Fenchurch. 'Paul got here as soon as he heard. Got me a coffee.'

'Least I could do.' Tears welled up in Temple's eyes. 'Sure you don't want me to leave?'

Fenchurch frowned at him. 'Are you okay, mate?'

'It's this hay fever.' Temple blinked away tears and rubbed his eyes again. 'Haven't had my spray today.'

'I've just come from Leman Street.' Fenchurch sat forward, the edge of the bed digging into his thighs. 'Thought you'd be leading the prosecution of those scumbags.'

'Docherty told me.' Temple held his hand out for a fist bump, like he could barely put any effort into it. 'I want to make sure Abi's okay.'

'Right.' Fenchurch bumped knuckles. 'They will go away for it, won't they?'

Temple scratched the skin on his hand. 'You know, maybe you shouldn't have gone industrial on Ingham.'

And then some.

'You try being in my shoes, Paul.' Fenchurch bunched up more of the sheet. 'But they won't get off, right?'

'Depends.'

Abi crushed her cup and dumped it beside the bed. 'That was good coffee, Paul. Better than the muck they've got in here.'

'Glad to be of service.' Temple hefted up his document holder. 'I'll best head back, see if I can be of use there.'

'You've been a great help here.' Abi lay back and yawned as Temple left them. 'These tests are taking forever.'

'You've only been here a couple of hours.'

'I want to go home and sleep, Simon.'

Fenchurch's fingers twitched. 'I'm going to go and chase this Dr Stephenson, okay?'

'*Mister*. He's a consultant. And one of the types who don't like to be called Doctor.'

'Right.' Fenchurch kissed her on the lips. She stank of garlic. He sniffed her breath. Really strong. 'What did you have to—'

'Simon!' She squirmed away from him. 'What's going—'

Fenchurch grabbed her by the shoulders. 'Abi, have you had any garlic today?'

'Simon? What are you talking about?'

'I said, have you eaten any garlic?'

'All I've had today is some bloody toast and that coffee.'

'Shit!' Fenchurch yanked the emergency cord and stormed into the ward. 'Doctor! Nurse! Help!'

'Simon! What's going—?'

The nurse's station was empty, just a ringing telephone.

Temple was over by the lifts, tapping a message into his phone. He locked eyes with Fenchurch and they bulged.

Fenchurch stopped dead.

Shit.

No . . .

No, no, no.

First Shelvey, now Abi?

Temple ran off, heading for the stairs.

Fenchurch sprinted after him, his legs groaning with the effort, and swung through the door into the stairwell. 'Paul! Stop!'

Temple was halfway down, feet clacking off the steps.

Fenchurch vaulted the handrail and leapt over. He landed on Temple, pushing him against the stairs. 'Stop!' He yanked Temple's arm behind his back, making him squeal. His document holder rolled down. Fenchurch tipped it up and poured the contents out onto the stairs.

Wallet. ID. Notebook. Documents. More documents. And a bag of white powder.

Fenchurch collapsed back on his heels. 'Paul . . . Why?'

Temple couldn't even look at him.

Fenchurch yanked Temple's arm back until it cracked. 'You stupid bastard!'

Chapter Forty-Two

Fenchurch pushed Temple into a chair and jabbed a finger at the lumbering security guard. 'Keep him here!' He darted over to Abi's room and raced up to the bed.

'What's happened to her?' Mr Stephenson was hovering over Abi, confusion twisting his grey face. 'She's—'

'She's been poisoned.' Fenchurch tossed the bag at him. 'If I'm right, it's arsenic.'

'Arsenic?' Stephenson stood, huffing out a breath. 'What?'

'You need to get Dr Gold in here, right now.' Fenchurch gritted his teeth, his eyes stinging. 'We had a death in custody two days ago. I think this is the same killer, the same MO. Abi's got garlic breath.' The coffee cup was on its side. His gut twisted into a knot. 'It's kicked in a lot faster than last time. It must be a higher dose . . .' He grabbed the coffee cup. 'This is how it was administered.'

'Okay.' Stephenson held up the cup. 'Can you get this tested? I'll work on this basis, but it needs to be confirmed, okay?'

'I'll do that.' Fenchurch bagged it up. A pair of nurses hung round Abi, delirious on the bed, but they didn't seem to know what to do. 'Is she going to be okay?'

'Let's hope so.' Stephenson glanced over at Abi. 'Right now, the best thing you can do is get out of my way and confirm that's arsenic. While I await the sainted Dr Gold, I shall administer MiADMSA and monitor your wife's condition.'

'Miasma?'

'MiADMSA.' Stephenson ran a tongue over his lips, focusing on Abi again. 'We use it to flush arsenic out of a subject's system.'

A subject . . .

'Right.' Fenchurch stepped away.

Paul Temple! How could he do this to Abi?

How could I let this happen?

'Guv?' Reed was out in the corridor. 'Your message didn't make any sense. What the hell's going on?'

'Him.' Fenchurch grabbed Temple's collar and hauled him to his feet. 'He poisoned her.' Couldn't even bring himself to look at Temple. 'Gave her arsenic in a coffee.'

Reed frowned at her old friend, her eyes widening. 'He . . . *What?*'

'It's him, Kay.' Fenchurch tightened his grip on Temple's arm. '*He* killed Shelvey. *He's* the one who's been phoning me . . . Leaking all this shit . . .' He pushed the bagged cup into Temple's face. 'This is how you did it, isn't it? Eh?'

The lawyer looked away. 'You need to get someone to fix my arm. I think it's broken.'

'The duty doctor will do that down the station.' Fenchurch stepped away and placed his hands on Reed's shoulders. 'Kay, you're the only person I can trust. Can you stay with her?'

———

Fenchurch barrelled along Commercial Street, just waking up late into its Sunday lunchtime, the hipster boutiques and bars starting to get some custom. He pulled up at the lights. In the rear-view, the squad car was close behind, keeping a good eye on him.

Fenchurch listened hard for a motorbike. Scanned around for people with guns, ready to jump out. Watched for any cars ready to ram into him and pull Temple out of the wreckage. He twisted the mirror to focus on Temple. 'Why aren't you talking to me?'

Temple folded his arms, the handcuffs clinking and rattling. 'No comment.'

'You can talk to me, Paul.' Fenchurch set off and hammered down the street, weaving out to overtake a trundling bus. 'I'm your guardian angel.'

Temple's face screwed up as he clutched his side. 'Simon, my shoulder is killing me.'

'You're lucky I haven't killed you.'

'You honestly think this is a good idea?' Temple's chin rested against the side window, his breath misting on the glass. 'Accusing me of trying to kill Abi and then taking me to the police station yourself?'

'I saw what happened the last time I didn't drive someone myself.' Fenchurch pulled up at the lights. Leman Street was just ahead, Aldgate Tower and its sister blocking out the sun.

His Airwave blasted out. 'Guv, it's Martin. I'm in reception and you're not here.'

'Two minutes.' Fenchurch dumped the Airwave on the seat next to the coffee cup and the white powder. 'Why did you try and kill Abi?'

'My arm's agony. I should be back at the hospital. I think my shoulder's broken.'

'Abi's your friend. You, her and Kay. Been mates for a long time. How can you do that?'

'You're stitching me up. You'll never get a conviction.'

'You're lucky I don't take you to some waste ground somewhere, a building site, and just smash your brains in.' Whitechapel High Street coiled off to the left. 'Could just drive off, get out to Essex, throw you in the North Sea. See how you like that.'

Temple held his gaze in the rear-view before looking away.

A car horn sounded from behind. The squad car flashed its lights. Fenchurch drove off, heading straight ahead, Aldgate tube spewing out a fresh wave of passengers. He pulled up in front of Leman Street station. The squad car behind opened up and two uniforms got out.

Could just put my foot to the floor and sail off. Take him to Southwark and dunk him in the Thames. See if he floats or sinks.

'I really need to see a doctor.'

Fenchurch opened his door, grabbed the evidence from the passenger seat and got out. He gestured at the uniforms to take Temple.

'There you are.' Martin stood on the top step, squinting into the light. 'We're full up in here.'

'Dump anyone not related to this investigation at Brick Lane. Use Wapping if you have to.' Fenchurch held the mirror door open to let them haul Temple inside, head bowed and wincing. 'Get the duty doctor to check his shoulder and his arm.' He followed them in.

Clooney was waiting by the security door, tapping his foot on the ground. 'Got that thing for me?'

Fenchurch passed him the evidence bags. 'Things.'

'Right. I'll give you a call when I'm done.' Clooney darted out of the door.

Fenchurch followed the uniforms and Temple through to the Custody Suite.

Ingham was hugging the desk. *Looked like someone had done a real number on him. Wonder who that someone was?*

'—you do say may be given in evidence.' Nelson stood in front of him. 'Do you understand?'

Ingham settled his focus on Temple. He gave him a slight nod, then back at Nelson. 'I understand.' Nelson pushed him towards the back of the Custody Suite.

Temple muttered something.

Fenchurch grabbed his arm. 'What was that?'

'You're hurting my arm!'

Fenchurch bent Temple over the desk. 'That's your boss, isn't it? Lord Ingham?'

'You're hurting my arm!'

Fenchurch let him go. 'Well, you'll be sharing photos in prison soon enough.'

Martin pushed Fenchurch away. 'Get yourself upstairs, Si. I'll make sure this didn't happen.'

———

Fenchurch met Docherty in the corridor. 'Take it you've heard?'

'Aye. Nasty piece of work.' Docherty screwed up his face. 'All that time and he's . . .' He blew air up his face. 'How do you begin to . . .'

'I want to speak to him, boss.'

'After what you did to Ingham?' Docherty shook his head. 'He says he's suing us. If this costs us the conviction . . .'

'It'll cost nothing, boss. We've got stacks and stacks of evidence against him.'

Docherty stopped at the corner and put his hands on his hips. 'Si, I know you've really been through the ringer, but this is where the cowboy shite stops.' He stepped aside to let some uniformed officers pass. 'I've got my work cut out to clear your name, so no more.'

'Guv, you switched off the recorder.'

'Yeah, I know.' Docherty winked. 'But no more of that, okay? You're going on holiday as of tomorrow.'

No bloody way am I going on holiday. I need to—

Fenchurch caught himself. Tears filled his eyes.

I need to spend time with Abi, get over what's happened. Work out how the hell to move on with our lives after all of this . . . all of this shit.

He smiled at Docherty. 'Boss.'

'Well, wonders will never cease.' Docherty clapped him on the back. 'I'll see what I can do about making these allegations go away.'

The door behind them opened and another hulking Custody Officer stepped out, followed by Temple, his head bowed. His eyes widened.

The CO pointed into the vacant interview room. 'We'll be in there.' He tugged at Temple's collar like it was a dog's lead. 'Come on, sunshine.'

Fenchurch set off to follow, but Docherty grabbed him back. 'You're the last person who's interviewing him.'

'Can I speak to him before his lawyer turns up at least?'

'Jesus, Si.' Docherty let his grip go. 'Right. But no monkey business, okay?'

'Cross my heart.'

'Go and light the brazier, then. I'll see if I can find the brand.'

Fenchurch entered the room, leaving the door open. He hovered by Temple, waiting for the Custody Officer to leave them. The door clicked shut and he crouched next to Temple. 'I'm not going to be interviewing you, Paul, but I just wanted a quick word.'

Temple shrugged. 'You should leave right now if you want any chance of me seeing the inside of a court room.'

'You've killed a cabbie.' Fenchurch rested one hand on the floor and leaned forward into Temple's face. 'You've betrayed the trust of a lot of people, and for what? You make me sick. You're Abi's friend and you tried to kill her. You know what Ingham, Ogden and their cronies are doing, don't you?'

'Enlighten me.'

'They're paedophiles, kidnapping children off the street, having sex with them and—'

'It's not like that.' Temple looked away.

'Oh? Try me.'

Temple brushed at his hair, the cuffs rattling. 'We didn't harm anyone. Those children weren't awake when they were . . .'

'When they were what?' Fenchurch grabbed his tie and pulled him close. 'They abducted my daughter, you little shit!'

'That was nothing to do with me.'

'Oh, you were only following orders, were you?' Fenchurch let the tie go. 'How long have you been involved in this?'

'I'm not telling you.'

'So help me, I will use some of your tactics on you.' Fenchurch grabbed the tie again and yanked it tight. 'I'll disappear you before you face trial. Just another missing person. A single man goes missing. Nobody will miss you.'

Temple held his gaze, his eyes narrow. 'You don't know anything.'

'I just want to know what you did to my daughter. Now, you tell me everything and we'll leave it at that.'

'I did nothing to her. I was on holiday at the time.'

'Single man in Thailand, was it? Buggering ladyboys?'

Temple snorted, tears welling in his eyes. 'It's not like that.'

'Try me.'

Temple laughed, snot bubbling in his nose. 'Piss off.'

'I'm serious. I just want the truth.' Fenchurch scraped the chair back, then sat opposite. 'I'm guessing you're one of them. Are you?'

Temple looked away, his Adam's apple bobbing up and down.

'Paul, are you a paedophile?' Fenchurch let the question ring around the interview room.

'I never—' Temple rubbed at his face, hands clawing all over it like he could change the past. 'Yes.'

'How long?'

Temple propped himself on his elbows, his face twisted up. 'Since I was a student.'

'At Southwark University?' Fenchurch waited for the nod, rubbing his chin. 'How did you get involved in that group? One wrong click and you're in some Facebook group? Then you're down some dark-web rabbit hole?' He frowned. 'Hang on, that's twenty years ago. Before the internet. How did it work back then? You can't just walk up to someone and say, "Oh, look at the lack of tits on that little girl?" or "I'd smash that little boy's back doors in." It doesn't work like that, does it?'

'It was a photography club. Ogden's an alumnus and he sponsored it, paid for the darkroom there. Gave us money for film, donated some cameras.' Temple scratched at his hair, like he was trying to tug the roots out. 'We got to know each other over the first year. Ogden was in the darkroom one day, developing some photos of a child. They were arty, you know? Black and white. A kid on a beach. I liked them. And that's when I think he knew.'

'That you're a paedophile?'

Temple let out a stuttering breath, eyes shut. 'He was very subtle about it. Next time, the kid was naked. I spoke to him about it and he showed me some other stuff, Scandinavian stuff. Magazines.'

'Porn?' Fenchurch waited for the nod, barely got anything. 'You could've got help, Paul.'

Temple pulled a tuft of hair from his fringe. 'I have this . . .' He snorted, his lips curling up. '. . . this disgusting urge, but I *never* acted on it. You've got to understand.'

'So why didn't you report him?'

'Don't you think I don't ask myself that every single day?' Temple wiped a tear from his eye. 'Ogden invited me to dinner at his house in Vauxhall. There were a few others there.'

'Lord Ingham?'

'Amongst others.' Temple scratched at his hair, tugging it into knots. 'They must've spiked my drink, because I blacked out. I woke up in a spare room, completely naked. On the pillow there were photos . . .' He pulled a tuft out. 'I was abusing a girl. She was young. Thirteen. Maybe younger.'

'Did you do it?'

'I don't remember.' Temple looked Fenchurch in the eyes. He was telling the truth, no varnish. 'This is before Photoshop. It wasn't fake.'

'What happened next?'

'Ogden came into the room and told me there was more. He had a video of it.' Temple's cheek was slicked with tears. This must've been the first time he'd talked about it, the first time the dirtiest of all secrets had come out of that skull. 'He told me one of the guys went to my flat. Put a load of child pornography on my computer. They had some cops on their payroll and they impounded it, but never charged me. It's just sitting in evidence somewhere, connected to a closed case. One little admin tweak and . . .'

Fenchurch sighed. 'They've used it to frame you ever since, haven't they?'

'They forced me to join the CPS as a trainee lawyer, helped me progress up the ladder. All so they could have power over me.'

'You sure it's just that one time, Paul?'

'I swear.'

Fenchurch got to his feet and paced around. His skin crawled, like there were maggots under the surface. 'I bet this blackmailing was a liberation for you. You were in the inner sanctum. You could now indulge yourself in it, fulfil your every whim, knowing that they had the worst on you. You couldn't get any deeper into the shit.'

Temple's chin dropped to his chest. 'I'm as much of a victim as those children.'

'What?' Fenchurch stopped beside Temple and put his hand under his chin. 'You're not a victim, Paul. You're a filthy pervert. You've ruined people's lives. People like me. People like Abi. You supported us through it, when you knew . . .' His throat was thick with mucus. 'When you knew what'd happened to Chloe. Where she'd gone. Who'd taken her. What they'd done with her.' He twisted Temple's head up, but his eyes looked away. 'Why did you try and kill Abi?'

Temple tried to jerk his head away from Fenchurch's grip.

Fenchurch tightened it. 'Was it to punish me? Like you punished me through my father?'

'You're getting too close to the truth.'

'About what? Abi didn't know anything that could make it any worse for Ogden or Ingham.'

Temple broke free and huffed out a sigh, but didn't speak.

'What, then?' Fenchurch crouched down to Temple's eye level. 'Close to what?'

'Chloe.'

'She's dead. And knowing . . .' Fenchurch swallowed the mucus down. 'Knowing what happened is the hardest thing in the world, but it's over.'

'Simon.' Temple shut his eyes and collapsed back into the chair. 'She's still alive.'

Chapter Forty-Three

What?' Fenchurch almost toppled over backwards. He had to grab hold of the table to steady himself. 'What did you just say?'

Temple clenched his jaw, kept his mouth shut.

'Paul . . .'

Temple's lips twitched, seemingly out of control. 'I said, she's alive.'

'So you gave the Simons my daughter?' Fenchurch pushed himself up to full height, his guts churning, the drums thundering through the effect of the pills. 'They let her die!'

'That was a cover.' Temple bit into his bottom lip. 'The whole thing was a cover.'

'You're lying!'

'Why would I lie?' Temple placed his hands on the table. 'I've got nothing left to lose.'

'To twist the knife.' Fenchurch batted at the light above the table, sending it spinning round, the glow wobbling over the dirty walls. 'To put me and Abi through it all over again. As if we haven't suffered enough.'

'I don't want you to suffer any more.'

Fenchurch crouched again as the light settled into the middle, slowing down. 'You just tried to kill Abi, you little shit.'

'That's the hardest thing I've ever had to do. I swear.'

'I don't believe anything that comes out of your mouth.'

'Simon . . .' Temple brushed a tear away from his eye. 'I'll tell you the whole, unvarnished truth, okay?'

Fenchurch tried to keep his voice level. 'You're getting nothing in return.'

'I know that.' Temple sniffed and tugged at his nose. 'I want to give you something back to make up for what I tried to do to Abi. That's all.'

'I want everything. No lies. No skipping bits.'

'Okay.' Temple sucked in a deep breath, like he was about to dive into a deep pool. He released it slowly, like ancient sand sliding across a desert. 'Cheryl Simon used to work as a City lawyer for Gerald Ogden. He caught her stealing a client's money. Quite a whack of it. Enough to piss off abroad.' His smirk betrayed some admiration. 'She didn't realise who she was messing with. Instead of going to the cops, he told her all she had to do was accompany someone in a car.'

'One of Flick Knife's child snatchers?'

'If you put it that way.' Temple wiped a hand across his forehead. 'This was early on, so she had to kidnap the kid.'

'And did she?'

Temple frowned at him. 'Can I have my phone?'

Fenchurch reached over to a table at the side and snatched up a plastic ziplock bag. 'I don't want you wiping this.' He tossed it onto the table. 'What's the code?'

'1976.' Temple looked away from the phone. 'You need to go into the Dropbox app. I'll show you what folder you need to look at.'

Fenchurch unlocked the phone and found Dropbox on the first page of icons. 'Which folder?'

'It's called Household Bills, then Car, then Garage. There's a video file in there.'

'Is this you having—'

'Just open it.'

Fenchurch tapped on the folders and opened up a list of video files. 'Which one?'

'It's marked "MOT 1999-04-30".'

Fenchurch found it at the bottom and tapped on it. A video opened up, taken from the inside of a car. Grainy camcorder footage.

Cheryl Simon sat on the back seat. She looked a lot younger but her Sloane mask slipped to reveal a lost girl underneath. She nodded at the driver and got out of the cab. The view swivelled round to track her into a park. Looked like Greenwich. The place was empty apart from a girl on a swing. Cheryl walked up to her and spoke to her. After a few seconds, she took her by the hand and led her back to the car. She stopped outside and waited. Then a voice said, 'Get in!' Cheryl nodded and helped the girl onto the back seat. The camera settled on the girl as the car drove off. The video faded to black.

Fenchurch looked up at Temple. 'Who is this?'

'You'll recognise Cheryl Simon. The girl is Tasmin Healey. Six months after that, she was rehomed with a couple in Lincolnshire.'

Fenchurch's stomach started bubbling, eating at him. 'And in those six months . . .'

'You've got it.' Temple couldn't keep his eyes off his phone. Like he could wipe it just by looking at it. 'They changed how they did it after that. The other woman almost got caught, so they had the drivers do the abductions. Cheryl got in the second car and pretended to be their mother.'

Fenchurch swallowed the bile down, letting it mix with the raging torrent in his guts. He nodded at the phone. 'That video was leverage, I get that. That and all the other kids she took. How did she get started?'

'She owed Flick Knife a favour.' Temple lifted his shoulders. 'Can't remember what it was. Money or sexual favours.'

'So how did she end up in Dorchester instead of doing this?'

'Because we had to use her as cover once. In 2002. Took a boy in Pinner. Undercover cops working a drug deal spotted it. Took her into the station, she gave them this story about losing her son outside a butcher. We had it all backed up and she got out.' Temple's breath hissed out slowly. 'You can't do it more than once.'

'So you gave her a house in the countryside as a reward?'

Temple sighed as he shook his head. 'We hooked her up with Flick Knife's accountant.'

'Larry Simon?'

'That's right. He'd helped set up Fresh Start. We had enough on him to keep him under our thumb.'

Fenchurch cracked his knuckles. 'Was he abusing children?'

'Not that.' Temple's dead eyes locked onto Fenchurch. 'All the paperwork was in his name. If he tried to blow the whistle, he'd be implicated. Everything led to him.' He held his gaze, blinking slowly. 'And we helped them adopt a daughter. Amanda. As you know, she died in 2002.'

Fenchurch stood up, looking over at Docherty and getting a flick of the eyebrows in return. Then he crouched again, squatting in front of Temple. 'So you gave them Chloe?'

'Not as such.' Temple huffed out a sigh. 'When they kidnapped Chloe, they realised who she was pretty quickly. A call went out on the radio. Naismith heard it and connected the dots. He told Blunden who she was. The plan was to kill her. Blunden didn't know who you were, didn't care. They're more than capable of losing people in the Thames or one of the many building sites around the city.'

That tallied with Johnson and Naismith's stories.

Fenchurch's knees groaned, but he stayed crouching. 'So why didn't they kill Chloe?'

Temple swallowed hard. 'Because I told him to stop.'

'And they just listened to you?'

'Ingham did.' Temple wiped another tear from his eye. 'He prided himself on not killing their victims. Maybe helped him sleep at night.' His lips twisted into a grimace. 'No harm done.'

'No harm—' Fenchurch stopped himself. Need to keep him talking . . . He pushed up tall and started pacing around the room. 'How did you persuade him? You were in hock to him for abusing a child.'

'I'd gained his trust by then.' Temple's tongue flicked over his lips. 'I said they should keep Chloe safe, then they could use her as leverage against you or your father when the time came. Your old man was a DS in the murder squad at the time, you were a newly promoted DI. Always useful to have influence over people like that.' He stared right at Fenchurch, drilling right down to the marrow. 'Amazing how much of what seems like incompetence is actually more sinister.'

Fenchurch frowned. 'The cop we spoke to mentioned a sister.'

'Holliday?'

'Not him. A local cop.' Fenchurch made a note. 'Is Holliday involved?'

'Maybe.'

'So, this sister?'

'Right.' Temple nodded slowly, his lips puckering tight. 'The Simons were adopting another girl from Fresh Start. Jennifer Hay. We made them adopt Chloe as well. Didn't give them a choice.' He wiped snot off his nose with his sleeve. 'The trouble was, Jennifer remembered what happened in the . . . sessions. She didn't react well to the . . . medication we used to make them forget.'

Fenchurch's gut lurched again. The depravity. The sickness. All thought through. All covered over, like entries in a ledger. 'In Peckham?'

'It was Vauxhall in those days, but yes.' Temple drew a circle on the table with his finger, then clicked it with his nail. 'Jennifer and Chloe looked pretty similar. Like fraternal twins. So when a bus hit them by accident, it was a chance—'

'What?' Fenchurch's gut lurched. The drums cannoned around his head. 'It hit them *both*?'

Temple nodded again. 'Killed Jennifer there and then.'

'What?'

'Jennifer's in Chloe's grave, not that there'll be enough left of her to prove it by now.' Temple swallowed hard. 'Chloe suffered a brain injury. She couldn't remember anything. Larry called me up and I visited her in hospital. She didn't recognise me.' He drew the circle again. 'I'd known Chloe all her life and she didn't recognise me. Didn't recognise her new parents.'

'So you swapped them?'

'I thought it was for the best.' Temple sipped some water from the plastic glass. 'It solved the problem in Larry and Cheryl's heads. They no longer had a cop's child.'

'But I was still looking. Dad was still looking. If we found out the truth, they'd still be implicated.'

'Lots of ifs there.' Temple crumpled his water cup, spilling droplets onto the table. 'I visited over the years, checking she didn't remember. Checking she was okay.'

'How the hell did they get away with it? Surely the pathologist would've noticed? What about at school?'

'It's easier than you think.' Temple shrugged. 'Cheryl home-schooled them. Home-schooled *Jennifer*.'

Fenchurch could do anything. Strangle the little shit. But his knowledge would die with him. 'I don't believe you.'

'I'm telling the truth.' Temple looked up at him, his eyes watering, and looked away. 'They're not bad people.'

'Of course they're bad people! They knowingly took my daughter!' The words echoed around the room. 'You warned them, didn't you? On Saturday, when Abi and I drove up there, you called them, told them what was going on. When we pitched up, they'd had hours to rehearse their story.'

'Simon, they gave her a good life. She was happy. I—' Temple broke off, wiping his eyes. 'I'm telling you this to help you and Abi.'

Fenchurch couldn't process it.

How could this be true? How could they just do that to him? To Abi? To his mum and his dad? To Chloe? Taking all those years of life away, just because they'd taken the wrong girl?

He folded his arms. 'So where is my daughter?'

'Jennifer's at university.' A bitter smile flashed across his face. 'Southwark, like her mother.'

———

Docherty roared across Lambeth Bridge, heading away from Millbank and its ancient political hub towards new-build London, his Audi growling with the effort, the siren and lights blaring. 'Is Nelson there?'

'Secured the perimeter, guv.' Fenchurch clutched the Airwave in one hand, the 'oh shit' handle in the other as Docherty swung a tight turn, keeping to the river. 'Not gone in yet.'

Docherty bombed past Lambeth Palace, weaving into the right-hand bus lane to avoid the thick traffic. A bus powered towards them. He thumped the headlights. 'Get out of the way, you stupid arse!'

The bus pulled in and a thin wedge appeared in the oncoming traffic. Docherty bobbed round it, flooring it when he got to the other side of the bus, following the road as it slalomed around some old brick buildings.

Fenchurch braced himself while Docherty switched into the oncoming road as the bus lane disappeared. He hammered towards a bulbous glass-and-chrome building and pulled right onto a road marked 'Local Buses Only', cutting off a Duck Tours amphibious bus. They joined a main road, horns squealing out from behind.

Docherty powered up to the roundabout, clogged with taxis and Sunday drivers, and veered out into the oncoming lane, ignoring the traffic lights. He bounced over the pavement to join the emerging bus lane. 'Are you sure it's her?'

Butterflies hammered at Fenchurch's stomach, beating their wings like tiny hurricanes. 'Of course I'm not sure.'

Docherty bombed around the BFI IMAX cinema, a squat glass cylinder built onto the roundabout, and screeched to a halt at a police cordon. He stopped the engine and got out. 'Well, here we are.'

'Come on.' Fenchurch flashed his warrant card at the uniform guarding the perimeter and stuck his Airwave to his lips. 'Jon, we're here. Where are you?'

'Out front, guv.' Nelson was waving by a bus shelter halfway along the street, the grey metal cowering between the opulence of the university buildings. 'No movement so far.'

'Okay.' Fenchurch jogged down the road, pocketing the Airwave, and stopped beside him. 'Lead on, then.'

Nelson buttoned up his jacket and led through the left-hand revolving door, the modern entrance sculpted into the Victorian facade. The pitter-patter of a heavy-booted squad of uniforms joined them.

A security guard burst out from behind a desk, looking like he was enjoying the first taste of action in a long career. He waved through an open gate to a locked door. 'Through there, officers.'

Nelson stopped by the door and smiled at him. 'Can you ensure the perimeter stays secure?'

The guard nodded furiously. 'Of course, sir.'

Nelson pushed the door open and headed down a long corridor, reeking of Lynx and Pot Noodle. Bass drums thudded from some doors, acoustic guitars from others. 'Just up here.' He stopped halfway down and stepped aside. 'After you, guv.'

Fenchurch sucked in stale air and knocked on the door.

'Just a minute!' The door slid open and a tall young woman stood in the doorway. Bright-red hair like that Spice Girl. She looked Fenchurch up and down. 'Yes?'

Fenchurch smiled. 'Jennifer Simon?'

She frowned at him, a dimple puckering her cheek. 'Do I know you?'

Fenchurch's heart just about stopped. 'I think you do.'

'And?'

Fenchurch fumbled out his warrant card and dropped it on the carpet. He bent down to pick it up, sweat pouring down his back. 'My name is Detective Inspector Simon Fenchurch. I need you to accompany me to the station so you can answer a few questions.'

'What's this about?'

'Does the name Chloe Holland mean anything to you?'

'Should it?' She stared at the ground. 'Wait, my sister . . . I had a sister called Chloe. She died when I was little, I think.'

Is it her? Could it be her?

'You think?'

'Sorry, who the hell are you?'

Docherty stepped between them. 'Madam, if you'd like to accompany me . . . ?'

Chapter Forty-Four

Fenchurch stood in the doorway. He couldn't speak. Felt like his ears had covered over, just flaps of flesh blocking out the sound.

Jennifer winced as Clooney plunged the needle into her arm.

He pulled the syringe back and squirted the contents into a vial. 'There. That's us.'

She rolled down her sleeves. 'So I can see my parents now?'

'That's not my department.' Clooney bagged up the DNA kit and put it under his arm, the swab rattling in its container. 'It'll be a couple of hours, okay? And that's after I get out to Lewisham.' He flashed his eyebrows at Fenchurch. 'All yours.' He walked off and shut the door.

Fenchurch sat next to Jennifer in the meeting room, trying to get his breathing under control.

She twisted her mouth. 'You said I should know you, but I don't.' Her accent was tinged with the West Country burr, all the vowels rounding out consonants, but still had traces of London. Maybe recently acquired. 'Who are you?'

The red hair. 'Is your hair dyed?'

'What?' Her scowl twisted further. 'Are you a pervert or something?'

'Chloe, what—'

'My name is *Jennifer*.' She shook her head, smiling like a superstar footballer who wasn't getting the rub of the green, their teammates just not up to it. Her dimple appeared on her cheek. 'Jesus . . . I told you, Chloe was my sister. She died. I don't remember her.'

Fenchurch bit his teeth together, feeling like he was pushing his fillings deeper in. 'You were adopted, right?'

Jennifer's cool-teenager mask slipped off, showing the scared girl underneath. She nodded.

'What happened to your parents?'

'They're in this police station, I guess.' She looked over at the door. 'You guys will be shouting at them or something. Trying to get them to admit to something they didn't do.'

'I meant your birth parents.'

She shut her eyes. 'They died when I was eight, I think.' Her eyes burned into him. 'It was only a few months ago that my parents told me I was adopted, okay?'

'Do you remember your birth parents?'

'Not much. They died in a car accident. I survived, but I got this injury.' She sniffed and slid her hair up above her ear, revealing an indentation in her skull, like a dent in a car covered in skin.

Everything clenched in Fenchurch. He couldn't breathe, his lungs felt like they were full of water. He blinked away tears. 'Who did that to you?'

'Are you not listening to me? I was in an accident.' She nibbled at her lip. 'Why do you care, anyway? You're acting all weird about this shit.'

'I need to—'

The door juddered open and Docherty peered round it. 'There you— Oh.' He coughed. 'I need a word, Si.'

'Boss, I—'

'Now.'

Mulholland entered the room. 'I'll look after you, Jennifer.'

Fenchurch joined him in the corridor but left the door open. Didn't want to leave her. Never again. 'What's up?'

'One of your lassies dug this up for me.' Docherty handed him a file. 'Check it.'

Fenchurch held it up. Jennifer Hay. He flicked through the pages, so fast they kept slipping. 'This is the girl in the grave?'

'It all tallies, Si. Disappeared from a park in Pinner. Timeline works.'

'So it's her?'

Docherty snatched the file back. 'Come walk with me.'

Fenchurch stared into the room, Mulholland smiling at Jennifer. Chloe. If it was really her and not just Temple twisting the knife again. 'Boss, I—'

'Si, come on. We need to get to the bottom of this, okay?' Docherty patted Fenchurch's arm with the file and paced off.

One last look at Chloe and Fenchurch joined him.

———

Docherty stopped outside the interview room and stuck his hands on his hips. 'All I'm saying is wait for Clooney, okay? If that's *not* her, then we're in for a whole heap of shit, okay?'

'Did you see the . . .' Fenchurch sucked in stale air. 'She's got a scar . . .'

'So they had to operate after the crash to save her life or whatever.'

'Or they—'

'Si, quit it, okay?' Docherty checked his watch. 'Howard's letting us speak to them just now while he' — he did air quotes — 'gets a coffee. So let's not waste this, okay?'

Fenchurch pressed his finger into the door. 'You're letting me interview him?'

'Come on.' Docherty entered the room and tapped Nelson on the shoulder. 'Give us a minute, Sergeant.'

'Sir.' Nelson got up and smiled at Fenchurch on his way out.

Docherty sat across from Larry Simon. 'So let me get this straight, you deny any involvement in the abduction of Chloe Geraldine Fenchurch?'

'Of course we do.' Larry's brow pinched together, made it look like devil horns. 'My wife and I are completely innocent of all these matters.'

Fenchurch sat next to Docherty. 'We spoke to you in a police interview room with you last night and you fed us a pack of lies about your lack of involvement in this case.'

Larry looked away. Couldn't even deny it.

'Then I sit down with someone who admits involvement in the case, who insists that my daughter, *Chloe*, is still alive.'

Larry's nostrils twitched. 'Listen to me very clearly. We told you the truth.'

'You said you and your wife had been rejected by the system.'

'We had.'

'I know how you met, Mr Simon.'

Larry looked away, clasping his hands like a newsreader. 'We lost our daughter and sought an adopted child. That was Chloe. We lost her as well.'

'So why is she sitting in a room downstairs?'

The strip lighting caught in Larry's glasses. 'What?'

'We just collected her from Southwark University.'

The lights flashed across the glasses as he swivelled his head, switching his focus between them. 'That's *Jennifer*. My daughter! You're going to pay—'

'Her name is Chloe Geraldine Fenchurch.'

'It's . . .' Larry licked his lips, frowning. 'We've been over this so many times. If young Chloe was your daughter, then you have our deepest sympathies. I know what you're going through, having lost two daughters, but you've got to understand me, Jennifer is our child.'

'Chloe was taken by a group of powerful men.' Fenchurch splayed his hands on the table, focusing on the triangle between his thumbs and forefingers. 'They kidnapped small children, drugged them, had sex with them, then got rid of them. This isn't like Operation Yewtree, where the kids went back to their orphanages or got let out of Jimmy Savile's caravan, confused and traumatised.' He squeezed the triangle tight. 'They hid these children by adopting them out to desperate people.' He bunched his hands into fists. 'Chloe was one of them. You adopted her and you raised her.'

'That's . . . Jennifer.' Larry scratched at his neck. 'I acted in good faith . . .'

Fenchurch sat back and waited. Give him enough time to scratch all the skin away. 'Jennifer Hay.' He got out a photocopied birth certificate and nudged it over the table. 'Born on the twelfth of August, 1996.'

Larry's eyes shot up. 'What is this?'

'She was abducted from a park in west London in February 2005.' Fenchurch leaned low, his hands splayed on the table. 'She was taken by the same animals who took my daughter. You adopted her. Along with my Chloe.'

'That's preposterous!'

'Only they had an accident. Jennifer died, but you didn't like having a copper's daughter in your house, so you pretended she was my Chloe, didn't you?'

Larry gritted his teeth. 'I've nothing more to say on this matter.'

'You set up Fresh Start for them, didn't you?'

'I— What?'

Fenchurch tapped at the sheet of paper. 'Jennifer Hay is the body in my daughter's grave. You covered your tracks by pretending *my* daughter died.'

'I have nothing more to say on this matter.'

'I can sympathise with you to a certain extent.' Fenchurch held his gaze for a few seconds, until Larry looked away. 'Someone took my daughter. Yours died of a sickening illness. I would've done *anything* to get Chloe back. Every day we didn't have her, I could feel the distance growing between my wife and me.' Acid bubbled away in his gut. 'But that doesn't give you the right to take someone else's child. To help these animals ruin someone else's family. You were complicit in this. I don't care how hurt you were. You destroyed my family.'

Larry's lips quivered, his eyes blinking furiously. 'I have nothing more to say on this matter.'

'We know what your wife did. She took children off the street for them.'

'She didn't have a—' Larry cut himself short.

'Didn't have a choice? Everyone's got a choice.' Fenchurch snarled at him. 'Some people think about others before they try and save their skin.'

———

DI Keith Holliday snorted, like he'd done a gram of coke on the flight back from the Algarve. Big, chunky, like he should be cracking pig bones on a farm somewhere. 'Why am I here?'

Fenchurch tossed the death certificate onto the desk in the interview room. 'You think we wouldn't notice?'

Holliday didn't even look at it. Some cop he was, bet Avon police were proud of him. He ran a finger across the page, like that could wipe away history. 'What am I supposed to have done here?'

'According to your case file, Chloe Simon died in a bus crash.' Fenchurch tossed a photo of Jennifer onto the desk. 'But here she is. Funny that.'

'You were sniffing around my old patch last night, weren't you? Trying to fit me up.'

'What, about the fact two girls were in the accident?'

Holliday shut his mouth and eyes. 'What?'

'The girl in the grave is one Jennifer Hay. We'll exhume that body and see if we can identify any DNA evidence. But Chloe Fenchurch was hit by that bus as well.'

Holliday tugged at his collar.

'You switched her identity.' Fenchurch produced a hospital report. 'This report states that Jennifer Simon was injured. The dates have been changed.'

Nothing from Holliday.

'If you know anything about this, it'll look a lot better for you if you tell us now.'

Holliday shifted to the other side of his collar.

'I get what was in it for you. Lowly PC in the arse end of middle England suddenly becomes a DI in Bristol. They helped that along, didn't they? Pushed you up the ladder.' Fenchurch gave him space, but Holliday just kept tugging at his collar. 'Looks like it wasn't just you. This accident happened on a main street. It wasn't just you. You needed help to cover this up.'

Holliday grunted out a cough.

'Whoever you're working for, they stole my daughter from me.' Fenchurch stabbed a finger in the air at him. 'Larry and Cheryl Simon raised her, took eleven years of her life from us.' He narrowed his eyes at him. 'You know who you're working for, do you? Do you know what they do to the children they abduct?'

Holliday shut his eyes.

'The kids think they're in some sort of queue for an adoption agency. These paedophiles call it Fresh Start.' Fenchurch cracked his knuckles. 'Only they slip something into their milk, don't they? After the kids fall asleep, they rape them. These men pass them around like sex dolls for six months to a year. After they've had their fun, they adopt them out, trying to pretend nothing's happened to them.' He let the words rattle around the interview room, let them batter Holliday. 'To get away with something like this, you need help from the judiciary, from police officers like you.'

'It's nothing to do with me.' Holliday tugged at his farmer's ears, far too big for his head. 'I've done nothing.'

'Did they pay you?'

'I did nothing!'

Fenchurch threw the case file up in the air, waiting for it to land with a thunk. 'This is your work. A fiction. Who was paying you?'

'I'm saying nothing.'

Fenchurch leaned forward, trying to get him to look up. 'Was it Ingham?'

'Who?'

'Ogden?'

Holliday looked away. 'I've no idea what you're talking about.'

———

'Might want to lose that key, Martin.' Docherty winked at Martin as he led Holliday into the cells.

Fenchurch stood in the Custody Suite, heart pounding. 'I don't know who's the worst. Him or the scumbags who . . .'

'Aye, you do.' Docherty rested his arms on the partition. 'He's just a cog in the wheel. We've got the whole car now.'

'I'm just waiting for the other shoe to drop, boss.' Fenchurch snarled, his nostrils feeling like they'd tear. 'Waiting for Ingham to pretend he's too senile to face a trial.'

'No way that's happening.' Docherty thumped his thumbs on the counter. 'We can get quite creative about which brutal rapists we house with which child rapists. He's sharing a cell with Big Barry, don't you worry.'

Fenchurch stared at the door Holliday was behind, down the long corridor, two down from where Steven Shelvey died. 'All that paperwork, covering over their tracks. No wonder I never found her.'

Martin clanked along the corridor with his keys, leading Dad out into the Custody Suite and patting him on the shoulder. 'Right, Ian, you're free to go.'

Dad frowned at him. 'What?'

'I'll get your possessions as soon as we've signed all the paperwork.'

'What?' Dad squinted at him. 'What's happened?'

Fenchurch wrapped his arm round Dad's shoulder. 'There's been a bit of a development—' His Airwave blasted out. Clooney.

'Sorry, Dad.' Fenchurch took a deep breath as he answered it. 'Mick.'

'Si . . .' Clooney exhaled down the line. 'Okay, two things. First, Mulholland got someone to do a quick examination. That scar is consistent with the injuries she'd received in the bus crash.'

Fenchurch sighed. All memories of him and Abi gone, deleted like a computer disk. 'What's the other news?'

'The old DNA test's come back. We're trialling one of those new American machines, quick as fu—'

'Mick.' Hope burning a hole in Fenchurch's gut. 'What's the result?'

'Here we go.' Clooney tapped at a keyboard. 'Oh, that poor girl.'

'Mick . . .'

Chapter Forty-Five

Fenchurch stood on Leman Street, looking up and down the thoroughfare. Where the bloody hell were they?

The rain was finally heading their way. He got out his phone and checked for messages. Still nothing.

A red Fiat 500 bundled down the street, rattling over the tarmac, and pulled in across from the bus stop. Reed got out of the driver's seat. 'Guv, you okay?'

Am I? I've no idea.

Fenchurch put his phone away and jogged across the road. He reached in to help Abi out. 'Are you all right?'

'I wish people would stop treating me like I'm a bloody invalid.'

Fenchurch let her take his hand and winch herself to her feet. 'Has the doctor cleared you?'

'Not yet. Says I'm out of the woods.' She rested against the car, wincing. 'But my system's going to be a mess for a few days. The arsenic didn't get much of a chance to get into it. They've flushed it out. The pain I've got is the medicine, all the side effects.'

Fenchurch tried to speak but nothing came out.

'Kay, why have you dragged me here?' Abi winced as she breathed out. 'This is supposed to be important, right?'

Reed scuttled round the front of the car. 'Guv, do you want to tell her?'

'Is this about Paul?' Abi crossed her arms. 'Because I know he poisoned me.'

'It's not that, love.' Fenchurch nodded at Reed. 'Can you give us a minute?'

'Sure.' Reed walked off, crossing the road.

Abi put her hands on her hips. 'What's happened?'

'Paul's involved in this whole sex ring. The ones who took Chloe.'

She stared into space. 'Did he know?'

'I think so. But we got a lead on what happened to Chloe.'

She frowned. 'You found who took her?'

'Better.' Fenchurch gave her a smile, not sure even he could believe it. 'We've found her.'

'What?'

'I had a DNA test done. The Simons' daughter, Jennifer . . . She's my daughter. She's your daughter. It's Chloe.'

'Can I see her?'

'Not yet, love.' Fenchurch stuffed his hands in his pockets. 'They haven't told her yet.'

Abi fiddled with her wedding ring, the other hand patting her stomach.

Reed stared at Fenchurch, her eyes almost hidden in their sockets. 'Is Paul Temple here?'

⌣

On the screen, Reed sat opposite Temple, neither of them managing to speak. Jon Nelson sat next to Reed, keeping quiet.

Fenchurch sat next to Abi in the Obs. Suite, silent, letting her come to terms with what Temple had done. Not that you could.

She glanced round at Fenchurch, arms hugged tight. 'I want to speak to him.'

'That can't happen, love. We just have to watch.'

Abi shook her head. 'This place.'

'We'll get him, don't worry. He'll go away for a long time.'

'I do worry.'

On the screen, Temple reached his hands across the table. 'Kay, you've got to believe me, I had nothing to do with it!'

'He caught you red-handed.' Reed held up the evidence. The bag with the empty coffee cup, the clear plastic smeared brown. The sachet of white powder. 'That's arsenic.'

Nothing from Temple.

Reed rattled the evidence bag. 'That's what you gave Shelvey, isn't it?'

Temple just shook his head.

'Simon found that arsenic on you.' Reed held up the second evidence bag, containing the white powder. 'This is open and shut. You tried to kill her just like you killed Shelvey.'

'I was trying to cut a deal with him.' Temple shuffled forward on the seat. 'I was trying to get him to confess, to save us all some time.'

'You weren't on the visitors' log, but I bet you were in there. Feeding him poison.' Reed twisted her head to the side. 'Why did you delete the CCTV?'

'Why do you think?' Temple sat back and folded his arms.

Reed broke the silence. 'You know what the worst part is? Aside from the betrayal and . . . and what you let happen to Abi. What really hurts is we're your friends. Why didn't you speak to us about this?'

Temple chanced a glance at her, then laughed. 'What could you have done?'

'We could've helped. It's what we're here for, Pau—' Kay broke off, her teeth bared. 'I can't even use your bloody *name*.' She shut her eyes. 'It's what we *were* here for. When did it start? Uni?'

Temple gasped out a breath. 'You wouldn't have understood.'

'You could've tried. We were your friends, Paul. We'd have made sure you got the help you needed. There's something wrong with you, and it's not criminal until you make it.'

'You wouldn't—'

Reed smashed her fist into the desk. 'We would, Paul. You were the one who helped me through all the shit I went through. Getting a third, not getting into that law firm. You were there for me. I could've helped you.'

'Kay . . . I'm so, so sorry.' Temple tugged at his hair again. 'You don't know what's happened to me . . .'

'What? What happened to *you*?' Reed spat the words at him. 'You're a paedophile, Paul. You make me *sick*.'

'I couldn't—'

'You could. Of course you could. Every day you didn't own up, more evil happened because of you.'

'It's not like—'

'Of course it is.' Reed cleared her throat. 'Every time you saw Abi or you worked with Simon or me on a case, you knew what you'd done.' Her voice wasn't hanging together, just a fragmented whisper. 'You're scum.' She thumped the table, sending ripples across the cup of water. 'Worse than any drug dealer or wife beater I've picked up. You're the cause of that shit. Your type, thinking you're better than all of us.'

Temple collapsed into his seat, digging his palms into his eye sockets. 'When Ingham told me to kill Abi . . . It was the hardest thing I've ever done.'

'You still tried to do it.'

Temple jabbed a finger at the door. 'But I told Simon what happened to Chloe!'

Like that could make up for any of it.

Reed leaned across the table. 'Did you kill Shelvey?'

'You know I did.' Temple shrugged. 'What's the point in even asking?'

'Who gave the order?'

'Ogden.' Temple ran a finger across the palm of his other hand. 'You let out the suspect's name. The person who'd raped and killed his precious goddaughter.' He looked up at her. 'Well done, Kayleigh. His death's on you.'

'That's not mine, Paul.' Reed was on her feet, looking ready to throw him through a wall. 'And stop bloody calling me that.'

Temple sniffed.

'Did you tell Connolly to kill Cassie McBride?'

He gave a nod.

'How did you know about her?'

'For a man in his position, Howard Savage is a bit loose with his lips.'

Fenchurch stormed down the corridor, Abi at the other end, speaking on her mobile.

'Wait up, son!' Dad was jogging behind him, panting hard.

Fenchurch stopped by Abi as she put her phone away. 'Dad, come on.' He tore open the door and entered.

Chloe was sitting on her own, the Custody Officer standing behind her, arms behind his back like he was on parade.

That social worker stood between them, Robert or something. Could be Jeremy Corbyn's brother — tweeds and tie. He smiled at Fenchurch, the usual one full of bitterness at thirty-odd years of dealing with the worst London had to offer.

Chloe got up and charged over to the door. 'When are you letting me out of here?'

'I'm afraid we've got some news for you.' Fenchurch blocked her exit and swallowed hard. 'You should take a seat.'

She folded her arms. 'Out with it.'

Robert walked over and smiled at Chloe. 'Jennifer, I suggest you come sit next to me.'

'I want to hear it. Now.'

Robert shrugged at Fenchurch.

'We've processed your DNA.' Fenchurch tried to pass her the report summary. She didn't take it. Just like her mother . . . 'You're our daughter.'

Confusion twisted her forehead into knots. 'What?'

'Your name is Chloe Fenchurch.'

She screwed up her lips, like a punk singer. 'My name is Jennifer Simon.'

Fenchurch swallowed down stomach bile. 'Abi is your mother and I'm your father.'

She waved him away. 'Quit it with the *Star Wars* shit.'

'Chloe, you were taken from outside our house.' He reached out to touch her hair. 'You're my daughter.'

She slapped his hand away. 'Get away from me, you pervert!'

'You're Chloe Fenchurch.'

'Stop calling me that!'

Fenchurch's gut plunged through the floor, like a lift with a snapped cable. 'Chloe, I know this is hard to—'

'You're not my parents!' Chloe pushed at Fenchurch's chest, almost toppling him over. 'Get away from me!'

Fenchurch bounced back into the door. 'Chloe, it's all true. You—'

'No!'

Fenchurch gripped her shoulders. 'I've been searching for you for eleven years. And now I've found you.'

'No!' She screamed and covered her ears. 'No, no, no, no!' She slapped his chest, stinging like a bee. 'Get away from me!'

'Chloe, come—'

Another slap, felt like it'd taken the skin off. 'My name is Jennifer!' She glared at him, shaking her head slowly. 'I want nothing to do with you.'

The elevator hit the bottom and the acid bubbled away. 'Come on . . .'

Chloe stabbed a finger at the door. 'They're my parents. They raised me. Loved me. They've done everything for me. You didn't! You're nobody.'

Abi stepped forward, tears streaming down her cheeks. 'Chloe . . . I'm your mum.'

Chloe screamed again. 'Get away from me!'

Robert stepped between them. 'Simon, you need to—'

'No!' Fenchurch reached past and grabbed her by the shoulders. 'Listen to me! Your name is Chloe Geraldine Fenchurch!'

'GET AWAY FROM ME!'

The Custody Officer grabbed Fenchurch's arm. 'Sir, I need you to get away.'

'I'm not—'

'Sir.' The grip tightened like a vice, chewing into his arm. 'Now.'

Chloe was led from the room. His daughter. Red-headed and scowling, ferocious temper like her father, stubborn like her mother. She slammed the door, cutting the cord between them.

———

Fenchurch entered his office, helping Abi in. Tears streamed down his face, burnt his sinuses and nostrils.

Abi stood there, shivering, arms tight around her torso. She couldn't seem to focus on anything. 'This is the first time I've been in here.'

Fenchurch perched on his desk and brushed at his cheeks. 'I've dreamed about this day. Bringing you and Chloe in here, reuniting us.'

He walked over and grabbed a tissue from Mulholland's desk. 'What just happened?'

'She's . . .' Abi slumped into a seat, tearing up, rubbing her knuckles into her eyes. 'What have they done to her?' She blew her nose into a tissue. 'I don't know what to do, Simon. I don't want to leave her side. I don't want anyone to take her away from me again.'

'Hey, hey, hey.' Fenchurch wrapped his arms around her and pulled her tight. 'We've got to give her time and space.' Tighter still. 'We've got time, love.'

'Have we?' Abi deflated, and he practically had to hold her up. 'She doesn't want to speak to us!'

'She's had a shock.' Fenchurch kissed her forehead and let her go. 'How you feeling?'

'How do you think?' She wrapped herself into his embrace. 'That's our daughter and . . . she doesn't want anything to do with us.'

'She's got to come to terms with the new world.'

'How long, though?'

'As long as she needs.' Fenchurch clasped her hands between his. 'There's a lot going on in her head. A lot still to process. But it's Chloe and we've got her back. It's just . . . I don't know how long . . . My baby girl . . .'

'Simon, that's our daughter! That's Chloe! They've . . . they've taken her from me!'

'Shh, it's okay.' Another kiss, pulling her tighter. 'We've got all the time in the world.'

'How could they do this to people?'

'There are a lot of evil people out there, love. These ones are paying for what they did to us. What they've done to everyone else.' Fenchurch let out a deep breath. 'And we've got a new baby on the way, Abi.'

'Christ, I almost forgot.' She put a hand to her forehead. 'The doctor. Stephenson . . . He's got the test results back. The Down's and . . . and the others.' Abi smiled. 'He's fine.'

Fenchurch's gut lurched. 'He?'

Acknowledgments

Thanks as ever to my agent and partner in crime, Allan Guthrie. Big, big thanks to James McKay for unpicking my police procedural blunders. Click.

To Kitty, for everything.

Thanks to everyone at Thomas & Mercer (Sana, Jane, Eoin, Hatty, Emilie and team) for all the support both ongoing and through this book, especially Jenny Parrott for the ninja editing and Emilie Marneur for, amongst all the million other things she does, tearing the initial outline apart and letting the story breathe.

And thanks to all the crime-scene writers who have kept me the right side of insane, especially Mason Cross for the name of Travis Cars.

About the Author

Ed James writes crime-fiction novels. *What Doesn't Kill You* is the third novel in his latest series, set on the gritty streets of east London and featuring DI Simon Fenchurch. His Scott Cullen series features a young Edinburgh detective constable investigating crimes from the bottom rung of the career ladder he's desperate to climb. Formerly an IT manager, Ed began writing on planes, trains and automobiles to fill his weekly commute to London. He now writes full-time and lives in East Lothian, Scotland, with his girlfriend and a menagerie of rescued animals.

1703